Heartfelt Praise for Dorothy Garlock and Her Unforgettable Novels

"Garlock is a master." —*Booklist*

"A gifted writer." —*Chicago Sun-Times*

"One of America's most endearing historical fiction authors."
—*RT Book Reviews*

SUNDAY KIND OF LOVE

"The latest of Dorothy Garlock's romances underscores why the author is a nearly permanent resident of the *New York Times* bestseller list. Garlock's mastery of momentum paired with captivating characters ensures a satisfying read." —*Bookpage*

"The undisputed queen of 20th century Americana romance... Garlock's realistic, heart wrenching romances have always touched readers who seek portraits of days gone by, but she doesn't gloss over the harsh truths, yet uplifts everyone in the end." —*RT Book Reviews*

"Realistic, poignant, and rich with Midwestern small-town flavor, this compelling story of a woman going after her dreams and the supportive, principled man who walks by her side brings the Fifties... to life as only this author can."
—*Library Journal*

"Another solid, touching romance laced through with flickers of tension and character building." —AllAboutRomance.com

TWICE IN A LIFETIME

"Garlock's terrific story, set in mid-20th-century Missouri, pairs a lonely single mother with a flashy auto racer...Garlock keeps readers so wrapped up in Drake and Clara's romance that it's impossible to put the book down...Thoroughly credible characters and the aw-shucks charm of their small town make this a winner." —*Publishers Weekly* starred review

"From the undisputed queen of Americana historical fiction comes a warm and realistic novel of a man's search for a dream and the woman who receives the gift of a second chance at love. It is the quiet beauty of the storytelling and the characters' struggles, as well as the convincing backdrop, that draw readers to Garlock's novels time and again. This is one her fans will cherish." —*RT Book Reviews*

TAKE ME HOME

"Garlock's lovely, sweet novel is a testament to the last great generation." —*RT Book Reviews*

"*Take Me Home* has a unique perspective for a historical novel set during World War II." —FreshFiction.com

UNDER A TEXAS SKY

"Garlock is a masterful storyteller who recognizes what her audience craves and consistently delivers a sweet, nostalgic

read that conveys the reality and romance of the era...There is enough depth of emotion in *Under a Texas Sky* to satisfy her fans."
—RT Book Reviews

"Who could resist a romantic summertime read from the 'Voice of America's heartland,' especially with 'Texas' in the title?"
—Fort Worth Star-Telegram (TX)

"The latest from romance doyenne Garlock mixes light suspense with traditional romance for an entertaining effect."
—Booklist

BY STARLIGHT

"Few authors can recreate the atmosphere of a 1930s small town as beautifully and faithfully as Garlock. She imbues each story with a classic American aura while creating a touching, realistic plotline peopled by authentic characters."
—RT Book Reviews

"An emotional tale of two people in an almost impossible situation...Dorothy Garlock has made the early twentieth century her own and has another winner in her latest novel."
—RomRevToday.com

The Nearness
of You

BOOKS BY DOROTHY GARLOCK

After the Parade
Almost Eden
Annie Lash
By Starlight
Come a Little Closer
Dreamkeepers
Dream River
The Edge of Town
Forever Victoria
A Gentle Giving
Glorious Dawn
High on a Hill
Homeplace
Hope's Highway
Keep a Little Secret
Larkspur
Leaving Whiskey Bend
The Listening Sky
Lonesome River
Love and Cherish
Loveseekers
Midnight Blue
The Moon Looked Down
More than Memory
Mother Road
Nightrose
On Tall Pine Lake
A Place Called Rainwater

Promisegivers
Restless Wind
Ribbon in the Sky
River of Tomorrow
River Rising
The Searching Hearts
Sins of Summer
Song of the Road
Stay a Little Longer
Sunday Kind of Love
Sweetwater
Take Me Home
Tenderness
This Loving Land
Train from Marietta
Twice in a Lifetime
Under a Texas Sky
Wayward Wind
A Week from Sunday
Wild Sweet Wilderness
Will You Still Be Mine?
Wind of Promise
Wishmakers
With Heart
With Hope
With Song
Yesteryear

DOROTHY GARLOCK

The Nearness of You

GRAND CENTRAL
PUBLISHING

NEW YORK   BOSTON

Copyright © 2017 by Dorothy Garlock
Cover design by Brigid Pearson.
Cover photo by MorganStudio/Shutterstock.
Cover copyright © 2017 by Hachette Book Group, Inc.

Grand Central Publishing
Hachette Book Group
1290 Avenue of the Americas, New York, NY 10104
grandcentralpublishing.com
twitter.com/grandcentralpub

First Edition: July 2017

Grand Central Publishing is a division of Hachette Book Group, Inc. The Grand Central Publishing name and logo is a trademark of Hachette Book Group, Inc.

The publisher is not responsible for websites (or their content) that are not owned by the publisher.

The Hachette Speakers Bureau provides a wide range of authors for speaking events. To find out more, go to www.hachettespeakersbureau.com or call (866) 376-6591.

LCCN: 2017934096

ISBNs: 978-1-4555-2735-9 (hardcover library), 978-1-4555-2734-2 (trade paperback), 978-1-4555-2733-5 (ebook), 978-1-4789-1613-0 (audio download)

Printed in the United States of America

LSC-C

10 9 8 7 6 5 4 3 2

For
Michelle Klein, Jodie McChesney,
Shannon Ruez,
Mary White, and Lois Woiwood
With love and gratitude.

The Nearness of You

Prologue

Hooper's Crossing, New York
May 1937

Sarah Denton lifted a damp blanket from the wicker basket at her feet and draped it across the clothesline, careful to smooth away any wrinkles before clipping it in place with wooden pins. Shirts hung next to tablecloths, napkins, bedspreads, and so on down the line. The spring air was filled with the scent of detergent and bleach.

High above, the early-afternoon sun shone brightly in a nearly cloudless sky. The blowing breeze was soft, unable to move the washings, but strong enough to stir the newly budded leaves on tree branches. Ladybugs momentarily lit on the line, their red-and-black shells standing out in stark contrast with the white fabric, before again taking flight. Bees weaved between the stalks of flowers. Birds collected twigs, looking for the perfect place to build a nest.

Sarah didn't have that problem. Her nest was right here.

Her family's two-story home wasn't much, but it was *theirs*. Sure, it had its share of problems: pipes that shook when the spigots were opened in winter; a staircase that creaked with every step; a jamb that hadn't been set quite right, making it impossible to shut the door; and from where she stood in the backyard, Sarah could see the spot just below the eaves where the squirrels squeezed their way into the attic. But for all of its faults, the house was as cozy and comfortable as a favorite sweater. She knew every inch by heart. It was crammed full of memories, of laughter, of good meals around the table in their cramped dining room. It was lined with photographs, holiday decorations, and boxes of toys. It was—

A sudden, lancing pain in her temple ended Sarah's reverie. It was so intense that she had to steady herself on the clothesline. Fortunately, it quickly lessened. The truth was, she hadn't been feeling well all morning. Most likely, she needed a glass of water and to lie down for a while. But there was still the half-full basket of laundry that needed to be hung. First, she would finish her chores, then she could take some time to rest.

That is, if Lily would let her . . .

As if in answer, Sarah's six-year-old daughter burst from the back door, the screen banging against the side of the house, before leaping off the porch. Her arms and legs pin-wheeled every which way, her blond pigtails bouncing as she laughed, a whirling dervish of energy. Lily made a bee-line for her mother, occasionally glancing back over her shoulder.

The girl weaved among the wash, darting in and out of sight until she collided with her mother's leg. Lily's face lit up like the sun, with fetching blue eyes, a smattering of freckles across the bridge of her nose, and a smile that was perfect even if it was missing a couple of teeth. Moments like this one, ordinary and innocent, were still capable of taking Sarah's breath away.

"He's coming!" Lily hissed in a whisper that was any-thing but quiet.

"Are you and your father playing a game?" Sarah asked.

"Hide-and-seek! He's looking for me right—"

Before the girl could finish, the sound of heavy foot-steps came from inside the house. "Now where did she go?" a voice boomed.

Lily burst into a fit of giggles, then tugged at her mother's skirt. "Hide me!" she insisted. Sarah did just that, tucking her daughter behind her, then raised a finger to her lips and made a soft shush.

Morris Denton stepped into the sunlight and gave his wife a knowing smile and wink, with no doubt as to where his child was hiding. "Now where in this big yard do you suppose Lily is?" he asked, which made the girl tremble, so desperate was she to hold back her laughter.

Sarah watched her husband peek behind the birdbath,

push apart bushes, and peer into flower beds, all while loudly announcing what he was doing as he came steadily closer. It was something of a comical sight. Morris was a big man in both size and personality; he liked to joke that the only thing larger than his waistband was his love for his wife and daughter.

"I wonder if she scurried down a rabbit hole," Morris said as he began to push his way through the drying laundry, giving his wife a wink. "Maybe she flew up into the treetops like a robin. Or maybe..." he continued, drawing the word out, "she's hiding right here!"

Morris pounced, landing beside his wife with his hands raised and fingers splayed, the huge smile on his face making him look comically ferocious. Lily squealed, half from delight, the other out of genuine fright. But instead of running away from her father, she dashed toward him, grabbing him tight.

"You found me!" the little girl exclaimed.

"It sure wasn't easy," Morris explained as he wiped sweat from his brow with a handkerchief, a playful smile teasing at the corners of his mouth. "Lily's the best in all Hooper's Crossing when it comes to hiding. For a while there, I thought she was gone for good!"

"Mommy helped," Lily admitted.

"Only a little," Sarah said.

"Partners in crime," Morris added, planting a kiss on his wife's cheek.

"Again, again!" Lily pleaded, jumping up and down.

"All right. One more time and then Daddy needs to sit

down for a bit," her father said. "Run away, little mouse, and hide as best you can!"

Lily set off to do just that, but when she turned she wasn't looking where she was going and ran right into her mother's laundry basket. Clean washing spilled and was then trampled underfoot.

"Watch where you're going, Lily!" Morris barked.

"I'm sorry!" the little girl replied, tears already filling her eyes.

"It's fine," Sarah soothed. "Nothing's ruined." She knelt down to pick up the laundry, but when she did the pain in her head returned, making her vision swim. Wincing, she fought it down, focusing on the mess and her daughter.

"She needs to be more careful," her husband continued.

Sarah ignored him. Instead, she gave Lily a smile, wiped a stray tear from the girl's cheek, and then planted a kiss on her forehead. "Hide really good this time," she said in a conspiratorial whisper.

And off her daughter ran, having already forgotten her chastisement.

But Sarah hadn't.

"You shouldn't be so hard on her," she told her husband. "It was an accident. She's just a kid."

For an instant, it looked as if Morris wanted to disagree, but then his features softened. "You're right," he said with a nod. "I just want Lily to grow up right, to be the sort of lady I know she can be."

"She will, even if she knocks over a laundry basket or two."

Morris chuckled, a sound that never failed to warm Sarah's heart. His laughter was one of the many things about her husband that she loved, part of a long list that included how he occasionally surprised her with a bouquet of flowers, the tuneless songs he hummed while shaving in the bathroom sink, the contented way he patted his belly after a big meal, and especially his ambition to become someone important, strengthening both his family and community. But even as Sarah smiled, another wave of pain washed over her, erasing it.

"Whoa, whoa, whoa," Morris said, rushing to his wife as her knees buckled, pulling her close, his strong arms keeping her upright.

Sarah managed to steady herself. "I haven't felt all that well today."

"Looks to me like you're the one who needs to lie down for a while," her husband replied. "Why don't you go inside and I'll finish the laundry."

She shook her head. "I'll be fine," she said. "Besides, someone is waiting for you."

"She won't be hard to find," he explained. "Lily will be either behind her bedroom door or under the bed. It's always one of the two. And even if, by some miracle, she decided to throw me a curveball and mix things up, all I have to do is follow the sound of her giggles. She won't stay hidden for long. I might even have time to stop off in the kitchen for a glass of lemonade first." But then Morris paused, looking at his wife with no small amount of concern. "Are you sure you're all right?" he asked.

"Go," Sarah answered, though her vision still swam a bit.

Morris looked at her for a moment longer, then leaned close and kissed her softly. "I love you," he said, then started for the house.

Watching him walk away, Sarah found herself thinking about the future. She understood that she would always be the one standing between Morris and Lily, tamping down her husband's high expectations for their daughter, as well as bucking up the little girl's spirits whenever she was feeling down. She would have to keep a close eye on Morris's expanding waistline and mend the items Lily broke as she tornadoed around the house. But for all the obstacles that they would need to overcome, Sarah believed there would be many happier memories, a veritable flood of smiles and laughter. Maybe there would even be an addition to the family; she was still young enough, and surely Lily would enjoy having a brother or sister to share in her mischief. Either way, with love, hard work, and the fact that they would always have each other, all their dreams would come true. She was sure of it.

It was then that the pain returned, stronger than ever.

This time, it struck hard and deep enough to force a cry from her lips. Sarah swayed, her face twisting in agony, then dropped to her knees. Desperately, she grabbed a damp sheet, not wanting to fall farther; the fabric stretched, straining against the pins that held it in place, before finally giving way. She collapsed to the ground, the basket once again knocked over, laundry crushed beneath her, the pain incredible and endless.

"Morris…" she managed, knowing that her voice was too soft, her husband too far away to hear.

Lying in the grass, Sarah struggled to keep her fear at bay as darkness closed in from all around. She fought against it as hard as she could, not wanting to give up, not wanting to lose all she had, but in the end it was a fight she couldn't win. She could feel the warmth of sunlight on her skin. She could hear the flutter of laundry in the gentle breeze. She could smell the scent of detergent mingled with spring flowers. She felt hot tears spill down her cheeks. She remembered the joy of watching her husband and daughter play hide-and-seek.

And then she was gone.

Chapter One

October 1952

L<small>ILY</small> D<small>ENTON</small> <small>STOOD</small> beneath the maple tree in front of her house, an ocean of fallen leaves at her feet. The night sky was cloudy, the moon playing hide-and-seek, and it was breezy enough to make her shiver, forcing her to pull her coat close, stamping her feet for warmth. She worried it might rain. A battered suitcase, painstakingly packed with what she thought she'd need, as well as a few treasured mementos, lay on the ground beside her. A dog's sudden bark startled her and she stepped deeper into the shadows, fearful of being seen.

"This is crazy . . ." she muttered to herself.

Every few seconds, Lily looked up and down the street, the sidewalks lit by streetlamps, hoping to see the familiar red Oldsmobile, but the road remained empty. There was no point in checking her watch again; she'd done it so many times that she knew it was a handful of minutes past eleven. She had been standing beneath the tree for almost half an hour and was chilled to the bone. Lily hoped that she wouldn't get sick, because the last thing she needed was to—

From the far end of the street, a pair of headlights interrupted Lily's thoughts, making her heart hammer. She bent down and grabbed the suitcase's handle, feeling both nervous and excited. But just as she readied to run to the curb, she saw that it wasn't the Oldsmobile but a dented pickup truck. As it drove past, she once again found herself alone.

Not for the first time, Lily thought about giving up. Her father would likely still be in his office, writing or talking on the telephone no matter the late hour, so she would have to sneak inside, but worry was starting to get the better of her. Even though she'd been planning this moment for months, daydreaming about it for years, Lily had always known it was a house of cards, and that one strong gust of wind would knock the whole thing to the—

The honk of a car's horn startled her.

She stared in amazement as a red Oldsmobile zipped down the street toward her before finally coming to an abrupt stop against the curb.

"Hurry up, slowpoke!" Jane Dunaway shouted out the driver's-side window. "Let's get this show on the road!"

Lily ran to the car, the suitcase banging against her leg.

She was convinced that every last person in the neighborhood had been woken, that porch lights were about to come on up and down the street. She didn't dare glance back over her shoulder, certain that her father would be at the window, watching her with an angry, disapproving look on his face.

"Keep your voice down!" Lily whispered fiercely as she opened the passenger's door. "You're going to give us away!"

Jane answered with a loud laugh. "Who cares?" she asked. "No one can stop us now. Throw your stuff in the back and get in!"

Before Lily could even shut the door behind her, the Oldsmobile was already moving, the engine loud as it sped down the street.

"Isn't this great?" Jane shouted over the cold wind rushing in through her still-open window, making her long black hair whip in every direction. She reached over and squeezed Lily's hand. "New York City, here we come!"

Lily managed a weak smile, but she couldn't match Jane's enthusiasm. The reality of what she was doing slowly began to sink in.

She was running away from home.

Hooper's Crossing was located in upstate New York, alongside a crook in the Porter River and nestled among the Adirondack Mountains. The town's name had come from a centuries-old British trading post that had long since burned down. It was a quiet, scenic place; few of its six thousand inhabitants caused much trouble. Victorian houses, complete with white picket fences, had been built on wide, tree-lined streets. Hooper's Crossing was the ideal American town.

But for as long as Lily could remember, she'd wondered what it would be like to live somewhere else.

She'd spent countless hours staring out the window at school, lying in her bed late into the night, walking down Main Street, and sitting in a church pew, daydreaming about other places. Lily had tried to imagine the bustling crowds of a big city, the quiet solitude of a farm or a windswept coastal town. She even fantasized about the exotic life to be had in a city like Paris or Honolulu. She wanted to spin a globe, drop her finger on some random place, and then be instantly transported there. Instead, she never left Hooper's Crossing.

Mostly because of her father.

Morris Denton had been the town's mayor for more than a decade; some of Lily's earliest memories were of her father campaigning for office. In the months and years after the sudden, tragic death of his wife, Morris had thrown himself into his work. He was a tireless advocate, welcoming businesses that created jobs, as well as fund-raising for a new roof over the elementary school and a pavilion in City Park. Morris knew everyone in town by name, from the president of the bank all the way to his paperboy. He'd made it his mission to help his community and, by nearly all accounts, had succeeded spectacularly.

He was also a loving father, indulging Lily in clothes

and books, whatever he could afford to provide. He championed her education, encouraging good marks at school. Morris had tried to broaden his daughter's horizons; he bought tickets to concerts, introduced her to everyone-who-was-anyone around town, and had once taken her to Albany to meet the governor.

But to say that Morris Denton was protective of his daughter would have been the understatement of the century.

When Lily was little, Morris had picked out what she could wear, had told her what to eat, where she could go, and especially what kids she could be friends with. No detail was too small to escape his attention. Any disagreement was met with a lecture that might last an hour. No matter how much Lily cried or argued, her father always won, not because Morris was mean or shouted at her, but because he believed so strongly in his convictions that he couldn't be persuaded. Deep down, Lily knew that her father had been trying to do right by her, that as a widower he didn't have a spouse to go to for advice, but all throughout her childhood, she'd felt smothered.

Even now that Lily was twenty-one, her father continued to meddle. When she'd wanted to move out, to find a place of her own, Morris had discouraged her. When she suggested going off to college, he'd gotten her a job at the library instead. Worst of all, Lily was convinced that he had chased away romantic suitors, men who might've asked her out on a date. No one was good enough for his little girl.

Because of Morris's standing in Hooper's Crossing, nothing was going to change anytime soon. The only way she could leave was in her dreams.

And so Lily had been caught off-guard the afternoon three weeks back when Jane had leaned against the library's front desk and asked in a soft voice, "Want to run away to the big city with me?"

Jane had been Lily's best friend since kindergarten. Her father owned Dunaway's Department Store and was one of the friendliest people in Hooper's Crossing. But while Jane's two younger sisters flew straight as arrows, she liked to dance to the beat of her own drummer. Jane had never been afraid of a little trouble. She had been the first among their classmates to skip school, to take a sip of alcohol and puff on a cigarette, and she always seemed to have a hemline shorter than what was considered acceptable for a young lady. She certainly wasn't shy when it came to flirting, laughing, or voicing her opinion. Any one of these reasons should have been enough for Morris to order his daughter to stay far away, but because of her father's standing in town, he reluctantly gave the girl a pass.

So because Jane could be prone to big, impractical plans and flights of fancy, Lily had laughed off her question. "How about tomorrow?" she replied with a smile. "I'll have to check my calendar, but I think I'm free."

"I'm serious," Jane said. "As soon as I have a little more money saved up, I'm gone. I want you to come with me."

Lily knew that Jane's reasons for leaving were different from her own. For one, she was a knockout, the sort of beautiful woman who could turn a man's head halfway around his shoulders just by walking down a sidewalk. With her friend's long black hair and sharp feminine features, Lily had always expected Jane to end up in Hollywood making movies or be on a billboard advertising clothes or cigarettes. Running off to New York City was likely a step in that direction. Jane believed that Hooper's Corner was holding her back from bigger and better things.

She wasn't the only one who felt that way. Lily knew she wasn't as attractive as Jane. Sure, her shoulder-length blond hair was curly and her eyes a sparkling emerald green, but whenever she looked at her reflection in her bedroom mirror, what she noticed was the smattering of freckles across the bridge of her nose and the soft curve of her cheeks and chin, details she thought made her look a bit childish. Lily didn't think she was an ugly duckling, but if she was standing next to Jane, few people would have thought her to be a swan. Still, Jane's offer was the opportunity Lily had been waiting for, a chance to finally escape her father's controlling ways.

In the end, it was an offer she couldn't refuse.

"I'll go," Lily had answered.

For the next few weeks, they'd made plans while talking on the telephone or meeting during Lily's lunch breaks at the library. She withdrew her savings from the bank, hoping the money would last until she found a job. They wrote out lists of what they wanted to take, crossing out some items while adding others; at first, Jane simply didn't understand why she couldn't take *all* her wardrobe. Everything was meticulously packed in the suitcase she then stashed in the back of her closet, though she constantly worried that her father would somehow find it. But he hadn't and the days kept ticking by until finally it was time to go.

That afternoon, Lily had gone to the cemetery, to her mother's granite tombstone where she'd talked and cried, often at the same time. Sitting on the grass, watching leaves fall from the nearby trees, she spoke of her hopes and fears, attempting to explain herself to someone who couldn't reply. Later, back home, she'd written her father a letter. In it, she tried to tell him why she was leaving, to make him understand. The crumpled pages scattered on the floor around her were a testament to how hard it had been to find the right words. At the end, she had told him not to worry, that she would write when they reached their destination, and that she loved him. Just before she snuck out, she placed the letter on her pillow; when Morris realized that she was missing, he would quickly find it.

This was a new beginning, the very thing Lily had always wanted.

So why did it feel so wrong…

Jane steered the Oldsmobile through the quiet neighborhoods. Rather than take the shortest route out of town, she turned onto Main Street as if she wanted one last look at the place before leaving. Staring out her window, Lily watched the familiar sights roll by: Will Burton's barbershop, the post office, Sally Lange's bakery, the Hooper's Crossing Bank and Trust, as well as the library in which she'd spent so many hours. On the corner opposite the movie theater was the business Jane's father owned and ran, Dunaway's Department Store.

"*There's* a place I never want to see again," her friend said, frowning as they drove past. "If I had a nickel for every box of mousetraps I unloaded, screwdriver I priced, or can of tomatoes I lined up on a shelf, there'd be enough money for us to fly to the city."

"I always had a soft spot for the candy counter," Lily replied. "Your dad always had the best lemon drops."

Jane shook her head. "Maybe so, but no candy is worth sticking around here," she said with a wink. "There's better where we're going, anyway."

Main Street ended where it ran into City Park. Wooden booths in various stages of completion lined the sidewalks under the streetlamps. Homemade banners advertised NEW YORK'S TASTIEST APPLES, WOOL SWEATERS—STITCHED TO YOUR SIZE, HAND-CARVED BIRD-HOUSES, and dozens of other goods. Strings of lights, currently unlit, had been wound into tree branches and stretched toward the pavilion in the center of the park, the very one Lily's father had been instrumental in having built; in a matter of days, musicians would play and the park would overflow with hundreds of people, many dancing under the stars. The Hooper's Crossing Fall Festival, an annual event that drew people from hundreds of miles in every direction and culminated in a Halloween night party and parade where almost everyone wore a costume, was about to begin.

"Aren't you going to miss this?" Lily asked as the Oldsmobile finally left town and headed for the highway.

"The fall festival?" Jane replied.

Lily nodded.

"Not in the least."

Lily couldn't help but laugh. "You make it sound like the worst thing in the world! You've had lots of fun there over the years!"

"All right, so it hasn't been *all* bad," Jane admitted a bit reluctantly. "Remember, that's where Jake Conroy kissed me behind the bandstand."

From there, it was as if the floodgates had been thrown open on their memories of growing up in Hooper's Crossing. Driving out of town, they reminisced about days long past: the summer afternoon they'd dared each other to jump off the bridge into the Porter River, both of them screaming the whole way down; Martin Bradley's ninth birthday party when Katie Sharp had eaten too much cake and gotten sick all down the front of her new dress; the shiveringly cold February day when Jane had caught Dave Cooke, the projectionist at the movie theater, shoplifting tins of hair pomade from her father's store. But even as laughter filled the Oldsmobile, Lily felt a strange sadness settle over her, and no matter how hard she tried to shake it off, it refused to let go.

On the road ahead, the car's headlights illuminated a large sign announcing that they were leaving Hooper's

Crossing. It quickly loomed before them, its colors bright, then vanished and all was dark.

And something inside Lily cracked.

"Stop the car," she said, the words quiet and mumbled.

When Jane didn't respond, still talking about the time Matt Hoskins had forgotten the words to "Silent Night" during his solo at the school Christmas concert, Lily repeated herself, this time loud and clear enough to be heard.

"What for?" Jane asked. "Did you forget something?"

"Just pull over!" Lily snapped, the sharp sound of her voice surprising even her, her heart racing faster than the speeding car.

Jane did as her friend asked, guiding the Oldsmobile onto the road's shoulder and pressing down hard enough on the brakes to make the tires slide in the soft gravel. For a long moment, neither of them spoke, the only sound the ticking of the car's engine.

Sitting in the silence, Lily searched her feelings, trying to understand why she'd suddenly gotten cold feet. The answer didn't take long to find; it was there in the silent stalls of the festival, the shops along Main Street, the billboard on the way out of town. Hooper's Crossing was her *home*. No matter how much she had dreamed about leaving, the truth was, she was scared to go. The grass might be greener elsewhere, but what if it wasn't? And even though her father meddled in her life, Lily still loved him. In the years since her mother's death, all they'd had was each other. If she left, especially like this, without telling him, she would be abandoning him. She wasn't willing to break his heart all over again.

"I can't do it," she finally said, staring at her hands, folded in her lap. "I can't go to New York City."

"Sure you can," Jane replied encouragingly. "It's easy. We take the highway once we reach Lewiston and from there, all we have to do is—"

"I'm not going," Lily interrupted, raising her eyes to look at her friend.

Jane's cheerful expression deflated. She nodded, then looked out the windshield into the darkness.

"I'm sorry," Lily said, feeling more than a little guilty. "I know you had your heart set on us going. But who knows, maybe next spring things will be different and we can try again. Both of us can save up more money and—"

"I'm still going," Jane interrupted.

Lily was too shocked to answer.

"When I came to see you in the library that day," her friend continued, "I'd made up my mind, and nothing that's happened since has changed it." She hesitated, then turned to Lily. "You might be able to keep living here, but I can't bear the thought of another day. I want more than Hooper's Crossing can offer."

Without another word, Jane turned the car around and started back in the direction they'd come.

Lily stood in the street with the door open. Jane had stopped at the end of the block, far enough away so that Morris wouldn't see them. They'd already shared a long hug, Lily apologizing for what felt like the twentieth time, but still she lingered, not yet ready for her friend to leave.

"It's awfully late," she said, looking up at the dark sky. "Are you sure you don't want to wait and go tomorrow?"

Jane shook her head. "It's like my dad always told me when I didn't want to unload boxes in the storeroom. There's no better time than the present."

"I understand," Lily said, and in a way she did. "Be safe."

"I will," Jane agreed as she put the Oldsmobile in gear. "And I promise I'll write just as soon as I can. I want you to know what you're missing." Lily smiled weakly at her friend's good-natured teasing. But then, just as she was about to say good-bye, Jane added, "It's not too late to change your mind. Again..."

Lily shut the car door without a word, then watched as Jane drove away, not moving until the car's taillights were out of sight.

Trudging toward home, Lily's suitcase felt as if it weighed a hundred pounds. Every step she took seemed to add another question for her to worry about. Was she making the right choice in staying? Had her father found her note? If he hadn't, would she be able to sneak back into the house without being seen? Would Jane be all right by herself in the big city?

This time, answers were hard to come by.

Her house came into view. Lily was relieved to see that light still shone from the window of her father's office; that meant that he was still awake, working on something, and likely hadn't discovered her note. She stashed the suitcase in the bushes in front of the porch, knowing that she could retrieve it in the morning before she left for work.

But then, just as Lily stepped onto the driveway, already considering how to get inside unnoticed, she was blinded by a glaring light. Then the quiet of the night was broken by a man's forceful shout.

"Freeze! This is the police!"

Chapter Two

LILY WAS TOO FRIGHTENED to scream. Her heart and thoughts raced. She spun around and was momentarily blinded by the light, forcing her to quickly look away. She struggled to make sense of what was happening, further worried that her father was about to come stomping onto the porch to investigate what was disturbing him at such a late hour.

But then the light vanished and laughter filled the night.

"You should see the look on your face! I got you good!"

And just like that, Lily knew who it was.

Garrett Doyle was nearly doubled over on the drive, one hand slapping his knee while the other held a flashlight. He wore his police officer's uniform, a badge pinned to the breast pocket, a gun holstered at his hip; he hadn't been lying when he announced himself. His squad car was parked across the street in front of his own house. Lily must have been so preoccupied with her father seeing her that she hadn't noticed it.

She should have. Garrett had almost always been a part of her life.

Lily had been eight when Garrett's parents were killed in a car accident and the orphaned seven-year old had come to live with his mother's folks, the Dentons' neighbors. At first, the boy had been quiet, shy, and plenty sad, understandable given the circumstances. But with persistence, as well as the knowledge of how lonely life could be without a parent, Lily finally managed to draw Garrett out of his shell. Together, they raced around on hot summer nights, collecting fireflies in Mason jars. They set up a lemonade stand on the sidewalk and used their earnings to watch Tarzan matinees and buy comic books. They pulled Garrett's wagon up and down the street, collecting tin cans and newspapers, doing their part to support the war effort against the Germans and Japanese. Where one went, the other was sure to follow.

Morris had never minded the two of them spending time together. As protective as he was when it came to his daughter, he found Garrett to be an honest, hard-working boy who was attentive and caring toward his elderly grandparents. Garrett hadn't hurt his case by becoming a police officer, either. As the youngest member of the Hooper's Crossing Police Department, he patrolled his community's streets, helping to keep it safe.

But while Garrett hadn't changed much on the inside, his outside was plenty different. He was no longer a skinny, somewhat awkward boy whose blond hair always stood up in the back, his elbows and knees covered in scrapes and scabs. His shoulders were now broad, his chest full, and his arms muscled. His unruly locks had been tamed, his chin kept free of whiskers, his smile as bright as the flashlight he'd shone in her face. But whenever one of Lily's friends commented on how handsome Garrett was, she couldn't help but laugh. She just couldn't think of him that way. After all, he was the brother she'd never really had.

Which was why he was so good at teasing her.

"You scared me half to death!" Lily hissed, her heart still racing.

"Sorry, but I couldn't resist," Garrett explained with a chuckle, making her doubt how sincere his apology really was. "I saw you and thought I'd have a little fun."

"At my expense!"

Garrett held up his hands. "Guilty as charged," he confessed, then asked, "What are you doing out here at this hour, anyway?"

Unable to stop herself, Lily looked toward the porch where she'd just stashed her suitcase; she could see the edge of it, poking out from under the bushes. She wondered how long Garrett had been watching her. Had he seen her coming down the street? Did he know about the bag? Quickly, Lily decided that he didn't, otherwise he would've already asked about it. Not wanting to give herself away now, Lily tore her eyes from the suitcase and moved a couple of steps to her right, drawing his attention away from the house.

"I couldn't sleep," she lied. "I thought that some fresh air might clear my head."

Garrett waved an arm toward the sky. "You didn't try counting stars?"

Lily smiled. When they were little, they'd counted the twinkling pinpricks of light outside their bedroom windows to help them fall asleep. The next morning, they would reveal the number they'd reached; the one with the higher tally was the winner. "Maybe I should have," she said.

"Used to work for me. Heck, it still does from time to time."

For a moment, looking at Garrett smile at the sky, Lily considered telling him that she'd nearly left town. For the weeks she and Jane had been planning their getaway, Lily had agonized over whether to confide in him, wondering what Garrett would think, worrying that he would tell her father or try to talk her out of going. In the end, though she felt plenty guilty, Lily had chosen to stay silent. Now she couldn't help but think that deep down she'd known she wouldn't go.

So instead she asked, "Did you just get off work?"

"About an hour ago," Garrett answered. "I forgot something in the squad car and had just come outside to get it when I saw you."

When his grandmother passed away last year, Garrett had inherited the home he'd grown up in and eagerly returned. Whereas Lily fantasized about being somewhere else, he'd never wanted to leave.

"Are things getting busier now that the festival's about to start?" Lily asked.

"A bit. There are new faces here and there. In a couple of days it'll be a circus and a half, but for now my nights are spent rousting Marvin Ungar from the tavern and changing Betsy Pepper's flat tire out on Simmons Road. About the same as any other time of year."

"Do you think there'll be trouble at the festival?" Lily asked.

Garrett shrugged, as if he wasn't all that concerned. "I'll break up a fight or two, likely a couple of guys from out of town who've had too much to drink. There might be a fender-bender or a pickpocket working the crowd, but nothing much more than that." He paused, then asked, "Are you planning on going?"

"My dad will want me to listen to him read some proclamation about the lights donated by the Women's Auxiliary Club or the day in honor of the Boy Scouts, but I'm sure I'll check it out on my own."

"On your own? What about Jane?"

She'll be too busy having the time of her life on Broadway to spare a thought for the Hooper's Crossing Fall Festival...

"With or without her," Lily said, "there are things I'd like to see."

"Like Cliff Anderson's booth?" Garrett asked with a chuckle. "I seem to recall that you're awfully fond of his candied apples."

"You know me well," she admitted. "But what about

you? Are you going to be able to have some fun or do you have to work?"

"Chief Huntington has me scheduled almost every night but I'm supposed to have Friday off." He hesitated, his eyes flicking toward Lily, then away. "Actually, that reminds me of something," he said. "I thought that if you didn't have anything planned, maybe you'd want to—"

But before Garrett could finish, the front door of the Dentons' house opened and Morris stepped onto the porch. Even as Lily heard the rusty hinges creak, a feeling of dread grabbed hold of her and squeezed tight. She couldn't help but feel like a child again, caught doing something she shouldn't. Somehow, she had been so wrapped up in her conversation with Garrett that she'd forgotten she needed to sneak back inside. Now it was too late.

Lily's father came to the railing and stared down at them. The mayor of Hooper's Crossing wasn't a small man; some would surely have called him fat, though never to Morris's face. His weight rose every year, slowly but surely, straining against buttons, stretching collars and cuffs. His growing waistline was likely the result of too many trips to the local diner, scarfing down greasy burgers and fries, as well as late nights dipping into the well-stocked candy jar on his desk; Morris's sweet tooth was well known around town. He was aware of his girth, maybe even a bit embarrassed, and wore a short beard to cover much of the hang of his jowls. Every year he vowed to shed some pounds but always failed.

Morris's personality was as large as he was. He over-flowed with good cheer and positivity. All of his life, he had been a tireless supporter of his community and the people living in it. Burning the candle at both ends, it sometimes felt as if he was everywhere at once, shaking hands, slapping shoulders, and laughing loud enough to make his belly jiggle. After his wife's death, Morris had thrown himself into his work. He'd been mayor for almost a decade now, each year seemingly busier than the last. When she was little, Lily often complained that her father wasn't home; plenty of afternoons were spent with Garrett and his family, evenings with a sitter. But when he *was* there, she complained that he was too strict, not letting her do this or that. In short, their relationship was more than a little complicated.

"I thought I heard voices out here," Morris said.

"Lily and I were just talking, Mr. Denton," Garrett ex-plained, formally addressing her father, as he'd done since he was a boy. "Sorry if we bothered you."

"No problem at all," Lily's father answered. "As a matter of fact, I'm thankful for the interruption. I had no idea it had gotten so late. Speaking of which," Morris added, turning to his daughter, "I'm surprised to see you out here at such an hour, young lady."

"I couldn't sleep," Lily lied for the second time that night. "I didn't want to bother you, so I slipped out the side door."

"She would've been back a while ago if I hadn't come over and pestered her," Garrett said, sugarcoating how he'd scared her half to death while simultaneously build-ing her alibi. "It's my fault she hasn't come in yet."

Even as the young police officer spoke, Lily kept ex-pecting her father to look down from the porch and notice her suitcase in the bushes, bringing the whole house of cards she'd built crashing down. But Morris's attention didn't waver. It was far too focused on her.

"Thank you for keeping an eye on her, Garrett," he said, "but it's late. I think it best that we all call it a night."

"Yes, sir." But before he started back across the street to-ward home, Garrett gently took Lily by the elbow. "Maybe tomorrow we can continue our conversation," he said, his voice low, as if he was trying to keep her father from hear-ing. "There's something I'd like to ask you." He allowed his touch to linger an instant longer, his eyes bright even in the dark gloom, until he finally walked away. Lily watched him go, wondering what he wanted to talk about.

She was supposed to be with Jane on their way to New York City, about to start a brand-new life. Instead, Lily was right where she'd always been.

And it looked like nothing would ever change.

"...those many long years ago when the first fall festival was held here in Hooper's Crossing. Back then, it was meant to celebrate the harvest, a time when friends and neighbors could come together, share a meal and con-versation, a moment of good cheer before the coming of winter when..."

Lily sat before her father's desk, struggling to pay

attention as Morris practiced his speech. He paced back and forth, one hand clutching his script while the other cut through the air, punctuating the perceived importance of his words. Lily stifled a yawn. No sooner had she trudged up the steps, taking one last look at her suitcase in the bushes, than Morris had asked her to listen to his remarks. Even though it was the *last* thing Lily had wanted to do—she would have much rather gone to sleep—her feelings of guilt, especially for having lied to both Garrett and her father, made her reluctantly accept.

"...note that we are especially indebted to the members of our business community who have made sizable donations of time and money. Without them, we wouldn't have new lights for the pavilion, posters that have been hung around..."

When Morris spoke, he was transformed. His blue eyes shone like precious stones and his chubby cheeks glowed a healthy red. He truly seemed to be enjoying himself. Lily had always suspected that her father was a performer, someone who was born to stand before an audience, the focus of everyone's attention. Still, he looked tired to her, even a bit disheveled with his shirttail untucked and a smattering of whiskers on his cheeks. The dish that had always sat on the corner of his desk, usually filled to the brim with butterscotch and peppermint candies, was nearly empty, a telltale sign that her father wasn't eating well.

"...get bigger and better with every year. We've had visitors from all around the state, from New England,

Pennsylvania, and as far away as California. Why, people have even made the long voyage across the Atlantic, traveling from France to visit relatives, but also to take in our wondrous…"

If things had been just a little different, if she hadn't gotten a case of cold feet, Lily would have been sitting beside Jane in the Oldsmobile, traveling darkened highways that led to the big city and a new life. Instead, Jane drove on alone while Lily was still at home, a place she wondered if she'd ever have the courage to leave. She glanced up, trying to act as if she was paying attention, and caught a glimpse of her mother's photograph on the wall. The picture had been taken a year before Sarah Denton's tragic death and captured her just as Lily remembered. She smiled brightly with a hint of mischief in her eyes, as if she was just about to laugh. It had always been Lily's favorite photo, but now it seemed like her mother's expression wasn't quite so cheerful, almost as if Sarah was disappointed in her only child.

"…hope you have the best fall festival yet!" Morris finished, then looked expectantly at his daughter. "Well?" he asked. "What did you think?"

"Uh…it was good…" Lily managed.

"Good?" her father echoed, looking disappointed. "I was hoping you'd like it a little more than that."

Hoping to right the ship, so to say, Lily said, "I especially enjoyed the part about the pavilion's new lights. They look great."

No sooner had the words left her mouth than Lily

froze, her heart beating wildly. The lights hadn't been strung to the pavilion until that afternoon; she'd passed the workers on her way home from the library. The only reason she knew what they looked like all lit up was because she and Jane had driven past the park on their way out of town. If she'd been in the house all evening like she wanted her father to believe, how could she have seen them?

But fortunately for Lily, her father didn't notice her slipup. "I like that part, too!" he exclaimed. "Those lights are the nicest addition to the festival in years." Morris paused, a wrinkle in his brow. "But that reminds me, I wanted to put something in about the Methodist church's bake sale. Betsy Abercrombie would have my hide if I forgot." He reached for a pen, then paused and looked at his daughter. "Thank you, Lily. You're always such a big help."

It was usually true, at least when she wasn't so distracted. For years, Lily had served as her father's sounding board, listening to speech after speech, everything from the dedication of a new building to a funeral eulogy, from Christmas well-wishes to the start of the Fourth of July parade. To his credit, Morris listened to her, too. Whenever Lily suggested a different word or reminded him of something or someone he'd forgotten, he made the necessary changes.

"One more thing, Lily," Morris said as he made an addition to his speech.

"Yes, Dad?"

"I know you were having trouble sleeping, but I don't

want you outside at such a late hour," her father explained, his eyes never leaving his papers.

"I was fine," she answered, her tone a bit defensive. "Garrett was with me."

"And I'm thankful he was there," Morris replied as his gaze finally wandered from his speech, rising to stare out at the darkness beyond the window. "But there will be lots of people coming to town for the festival whom I wouldn't know from Adam. Most will be good, honest folks who won't cause a lick of trouble, but there'll be a few bad apples. There always are. Because of that, I'd feel better knowing you were safely at home." Morris looked over and gave his daughter a smile. "Next time you can't sleep, try a glass of warm milk instead."

For a moment, Lily wanted to argue, to tell her father that she wasn't a child anymore, that she could take care of herself. She was even tempted to confess to nearly leaving town with Jane. Unlike when she'd considered telling Garrett, to confide in him, now Lily wanted to shock, to show Morris that there was much more to her than he suspected. She could only imagine his reaction. But then Lily once again looked at her mother's photograph, and understood that she wouldn't say a word. It was already too late.

After all, this was the choice she had made.

Now she just had to live with it.

Chapter Three

BOONE TATUM STOMPED his feet and blew on his bare hands in a futile attempt to warm himself. A brisk early-morning breeze blew across the Hudson River, beneath the towering bridges, to where he stood on a Brooklyn dock. The sun was still a good twenty minutes from rising, only now coloring the bottoms of the scuttling clouds in shades of purple and orange, and far longer from providing warmth. But Boone wasn't leaving anytime soon, so he jammed his hands deep into his jacket pockets and turned away from the teeth of the wind.

He had a picture to take.

For the last four years, Boone had worked as a photographer for *Life* magazine. At twenty-six, he had seen far more of the world than he would ever have expected, with plenty more traveling to come. Assignments had taken him from war-ravaged and rebuilding Europe and Asia, to the jungles of South America and the deserts of Africa.

His camera had captured elephants bathing in an Indian river, an outdoor market in a Mexican village, two lovers embracing on a California beach, and dozens of other moments, sad, celebratory, frightening, and every other emotion in between. But sometimes he wanted to photograph something simple.

And that's why I'm here, freezing my ass off…

New York City was home. Every time Boone returned from some far-flung corner of the globe, he felt a familiar itch, the siren call of a picture he'd always longed to take. It would be of the river, parts of it still swathed in morning fog, backlit by a rising sun that would illuminate tugboats and the towering buildings beyond. Boone could have taken this picture in dozens of cities worldwide; Marseille, Istanbul, San Francisco, or Buenos Aires were all on the water and would've given him something similar. But none of those places was *New York*, the biggest and brashest city in the most powerful nation on earth. None would've looked quite right, like a giant rising from a night's slumber. And so, after years of putting it off, complaining that he was too busy or that the conditions were wrong, Boone had risen before dawn, hailed a taxi, and set out to capture the perfect picture.

He'd been picky. Searching along the shoreline, making his way through the near-dark, Boone had rejected one place after another; the light wouldn't be enough or there weren't enough skyscrapers in the background. Finally, he had found the right view. Unfortunately, it was behind a chain-link fence on which hung a sign warning away trespassers.

"Like that's going to stop me," he'd said to himself before climbing the fence and dropping down on the other side.

Wishing that he'd brought a heavier coat, Boone lifted his brand-new Mycro out of his camera bag and looked through the viewfinder. He was still getting used to it—there were a few more bells and whistles than his old Perkeo—but it took one hell of a picture. He was careful with it, too, which made sense since it was the most valuable item he owned, probably worth more than the rest of his stuff combined. Boone wasn't satisfied with the shot, not yet, but once the sun had another five minutes or so to rise, he would be able to start snapping photos.

Then he'd have to find someone to buy them.

No one had asked him to come down to the docks before sunrise. He was freelancing it, all the way. But if this shot turned out the way Boone expected, he felt confident that he could plop it down on the desk of Walter Bing, his boss at *Life*, and name his price. Hell, it might even make the cover.

Not for the first time that morning, Boone thought about Daisy. She hadn't moved a muscle as he was getting ready to leave the apartment. She would have come along if he'd asked, but he hadn't had the heart; he knew how much she liked her sleep. Maybe when he got back, they could go out and—

"Hey!" a voice suddenly shouted behind him. "You there!"

Boone turned and saw a man striding purposefully toward him. He was big, considerably broader across the shoulders than Boone. Dressed like a longshoreman, he also wore an ugly scowl.

"Aw, hell..." Boone muttered to himself.

"This is private property," the man snapped once he'd reached the trespassing photographer. Up close, he was even more intimidating, with hands as big as canned hams and muscles that strained the fabric of his shirt. "You ain't supposed to be here." Pointing at the camera, he added, "Especially not with that."

Boone chose to put on an easy smile. He'd been in plenty of situations like this before, caught somewhere he wasn't supposed to be, needing to smooth things over before they got worse; at least this time the other guy spoke English. If he played things cool and used his charms, he'd get what he wanted, then be out of this guy's hair. "I wasn't trying to cause trouble," he said in a friendly tone. "I just—"

"I don't give a damn why you're here," the man interrupted, taking a menacing step forward, "only that you beat it."

"Look, buddy," Boone said, some of his fake good cheer falling away. He waved an arm toward the brightening city skyline. "I only need a couple more minutes to snap some pictures and then I'll be on my way. Just let me—"

Once again, the longshoreman cut Boone off, this time with a shove to the chest hard enough to make the photographer take a staggering step back. "What're ya, deaf?" he shouted. "You either start makin' tracks right now, or I'm gonna knock you on your ass and carry you out! Either way, you're leavin'."

Boone frowned, then reached into his back pocket to pull out his wallet. There had been plenty of times in the past when slipping a handful of bills into an angry person's palm had gotten him what he wanted. If that's what it now took to get the shot he needed, that he had gotten up so damn early for, then so be it. "What's it going to take?" he asked, hoping it wasn't much. "How's about—"

"Ain't no amount of money gonna delay me throwin' you outta here," the longshoreman cut in.

Boone stared back hard at the man for a long moment, his jaw tense, then nodded. He put his wallet away and then bent down and placed his camera back in its bag, as if he was intending to leave, but the truth was he wanted to keep it safe from what he knew was likely to come next. When he leaned up, he folded his arms across his chest. "I'm not going anywhere."

The other man's scowl deepened. "What did you say?"

"I've been dreaming about snapping this picture for so long, there's no way I'm leaving until it's taken, whether you like it or not."

In his time as a photographer, Boone had talked his way out of plenty of pickles, but sometimes words couldn't get the job done. Watching the other man sneer, then walk toward him, Boone understood that *this* was one of those times.

Every once in a while, he needed to use his fists.

Boone stewed in a chair in his editor's office on the third floor of *Life* magazine's building on West 31st Street. He was alone, but the familiar sounds of the newsroom barged in through the cracked door. There was the rat-a-tat-tat of typewriter keys as columnists hurried to meet their deadlines. He heard the incessant ringing of telephones, like some strange symphony where every musician had different sheet music. A dozen people were talking at once, their conversations occasionally punctuated by a burst of laughter or a name being shouted across the room. The stale smell of cigarettes and burnt coffee filled the air.

Leaning forward, Boone took a picture frame off Walter Bing's desk. The photograph was of a middle-aged woman and a youngish boy; Boone didn't recognize either of them, though the kid shared enough of a resemblance to his old man that it was clear this was Walter's family. But Boone hadn't picked it up out of curiosity. He tilted the frame so that he could see his reflection in the glass.

"Aw, hell," he said for the second time that day.

A dark bruise blossomed on Boone's cheekbone, the result of a punch he hadn't been able to avoid. Gingerly, he touched it with his fingertips, wincing from the sudden pain. The brawl with the longshoreman had been short but ferocious. Boone felt that he'd given as good as he'd gotten, better than might have been expected given the size difference between him and his opponent. But things had taken a turn for the worse when a couple of other workers had noticed the commotion and come running, tipping the balance and not in his favor. Fortunately for Boone, a beat cop had walked past the fence at that moment, blowing his whistle and putting a halt to the brawl. He'd hauled the photographer off to the precinct house and charged him with trespassing, but Boone knew he was lucky. Things could have been much, much worse.

And they still might be...

Boone was still looking at his nicks and bruises when the door to the office banged open and Walter Bing entered. The editor snatched the frame from Boone's hand and put it back on his desk. "You want a better look at yourself, use the mirror above the sink in the bathroom," he said, then took a longer glance at the photographer before settling into his chair. "Although I wouldn't advise it."

"Thanks a lot," Boone grumbled.

Walter Bing had been in the publishing industry for longer than Boone had been alive. He'd gotten his start in newspapers, moving from the street corner hawking the evening edition to the office, then on to the glitzy "slick" magazines that made their money on Hollywood news and gossip, before finally joining *Life*. Walter was in his mid-fifties, thin with perpetual dark bags beneath his eyes, a testament to the late hours he kept and the countless cigarettes he smoked. Both demanding and fair, he didn't play favorites and rewarded talent wherever he saw it, but employees quickly learned that they crossed him at their own peril.

The editor leaned back in his chair. "You know, I'm not going to pretend that we don't know why you're here," he said with a sigh. "It's not as if this is the first time you've been sent to the principal's office."

And it wasn't. Far from it.

Even though he was a talented photographer, Boone seemed to attract trouble like a magnet. There was the time he'd been chased out of Broxton, Florida, with the speedometer buried, racing to stay just ahead of an angry mob. After dashing into a burning building in Madrid, a fireman had barely yanked him out before the ceiling collapsed. And then there were the fistfights in Honolulu, Cairo, and Copenhagen, to say nothing of what had happened that morning.

"It was a misunderstanding," Boone said, defending himself.

"Isn't it always," Walter replied, clearly not believing that explanation.

"If that big lug would've just done what I told him and backed off, I would've taken my picture and been out of his hair. He's nursing a black eye and a fat lip because he wouldn't listen."

"You're just lucky they didn't charge you with more than trespassing."

"About that," Boone began. "Thanks for bailing me out."

Fortunately, he'd only had to stew in a jail cell for a

couple of hours, mostly spent fending off the drunks and drifters who thought pestering him would be a fun way to pass the time. When a policeman shouted his name and unlocked the door, Boone had been given back his camera bag and made a beeline for the *Life* offices.

Walter shook his hand. "No thanks needed," he said. "I had nothing to do with it. If it had been up to me, I would've let you spend a night or two in jail to knock some sense into that thick skull of yours."

"Well if you didn't do it, then who did?"

The editor pointed at the ceiling. "The higher-ups around here admire your talent for taking pictures. They figure you're worth the headache," he explained. "Then again, they don't have to deal with your crap as often as I do."

Boone thought about apologizing again, but couldn't; he'd already done more of that than he liked.

"And after all that, you didn't even get the picture."

"No," Boone said with a frown, a flare of anger igniting in his stomach. "And to make matters worse, I'm out a camera."

As soon as he'd gotten out of jail, Boone had opened his camera bag on the precinct's front steps and found that his brand-new Mycro was broken. He had no idea if it had happened during the brawl or if the policeman had been careless with it when he'd hauled Boone away. Either way, he was now out one valuable piece of equipment. He'd have to make do with his old Perkeo for a while.

"That's too bad," the older man said without much sympathy.

"Look, Walter, I give you my word it won't happen again," Boone began, laying on the charm for a promise he wasn't certain he could keep. "Now, if you could help me out with the camera, maybe get the magazine to front me the money for a new one, then I can head down to Havana next week and take the—"

"You're not going," the editor interrupted.

Boone was momentarily stunned into silence. "Wait...what're you saying...?" he stumbled.

"You might have skated out of that jail cell without much of a scratch," Walter answered, pointing at the mark on Boone's face, "but you didn't think there weren't going to be consequences for this, did you? You're off any plum assignments, effective immediately."

"Oh, come on!" Boone snapped, rising out of his chair. The Havana trip had been planned for months, long enough for him to have spent plenty of time imagining the sandy stretches of beach, cold beer, and lovely senoritas waiting there for him. He wasn't going to let it go without a fight. "I just got in a little scrape, that's all! Now you're telling me I'm shelved? This is ridiculous!"

"First things first, sit back down," Walter said with a hint of steel in his voice, pointing at Boone's recently vacated chair. Once the young photographer had reluctantly done as he'd been told, he continued. "Second, I didn't say you were being suspended, only that you're not going to Havana." He slid a folder across the desk toward Boone. "I've got somewhere else in mind for you."

Boone snatched up the folder and began to quickly

read its contents. With every passing word, his mood soured. "You've got to be kidding me."

"Hooper's Crossing, New York," the editor said with a smile, crossing his arms behind his head. "They have a fall festival that apparently draws quite the crowd. Music, crafts, food, that sort of thing. Hell, maybe there's even a hayride, a barn dance, or a contest where you bob for apples."

"I've never heard of this place."

"It's upstate somewhere," Walter replied with a shrug. "There's a few thousand people, one of countless other towns just like it. I'll get you a map."

"And *Life* wants pictures?" Boone asked in disbelief.

"It's for a new section that's going to go in the back of the magazine. 'Slices of America' or something like that. Little snapshots of here and there to make readers feel as if they know the rest of the country." He grinned broadly. "And you're going to take the pictures that will show them what they're missing."

Boone tossed the folder back on the desk. "I'm not doing this."

Walter shrugged. "Then you're fired."

"You're bluffing," Boone said, although he was pretty sure he didn't sound as confident as he hoped.

Once again, Walter pointed toward the ceiling. "It was one of the conditions of bailing you out," he explained. "Besides, think of how many photographers are out there waiting for you to fail so they can have your job. Hotshots fresh out of school who only want a chance to show what they can do. I bet that I could hire someone within an hour of you walking out that door. And to keep that from happening, all you have to do is drive up there, take some shots that really capture the festival, the people there, and bring them back to me."

"I'm too good a photographer for this."

"You are," the editor agreed. "One of the best I have, but that doesn't change the assignment. This is what you've got."

"Fine," Boone grumbled, grabbing the folder. "I'll go."

Walter started to chuckle.

"What's so damn funny?"

"It's just that you're already bent out of shape and I haven't even told you the best part."

"Which is?" Boone asked, a shiver of dread running down his spine.

"Clive Negly is going with you."

Up until that moment, Boone had assumed that things couldn't get much worse for him, but Walter had just shown him how wrong he could be. Clive Negly was the newest writer the magazine had hired. Fresh out of college, he was as green as May grass. The few times Boone had been in the office with Clive, he'd been bombarded with questions about his travels, quizzed on how to get ahead in the business, about practically everything under the sun. The idea of traveling to Hooper's Corner or Crossing or whatever the heck the place was called, with Clive beside him, couldn't have appealed less to Boone.

"Are you *trying* to make me quit?" he asked.

"From where I'm sitting, it makes a lot of sense," Walter replied. "The kid needs experience and who better to give it to him than someone who's seen it all. Show him the ropes, keep him from making the same mistakes you did."

Boone frowned. "What could I possibly teach him? Clive's a writer and I take pictures. We aren't speaking the same language."

"Sure you are," the editor disagreed. "How different is looking for just the right word from finding the best angle for a shot? In either case, you're trying to be professional, to tell the story as best you can. You're saying that there wasn't a writer you've worked with who taught you a thing or two?"

Deep down, Boone knew Walter was right, even if he refused to admit it.

"If I go, I'm taking Daisy with me," he said, desperately trying to throw a monkey wrench into the works.

"Fine by me," the other man replied. "She'd love to get out of the city for a while. The poor girl probably spends too much time cooped up indoors anyway." Seeing that Boone's mouth was opening to raise another complaint, Walter added, "My advice to you it to take this seriously. Do it right, work with Clive, bring me back some good pictures, and you'll get the good assignments again. But if you screw up, well..."

Walter may have left the rest unsaid, but Boone heard him loud and clear.

Another mistake and he was out on his ass.

Without another word, Boone took the folder and left

his editor's office, stomping across the newsroom, headed for the door. By the time he reached it, he was already for-mulating a plan, one that would get him in and out of this Hooper's whatever-it-was as fast as conceivably possible.

Walter, Clive, and everyone else be damned.

Chapter Four

"WHO COMMANDED THE BRITISH FORCES at the Battle of Yorktown?"

Lily looked up from her place behind the front desk of the Hooper's Crossing Library to find Sherman Banks staring expectantly at her. Eighty-six and as wrinkled as a prune, though dapperly dressed in a tweed suit, Sherman was one of the library's regular patrons. Every weekday morning like clockwork he came slowly through the front door carrying the newspaper and a pencil, bound and determined to complete the crossword puzzle. It was a task that usually took him until lunch, sometimes longer. He perused dictionaries and encyclopedias, examined biographies and pored over novels, searching for answers. But when he was really stumped or couldn't find the resource he needed, he asked Lily for help. Over the years, she'd answered plenty of questions.

"What is the chemical sign for table salt?"

"In what key did Beethoven write his Fifth Symphony?"
"Where is Victoria Falls?"

And on and on and on. Lily didn't mind; in a way, she learned right along with him. "Why don't we go find out," she said, and started for the stacks with Sherman shuffling behind her.

The library was one of the oldest buildings in Hooper's Crossing, having been donated by the grandson of the town's founder. Steps led from the front door to an impressive wall of shelves holding thousands of books. Past the card catalog and the desk where Lily worked, another entryway opened onto a space with large windows; bright sunlight streamed across the wooden floor. Reference tomes, newspapers and magazines, as well as desks and chairs, were arranged around the room.

"You said the Battle of Yorktown?" Lily asked as her finger slid across the spines on a history shelf, looking for just the right book.

"The seventh letter is an *l* but that's all I have," Sherman answered, still staring at the folded newspaper in his slightly shaking hands.

"Ah, here it is!" Lily exclaimed as she finally found the volume she was looking for, then pulled the dusty book from the shelf and handed it to the older man. "This should give you the answer you need."

"Thank you," Sherman mumbled as he began shuffling back toward his usual corner desk, already flipping through the pages.

Lily smiled. Another satisfied customer.

But before she could turn around and head back to the front desk, a woman's voice hissed behind her. "Now that you're done with all of that nonsense, maybe you can do some actual work for a change."

Just like that, Lily's good cheer faltered. Ethel Wilkinson had a way of ruining the best of moods.

For several generations of patrons, Ethel had been the bitter pill that had to be swallowed in order to use the library. In her late fifties, she was a self-proclaimed spinster, though Lily had trouble imagining the sort of man who'd want to romance Ethel. She dressed matronly, with blouses buttoned all the way to their collars, drab skirts and plain shoes, as well as butterfly glasses that hung around her neck, attached to a bulky silver chain. But it was Ethel's personality that was truly as sour as a lemon. Nothing Lily did could please her, and no mistake was too small to escape being pointed out. But she wasn't the only one who had to face the librarian's wrath. Ethel shushed children for making the slightest of noises. She frowned disapprovingly at patrons who forgot their library card. Once, Lily had watched her berate Pastor Matthews for bringing a book back a day late, arguing that he was setting a poor example for his congregation.

It was a struggle, but by the time Lily turned, she'd regained a sliver of a smile. "I was helping Sherman with his crossword," she explained.

"When I think about how many hours and how much money is wasted every year on that man's ridiculous puzzles, it's almost enough to make me sick," Ethel said with a sneer. "Mark my words, people like Sherman Banks are what's wrong with this world. Selfish! They think only about themselves."

Lily held her tongue. She knew from experience that if she argued with Ethel, if she tried to explain to the old librarian that she was wrong about Sherman, that he was *exactly* the sort of person they were meant to help, it would just make things worse. Much, much worse. Ethel didn't just hold grudges, she squeezed them until they'd been strangled. For years, Jane had tried to get Lily to complain about Ethel to her father, to ask him to use his influence to make the old crone come down off her high horse, to be a little nicer to people. If that failed, Jane hoped Morris would fire the witch. But Lily never complained about Ethel, for several reasons. First, she doubted it would work. Ethel wasn't the least bit intimidated that Lily was the daughter of the mayor. In fact, it gave her an excuse to complain about all the ways that the town neglected the library, that they didn't properly care for the books, that there was never enough money for the things she needed. But second, and more important, Ethel was Lily's problem. She wanted to deal with the belligerent woman on her own.

And so, sidestepping Ethel's gripe about Sherman, she asked, "What was it that you needed me to work on?"

"The card catalog is an absolute mess!" the older woman snapped. "I started to insert the ones I just finished typing and found an inch-width of J's stuck in the middle of the F's. It's a disgrace! It has to be fixed immediately."

By some miracle, Lily didn't sigh. This was the same job Ethel had had her doing two weeks ago, and the month before that, and then back in midsummer. Whenever she found even one card out of place, it was an excuse to start Lily combing through the whole thing. Ethel considered herself above such menial work.

"I'll get right on it," Lily replied and started to walk away, not because she was excited to begin collating the card catalog, but because she'd reached the absolute limit of how long she could stand Ethel's company.

"One more thing," the older woman said before Lily got very far. "As you know, that wretched fall festival starts tomorrow," she began, wrinkling up her nose with disgust, as if she'd just found a dead fly in her sandwich. "Just an excuse for everyone to act like utter savages, if you ask me!"

Lily wished she could point out that no one had.

"That means that there will be plenty of strangers coming in from out of town," Ethel continued, echoing a similar sentiment made by Lily's father the night before. "Whenever you see someone in the library who you don't recognize, pay close attention to them. Likely, they'll be here to steal things!"

"I don't think that anyone would—"

"Why, if we let them, they'd likely rob us blind," Ethel continued as if Lily hadn't spoken a word. "Whole shelves of books would be gone in an instant. Imagine the sad state of affairs then! Who would pay to replace them? The town? I think not!" Before Lily could respond, the old librarian stalked off, throwing a disapproving glance at Sherman Banks for good measure.

Lily wondered why Ethel was getting so worked up about people coming to town for the festival. Odds were, this year wouldn't be all that different from any other. A bunch of visitors would come to eat, drink, dance, and dress in Halloween costumes, and then they'd all leave. Two weeks from now, everything would be back to normal, at least until next October. Ethel, and her father for that matter, were worrying about nothing.

But before Lily could start dealing with Ethel's "emergency" at the card catalog, she felt a tug on her sleeve. Sherman had returned.

"What's the biggest export of the Belgian Congo?" he asked.

Here we go again...

Lily rose from her stool in front of the card catalog and stretched, trying to alleviate the dull ache in her lower back. She'd been leaning over the sliding drawers for hours now, searching for the disorganization Ethel had described, but so far had found little out of place, only a stray entry here and there; the "inch-width" the older librarian had described turned out to be one card for a book about the history of Japan. Still, Lily would keep at it until the job was finished.

And then I'll do it again in a month or two, then a few after that...

Over the course of her morning, Lily had checked out

patrons and answered the telephone. Maybe it was because she'd nearly left Hooper's Crossing with Jane the night before, but today it seemed as if every conversation she had, every smiling face that greeted her on the other side of the counter, reinforced all the things she loved about her job, about her town. People asked about her father, wondered whether she was excited about the festival, or commented about the warm autumn weather. Even Sherman had warmed her heart a little by offering thanks for all of her help as he puttered toward the door, his crossword puzzle finally completed. This was what had drawn her toward being a librarian: to help people, to share in their day, no matter how briefly.

And so, Lily had slowly begun to convince herself that she'd made the right decision after all. She still wanted to leave someday, to discover what sort of excitement could be found outside her little corner of the world, but not yet, not now. She would wait until she was well and truly ready. And then she'd—

Her thoughts were interrupted as the telephone began to ring. Lily answered it with a practiced, "Hooper's Crossing Library."

"Hello from the big city!" the voice on the other end of the line greeted her.

Lily's heart felt as if it had come to a sudden stop before it started pounding away at triple time. For an instant, she was speechless. "Jane?" she blurted loudly when she rediscovered her voice. Lily nervously glanced around the library, hoping with all her heart that Ethel wasn't nearby. "Is it really you?" she whispered into the receiver.

"None other," her friend replied. "I'm all bright-eyed and bushy-tailed even though I drove almost the whole night. I stopped about halfway in some nowhere town whose name I'll never remember and caught a few winks in a grocery store parking lot," Jane explained, talking a mile a minute. "When I woke up a couple of hours later, I got back on the road and now, here I am!"

"You're there? In New York City?" Lily asked, having trouble believing that her best friend had actually followed through with their plan.

"Can't you hear it?" Jane asked, then turned the pay phone's receiver toward the street. Lily could make out the frenzied sounds of vehicles honking, people talking, and feet click-clacking on the sidewalk, all the noises that were part of a metropolitan city as it went about its day. For a couple of seconds, Lily felt as if she was there, too, a part of the hustle and bustle.

But she wasn't. Not really.

Not at all.

"You won't believe the things I've seen already," Jane told her. "There was a man selling peanuts from a cart who threw packets up to the second floor of a building, then caught the money people tossed back down to him. Then this woman got out of a fancy car wearing a necklace with a diamond on it that I swear was as big as my fist. Oh, and I even saw a musician grinding a hand organ for a dancing monkey. He took a dime right out of my hand!"

The moment before Lily had answered the telephone, she had come to understand that she'd made the right choice by staying in Hooper's Crossing. Now she felt the exact opposite. A pang of jealousy flared in Lily's stomach, but she stamped it down. What right did she have to be upset? After all, it was her choice to remain behind, too scared to chase her dream.

"Did you find your cousin's apartment?" Lily asked, wanting to change the subject, if only a little. Part of their plan had been to stay with Jane's distant relative Samantha, who lived on the Lower East Side of Manhattan, at least until they got their feet under them and could find a place of their own.

"Piece of cake," Jane answered. "The only trouble was that I had to drive around the block five times before I could find a place to park. Samantha's apartment is small and the room I'm staying in isn't much more than a closet, but I don't care. If everything goes the way I hope, I won't be there for long."

Lily thought her friend was probably right. If confidence was currency, Jane was as rich as the lady she said she'd seen with the big diamond. In no time at all, her face would be up on a movie marquee or billboard, advertising a Broadway show.

"What about you?" Jane asked. "Did you have any trouble with your dad?"

As she answered, Lily couldn't help but feel embarrassed. The story of hiding her suitcase in the bushes, being scared by Garrett, and then listening to her father's speech into the wee hours of the night seemed childish to her ears. "I'm sorry I didn't go with you," she finished.

"Don't worry about it," Jane replied. "Like I said, this isn't forever. Whenever you're ready, let me know and I'll be at the airport, the bus station, the train depot, or out on the sidewalk waiting for you."

"Okay," Lily said, fighting back tears.

"Hey, there's one more thing I wanted to tell you," her friend said.

"What's that?"

"Remember how you wrote your father a letter telling him that you were leaving town and going to the city?"

"Yes," Lily answered, remembering how relieved she'd been to find it still on her pillow, and how she had then torn it into hundreds of pieces.

"Well, what I wrote will make sure that no one around town will ask about where I am, at least for a little while. But part of that explanation involves you. See, I..." but as Lily listened, static hissed across the connection, making Jane's words a garbled mess. All she heard was, "...left it...mentions that...just thought that you should know that...but only if...least I could do for..."

"I didn't catch much of that," Lily said, instinctively knowing that whatever Jane had said, it was important. "Tell me again."

But before another word could be said, Ethel Wilkinson rounded the stacks and noticed that Lily wasn't at the card catalog. She looked toward the front desk, caught Lily's eye, and glared. Immediately, she began to march over.

Panicked, Lily said, "We'll call you as soon as the book arrives," and slammed the receiver into its cradle with a bang, hanging up on Jane.

"I should have known you'd be shirking your duties," the older librarian commented.

"I was helping someone find a book," Lily lied, her head still swimming from her conversation.

"Lollygagging is more like it. Why, I bet that—"

"The phone rang and I went to answer it," Lily interrupted, irritation getting the better of her. "What was I supposed to do? Ignore it?"

Ethel's mask of smug superiority slipped as she was momentarily caught off-guard by Lily's outburst, but she quickly recovered. "There's no need for smart talk," she complained haughtily. "Your work is slipping, that's all. Why, if you can't accept a little criticism now and then, maybe you should start thinking about another career." Without giving Lily a chance to respond, Ethel turned on her heel and quickly walked away.

Lily sighed. What was she thinking? She knew better than to argue with Ethel. No good would come of it, that was for sure. But she wasn't thinking straight. It was bad enough that she'd nearly left town last night and had lied to both Garrett and her father. Her talk with Jane had upended the work she had done convincing herself she'd made the right decision. So while her friend was in a city teeming with people, adventure beckoning in every direction, Lily remained in Hooper's Crossing, convinced that nothing exciting was ever going to happen to her.

No matter what choice she made, it seemed like it was the wrong one.

"That's one heck of a deposit. You must've been saving up for quite a while."

Gladys Martin smiled warmly at Lily from the other side of her teller window at the Hooper's Crossing Bank and Trust. Laid out between them was a stack of bills, almost two hundred dollars' worth, all the money Lily had painstakingly set aside to help get her started in New York City.

"I was," she admitted, offering a sliver of the truth. "I thought I knew what I wanted to do with it, but at the last second, I changed my mind."

"Probably a good thing you brought it back, then," the teller said. "Whenever I have a couple of extra dollars in my purse, they always seem to get spent, no matter how hard I try to hold on to them."

Lily nodded but didn't say more. Bringing the money back to the bank had been a hard decision to make. She could have kept it at home, secreted in her closet or somewhere else thought it would be safe, but there'd always be the worry that her father might accidentally stumble across it and start asking questions. Lily was sure she could have come up with an excuse, that she was setting it aside for something or other, but she'd already done enough lying. In the end, the bank seemed the best choice. It wasn't as if she was going to change her mind and hop on the next bus or train to join in Jane's adventures. No, she was going to be in Hooper's Crossing for a while longer. It would be here if she needed it.

Once she'd finished her business, Lily headed for the door. There were a few other people in the bank and she nodded and smiled on her way out, but she was distracted, her thoughts a swirling mix of her conversation with Jane, whether there'd be trouble with Ethel when she got back to the library, and even what she might order for lunch at the diner.

That was why when she stepped outside, the autumn sun bright in her eyes, Lily didn't pay any attention to man coming toward her down the sidewalk.

But he *definitely* noticed her.

Chapter Five

WHEN RANDALL KANE saw the blonde walk out of the bank, he couldn't help but whistle; fortunately, or was it unfortunately, the gal was too far away to hear. Damn, she was a looker. Just his type, as a matter of fact. She wasn't a Hollywood starlet, the sort of gal who turned the heads of every guy she met, a broad who knew she was the bee's knees. No, this one seemed quiet, innocent even. Randall wondered if she was a schoolteacher or a librarian, prim and proper on the outside but a real minx in the sack. As she walked toward him, her attention obviously elsewhere, he smiled, showing some teeth.

I may get in trouble for this, but what the hell...

Just before the woman reached him, Randall inched to his left, straight into her path. Their collision was strong enough to force a gasp of surprise from her lips and cause her purse to drop to the sidewalk. She would've fallen, too, if Randall hadn't grabbed her elbow and kept her upright.

"Sorry about that, darlin'," he offered with fake sincerity. "I wasn't payin' attention to where I was goin'."

"No, it was my fault," she apologized, her cheeks flushing with embarrassment. "I . . . I was lost in thought . . ."

"That can happen on a beautiful day like this," Randall said, laying it on thick. "Here, let me get your bag." He knelt down, making sure to take a long look at her legs on the way, definitely liking what he saw, and picked up her purse. "There you go," he said, handing it back.

"Thank you," she replied, still a bit out of sorts.

"Now, where are my manners?" Randall asked, reading the next line of a script he'd performed dozens of times before. "I'm Mike," he lied, offering her his hand. "Mike Detmer."

"Lily," she replied, giving him a shake but no last name. Being a pretty perceptive guy, Randall noticed the way her eyes kept roaming away from his, to the street and back again, like an animal that sensed danger, that wanted to run. But he wasn't going to let her get away that easily.

Randall turned his smile up to full wattage. He knew he was a good-looking man with no shortage of charm. Just barely thirty, he was trim and well dressed with a conservative haircut. But the feature that most woman he met noticed was the hint of danger lurking in his dark eyes. Hell, that was what attracted most of them in the first place, that chance to walk on the wild side. It was intoxicating. He liked things raw and rough, but he could be kind, suave, even sophisticated if he needed to be. He had a gift of gab, too, just as likely to talk himself out of trouble as into it.

"I just got into town for the festival," Randall said, which was the honest-to-God truth, "and was thinking about getting a bite to eat. Might be nice to have some company. How about I buy you lunch? Make up for bumping into you?"

He'd been hoping to see a glimmer of a smile, a flicker of curiosity in Lily's eyes that might end up with them spending the afternoon in a hotel room bed. It had happened before. Instead, her expression soured.

"I'm sorry," she said. "I need to get back to work. It was nice to meet you," she added, a polite formality, and then started to walk away.

Randall stood there and watched her go, paying particular attention to the way her ass swiveled in her skirt.

"You win some, you lose some..." he muttered to himself.

Though he was a bit disappointed, Randall knew that it was probably better this way. If she'd accepted his offer and they had headed off down the sidewalk, there would've been trouble. Lots of it. After all, Randall was in Hooper's Crossing for a very specific reason. He had a job to do.

He was there to rob a bank.

For as long as Randall could remember, he'd liked to steal things. It didn't matter if it was a kid's prized marble, an apple at the grocer, a bicycle or car, a family member's trust, some young girl's innocence, or a wad of money, he got an electrifying thrill out of taking something that didn't belong to him. Stealing was a drug coursing through his veins; when he was high on it, he left chaos and confusion in his wake. And Randall was good at it, too. He might escape by the skin of his teeth, dropping out of a window into the dark of night right as a light was turned on, or racing around a corner just as the sound of police sirens rose in the distance.

But he *always* got away.

What Randall was best at, though, was cracking safes. He had an ear for it, literally. Whenever his fingers held a tumbler, spinning it first one way, then another, he swore he could hear the lock fall into place. When he landed on the right number, it was as if an alarm had gone off, sending an electrical jolt coursing down his arm. To this day, he'd yet to meet a safe he couldn't get into. The criminal who had taken him on as a sort of apprentice was an old con named Tom Muntz, who claimed that he'd once worked with John Dillinger, but by the time his path crossed with Randall's, he'd been ruined by drink. Tom often claimed that safecracking was a lot like courting a young woman.

"If you pay attention to her, if you give a listen to what she's tryin' to tell you, odds are she'll give you what you're after," he'd said.

For more than a decade, Randall had hopscotched the country, running whatever cons and jobs would put money in his pocket. He'd stolen cars in Maryland. He had scammed a widow out of her life savings in Kentucky. For almost four months, he'd pretended to be a preacher in Indiana, bilking his naive "followers" for more and more "contributions." During the war, he had illegally trafficked in gasoline, rubber, and ration cards, always managing to stay one step ahead of the law, as well as the draft board. And he'd cracked safes from Iowa to New Hampshire. He'd been known as Mitchell Givens, Carlton Bow, Freddie Spencer, Boyd Reeder, and another alias he had dusted off that very afternoon, Mike Detmer. But no matter how many crimes he committed, no matter how much money he made, Randall never seemed to have enough.

And that was because he couldn't stop gambling.

It didn't matter if it was cards, dice, horses, dogs, or even a wager over whether it would rain or shine, Randall couldn't resist the lure of a bet. But unlike his success at opening locked safes, where Lady Luck always seemed to be perched on his shoulder, fortune rarely seemed to smile on him when he gambled. Thousands of dollars had passed through his hands over the years, all of his misbegotten earnings and then some. Randall could never set foot in Arkansas again, thanks to some unpaid debts he'd left behind in Little Rock. Wiser men might've taken the hint, found another way to spend their time and money, but the siren's call of the bet enthralled him. He was convinced that the next hand of cards, roll of the die, or pick of the ponies would be a winner. But still he lost.

And now he needed a big score. Something that would balance his ledgers, get him back in the game. That was why he was here, in upstate New York, scoping out a little bank in Hooper's Crossing.

It was also why he wasn't here alone.

Randall opened the door to the bank, held it as an older gentleman exited onto the sidewalk, then stepped inside. The Hooper's Crossing Bank and Trust was like dozens of others he'd seen in small towns all over the country. It was decorated with a handful of chairs and a desk, the marble floor covered with a few well-worn rugs. A quartet of teller windows faced the high-ceilinged vestibule. Just behind those was a good-size vault; the safe door wasn't even half-way shut, which made Randall almost shake his head in disbelief. Offices were over to the side, with blinds drawn over their windows; odds were high that the fattest cat in this rinky-dink town sat inside, counting his money. He didn't see a guard.

Robbing this place was going to be easier than he thought.

Two of the teller windows were staffed and both were serving bank patrons; at one, a farmer in overalls who smelled like he'd been rolling around in his livestock's shit guffawed at his own joke, while at the other, a wrinkled prune of a woman was counting out coins one at a time. Randall got in line behind a businessman and took in every detail he could. He imagined what he was about to do, how it had to be done, imagining potential obstacles. Preparation made perfect, like Tom Muntz used to say.

When the farmer waddled away and the businessman took his place, Randall stepped forward. He was next. Now that he had on unobstructed view, he took a longer look at the tellers. Both were women, which wasn't surprising. In Randall's experience, men in banking counted the big bills in the office; they couldn't be bothered to hand out change up front. Neither of these ladies was much to look at. Both were getting long in the tooth, whatever passed for their best years already in the rearview mirror. He figured they were either deep into spinsterhood or unhappily married, whatever interest their husbands had in them far in the past. The one helping the businessman looked unfriendly, bitter even, her lips pursed in a caterpillar of wrinkles as she went about her business. The other teller at least had a sliver of light in her eyes, even if it was dim. That was the one he wanted. Seconds later, when the grandmother finally finished depositing her spare change, he got his wish.

Here we go. Time for the show to start.

"Can I help you, sir?" the woman asked as friendly as could be when Randall approached her window.

"I sure hope so, ma'am," he answered with a sincere smile, the kind seen just as easily in his eyes as on his mouth. It was different from the one he'd given Lily; neighborly was the way he would have described it, letting the teller see that she didn't have a thing to worry about. "I've got a little problem I was hoping you could fix for me."

"And what's that?" she asked, right on cue.

Without his eyes leaving hers, Randall slowly reached his hand into his trouser pocket. "Well, I've got something I've been carrying around with me all day," he explained, "and this seems like the right time to put it to use."

If only it was my gun.

He slapped a ten-dollar bill down on the counter. "Could I change this for some silver coins? Got a buddy who collects 'em."

"I think I have enough," she said pleasantly.

"Peace are fine, but Morgans if you have 'em," Randall added as he watched her go about her work, making a note of where she kept things. He noticed that her fingernails were all bitten down to the quick. Meant she was nervous.

"Are you in town for the festival?" the teller asked, making small talk.

"Yep," he replied cheerfully. "My first time here."

"You'll love it. Everyone does."

"That's the plan," Randall said, their conversation unspooling almost exactly as he'd expected. As they talked, he took a long look at the safe over the woman's shoulder. It was a York, a little fancier than he might have expected from a backwater town like this, but hardly a challenge for his considerable skills; he'd broken into that make plenty of times before. Odds were, the people running the bank were so comfortable in their daily routine that they didn't bother spinning the tumbler after they opened it in the morning, which would make one number easy, at least. Heck, the whole thing was probably written down somewhere close in case they forgot it. "How about you?" he asked, carrying on his charade. "Will you get to have some fun or do you have to work the whole time?"

"My nights are free, but I should get an afternoon off, too," she explained. "Fortunately, the bank always hires extra help during the festival."

"That much more business?"

"Oh, yes," the teller said as she began to count out his coins. "What with hundreds of people coming to town, everyone will bring money to spend. Why, some years businesses and vendors are lined up out the door to make deposits."

"You might need a bigger safe," he joked.

"Maybe," she said, then held up a single coin. "Sorry, just the one Morgan."

Randall took it from her. The silver dollar had passed through a lot of hands over the years, the image on its face worn smooth in parts. He deftly maneuvered the coin across his knuckles, raising one finger at a time to roll the silver dollar along, flipping it over and over, one way and then back again, a sleight of hand he'd learned years ago in a Philadelphia bar. It always impressed the ladies.

"That's quite the trick," the teller said, no exception to the rule.

"Just a way to pass the time," he said, slipping the coin, along with all the others, into his pocket. If Randall had been wearing a hat, this was when he would've tipped it to her. "Thanks for the help, darlin'."

"Enjoy the festival," she told him.

I plan to. You can bet every last cent in this bank on it . . .

"You were doin' it again."

Leo Burke drove the Plymouth down Main Street toward the park. It looked as if the whole damn town was there putting the finishing touches on the festival. The afternoon air was filled with the sounds of hammers and saws, workers directing the installation of signs and lights, even a policeman with a whistle routing traffic this way and that; when Leo went by, he gave the cop a friendly raise of his fingers from atop the wheel.

"Doin' what?" Randall asked, slouched in the passenger's seat.

"Flippin' the coin across your knuckles. We talked about that, remember?"

The younger thief shrugged. "So what?"

Before he answered, Leo glanced at himself in the car's rearview mirror. He was in his mid-forties, and crow's-feet marred the corners of his icy-blue eyes, a deep crease ran across his forehead, and a smattering of gray was sprinkled in at the temples of his otherwise black hair. Compact, muscular, a bit rough around the edges, he wasn't the sort of man who made others feel comfortable. Usually, it was the opposite.

"So if you keep doin' it, someone is gonna notice," he explained, his voice rising as he struggled to keep a lid on his temper. "That's the sort of detail a teller might remember. If she tells the cops or some newspaper reporter . . ."

"Who cares if she remembers?" Randall responded dismissively. "Mine'll be just another face in a long line of strangers coming to town. Pretty, sure, but not all that different from dozens of others. Besides," he added, "it ain't like she's gonna be there when we rob the place. She'll be celebrating with everyone else. You're making somethin' out of nothin', old man."

Just like Randall, Leo made his living by taking from others. But where his fellow criminal specialized in safes, Leo excelled at masterminding jobs. Poring over building plans, hours spent watching a security guard's patterns to find that one weakness, staking out a Brinks truck's route on a cold February morning: these were the ways Leo went about his work. Get in, get out fast, and triple-count your take. Over the years, he'd hit banks, theaters, restaurants, racetracks, anywhere that was fat with cash for the taking.

But he was getting older now. Leo had come to the realization that stealing was a younger man's game. What a buck like Randall might lack in wits or wisdom, he more than made up for in physical talents. Running into a cornfield to escape the police wasn't as easy as it used to be. Leo had become convinced that if he kept traveling down the same road as always, he was bound to slip up and go to jail. Maybe even worse. He needed a big score, enough money to allow him to coast, to retire from the game.

And so Leo had come up with the idea of robbing the Hooper's Crossing Bank and Trust.

For years, the thought had been bouncing around in his head, tempting him. He'd heard talk about this little town in the middle of nowhere with a fall festival that drew a huge crowd, everyone flush with cash, most of which would get deposited in one spot, a bank without much for security, ripe for the plucking. Under the cover of darkness, while the town enjoyed Halloween, a couple of skilled thieves could break into the safe, fill their sacks with loot, and disappear back into the crowd before anyone got wise to their heist. There were risks involved, just like any job, but the potential rewards made them worth taking.

Because Leo knew he couldn't do it alone, he'd brought in Randall. The kid had come highly recommended by Larry Galvin, a guy Leo had worked with a couple of times before. The way Larry made it sound, there hadn't been a safe invented yet that Randall couldn't crack, which had better be true, since Leo was starting to get fed up with the way the kid handled himself.

"What were you doin' talkin' to that blonde on the sidewalk?" he pressed. Leo had been outside doing his own reconnaissance of the bank, and had seen the whole thing. It looked as if the kid had bumped into her on purpose, and then started hitting her up for a date.

"Lily," Randall answered flatly. "Her name was Lily."

"Jesus Christ," Leo spat. "What did you do, introduce yourself?"

"Yeah, I gave her my real name and told her I was plannin' on robbin' the bank," he answered sarcastically. "Give me a little credit, huh?"

"All I'm sayin' is that you're takin' too many risks."

"And what *I'm* sayin' is that you're acting like an old woman. Relax. I may be twenty years younger than you, but this ain't my first time on the merry-go-round. I know what I'm doing."

Leo took a deep breath, struggling to put a leash on his frustration, something he seemed to be doing a lot of these days. The kid was goading him, but he didn't want to take the bait. "Did you see what you wanted in the bank?" he asked.

"The vault's a York," Randall answered, looking out his window. "Thirty years old at least but nothing I haven't encountered before."

"Can you crack it?"

"Does a bear shit in the woods?" the younger man replied, then laughed halfheartedly at his own stale joke. "You get us in the door, I'll open the safe, and if there's as much cash as you say there'll be, we'll be set up like Howard Hughes."

The kid might have been exaggerating, but Leo knew that if everything went the way he'd planned, both of them would be plenty rich. Maybe he would even have enough to leave this life for good, retire to Arizona, Utah, or California, somewhere warm, find a fishing hole, and enjoy whatever years he still had ahead of him. But first things first. He had work to do before Halloween.

And who knew what could go wrong between now and then.

Chapter Six

BOONE STOOD AT the door to his apartment, fishing in his pocket for his keys. He lived in an old building on 109th Street, near Amsterdam Avenue and west of Central Park. His place was on the fifth floor; without a lift, he had to trudge up the stairs that were hotter than an oven in summer, cold like an icebox in winter. Since the magazine kept him hopping around the globe snapping pictures, he wasn't home much, and thought of his apartment more as a place to store his stuff than somewhere to live. There was, however, one notable exception.

"Daisy!" he hollered once he'd let himself inside. "I'm home!"

Immediately, the excited sound of racing footsteps pounded down the hallway toward him. An instant later, a yellow Labrador retriever raced into the room, heading straight for Boone. Her pink tongue lolled from her mouth and her tail wagged faster than windshield wipers on a rainy day; it was clear that the dog was happy to see him.

"Hey, girl," Boone said, rubbing her head. "I'm glad to be back, too."

Daisy had shared his life for a little more than three years now. Boone had come across a dirty, malnourished puppy while on assignment in Tijuana and had been instantly smitten with the dog. Even as he'd snapped pictures, he couldn't stop thinking about her. And so, bound and determined not to let the animal die on the streets, Boone had smuggled her back home. He'd named her Daisy to be cute; she was *nothing* like a delicate flower. Fortunately, Mrs. Rodriguez, an older widow who lived on the second floor, was a dog lover; whenever Boone was traveling for *Life*, she took Daisy for afternoon walks and made sure the dog had food and water.

Suddenly, the dog ran off but quickly returned with a rubber ball, which she dropped at Boone's feet.

"I don't get some time to relax?" he asked.

The dog tilted her head as if to say, *Are you kidding?*

Boone chuckled. "I didn't think so."

He picked up the ball and sent it flying down the hallway. Daisy raced after it, a tornado of panting, drool, claws, and fur.

Even as he watched her go, Boone realized that for the first time since he'd left Walter Bing's office, he wasn't thinking about the utter unfairness of his punishment. The whole walk to the subway, each jarring stop on the ride, and every step since, he'd been grumbling to himself, wishing that the damn longshoreman had minded his own business, still in disbelief that he had to go to Hoover's Junction and take pictures of a bunch of rubes prancing around in their Halloween costumes. It was beneath him, plain and simple. But Walter had made it clear: either he went or he was out on his ass. No *Life* magazine job. No Havana. No nothing.

So Boone was going, whether he wanted to or not.

Before he had left the office, Boone called Clive Negly, the writer he was supposed to babysit. As soon as Clive picked up he'd launched into a gushy speech about how excited he was to be paired with such an experienced photographer, how he was sure they were going to produce the best story possible, blah, blah, blah. Boone had quickly cut the man off, given directions to his apartment, then hung up.

After playing awhile longer with Daisy, he went into his bedroom and started packing a suitcase. He picked the smallest one he had, since he didn't plan to be in Harper's Corner for long. He threw in a couple of days' worth of clothes, his toiletries, a map, and a few other odds and ends.

"You get to come this time, girl," Boone told the dog. Daisy rose from the doorway and trotted off as if she'd understood and needed to pack her things, too.

Boone next went to the hallway closet. His Perkeo camera was right where he'd put it. Since the longshoreman had busted up his new Mycro, he had no choice but go back to the older model.

"One more time, huh, old buddy?" he muttered.

He was about to shut the closet door but then paused. Rows of bottles lined the shelves, full of chemicals he used developing pictures. Briefly, Boone considered leaving them behind; after all, he was just going to zip upstate, snap a handful of shots, and then be on his way. He could always develop them once he got back to the city. But something nagged at him. He suspected that it would be better to have them and not need them than the other way around. He sighed, then started grabbing bottles.

When he was finished, Boone looked at his watch. He still had a couple of hours before Clive showed up, more than enough time to go over the finer points of his plan, to correct any mistakes. He was sure it would work.

Walter would get what he wanted.

Clive could go back to writing about cats stuck in trees.

And he wouldn't have to spend twenty-four hours in Hillman's Corner. If he played his cards right, this would be over before it had really even started.

Daisy was in the Chrysler's backseat panting and fogging up the windows, the rest of his things in the trunk, when Boone saw Clive Negly making his way down the sidewalk almost twenty minutes late. The young writer was struggling along, overburdened by three large suitcases; as Boone shook his head, Clive dropped a pair of them to the ground with a clatter.

"Why in the heck did you pack so much stuff?" Boone demanded.

Clive shrugged. "I couldn't make up my mind so I decided to bring it all."

"This isn't a damn safari!"

Clive Negly wasn't much to look at. His department store suit, complete with bow tie, hung awkwardly on his thin frame, like he was a boy playing dress-up, parading around in his father's wardrobe. A prominent Adam's apple, dimpled cheeks, and a smattering of acne at the corner of his mouth didn't do him any favors, either. Oddly enough, Clive's strawberry-blond hair was already thinning on top, not the least bit disguised by his rather severe attempt at a comb-over; Boone would've bet the kid would be bald as a cue ball by the time he was thirty.

But as out of sorts as the young writer's appearance was, his social skills were even worse. He stood too close, talked too loud, and stayed too long. Scuttlebutt around the office was to never get pinned in a corner by Clive because you'd never get back out. Questions left his mouth like machine-gun fire. To the kid's credit, Boone had heard he was talented with the typewriter, capable of finding angles that hadn't been explored and writing about them. Still, Boone had been thankful to have avoided working with Clive.

Until now, that is.

"Give me those," Boone said, pointing at Clive's luggage. He popped the trunk of the Chrysler and frowned. Even though he'd brought hardly anything of his own, there still wasn't a lot of room on account of the odds and ends he'd been hauling around for years. He snatched up the writer's bags and tossed them in; the first two fit fine but the third didn't want to cooperate.

"Be careful with those," Clive said. "They're handmade, crafted from the finest leather. My parents gave them to me as a graduation gift."

"Sure, sure," Boone said, wedging the suitcase in even harder.

"Why not just put it in the backseat?"

"'Cause that's where Daisy's sitting," Boone answered, turning the bag this way and that, growing frustrated that it still wouldn't fit.

"Daisy?" the writer echoed. "Walter didn't tell me someone else was coming along." He stooped to look in the rear windows. "Wait...is that a *dog*...?"

Holding the luggage at just the right angle, Boone grabbed the trunk lid with his free hand and slammed it shut in one fast motion. He suspected that Clive's suitcase was a little crunched, but at least the lid stayed shut. "Good powers of observation you got there, pal," he answered.

"No, no, no," Clive said as he shook his head, his arms folded across his chest. "That animal isn't going with us to Hooper's Crossing."

"The heck she isn't," Boone disagreed. "You'll stay behind before she does."

Clive's look of defiance faltered, quickly turning into something that resembled pleading. "But you don't understand," he said. "I *can't* ride with her."

"Why not?" Boone asked.

"Because I'm allergic to dogs."

"How so?"

"Anytime I'm around them," Clive explained, "I break out in hives, I can't stop itching, my nose runs and my eyes water, to say nothing of the…of the…of the…" While he stuttered along, the writer's face got all screwed up, his nose twitched, and his mouth fell open before he finally let loose a titanic sneeze, spraying the sidewalk; a woman who'd been walking past raised the lapel of her coat to her face and hurried away. "The sneezing…" Clive finished, although it was hardly necessary.

"It can't be *that* bad," Boone said, unmoved and unconvinced.

"It's been like this since I was a kid," Clive replied. "Whenever I'm around a dog, I can't seem to stop myself from—" Before he could say more, he was overcome by a series of violent sneezes that shook his paltry frame. Boone didn't know if the man was as allergic as he claimed, or if it was all in his head and the sight of a dog set him off. In the end, he decided that it didn't matter. It was bad enough that he'd been given this assignment in the first place. He wasn't leaving Daisy behind.

"You'll get used to it," Boone said.

"But I won't," Clive insisted, sounding sort of whiny.

"Then ride with the window down. The fresh air will do you good."

"For ten hours?" the writer blurted. "By the time we get there, both of us will have caught our death from cold!"

"No, we won't. This girl's got one hell of a heater,"

Boone replied, giving the Chrysler's roof a pat for good measure. "C'mon. Don't be a baby."

Clive's frown deepened. "Maybe we should go inside and call Walter..."

Boone's jaw clenched. He was starting to get angry. For a moment, he thought about lighting into Clive, maybe even tossing the writer into the car himself. It wasn't like the scarecrow of a man could put up much of a fight. But then he thought of another tack he could take.

"You want to be a writer, don't you?" Boone asked.

"Of course," Clive replied, as if it was the most obvious thing in the world.

"I mean, you want to make a career for yourself with *Life* magazine," he clarified. "Trotting around the world. Writing important articles."

A big smile opened on the young man's face. "I do," Clive insisted. "It's what I've been working for my whole life."

"So what happens if you're in the war-torn streets of Berlin or some Mexican village just after a hurricane and a dog trots over to say howdy?" Boone asked. "Or what if it isn't a dog but some sniper shooting from a wrecked bell tower or a fire in a factory? Are you going to let an obstacle stand in your way or are you going to go get that story no matter what?" He remembered what Walter had told him, about how he should mentor Clive, let a little of his experience rub off on the kid. "I've been there, you know, when things don't go the way you planned. All I've gotten as a photographer, all the praise and bylines, happened because I didn't let the little things hold me back."

From the look on Clive's face, it seemed as if Boone had managed to push the correct buttons. "You're right," he said, nodding his head. "If I want to become a famous writer, I can't let an allergy keep me from my story." He yanked open the passenger's door. "Let's go!"

"Thank God," Boone muttered under his breath.

But by the time he'd put the key in the ignition, a jazz tune on the radio beating along in perfect time with the sound of Daisy's tail thumping against the upholstery, Clive was already sneezing.

"Roll down the window," Boone told him.

The writer did as he'd been told, but his allergy showed no signs of slowing. "I'll be...I'll be fine..." Clive claimed, then went right back to sneezing. "This...this is going to be the...be the..." Another sneeze. "...best trip ever..."

Boone had plenty of doubts about that dubious claim. As a matter of fact, they hadn't left the curb and he was already exhausted.

Boone drove them north and out of the city, crossing the Hudson River as the crowded metropolitan center gave way, slowly at first, to rolling fields and woods thick with trees, their leaves the bright red and orange of autumn. They passed through a steady stream of towns, Highland Mills, Mountainville, Newburgh, and on and on. And with every mile that they drove, Boone learned the hard way that the rumors about Clive were true.

He never shut up. Ever.

In the couple of hours that they'd been on the road, Boone had learned that Clive had grown up in Salisbury, Maryland, only twenty minutes from the ocean; that he'd been the youngest child and only boy among six sisters; that he had swung hard at the first baseball pitch he'd ever seen, nicked the ball and fouled it back, breaking his nose, causing him to never play the game again; that Clive thought Faulkner was overrated as a writer; that the perfume Chloe wore in the office made him sneeze even harder than when he was around dogs; that his upstairs neighbor played his records too loud; and a good two dozen other useless tidbits that Boone had struggled to tune out, staring at the road and squeezing the steering wheel ever tighter.

The worst part was that Clive had carried on his mono-logue through a series of sneezes. Even with the cold wind blasting through his open window, his allergies never re-lented. Water streamed from the corners of the writer's eyes and he'd blown his nose in his handkerchief with such force that it sounded like an elephant's trumpet. Un-fortunately for Boone, none of this silenced Clive's tongue. Occasionally, Boone snuck looks in the rearview mirror at the source of his passenger's irritation, but Daisy was peacefully dozing away, chasing a ball in her dreams, com-pletely unaware of the chaos she was causing.

"Do you have a girlfriend?" Clive abruptly asked.

"What?" Boone blurted, yanked out of the trance he'd been in.

"I asked if you…if you…" Another sneeze. "…had a girlfriend."

"No, I don't."

"Huh…" Clive responded. "That's surprising."

Boone looked at the writer. "What makes you say that?" he asked.

"I would've thought that a guy like you, good looking and with a job that takes him all around the world, would have women flocking to him like chickens at…at…at…" Another sneeze. "…feeding time. The second you said 'Daisy' back on the sidewalk, I expected to find some voluptuous brunette in the backseat, checking her lipstick in a…in a…" Sneeze. "…compact or looking at me through stylish sunglasses like the Hollywood vixens wear. Quite frankly, it doesn't make sense to me that you're single."

Staring at the road stretching out before them, Boone didn't answer. The truth was, it didn't make a lot of sense to him, either. There were women in his life and it *was* largely on account of his work. He had sipped sake with a cute Japanese girl in Kyoto. He'd kissed a California blonde on a beach beneath a sliver of a moon. He had danced the tango with a brown-skinned beauty in Madrid. But none of these romances had lasted. Each was a brief moment that had burned bright and hot before it went out. The demands of being a professional photographer always kept him on the move, leaving little time for dinners by candlelight, dates at the movies or a ballgame, love letters, whispered phone conversations, or tearful good-byes at the train station.

His parents hadn't provided much of an example for him to go by. Boone's mother and father had always seemed to be married more to the Lord than each other. All through his childhood, they'd dragged him to and from church, traveled around the countryside sermonizing from door to door, and even stood on street corners holding signs announcing the upcoming return of the Savior. Nights weren't wasted listening to the radio or talking around the fire but were to be spent reading the Bible and lecturing their only child about the dangers lurking outside their door. Their warnings had clearly fallen on deaf ears, for as soon as Boone was able, he'd left his folks behind and moved to the city, more than a little curious about what was really out there in the larger world.

If he found love one day, Boone was confident that it wouldn't look anything like what he'd known growing up.

But what it *would* look like was anyone's guess.

"So what about you?" Boone asked Clive. "You got a lady?"

The writer sneezed twice, then wiped his dripping nose with his handkerchief. "Mandy Pitlor," he said. "She's the girl of my dreams."

"Does she live in the city?"

"No," Clive answered. "Mandy's back in Maryland where we grew up."

Boone nodded. "A long-distance thing, huh?"

"Sort of. She's...she's..." Sneeze. "...married with a couple of kids."

The car swerved slightly as Boone struggled to contain his surprise. "I thought you said she was your gal!"

"I wanted her to be," Clive said. "She lived down the street from me when we were growing up and I always... always..." Sneeze. "...thought we'd end up together, but I never got up the nerve to ask her out, so...so..." Yet another wrenching sneeze. "...Sam Donovan beat me to the punch."

Somehow Boone held his tongue. His first instinct was to tell Clive that if you wanted something bad enough, you had to go get it. Nothing was just going to fall in your lap. Just that morning, he had taken a risk by sneaking over the fence to snap a picture of the Manhattan skyline, and while things hadn't worked out like he had planned, at least he'd tried. Fortune favored the bold. But then Boone thought better of it. What good would it do to give the guy grief? Clive would either figure it out one day or he wouldn't. It was as simple as that.

"I bet *you* don't have any problem with girls," the young writer said.

"I do fine," Boone admitted. "Job makes it tough."

Clive frowned. "I'd think it would be the opposite. All those glamorous places and pretty faces from around the world." His face suddenly lit up as if he'd had a brilliant idea. "As a matter of fact, I bet you manage to meet someone while we're in Hooper's Crossing."

"What're you talking about?"

The writer dug around in his back pocket before finally pulling out his wallet. He yanked out a bill, holding it tight on account of the wind whipping in the open window. "I've got five bucks that says you at least get a kiss."

"Whoa, whoa, whoa," Boone said. "You're willing to bet money on me mashing with some broad?"

"Why not?"

Boone knew that Clive was just trying to bond with him, to come up with something that would bring the two of them a little closer. But the more he thought about it, the more he saw it as a win-win situation. Either he got a kiss from some cute number, which would only set him back a fiver, or he got a little extra padding for his pocket. After all, another Mycro cost money, and every bit helped.

"All right," he said. "You're on."

"Four days is plenty of time for you...you..." Sneeze. "...to come through."

Once again, Boone didn't answer. He hadn't broken it to Clive that Walter's plan for them to be in Hoover's Crossing for four days, snapping pictures of some ridiculous fall festival, wasn't going to happen.

If he had it his way, they wouldn't be there for more than one night.

But who knew? Maybe that was still enough time for a kiss.

Chapter Seven

SHORTLY AFTER FIVE O'CLOCK, Lily slipped her key into the library's front door and turned the lock, another workday done. Her afternoon had been much like her morning. Between checking out books, helping people find what they were looking for, and answering the telephone, she'd continued to search the card catalog for mistakes; by the time the boring task was finished, she had found a grand total of six. Every time Ethel appeared between the stacks, she frowned at Lily, acting as if her younger colleague was doing something wrong or lazing about. Finally, the clock had wound its way to closing time and Ethel had hurried out the door, leaving Lily to finish up.

Just like she does almost every other day . . .

Not that Lily was in a big hurry to get home. Tomorrow was the day of her father's big speech opening the fall festival, which meant that Lily was going to have to sit through more practicing as Morris nitpicked every detail, trying out inflections and hand gestures, changing a word here and there, all while driving his daughter completely out of her—

The sudden honk of a car's horn startled Lily so badly that she dropped her keys. She spun around to find Garrett Doyle smiling sheepishly as he leaned out the window of his police car.

"Looks like I'm making a habit out of scaring you," he said.

"It most certainly does," Lily replied as she bent to retrieve her keys, thinking about how badly she'd jumped the night before when Garrett surprised her outside her house, the command of his voice and the glare of his flashlight making her heart race.

"Would you believe me if I told you it wasn't on purpose?"

"Probably not," Lily told him, although she was smiling as she walked toward his car. "Is your shift just starting or are you done for the day?"

"Neither," Garrett answered. "I'm supposed to be on my dinner break but I've been too busy to take it. When I saw what time it was, I thought I'd swing by and see if you wanted a ride home. With the way I startled you last night, I figured it was the least I could do."

"But then you end up frightening me all over again."

He laughed easily. "Like I said, it's becoming a habit. So how about it? You want a lift?"

"Sure," Lily said, then opened the passenger's door, thankful that she wouldn't have to walk home and for a little friendly company.

But once she was inside, Garrett whipped a U-turn in the middle of the street and headed in the opposite direction from where they lived.

"Didn't you say you were taking me home?" Lily asked. "Don't tell me you've forgotten the way."

"I have to run a quick errand first," he explained, then patted the seat between them, jostling a small paper sack stained with a smattering of grease spots. "Louise Hickman flagged me down when I was going past her house and asked if I'd mind taking her husband his dinner. Ken's working at the festival grounds and forgot it on the way out the door. It'll just take a minute."

"Is this why you're too busy to eat?"

"It's no big deal," Garrett answered with a shrug. "Besides, the Hickmans are good people. Last Fourth of July, Louise left a plate of barbecue sandwiches in her mailbox for all the police officers who had to work. It was one heck of a nice snack in the middle of the night, that was for sure."

For the rest of their short drive to the park, they chatted about their respective days. Garrett told her about some of the goings-on around town, all the new faces he'd seen, as well as the blown tire of a delivery truck out on Route 5. But when it was Lily's turn, she chose not to be as forthcoming. Like Jane, it wasn't as if Garrett didn't know from experience how grouchy Ethel Wilkinson could be. But Lily didn't want to sound like she was complaining, so she held her tongue.

Garrett pulled to the curb beside City Park. Out her

window, Lily watched what seemed like half the town working on the festival. Even in the short time since she'd last seen it, the night before when she and Jane had driven past, things had changed. The booths looked ready to open for business. The strings of lights in the trees shone as the bulbs were inspected. Bunting hung along the stage on which her father would give his speech. The air was filled with the strange symphony of hammers and saws, shouts and laughter.

"I'll be right back," Garrett said before grabbing Ken Hickman's forgotten meal and heading into the crowd.

As he went, Lily watched the way people greeted Garrett. As a police officer, cutting a fine figure in his uniform, he commanded a certain amount of respect, but it was more than that. Lily saw it in the smiles, shouted greetings, and pats on the shoulder that her life-long friend received.

But then she noticed something else.

Patsy Vowell looked up from where she'd been painting a sign to hang above her family's booth of baked goods, and noticed Garrett. A couple of years younger than Lily and only recently graduated from high school, Patsy's face instantly lit up; a grin blossomed across her pretty face as her eyes focused on Garrett before darting away, then back, and then away again. Her feelings for him were as obvious as if they'd been written on her sign. She was smitten with Garrett.

And why shouldn't she be? He was a handsome, friendly, charming young man who had a bright future ahead of him as a police officer. If Garrett played his cards right, there was no reason to think he wouldn't someday become chief. Any girl would be lucky to have him for her husband. Surely Patsy Vowell wasn't the only potential suitor he had in town.

So why was he still single?

When Garrett returned after receiving a hearty thanks from Ken Hickman, Lily decided to find out.

"Did you see the way Patsy Vowell was looking at you?" she asked.

Garrett peered through the windshield even as he backed the squad car into the road. "No," he answered. "Should I have?"

"It would've been awfully hard to miss," Lily joked. "She was practically sizing you up for a tuxedo to wear at your wedding."

"I thought she was going with Shane Gritton," Garrett said, gaze steady on the road. To Lily, it felt as if he was deflecting the conversation, like the subject made him a little uncomfortable.

"Maybe, but I don't think Shane would stand a chance if you wanted to take Patsy to the festival."

"What about you?" he asked, finally turning to look at her, pouncing on what she'd said. "Are you going with anyone?"

Oddly, Lily's first thought was of the man she'd spoken with in front of the bank. Even though he was handsome enough, there was something about the stranger that had bothered her from the start. Maybe it was that his smile was too bright, his words too polished, as if he had used them dozens of times before. Later, as her mind had wandered while she sat in front of the card catalog, she'd even wondered if their meeting hadn't been an accident, if he hadn't bumped her on purpose. Regardless, Lily was glad she'd likely never see the man again.

"No, I don't," she answered.

"Well, neither do I, which got me thinking," Garrett said. He paused to lick his lips. "What would you say if I picked you up Friday night, we got a bite to eat, played a few games at the festival, and then maybe danced a little in the square? Would that interest you?"

Listening to her oldest friend, someone she considered the brother she'd never had, Lily felt something tickling at the edge of her thoughts, a kind of suspicion. She couldn't be hearing him right, could she? In the end, there was only one way to find out for sure.

"Are you . . . are you asking me on a *date* . . . ?"

For as long as Garrett could remember, he had been in love with Lily Denton. He didn't know when it had happened, not exactly. It could have all started out on the playground at the Hooper's Crossing Elementary School, the two of them racing around among the other kids. Maybe his feelings for her had suddenly sparked to life as they sat side by side at the drugstore's soda counter, sipping chocolate milk shakes. Or it was possible that it went all the way back to the beginning, as Garrett stood in his grandparents' front yard, scared and nervous to start a new life, staring across the street at a little girl, his heart beating a little faster as she raised her hand to wave. In the end, it didn't matter. All he knew was that he couldn't remember a time when he wasn't completely smitten with her.

After all, what was there about Lily that wasn't to like? Without question, she was the prettiest girl he had ever laid eyes on. Her long blond hair, the intoxicating depth of her eyes, the gentle sweep of her smile, the smattering of freckles across her cheeks; to Garrett, no Hollywood starlet could hope to hold a candle to Lily. But it was more than that. Much more. She was fair and honest, kind and considerate. He could listen to the sound of her voice for hours. Whenever Lily laughed, Garrett couldn't help but smile; strangely enough, on the few times he'd heard her cry, there had been a sort of beauty in that, too. He wanted nothing more than to be by her side, to hold her hand, to love her and be loved in return.

But there was a problem. A big one.

Garrett had never been able to tell Lily what was in his heart.

Over and over, he'd practiced the things he wanted to say to her. He rehearsed his lines while lying in bed at night, unable to sleep. He daydreamed about conversations they might have while sitting at his desk in school. He paced back and forth on the sidewalk, muttering to himself, his hands waving through the air, probably looking like a crazy person to anyone passing by. He did it so often that he thought he had an answer for any response Lily might give.

But whenever Garrett told himself that today was the day, that he would confess his feelings for her after school or sitting in the park or as soon as the movie was over, his courage failed him. He just couldn't bring himself to do it.

Though one time, he had come awfully close...

It was the January when both Garrett and Lily were fifteen. They'd been sitting on the railing of the Dentons' porch, their feet swinging above the white-capped bushes, watching as snowflakes fell from the dishwater-gray clouds. A big storm had blanketed the area with so much snow that school had been canceled, which was rare for their neck of the woods. The street was still and quiet save for the scrape of a neighbor's shovel. Garrett watched as Lily, blond hair peeking out from under her wool hat, stuck out her tongue to snag the drifting flakes, the snow melting the very instant they landed. He couldn't help but notice how beautiful she was. He was still staring when she turned and caught him.

"What is it?" Lily asked.

"Nothing..." Garrett muttered then looked away, hoping she'd think his cheeks were red from the cold rather than embarrassment. "I was just daydreaming."

Lily nodded, then said, "Days like this make me think of my mother."

Garrett froze. Sarah Denton had died shortly before he'd come to live with his grandparents and in the years since, he had only heard Lily talk about her mother a handful of times. "Really?" he asked tentatively.

"All the memories I have of her are in the spring and summer," she explained, staring off into the distance as snow swirled around her face. "I remember chasing fireflies in the backyard, helping her tend to the flower beds, standing together in the driveway at night as she pointed up at the stars, but there's nothing in the winter."

At that, Lily fell momentarily silent. Even if Garrett had had an idea of what to say, he would've held his tongue.

"I mean, I know we had to have baked cookies, sat in front of the fire, or built a snowman," she continued, "but I don't even remember Christmastime, hanging decorations or opening presents. Nothing." Lily paused, then took off her mitten and held her bare hand out to the snow; flakes peppered her skin, melting much as they had on her tongue, though some lingered for a second before disappearing. Garrett saw tears in her eyes. "So whenever it snows I think about her. About all the memories that are gone for good no matter how bad I wish I could find them."

Garrett knew exactly what Lily was talking about. He'd lost both of his parents and his own memories were just as scattered, a piece here, another there. In the end, maybe that was why Lily confided in him, because he alone could understand.

"Do you think about your parents much?" she asked.

"Sure," he answered with a shrug. "Usually around my birthday and during the holidays. Times that I can remember us all together."

"Does it ever make you cry?"

For a second, Garrett thought about lying, about pretending to be tougher than he was, but it quickly passed. "Every once in a while."

"Sometimes I wonder if I'll ever stop," Lily said as one of the tears that had been building broke free and slid down her cheek.

"Maybe it gets easier when we grow up," he suggested hopefully.

"I'm scared of getting older."

"Why?" Garrett asked, surprised by her words.

"Because it's so easy to get hurt," Lily answered.

"What do you mean? How?"

"Look at my dad," she explained, glancing over her shoulder toward the house; Morris was inside, working in his office. "He loved my mom with all his heart, enough to marry her and start a family, but one day she was just gone and there was nothing he could do to stop it. Now he's all alone."

"He still has you," Garrett said, trying to cheer her up.

But she shook her head. "It's not the same."

They fell silent as a car struggled down the snow-covered street, its back end fishtailing, the driver pushing the engine too hard.

"Do you think you'll ever get married?" Lily asked.

The suddenness of her question caught Garrett completely off-guard. Without thinking, he nearly answered. The words were right there on the tip of his tongue.

I want to marry you.

For so long, Garrett had been searching for the

perfect time to tell Lily how he really felt about her. Should he just blurt it out? He'd considered writing her a letter or saying it over the telephone. But right here, right now, was the perfect opportunity, the one he'd been waiting for.

But when he opened his mouth, nothing came out.

In that moment, Garrett told himself that because of the quiet of the snowy afternoon, his declaration would be heard all over town. But that was just an excuse, a pathetic one at that. Staring at Lily, Garrett understood a painful truth. Deep down, he knew that if he uttered those fateful words, all he'd get in return was disappointment. Lily didn't look at him the same way. She saw him as a brother, not a boyfriend. He was as close as family, but there would always be a distance between them.

"Someday, maybe..." he mumbled as he looked away, the inside of his head a mix of confusion and sadness, with a touch of anger for being such a coward added for good measure. "What about you?" he asked.

Looking back on that long-ago conversation, Garrett couldn't remember Lily's answer. Another man, or in this case boy, might have paid closer attention, attempting to glean some pearl of wisdom from her words, but he'd been overwhelmed, struggling to make sense of his weakness. Eventually, he had returned to pining for her, doing his best to convince himself that his assumptions were wrong, that they could be together, that someday they would be married. And so the question remained the same it had always been.

Could he tell Lily the truth? Could he confess to loving her?

Slowly, Garrett turned to look at her. Lily watched as his mouth opened as if he was about to say something, but then it abruptly shut. His expression seemed conflicted. Finally, his eyes returned to the road. "No . . . it's nothing like that . . . " he said. "I just thought that if you didn't have anything planned . . . " Garrett's voice trailed off, leaving an awkward silence behind.

Staring at him, something teased at the edges of Lily's thoughts. Surely, he hadn't been asking her on a date. Not Garrett. The idea was ridiculous. They had been neighbors for as long as she could remember. Garrett was one of her oldest friends, her partner in mischief, as close as a shadow, the brother she'd never had. There weren't any romantic feelings between them. There *couldn't* be.

"I'll have to check with Jane and see if—" she began before catching herself. Jane was far away in New York City and wasn't coming back for the fall festival. Not a chance. But making plans with Jane was such a habit that Lily hadn't thought twice before speaking.

Garrett replied with a short nod, looking so dispirited that Lily couldn't help but feel bad for him. So she decided to cheer him up.

"But if I'm free on Friday, I'd love to spend some time with you."

His face instantly brightened. "You would?" he asked.

"Sure. It'd be fun."

Just like that, whatever awkwardness there had been between them vanished and things went back to the way they'd always been. They spent the rest of the short drive home talking and laughing, both of them unaware that the next day, something would happen that would change both of their lives forever.

Chapter Eight

THE SUN WAS SINKING toward the treetops when Boone drove past the sign announcing their arrival in Hooper's Crossing. The trip had been long, periodically broken by bathroom breaks, refills at gas stations, what passed for a meal at a roadside diner, and occasional stops so that Daisy could run into the woods to do her business. And through it all, Clive had never stopped talking.

"Look at this place! Isn't this exciting!" the writer gushed, punctuating his words with another sneeze, his allergy to dogs still as strong as ever.

Boone stared out the Chrysler's windows as they neared the center of town. He wasn't impressed. It wasn't all that different from dozens of other forgettable places he'd been to over the years. There was a department store, a barbershop, a post office, and on and on, although there were more cars and people than Boone had expected; the festival really did seem to be a big deal, not that it mattered. He already couldn't wait to leave.

But the way Clive was acting, it was is if he wanted to move here. "A bakery!" he said, pointing like a tourist. "And...and..." he began before dissolving into another fit of sneezes, "...and a movie theater, too!"

"What are you getting so worked up about?" Boone asked, shooting the young writer a confused look. "You live in New York City. We've got everything this place has a thousand times over."

"I don't know," Clive answered with a shrug. "I just like it. It reminds me of those...those..." Another sneeze. "...towns you see in the movies."

"That's all make-believe. Places like those don't exist."

"Sure they do," he said, pointing to the buildings as they drove past.

Boone shook his head. What was the point in arguing with someone so naive? "So where's the hotel?" he asked. Just then, all he wanted was to get out of the damn car, stretch his legs, grab a bite to eat, take a hot shower, and get some sleep. The sooner all of that happened, the better.

But then Clive threw a bucket of cold water on his plans. "Hotel?" he repeated. "We're not staying in one."

"What in the hell are you talking about?"

"Well, there are only two hotels in town and both of them are...are..." Sneeze. "...full up with all the people who've come to see the festival."

"So where *are* we staying?"

The writer smiled. "Don't worry. We won't have to sleep in the car," he explained, throwing a glance at Daisy as if he was thankful he wouldn't spend the night sneezing. "The magazine rented us a room in a lady's house."

"And you didn't see any reason to tell me this before now?"

Clive's smile faltered. "You didn't ask."

Boone struggled to hold back his temper, angry at yet another indignity to add to the growing pile. He was convinced that all Walter would've had to do was pick up the phone, call one of the hotels, explain that he was sending someone from *Life* magazine to cover the festival, and they would have been immediately booked in the nicest room in the joint. But Walter hadn't done that. No, this was another form of punishment Boone was meant to suffer.

"I hope you're not mad," Clive said, sensing Boone's displeasure.

"In the end, it doesn't really matter," he replied. "We're only going to be staying in this two-bit town for one night, anyway."

"Wait...what...but I thought we were going to...to..." More sneezing. "...be here until the festival was over. We're supposed to interview the mayor and people around town. Walter said that we had to—"

"I don't care what Walter said!" Boone argued, his frustrations finally boiling over. "Listen close, because this is how things are going to be. We'll get up tomorrow morning, I can take a few pictures, you'll jot a few things down in your notebook, and then we're getting the hell out of this nowhere town. You got that?"

For a moment, Boone thought that Clive was going to argue, but instead the writer looked away. "Sure thing," he said. "Whatever you say."

"Now, where's this place we're staying?"

Clive gave him the address, explaining through another hail of sneezes that it was somewhere on the north end of Main Street.

For the first time since they'd left the city, Boone drove on in silence.

It took them a while to find the right address; Boone felt like he was driving in circles as he peered through the fading light at street signs. Clive continued to sneeze as he struggled to make sense of the directions he'd been given. But eventually Boone slowed in front of an impressive, two-story house.

"That's it," Clive confirmed, checking the numbers on the mailbox.

The home rose among a quartet of evergreens, as if it, too, was reaching toward the sky. There was a wraparound porch, gabled windows, a stand-alone garage, and well-manicured bushes. Boone turned into the drive and shut off the engine, the motor clicking as it began to cool.

He'd just gotten out of the Chrysler, pausing to stretch his back from too much time spent behind the wheel, when he heard a door open on creaky hinges.

The porch had steps going to the walk in front of the

house, but also a set that led to the drive. Boone watched an older woman shuffle into sight. Her shoulders were stooped, her hair as white as freshly fallen snow, and the arms poking out from beneath her blouse were so thin and wrinkled that she looked as if she might break apart in a stiff breeze. But there was something in the way her gaze never wavered from her visitors, in the determined set of her mouth, that told Boone she was stronger than her appearance would lead one to believe.

"Are you the fellows from the magazine?" she asked.

"We are, ma'am," Clive spoke up, then introduced them both.

"None of that 'ma'am' nonsense for me," the older woman replied. "My name is Marjorie Barlow, but Mrs. Barlow will do fine."

Slowly, carefully, she made her way down the steps to the drive, one hand holding tight to the railing for support. Neither man offered to help; Boone suspected that it wasn't because they were being rude or didn't think she needed it, but rather because each was convinced she'd be offended they had asked.

"Now, I'm sure young men like you two, coming from the big city, you're probably used to lots of noise, coming and going whenever you please, but around these parts, and my place in particular, you should know up front not to carry on that way," Marjorie explained. "You'll be staying in a room at the back of the house that's reached by its own door. Years ago, my husband had this harebrained idea that we should open it up and take in—" The older woman suddenly stopped midsentence and stared at the Chrysler. "You have a dog," she said, a statement of fact, not a question.

Boone took a deep breath. He was already on edge from the crappy assignment, the long drive, and Clive's endless talking. Now some old lady was about to tell him that his dog wasn't welcome in her home. In a way, he couldn't have cared less. He didn't want to be there anyway. He and Daisy would scrounge up a place to sleep, even use the Chrysler if they had to.

For her part, Daisy seemed just as curious about the older woman. The Lab stood on the backseat, her nose close to the window, her panting fogging over the glass as her tail wagged up a storm.

"Is that a problem?" Boone asked a bit defensively.

Instead of answering, Marjorie stepped closer to the car and asked another question. "Boy or girl?"

"Female."

"What's her name?"

"Daisy," Boone answered.

At that moment, Clive sneezed, as if the mere mention of the dog was enough to cause his allergies to flare up. "Pardon me," he said apologetically.

"Can I see her?" the older woman asked, turning to Boone with an expression that surprised him; her hard exterior had softened, her eyes a bit brighter, a hint of a smile curling her thin lips.

When Boone opened the rear door of the Chrysler, Daisy bounded out and hurried around the trunk, overflowing with excitement to meet the person who was paying her so much attention. For a moment, Boone worried that the dog's exuberance would be too much, that she might accidentally knock down Mrs. Barlow, but as soon as Daisy reached the older woman, she sat and presented her head for petting. Marjorie immediately obliged, scratching behind the animal's ears, her smile growing wider by the second.

"I've always loved dogs," Mrs. Barlow explained cheerfully, scarcely resembling the curmudgeon she'd been when they arrived. "My husband and I always had one for all the long years we were married. Some of those dogs were scamps, leaving hair on the furniture, digging holes in my garden, or snatching a freshly cooked chicken off the kitchen counter. But some were sweeter than honey, too." By now, Daisy had closed her eyes, Marjorie's petting a sort of paradise. "We had us a Labrador once, just like this one, only black. Maggie was my constant companion, like a shadow really. She followed me everywhere I went. When she died, almost two years to the day after my husband passed, it broke my heart all over again."

"Why don't you get a...a..." Clive began, then sneezed and moved a couple of steps farther away from the dog. "...another one?"

Mrs. Barlow shook her head. "I'm too old to care for a dog now," she explained. Giving Daisy's ears another scratch, she added, "Though I'm happy as can be at the thought of sharing this one's company for a while."

Marjorie showed them to their room at the back of the house. It was better than Boone had expected, with a pair of beds, a couple of other odd pieces of furniture, a bathroom, and a small kitchen. He peered into the kitchen and saw that it had been built without windows; with very little work, not much more than a blanket or two, he could have converted it into a makeshift darkroom, if he really needed one.

"It's perfect," Clive declared as if it was a suite at the Ritz.

"That's good to hear since it's yours till the end of the festival," the older woman said as she gave Daisy's ears another scratch. "Least that's how long the lady at the magazine said you'd be here when she called for a reservation."

Boone saw Clive's good cheer falter; no doubt, he was thinking about what had been said shortly after they'd arrived in town.

"We'll be here as long as it takes to get a story and some pictures," Boone explained, which in a way was true.

Clive nodded, still looking uncomfortable.

Mrs. Barlow nodded, then fished a set of keys out of her pocket and handed it to Boone. "I'll leave you fellows to unpack. If you want a suggestion about a good place to eat, I'd be happy to give it." With a final pet of Daisy's head, she added, "Remember what I said about the noise." Then she left.

Boone watched Clive as he halfheartedly began to unpack the one suitcase he'd brought in from the Chrysler. He remembered what Walter had said in the editor's office, that he should take the young writer under his wing and teach him something. An unexpected pang of guilt gnawed at Boone's gut. "This is all gonna work out," he said, trying to reassure the other man. "You'll get the story you need, I'll snap a few rolls of film, and then we'll both move on to bigger and better assignments."

"Yeah, sure," Clive said, though it didn't sound like he believed it.

Which was fine. If things went the way he'd planned, by this time tomorrow, they would already be driving back to the city.

To hell with Hoover's Crossing! Havana, here I come!

"I need to go take another look."

Randall Kane glanced over the top of his cards. He and Leo had been playing poker, a favorite pastime of his. There was a wadded pile of dollar bills lying on the table between them, far lower stakes than Randall was used to betting. A half-empty bottle of whiskey sat beside a pair of half-full glasses. Thick cigarette smoke hung in the small cabin like a blanket. Outside, night had nearly arrived, only a faint smear of light on the horizon to mark the sun's passage.

Leo stared back at him hard, his eyes slits. "Another look at what?" he asked.

"The bank," he answered, then picked up his glass and drained the last of the amber liquid, the booze burning a trail down his throat. "The more I think about that safe, the more I—"

"Cut the bullshit!" Leo snapped and tossed down his hand, the cards landing faceup. Even though he now needed to deal with an angry partner, Randall couldn't help but sneak a peek at what the other man had been holding.

Just a pair of sixes? He's a better bluffer than I thought.

Truth was, Randall was bored half to death. Leo hadn't wanted them to stay too near Hooper's Crossing, so he'd chosen a cabin in Clayton, another nothing town twenty miles away. They had been there four days, provisioned with groceries they'd brought with them. So far, the only time they had left was to case the bank. Every other moment had been spent in the cabin or just outside, playing cards, smoking cigarettes, or eating crappy food out of cans. They were so far out in the sticks that Randall couldn't even pull up a ball game on the radio.

He was going stir crazy.

"Look, you're the one who's always carrying on about things being done right," Randall said. "The last thing we want is a screwup."

In all the while Randall had been committing crimes, he'd never met someone as meticulous as Leo Burke. Every single detail was accounted for. Nothing was left to chance. He wrote out time lines and drew up crude maps. He talked about maybes, what-ifs, and who-knows at all hours of the day and night. Randall had listened to him talk about their plan so much that it sometimes felt as if they'd already robbed the joint.

"You're right about that," Leo agreed, then frowned

deeper. "And that's why we ain't goin' back until it's time to do the job."

"Remember when I told you the safe was a York?" Randall asked.

"Yeah, what of it?"

"Well, I forgot to look to see if it had a bracer's cap on the gate hinge. Some of the newer models have those."

"And that makes a difference?"

Randall nodded. "If it has one, I'll have to take a whole different set of tools," he explained. It was a lie, of course. York safes were all about the same with only the smallest of things separating each model. Also, there was no such thing as a bracer's cap on the gate hinge, but he felt pretty sure that Leo didn't know that.

The older thief's eyes narrowed. "Why didn't you think about this before?"

"Honest mistake," he answered, setting down his cards since the game was clearly over. "But they leave the safe door open during the day so it's easier to get more coins or bills, so I'll be able to see it easy enough."

"We go back, someone could see us."

"It'll be the same rubes as before," Randall argued. "'Sides, we're just another couple of strangers come to town for their damn festival."

"It's still a risk."

"The way I see it, it's less of one than us bustin' our way in only to find out I can't open the safe."

Leo's frown grew even deeper, but it was clear that he was chewing over what Randall had said. "All right," he finally agreed. "We go in and out quick, no more time in town than we need. We do it tomorrow, not too early, when there are enough people millin' around that no one pays us any mind. You go back in the bank, look closer at the safe, like you should've already done," Leo said, adding an accusation, "then we don't go back until it's time to do the job."

"Sounds good to me," Randall said. "Now, how about we play another hand of—" But before he could scoop up more than a couple of cards, Leo's hand shot out and grabbed his wrist, squeezing hard.

"Listen close, boy," the older man said, his voice a low growl. "If this is bullshit, if you're just bored of bein' cooped up here and want to stretch your legs, if you end up screwin' us outta all the money in that bank, I will kill you. Do you understand me?" When Randall didn't immediately answer, Leo gave his wrist a yank, pulling him closer. "I asked if you got that."

"Sure, sure thing. I heard you," the younger man quickly replied, figuring that placating the older man was the way to play things, at least for now.

"Good." Leo abruptly let go, rose from his seat, and made to leave.

"Ain't we gonna play more poker?" Randall asked, but the other man was already gone, the door slamming shut behind him.

Randall rubbed his wrist. So what if he was lying? And even though there was a tiny risk that someone in Hooper's Crossing might remember them, who cared? Leo was being paranoid. This way, they'd get out of the cabin for a day, have some fun, and then they could start preparing to rob the bank in earnest. Who knew, maybe if he was lucky, he would get another look at the cute blonde he'd met on the sidewalk.

Lily . . . that was her name . . . pretty, pretty Lily . . .

Chapter Nine

...But I'm the happiest of all to see so many smiling faces here today. When I think of all the hard work that has gone into getting our festival ready, all the banners made, the booths built and painted, the delicious pies baked, I see a community coming together, joined in the celebration of Hooper's Crossing and everyone in it. And because of that, I say..."

Lily stood off to the side of the crowd that had gathered to hear her father's speech opening the fall festival, doing her best not to look bored. It wasn't that she didn't find his words exciting, not necessarily, but rather that she'd been forced to listen to him practice it a dozen times the night before; truth was, Lily knew the speech so well she felt fairly confident she could give it herself.

"...and that spirit goes all the way back to when the first settlers arrived, struggling through their first winter but managing to survive, demonstrating a fighting spirit that can still be seen here today. Why, only yesterday..."

That morning at the library, Ethel had again snapped at Lily, claiming that she wasn't paying enough attention to her work. But unlike most days, this time, the older woman's criticism was likely spot-on. The truth was, she'd been preoccupied thinking about her conversation with Garrett, how much fun and mischief Jane was getting up to in the city, as well as the start of the festival. What she hadn't been focused on was the proper shelving of returned books.

"All day with her head in the clouds," Ethel had grumbled.

When Lily grabbed her coat and headed for the door—as the mayor's daughter she was expected to attend the opening ceremonies—Ethel had made a show, whining that she couldn't possibly be expected to do an afternoon's work all by herself. She was likely worrying about nothing. Almost everyone in Hooper's Crossing would be at the festival; even Sherman Banks hadn't come to work on his crossword puzzle. But Ethel wasn't the sort of person who would let the truth get in the way of some quality complaining.

"...and so I'm confident that this year's Hooper's Crossing Fall Festival will be the best one yet! Let the good times begin!"

With a hearty round of applause from the crowd, and some celebratory music from a small brass band, Morris's speech ended. Lily lingered off to the side as her father moved from one person to the next, smiling, shaking hands, and laughing loudly. When he finally reached her, taking her by the elbow, he asked, "So? What did you think?"

"Fantastic. The best version of it yet," she said, although she would have had a hard time telling it apart from the other renditions she'd heard.

"I thought so, too!" he enthusiastically agreed, congratulating himself in the process. "But it was hard to concentrate, what with knowing that I have an interview with *Life* magazine this afternoon! Did I tell you?"

Only about a dozen times...

"You might have mentioned it," Lily said instead.

"What a golden opportunity this is, for me, for the whole town," Morris began, pausing to shake a few more hands. "If word gets out about the festival, think of all the people who will come to Hooper's Crossing. Why, families will travel from Boston, New York City, Philadelphia, Baltimore, Washington, heck, all over, just to see us, and not just in autumn but all year round! Isn't it great?"

Lily smiled and nodded, though she didn't feel all that happy about it on the inside. For as long as she could remember, she'd wanted to leave *here* to go *there*; it made her feel conflicted, torn in two different directions at the same time. If her father was right, and she suspected he was, the closest she might ever get to city life would be by mingling with the tourists who came to next year's festival.

I'm never going to leave...

I can't wait to leave...

Boone picked his way through the crowd as Clive

hurried along behind him. There were more people then he'd expected, everyone smiling, laughing, having a much better time than he was. Vendors hawked their homemade goods and peddled fine-smelling food and drink. From somewhere ahead, the tinny sound of a man's voice could be heard on a loudspeaker. The autumn sunlight felt warm on his skin, a nice contrast with the crisp breeze.

"Take a look at that!" Clive gushed over something or other. That declaration was followed seconds later with another. "I've always wanted to try one of those!" Boone bit his tongue. It was like he was dragging a kid through a department store a week before Christmas, the greedy tyke pointing at all of the shiny presents he hoped Santa Claus would put under the tree. Finally away from Daisy, Clive's sneezing had subsided, making him more talkative than ever. "Oh, my goodness! I can't believe it! They even have a—"

"You're acting like a rube," Boone interrupted.

Clive stared, looking a bit taken aback. "No, I'm not."

"Yes, you most certainly are."

"Aw, you're no fun," the young writer replied. "Why are you so grumpy? What's not to like about this place?"

For starters, it sure as hell isn't Havana.

Every once in a while, Boone lifted his camera and half-heartedly snapped a picture. He caught a couple of kids carving a pumpkin, two older ladies as they admired a garishly painted birdhouse, a young police officer giving directions to a group of out-of-towners, and a handful of other mundane photos. Any one of them would look fine in the puff piece Clive would write, tucked in at the back of the magazine, forgotten a week after publication, destined to line the bottom of countless birdcages and litter boxes another month down the road.

"When are you supposed to meet with the mayor?" Boone asked over his shoulder as he eased between a pair of parked cars.

Clive looked at his watch. "About thirty minutes." He paused, then asked, "You're coming with me, right?"

"What for? It's not like Walter's going to run a picture of some small-town mayor with the piece."

The writer frowned. "I was just hoping that you'd be there to help, you know, if I started asking the wrong kind of questions."

"You want me to hold your hand?"

"It's not like that!" Clive said defensively. "I just thought that since we're a team on assignment, we should look out for each other."

"Fine. Whatever," Boone said, shaking his head as a sudden gust of wind blew, strong enough to tug leaves from their trees, causing a slowly falling storm of crimson and orange.

In the end, it didn't matter. In a couple of hours, he'd be gone from this place, headed back to the city and the life waiting for him there. His things were already packed. All he would have to do is throw them in the trunk, put Daisy in the backseat, and off they'd go. Clive would probably complain a bit, whining between sneezing fits about their responsibility to their assignment, that they owed it to the magazine. More blah, blah, blah. But his words would fall on deaf ears. A week from now, Boone would've forgotten all about Hoover's Crossing.

In a way, he supposed that Walter had succeeded in making his point. For a while at least, Boone would walk the straight-and-narrow path, because the last thing he wanted was another punishment like this one.

"Come on," he grumbled. "Let's get this over with."

"This is a bad idea."

Randall stopped, the passenger's door open, his foot already out on the curb. Leo remained behind the wheel of the car, coldly staring out the windshield, his thumb absently drumming against the steering wheel. That morning, they'd left the cabin and driven toward Hooper's Crossing as planned, but the roads had been heavy with traffic and the trip had taken longer than expected. Leo had skirted downtown, both of them looking warily at the throngs of people, before he finally parked down a side street in a quiet neighborhood a five-minute walk away. Randall figured they'd get right to it, but apparently not.

"It's like I said. I need to take another look at that safe." He'd used the lie enough times now that it had started to feel a little bit like the truth. "We don't want any mistakes when the time comes."

"That's what I think this is," the older thief grumbled. "A mistake. Tell me again why you can't just bring along extra tools."

Randall sighed. "'Cause the more I'm carryin', the

slower I'll move and the less room there'll be for what's in-side that vault. You want me to have to leave behind a wad of cash 'cause I'm haulin' an extra hammer?"

"Why can't you just leave the hammer behind? What with all the money you're gonna have, you shouldn't have a problem buyin' a new one."

"I thought you was dead-set against us leavin' behind any clues that could be tied to us," Randall answered, not anticipating his partner's line of thinking but react-ing quickly. "Besides, this is gonna be easy as pie. You saw all those people. No one's gonna pay either of us any mind."

Leo shook his head. "Not us. Just you. I ain't goin'."

Randall's first reaction was one of relief. He didn't want the older man tagging along anyway. It'd make it a hell of a lot easier to stretch his legs, get some fresh air, and enjoy being out of the cramped cabin. Still, he was curious about the reason. "Why not?" he asked.

"'Cause I'm smart. 'Cause I'm not willin' to risk some yokel rememberin' my face. 'Cause I did my job right the first time."

By now, the barbs were starting to piss off Randall. He got out of the car, slammed the door a little harder than needed, then bent down to look through the open win-dow. "Suit yourself," he said. "Have fun listenin' to the radio or playin' with yourself, whatever you got planned while you're sittin' here."

"I'm leavin'," Leo replied. "Ain't worth the chancin' some housewife lookin' out her window, seein' a suspicious car, and callin' the cops to come check it out. I'm gonna go for a drive instead."

"So what am I supposed to do when I'm finished? Hitch a ride?"

"I'll be back here in an hour, so make sure you're ready to go. I wait longer than a minute or two, the job's off and you're on your own."

Randall glanced at his watch, marking the time. "I'll be here."

"You better be," Leo said, then added, "And without any screwups." With that, he pulled the car away from the curb and down the street. Randall watched him until the Plymouth was out of sight, then spit in the grass.

That guy needs to loosen up. He's too much of a hard-ass for his own good.

As annoying as Leo could be, Randall couldn't help but feel a little triumphant that he'd gotten his way. Hell, it was even better than he'd expected. Now he could go to town and not even have to poke his head in the bank. He wouldn't have someone looking over his shoulder. He could enjoy himself a little. With a spring in his step, he set off for the festival.

Today was going to be a good day.

Lily said good-bye to her father, making sure to wish him luck for his big interview, then paused, undecided about what to do next. She glanced in the direction of the library. It was still late morning, too early for her to take her lunch break. She supposed that she should go back and help

Ethel; even if not a single patron had entered the library since Lily had left, the older woman was likely beside herself by now, fretting at imaginary indignities, all of which were surely Lily's fault. Still, the thought of taking another dose of Ethel's abuse didn't hold much appeal. Lily could practically hear the old battle-axe now, complaining about everything under the sun.

So why go back? It wasn't like that was her only choice.

Lily allowed the lure of the festival to tempt her, with all of its sights, sounds, and smells. Who would know if she spent some time wandering among the crowd, enjoying the beautiful October day?

She smiled.

Ethel was just going to have to get along without for a little while longer.

Boone raised his camera and snapped a shot of a man playing a harmonica, a pair of children dancing at his feet. It was a nice-enough image, but something was off, likely the lighting, so Boone moved a couple of paces to his right and tried again. Even though he wanted to leave this nowhere town as quickly as possible, when it came to taking pictures he was a professional. But even as he reshot the image, something continued to nag at him.

Well, not something. Someone. Clive.

"You want some cotton candy?" the writer asked as Boone clicked away.

"No. What I want is for you to get lost for a few minutes."

"But why . . . ?" he asked.

"Because you're bothering me. I'm not used to having someone look over my shoulder while I work, blabbing in my ear. So scram."

Clive looked around. "And do what?"

"I couldn't care less," Boone replied. "Go get damn cotton candy."

The writer must have agreed that it was a good idea, smiling brightly. But then the grin faltered. "Wait, aren't we supposed to be on our way to interview the mayor?" he asked.

"We've got time," Boone answered after he glanced at his watch. "I'll take some more pictures, then we'll meet up."

Clive still looked uneasy. "Where?"

Boone searched over the crowd. "There," he said, pointing at the movie theater. "Under the marquee in fifteen minutes."

"Are you sure that's enough—" Clive started, but then he stopped as soon as he noticed the irritated look on Boone's face. "Fine. Fifteen minutes."

Watching Clive disappear into the crowd, Boone let out a long sigh. Finally, there'd be some peace and quiet, if only for a short while.

He raised his camera and got to work.

Lily walked along the edge of the park admiring the festival. She bought a bag of homemade butterscotches from Mort Crawford, savoring their sweet taste. She listened to

Margaret Hoskins play her violin, clapping along with the appreciative audience. She even considered purchasing a beautiful scarf from Joe Knapp's booth, the wool luxuriously soft beneath her fingers, but decided to wait, at least for a little while longer. In short, she was having a wonderful time.

By now, the crowd had gotten larger, slowly but steadily swelling with every passing hour. Lily knew she should probably get back to the library before Ethel went completely out of her mind. Excusing herself, she squeezed between some people, then stepped off the sidewalk and into the street. She'd figured the going would be easier there, but Lily had only managed a couple of steps before she was bumped hard on her side and her balance was thrown off so badly she feared she would fall. She reached out, searching for something to hold on to, but her hands came up empty.

Instead, for the second time in as many days, she slammed into someone and her purse was knocked to the ground.

"I'm so sorry," Lily said, too embarrassed to find out who she'd hit, already crouching to scoop up her belongings.

"It's fine," a deep voice answered. "Let me help you."

It was then, just as she was about to grab her lipstick and the last of the butterscotch candies, that Lily looked over. A man knelt beside her. His attention was on a runaway pen and some coins, but she could clearly see his profile.

He was the handsomest man Lily had ever laid eyes on.

With his short dark hair, a strong jaw, and narrow blue eyes, he reminded her of the men she was used to seeing up on the big screen, the Hollywood heroes who always saved the day just in the nick of time. Whiskers peppered his cheeks, adding a whiff of ruggedness. Even his clothes, a leather jacket and jeans, said that he was stylish and not from around here. Lily found herself staring, fearful he would notice but too entranced to look away.

"Here you go," he said, holding out the items he'd re-captured as his eyes rose to meet hers.

But then the strangest thing happened.

He stared back.

Lily saw a quick, almost imperceptible surprise cross his face. Just then, the two of them crouched beside each other in the street, it felt like a moment frozen in time. Neither of them moved or spoke, a powerful *something* be-tween them. Strange as it was, Lily felt as if they were alone even as they were surrounded by hundreds of people. Her heart pounded and her body was tense with excited nerves, but she didn't look away. She couldn't.

"Do you have everything?" he finally asked as they both stood, breaking the spell that had held them both, though his eyes never left hers.

"Everything what?" she answered, feeling dazed.

A grin spread across his face. "The stuff that fell out of your purse."

Lily looked down. Between what she'd picked up, all that the stranger had handed her, and what was still in her bag, she thought she had it all. But then the man said, "Wait a second." He bent down and plucked a hair clip from the street. "This one was hoping to make a clean getaway."

When Lily took it from him, their fingers briefly touched, sending a shiver of electricity racing across her skin. "I'm sorry," she apologized. "I didn't see you. There were so many people that when I—"

"It's all right," the man interrupted. "It was an accident. Just don't go making a habit of it," he jokingly added.

But the fact was that Lily had. Just the day before, she'd run into that other stranger in front of the bank—or, more accurately, he had run into her. But while that man had unsettled her, his smile too slick, his wanting to spend time with her too insistent, *this* man made her feel the exact opposite.

"I'm Boone," he said, extending his hand.

"Lily," she answered, taking it.

"Don't take this the wrong way," he said with a grin, "but when we bumped into each other, I'm glad it was your purse that fell."

"Why is that?" she asked.

"Because I might have burst into tears if this thing had hit the pavement," Boone answered, holding up the fanciest camera Lily had ever seen; she was surprised to realize that she'd been so focused on Boone that she hadn't even noticed it.

"That looks expensive."

"It is, though I have one nicer," he explained. "I need

it for my job." When she looked at him quizzically, he added, "I'm a photographer."

"For a newspaper?"

"Close," Boone said. "I take pictures for *Life* magazine."

Just like that, the puzzle pieces slid into place in Lily's head. "My dad!" she exclaimed, then hurriedly added, "You're supposed to interview him this afternoon. He's the mayor."

"That's right," Boone said. "Clive, my . . . colleague . . . will talk to him," he explained, though his grin wavered a bit when he mentioned the other man. "I'll be there to snap a picture or two."

"I can't believe *Life* is here in Hooper's Crossing," she gushed.

"Me either," Boone agreed as he ran a hand through his dark hair. "I can tell you one thing, this place is nothing like New York City."

"That's . . . that's where you're from . . . ?"

"Yep. Ever been there?"

She shook her head.

"Too bad. With everything it has to offer, I reckon a girl like you would fall in love with it faster than you could snap your fingers."

Lily suspected that he was right; after all, it was the place she had been dreaming about for so long. Her thoughts raced. She imagined Jane, likely already on her way to becoming a movie star or fashion model. And here Lily was, still in Hooper's Crossing, still living with her father, still working at the library, and still going nowhere.

What could she possibly have to talk about with a man like Boone, someone who lived in the midst of the city's hustle and bustle, who worked for *Life* magazine, and who had probably seen more of the world in the last week than Lily would see in her whole life?

Then, feeling plenty sorry for herself, she glanced up at Boone and found him looking at her expectantly. Instantly, Lily understood that he must have asked her a question, one she hadn't heard.

"I'm sorry," she again apologized. "What did you say?"

"That I want to take your picture."

Lily froze. "Me?" she blurted. "Why would you want to do that?"

"Because it's my job, for one thing," Boone answered with a chuckle. "I'm supposed to be walking around the festival, taking photos that interest me." He paused, his expression growing a bit more serious, then edged a step closer to Lily. "And you most certainly interest me."

Most days, Lily would have allowed herself to be flattered by a handsome man's words and let him take her picture. But with her head spinning about Jane, the city, and the cowardice she'd shown in staying behind, she couldn't bring herself to accept Boone's offer. Lily believed that the camera would see the truth, that her weakness would be there in the picture.

"I can't," she told him, shaking her head.

Boone looked genuinely surprised at her rejection. "Why not?"

"I...I...just..." Lily started but stopped. It was too

complicated a story to tell, especially to a man she'd just met, even if there was something about Boone that made her believe he would listen. "I've got to go," she added, certain that if she stayed much longer, she would start to cry.

And so Lily turned and left.

Chapter Ten

WHEN BOONE WAS BUMPED INTO, his hands reflexively tightening around his camera, he hadn't thought much of it. There were a lot of people milling around, so it was no surprise that it had happened. Besides, he was from New York, a place where pedestrians slammed into each other a dozen times a day. When the woman's purse hit the pavement, he'd bent over to help her pick up her things, behaving like a gentleman. But when he got a good look at her, everything changed.

She was gorgeous, a true beauty who made his heart pick up speed.

Coming from a man like Boone, someone who had walked the streets of Rome in summertime, snapped photographs of a swimsuit contest in Sweden, and strolled along the beaches of Hawaii, this was high praise indeed. But Lily deserved it. She wasn't a statuesque blonde all glammed up with lipstick and dripping with jewels.

Instead, she had that rare and special something that grabbed hold of a man's heart and squeezed hard enough to make him see stars. From the moment Boone saw her, he'd wanted to hear her voice, to discover her name, to know her better.

And he most definitely wanted to take her picture.

For the life of him, Boone couldn't understand why she'd turned down his offer. Most women he knew, especially those from small out-of-the-way places like this, would have jumped at the chance if an honest-to-goodness photographer asked to snap their picture. But not Lily. She'd turned him down cold. In an odd way, her rejection made her *more* interesting to him. And so, as he watched her move toward the crowd, Boone made a quick decision.

He lifted his camera, sighted down the viewfinder, and took a deep breath.

Randall walked the sidewalks, taking in the sights and sounds of the festival, happy as a bird set free from its cage. He bought a candied apple, mostly eating the good stuff on the skin before pitching what remained on the stick into a garbage can. He picked up a newspaper at the drugstore, leaving the old man behind the counter a couple extra cents on account of his good mood. He tipped his hat in greeting to every pretty lady he walked by.

To hell with Leo and all his damn worryin'. Unless I run naked down the middle of Main Street, ain't a one of these people is gonna remember me.

As he neared the bank, Randall entertained the idea of poking his head inside for appearance's sake. He wondered if Leo wasn't somewhere in the crowd watching him, wanting to know if all this talk about vault doors and hinge caps was a lie, which it most certainly was. In the end, Randall walked right on past. He was just being paranoid. Besides, he only had an hour before he had to be back at the car. Best not to waste any of it.

But then, just as he was passing beneath the movie marquee, wondering what he might do next, Randall saw something that stopped him short.

There, in the middle of the street, was Lily.

Ever since he'd run into her, literally, the cute blonde had been on his mind. Randall had even dreamed about her the night before, a fantasy that found him covered in sweat when he woke up. And now he'd found her among hundreds of people. It must be fate.

Randall almost shouted her name but then thought better of it; she wouldn't be able to hear him over the din of the crowd, anyway. But when he started toward her, already practicing what he wanted to say, he noticed that Lily wasn't alone. A man was with her. They were talking. She was smiling.

What in the hell is this shit?

Randall was the possessive type, the sort who quickly got jealous. And he could no more change the way he was than a leopard could change its spots. He wanted to walk over and punch the stranger in the face, to grab Lily's arm, to drag her away. But he didn't. Impetuous as Randall could be, he knew that *that* would surely draw the sort of attention that Leo was hell-bent on trying to avoid.

Instead, he watched.

As he waited, Randall grew more impatient by the second. But just when he thought he couldn't bear it any longer, something between Lily and the other man changed. He saw her shake her head. The guy looked confused. Then Lily started walking in Randall's direction. He smirked. He must have misunderstood something.

Whatever. Here was his big chance.

Randall started toward Lily. Wouldn't she be surprised to see him? They'd pick up right where they left off, cram as much fun as they could into what little time he had left, maybe do some necking in a secluded doorway, and make plans for more. She was almost close enough to touch.

Then he heard her name, spoken loud and clear in the autumn afternoon.

The only problem was, Randall hadn't been the one to say it.

Lily turned around quickly at the sudden sound of her name, her blond curls falling from her shoulder and brushing against her cheek. Boone was right where she'd left him, but now he had his camera raised to his eye. A second later he lowered it, smiling slyly at having gotten what he wanted despite her wishes.

"Sorry," he told her. "I couldn't help myself."

A spark of anger ignited in Lily's chest. She thought about marching over and arguing with him, but she didn't

move. She didn't say a word. Truth was, there was something about Boone that flustered her. Maybe it was his
good looks, his quick tongue, or the fact that he was from
the city, giving him an air of both street smarts and sophis-
tication. Whatever the reason, Lily knew the picture wasn't
worth fighting about. After all, Boone was a stranger who
had come to town for the festival, a man she'd never see
or speak to again. This wasn't some sappy novel or Hollywood romance. They weren't going to fall in love. By this
time next week, he wouldn't even remember her name.

Let him have his photograph.

Without a word, she again started to walk away.

"Wait, Lily!" Boone shouted, but she kept going.

Incredibly, Lily had only gone a couple of steps before
she ran into someone else. It wasn't a big bump, more of
a brushing of shoulders, but she was so embarrassed that
she didn't even look up to see who she had hit, just mumbled an apology and kept going, making a beeline for the
library.

This time, at least, she had managed to hold on to her
purse.

"Wait, Lily!" Boone yelled, but she didn't slow. Taking her
picture hadn't gone like he had expected. Not at all. He'd
thought she might laugh, give him some teasing grief, and
then share more of his company. The one thing Boone hadn't
counted on was her looking angry and stalking away.

But just as he decided to go after her, a hand grabbed
his arm and halted him in his tracks.

"There you are," Clive said, looking relieved, a half-eaten bag of popcorn in his other hand. "You were supposed to meet me under the movie marquee, remember? That was five minutes ago. I figured I'd better come find you or we'll be late for our interview."

Annoyed at the interruption, Boone spun back around, but Lily had already vanished into the crowd. She was nowhere to be seen.

"Damn it," Boone swore.

"What's wrong?" Clive asked.

"Nothing. Everything," he said, his words as out of sorts as he felt. "I met this girl, we talked, I took her picture, but then she left."

"A girl? Was she pretty?" the writer asked.

"Shut up," Boone grumbled. The last thing wanted was to talk to Clive about Lily, or anything else for that matter.

"You keep this up and you're going to win our bet."

"Bet?" he echoed, still craning his neck, looking for Lily.

"About whether you'll kiss a girl while we're here? Don't tell me you've already forgotten about it."

But he had. Boone didn't give a damn about any wager. Hell, he would have gladly forked over the money if it had meant he could talk to Lily again, to smooth over whatever it was that hadn't gone right between them. But no amount of wishing was going to get her to come back. She was gone and all he had left was the memory of her face, the sound of her voice, and the feel of her touch.

And the film in his camera.

"I hate to cut your romantic moment short," Clive said,

"but we need to get to the mayor's office. I don't want to be late."

"Go on without me," Boone told him, already wondering how long it would take to race back to their rented room, scrounge together his chemicals, transform the small kitchen into a darkroom, and develop his roll of film.

"By myself? But...but you said that you'd go with me..."

"C'mon, Clive. Grow a backbone. You can handle an interview with a rinky-dink mayor, can't you? You work for *Life* magazine, for Christ's sake!"

"Well...sure, I do...but..." the writer said, then nodded, looking as unsure of himself as possible. "I just thought we were a team..."

Boone took a long, deep breath. While a part of him desperately wanted to blow Clive off and develop his pictures of Lily, another knew he couldn't. Like it or not, just as Walter had told him, he did have a measure of responsibility to the writer and his publisher. It frustrated him to no end, but he had an obligation. Besides, it wouldn't take long, an hour at the most, and then he'd have what he so desperately wanted. He would be looking at Lily's face again, this time in a photo.

"All right, all right," he agreed. "Let's go do the damn interview."

Clive's face instantly brightened. "Thanks, Boone!" He held out his bag of popcorn as if in celebration. "Want some?"

"Not in the slightest."

No, what Boone really wanted was to see Lily again, but doing that might not be easy. He didn't know where she lived, her telephone number, if she had a job or boyfriend. Finding out any of those things would take time...

Boone suspected he might not be leaving town so fast after all.

Randall didn't see a flash, no one told him to smile or say cheese, but the second he looked up at the sound of Lily's name, he'd known that the man had taken his picture. Stunned, he froze, then turned his head away. His thoughts raced. He was struggling to figure out what to do when Lily bumped into him, their shoulders touching, but Randall paid her no mind. For now, he had to forget about her.

All that mattered was the man with the camera.

As casually as he could, trying to be just another face in the crowd, Randall moved closer to the stranger, wanting to get a better look, to see his face, hoping he might find out who he was. But before Randall could make out much, another man approached the one with the camera and the two of them started talking. Leaning against a big blue mailbox, glancing at his watch like he was waiting for someone, Randall listened.

What he heard stopped him cold.

"...work for *Life* magazine, for Christ's sake!"

No. No way. It couldn't be. Was that who these jokers were with? If so, this was a problem. A huge one.

Shit, shit, shit...

Standing on the sidewalk, struggling to maintain his composure, Randall felt as if the bottom had fallen out of his stomach. If the guy Lily had been talking to was a goddamn photographer for *Life* magazine, then that meant the picture he'd just taken could end up in print. If so, then thousands, even millions of people might see it. Once the bank had been robbed, if someone understood that Randall Kane had been in Hooper's Crossing at the same time, it wouldn't take a rocket scientist to put two and two together. He'd be on the run for the rest of his life. He tried to calm himself. What were the odds that it would be used? But was it a risk worth taking? No, he had to do something. But what?

Randall knew the answer.

As much as he didn't want to do it, he needed to talk to Leo.

"...every bit as much to offer as a big city, in our own way, of course. Why, the fall festival has surely already proven to fine young gentlemen such as yourselves that..."

Stifling a yawn, Boone raised his camera and snapped a picture of Morris Denton. He was only halfheartedly listening to the mayor as he proudly droned on about his town. Over the years, Boone had met dozens of people just like him, men who couldn't get enough of the sound of their own voice. Government officials, lawyers, clergymen, anyone who had something to sell. Usually when interviewing someone like that, the thing to do was to periodically interrupt, to cut them off and steer the conversation where you wanted it to go, ending in a final question that made it clear that your time together was over.

But that wasn't what Clive was doing. Not by a long shot.

Boone glanced over and saw the young writer scribbling furiously in his notebook, as if every word the mayor was saying was worth its weight in gold. Boone shook his head. He doubted that more than a line or two of this drivel would make it into the magazine, if that. Or any of his photos, for that matter.

"...and if you'd seen it last year or the one before, you'd know that the festival is only getting bigger and..."

Normally, having to listen to this nonsense would have driven Boone up the wall. He would have tapped his foot on the floor. He would've kept glancing at his watch. He would have yawned or stretched, anything to not-so-subtly voice his displeasure. But not today. Not after what had happened earlier.

Not after meeting Lily.

It was hard for him to understand, to explain to himself, but she had captured his attention in ways dozens of girls from all around the world had never done. Since he'd met her, Boone hadn't been able to stop thinking about her. Something about her had bewitched him, grabbing tight. All he wanted was to look into her eyes again.

And in a way, that was exactly what he was doing.

A framed picture sat on the corner of the mayor's desk. From where Boone was sitting, he could easily make out its subject. Lily was Morris Denton's daughter, just as she had said. In the image, she was looking directly at the camera; it appeared to have been a professional sitting. Her eyes were bright and there was a hint of a smile on her lips. Blond hair spilled over her shoulders. She was as beautiful as he remembered. Still, Boone was convinced that the undeveloped photograph he'd snapped of her on the street would be even better.

Before he and Clive had gone to the mayor's office, Boone had carefully removed the roll of film from his camera. But instead of tossing the canister in with the others he'd already snapped, Boone zipped it up in his jacket pocket. He wasn't taking any chances that something bad would happen to it. In order to see it developed he just had to keep from dying of boredom.

"... until you see what happens on Friday night! Everyone together, under the stars, dancing to the music. What a sight! And then there's the pie-eating contest, the potato-sack races, and the ..."

Clive flipped a page, nodding along as the mayor talked.

Boone sighed. Staying awake was going to be harder than he thought.

"So what do we do now?"

Leo took a deep breath. Well, that was the question, wasn't it?

Sitting impatiently behind the wheel of the car, watching the street, his watch, and the surrounding houses all at the same time, Leo had waited for Randall to return. When the younger man finally strolled down the sidewalk, only a couple of seconds before he was to be left behind to fend for himself, Leo had instantly understood that something was wrong. It was in the way Randall carried himself, his shoulders slumped, his pace nervous-quick as he chewed on his lower lip. When he opened the passenger's door and got in, Leo was on him quick.

"What happened?" he asked, already dreading the answer.

To his credit, Randall came clean, even though he had to have known Leo would be angry.

And he was. In spades.

For good reason. Over and over, Leo had railed against making this trip to town. He'd worried that something would go wrong, that his meticulous plans would be ruined, but Randall had just kept telling him to relax, that he was overreacting. In the end, it turned out that Leo's fears had been justified. It was all he could do not to slug the son of a bitch in the face.

Leo's instincts told him to walk away. If a photographer from *Life* magazine had a picture with Randall's face on it, then to go through with robbing the bank would be a hell of a risk, for both of them; if the police managed to hunt Randall down, Leo doubted the other man could keep from revealing his partner's identity for long. What had drawn Leo to this robbery was the anonymity the festival would provide. One click of a camera had ruined everything. The younger thief had gambled and lost.

Still, Leo couldn't help but think about the crowd he'd

seen while driving through town. That many people meant lots of cash changing hands. Just imagining the pile of money that would be sitting in the bank's vault at the end of the week was enough to make his heart skip a beat. It was the answer to all his troubles, an end to a hard way of life. So was Randall's mistake enough to make Leo turn his back on all that money?

No, it wasn't. Not yet, at least.

"Would you recognize either of those guys if you saw them again?" he asked.

Randall nodded. "Sure, but why?"

The plan was still coming together in his head, but Leo said, "We'll come back tonight, after it's dark, look around, and maybe we see them."

"And if we do?"

Well, that was *another* question, wasn't it?

Chapter Eleven

Early the next morning, Boone stood in Marjorie Barlow's driveway while Daisy did her business, then began sniffing around the bushes, following the scent of squirrels, rabbits, and any other creature that passed by in the night. High above, clouds scuttled across the sky. Birds called from the trees, heralding the arrival of the new day. An autumn chill hung in the air, a reminder that winter was slowly but steadily approaching.

Boone noticed none of these things.

He couldn't take his eyes off the picture he held in his hand.

When he and Clive had returned to their room after interviewing the mayor, Boone had immediately begun setting up his makeshift darkroom. He laid out plastic trays and lined up the bottles of chemicals he would need. He rolled a heavy wool blanket to butt up against the bottom of the door, making sure that no light seeped in. He screwed in a red lightbulb so that he'd be able to see as he developed his shots. Finally, he poked his head out of the room. Clive was sitting in a chair, leisurely reading a magazine. "If you open this door and ruin my pictures," Boone warned, "the next place you're going to visit will be the hospital."

The young writer chuckled, then sneezed, then finally asked, "Wait... you're not joking, are you?"

"No, I'm not," Boone said, then slammed the door shut behind him.

He got to work just as he had done countless times before. It wasn't long before he was holding the photograph of Lily up to the light, his heart beating faster as he took in the image. She was as beautiful as he remembered, maybe more so. The camera's lens had captured her just as she'd turned, her expression tinged with surprise at his shouting her name, a few locks of blond hair brushing against her cheek. She looked different than in the photo on her father's desk, more natural, more *real*. The only problem with the picture was that a man had wandered into the shot, his face visible off to the side of Lily's shoulder. But it was easily fixed. Boone took a razor and cut the stranger away. Standing in the darkroom, holding the picture as if it was a treasure, Boone knew he had to see her again.

When he finally opened the door, Boone was taken aback to find Clive wearing his coat, all of his suitcases at his feet. "I'm... I'm..." he started before sneezing. "I'm ready to leave whenever you are."

"We aren't going anywhere." The words came out of his mouth strong and firm, just like his resolve to follow them.

"Wait...we're not?" the writer asked, looking plenty perplexed. "But I thought you said that we were—"

"Not anymore," Boone cut him off. "We're staying."

"What about Havana?"

What about it? Just like that, in a matter of hours, his desire to get there had evaporated. "It'll still be there when this assignment's over."

Clive looked genuinely happy and immediately set about unpacking. Boone had spent the rest of the night thinking about Lily.

And come morning, picture in hand, he was still doing it.

Finally pulling himself away from the photograph, Boone whistled at Daisy. The retriever raised her head from a tree trunk and came running. But instead of stopping at her master's feet, the dog raced past and bounded up the porch steps, skidding to a halt where Marjorie sat in a chair, drinking a steaming cup of coffee.

"I was wondering when one of you would notice me," the older woman said as she scratched Daisy's ears. "Whatever's in that picture must be mighty interesting."

"It is," Boone told her.

"Something you shot at the festival?"

He nodded.

"Can I have a look at it?" Marjorie asked.

Boone hesitated. There was a part of him that wanted to keep Lily's picture private, for his eyes only. If he had

to guess, he supposed it was embarrassment to be moon-
ing away over a pretty face, or maybe some odd sort of
possessiveness. But in the end, he chose to ignore those
ridiculous feelings and handed over the photo.

Marjorie held the image at a distance, letting her eyes
find their focus, then she smiled. "Lily Denton," she said,
nodding at the same time. "I can see why this picture has
such a hold on your attention."

"I met her yesterday," Boone explained as he leaned
against one of the porch's posts. "She didn't want me to
take her picture but I couldn't help myself."

"Do you know her father's the mayor?"

"I do," he said, then chuckled. "He sure likes to hear
himself talk."

"If a person got paid by the word, Morris would be a
millionaire," Marjorie agreed, then paused to take a long
drink of her coffee. "Still, he's a good man. He cares an awful lot about this town and his daughter. It couldn't have
been easy raisin' Lily on his own," she said, then handed
back the picture.

As Boone took it, he echoed her words as a question.
"On his own?"

"Lily's mother died when she was little. Her heart just
gave out one day. Sad set of circumstances."

Boone didn't know how to answer. His relationship
with his own parents was complicated, but they had been
a constant presence in his life while growing up. It was
hard to imagine what it would've been like without either
of them.

"Lily's caught your eye, hasn't she?" Marjorie asked.

"She has," he answered.

"I reckon it makes sense, a city fella comin' to a little town like this, figures he might as well have himself some fun while he's here."

"It's not like that," Boone replied defensively, the words coming out a little harder than he had intended.

"So what is it, then?" the older woman prodded.

"I don't know," he admitted. "All I can say for certain is that I liked what time I had with her and want more. A chance to know her better."

Marjorie was silent for a while as she drank her coffee and continued to scratch Daisy's head. As he waited, Boone started to wonder if what she had implied—that he was just looking for some fun with a local girl—had been a test to see what sort of man he was. If so, he hoped that he'd passed.

"Do you reckon Lily would be happy to see you?" Marjorie finally asked.

"I do," Boone answered truthfully.

"Then you're right. You should go talk to her again."

"Problem is, I don't know where she lives. I could look it up in the phone book but it might be awkward to just drop by out of the blue."

"You don't want to go there anyway," Marjorie said.

"Why not?" Boone asked.

"Because the only word that better describes Morris Denton than *talkative* is *overprotective*," the older woman explained. "I don't care if you are some fancy picture-taker

from New York City, if you show up at his door lookin'
to court his daughter, Morris is more likely to run you off
with his gun than let you talk to Lily."

"Well, if not there, then where do I find her?"

"Go to the library," Marjorie explained. "That's where
she works."

"Lily's a librarian?" Boone asked.

The older woman nodded, then went back to her coffee.

Just like that, Boone knew what he had to do. He'd go to
the library that very morning. He wouldn't be able to wait
any longer than that. Maybe he was imagining that there
was something between them. Or maybe he wasn't . . .

There was only one way to find out.

"Thank you," Boone said, then started down the porch
steps.

"Hold on there," Marjorie stopped him. "The reason I
told you those things was 'cause I've got the impression
you're the sort of young man who wouldn't take advantage." She paused, staring intently at him. "I'd hate to be
proven wrong about that."

He shook his head. "You won't be."

"For your sake, I hope you're right," she said. "I may be
old, but that doesn't mean I'm not dangerous with a frying
pan in my hand."

Boone might have chuckled in response, but deep
down, he knew that Marjorie wasn't kidding.

From the moment Lily had walked away from Boone
Tatum, she'd done little else but think about the *Life*

magazine photographer. She had thought about his handsome looks while halfheartedly listening to Ethel's endless complaints. Walking home from the library, she'd remembered the sound of his voice, how he had shouted her name. Sitting at the dinner table while Morris talked about his interview as if he was going to be featured on the cover, Lily had had to tamp down the urge to ask her father about the man who'd taken his picture. Then later, as midnight came and went on the clock beside her bed, she'd replayed their conversation over and over again, parsing every word until sleep finally came.

But in the end, Lily knew that it had all been a waste of time.

Standing behind the front desk of the library as late-morning sunlight streamed through the windows, Lily understood that she was never going to see Boone again. While he had made one heck of a first impression on her, he wouldn't be making a second. He'd be back to his life in New York City in a couple of days, if he hadn't left already. He probably wouldn't give her photograph more than a quick glance. It would end up in the bottom of a desk drawer or trash can, most likely.

All of which was fine, really. She had plenty of other things to think about. There was whatever it was between her and Garrett, what would happen when people finally *did* notice that Jane was gone, her father, and of course Ethel. Boone Tatum had been a distraction, someone who had stumbled into her life and just as quickly left it. She could dream all she wanted, but in the end, it was just—

And that was when he came through the library door, a camera bag slung over his shoulder. Boone looked around and spotted her, a bright smile creasing his handsome face.

"Hi, Lily," he greeted her.

"Hello, Boone…" she managed, still not quite believing he was there.

"You remembered my name," he said as he leaned against the counter. "That must mean I made a strong impression on you."

"But not necessarily a good one," Lily told him, her tone neutral.

His gaze narrowed, looking at her closely, though his smile never wavered. "I'm not too worried," he replied.

Lily stood up straighter, trying not to let Boone's self-assurance fluster her. There was something about the photographer's confidence that was endearing and frustrating at the same time. "Was there something I can help you with?" she asked. "Did you come to check out a book?"

Boone laughed loudly, as if she'd told a really funny joke. "Of course not," he answered. "I came to see you."

"How did you know where to find me?"

"I asked around."

"And here you are," Lily said, fighting back the surprise she felt that he had been talking to people about her, trying to find out where she was. Once again finding her bearings, she folded her arms across her chest, trying to act defiant even if she wasn't entirely sure why.

Noticing her expression, Boone tilted his head and asked, "Don't tell me you're still mad that I took your picture."

"Shouldn't I be?"

Boone shrugged. "I could apologize if you wanted me to, but I have to warn you, I wouldn't mean it."

"Did you develop it?" Lily asked.

This was one of the questions that had kept her up half the night. If he had, Lily wondered what she'd looked like, and especially what Boone had thought of it. A part of her was nervous, almost afraid to know the answer.

"I did," he replied, then paused. "Would you like to see it?"

Lily nodded without hesitation.

Boone pulled the photo from the inside pocket of his jacket, placed it on the counter, then slid it toward her. Lily picked it up and took in the image. She didn't know what she'd expected, but what she saw in the picture surprised her. The expression on her face, a look that was hard to define, was one that Lily had never seen before. It was natural, authentic. And it was beautiful. Gingerly, she reached out and touched the photograph, half expecting it to change, shifting like smoke, as if she couldn't quite bring herself to believe that it was her.

"You can tear it up if you want."

Lily looked up and found Boone staring at her. "Excuse me?"

"If you're still bent out of shape at me for taking it, then rip it to pieces," he explained. "That there is the only copy

I developed. If you don't like what you see or if it embarrasses you, have at it. It's up to you."

Once again, Lily looked at the picture. It was true that she hadn't wanted it taken and that it had upset her when Boone ignored her request.

Still, it was hard to argue with the results.

"No, you keep it," Lily said, and handed it back.

Boone took it, then chuckled.

"What's so funny?"

"Can I make a confession?" he asked, smiling slyly.

"Of course."

"Even if you *had* ripped it up," Boone explained, running a hand through his dark hair, "I would've just developed another copy from the negative."

Though a part of Lily was annoyed with Boone for misleading her, there was another that was flattered he wanted to keep hold of her picture so badly. "Do you like it?" she asked.

"That I do. It's got good lighting, the focus is just right, but it's the subject that has really grabbed my attention," Boone said, then raised his eyes from the photo to hers. "She's a real beauty, that's for sure. But..." he ended, letting that last word hang there between them, like bait on a line.

"But what?" Lily asked, unable to resist the word's lure.

"But a picture isn't enough. I want more," he replied. "Come with me, right now. Let's go get something to eat or take a walk. Anything, just so long as we're together."

The photographer's bluntness caught Lily off-guard.

She wasn't used to anyone, let alone a handsome man like Boone, talking to her in such a way and didn't know how to react. "I...I can't..." she managed, though the thought of spending some more time with him was tempting. "I'm not supposed to go to lunch for almost another hour and—"

"Who cares about 'supposed to'?" Boone interrupted. "Would you rather be here," he asked, his arms spreading to indicate the library, "or out showing me the festival and having a little fun?"

Put like that, Lily knew her answer. Still, it wasn't that simple. But before she could respond, Ethel chose that moment to walk out from the stacks, her mouth pinched in a tight grimace, as if she'd just taken a bite of a particularly sour lemon.

"If you're done loafing around," she groused at Lily, "I have a whole list of things that require your attention, starting with the—"

"How do you do, ma'am?" Boone cut in before Ethel could say more, stepping between the two women and extending his hand. He introduced himself, then added, "I'm a photographer with *Life* magazine," patting his camera bag for emphasis.

"Oh, well, hello..." Ethel replied awkwardly, taking his offered hand.

"I'm sorry to have to do this on such short notice, but I'm afraid Ms. Denton is going to have to come with me."

"She is? But...but whatever for...?"

"There are some pictures that need to be taken for our

upcoming story on the festival," Boone explained, nodding gravely, as if he was talking about a matter of national security. "I'll bring her back just as soon as we're finished, though as to when that might be, I'm afraid I'm not entirely sure."

"But...but..." the older librarian stumbled, completely out of sorts.

Boone turned back to Lily, flashing her a hint of a smile. "Are you ready?" he asked.

Lily had a choice to make. Boone was, in almost every way, a stranger, someone who came from the city, almost another world entirely. But there was no use in denying that he interested her. Still, if she left with him now, she'd be shirking work, a fact that Ethel would be sure to make her pay for ten times over. Yet in the end, maybe Boone was right. What harm could there be in having a little fun?

"Let's go," she answered, then came out from behind the counter and walked with him toward the door.

"Now, wait just a minute!" Ethel practically shouted, finally finding her voice. "I don't care what magazine this is for, that's no reason for—"

But Lily never heard the rest. She and Boone were already gone.

Chapter Twelve

AFTER THEY LEFT the library, Lily and Boone walked through town. The late-morning sun felt warm on Lily's bare skin, but the autumn air was still crisp enough to make her pull her jacket tight. As they went, she pointed out familiar places, businesses and the homes of friends, often adding little stories about what things had been like when she was growing up. For his part, Boone nodded along and even asked the occasional question. They weaved among the festival stalls, most of them just opening for the day. Lily greeted the people she knew, although there were plenty of faces she didn't recognize, out-of-towners like the man at her side. Here and there, Boone spotted something he liked and pulled out his camera to snap a quick picture, though he never turned the lens in her direction. Eventually, they made their way to Fisher's Diner, mostly empty at that hour, and snagged a table for a late breakfast or early lunch, depending on how one chose to look at it.

"So is that lady you work with always like that?" Boone asked after they'd placed their order.

"Ethel? Most days, yes," Lily explained. "She's one of those people who aren't happy about anything. Since we're the only two librarians, most of her grumpiness is directed at me. No matter what I do, it never seems to be good enough."

"That doesn't sound like a lot of fun."

"It isn't, but I try not to let her get to me, which is easier said than done," she added with a chuckle. "Strange as this might sound, part of me pities her."

"Really?" Boone asked, looking genuinely surprised.

"I can't imagine going through life that angry. It seems like a waste. Besides, it's not like I'm going to quit. I like books and helping people too much."

Boone leaned back in his seat. "You're a better person that I am," he said. "I wouldn't be able to put up with someone nagging me all the time."

"Isn't there anyone you don't get along with at the magazine?" Lily asked.

"Well, there's Clive, the writer I got stuck with for this job," Boone answered. "He sure can drive me up the wall, but that's 'cause he's new to this and doesn't know the tip of a pencil from its eraser."

"There you go, then."

"It's not the same. My job isn't like yours."

"How so?"

"For one thing, I'm always out in the field. Even my editor, a guy who, like Ethel, looks like he's been there since they hung the sign out front, almost never leaves his office," he explained. "Those people I do work with on assignments know enough to stay out of my way. The last thing I want is someone looking over my shoulder, telling me what pictures to take. Any writer worth his salt would say the same thing. Working that way has gotten me where I am."

"Are you a good photographer?" Lily asked.

"I am," he answered simply.

"Modest, too, I see."

Boone looked at her with a wry smile. "Modesty is for people who don't have anything to brag about."

"So you're saying that you're a braggart?"

He chuckled easily. "The way I see things, if you can back up what you say, then it isn't bragging. It's just the facts."

Lily stared across the table at Boone. Here was his strong sense of confidence again. But it wasn't as if he was crowing about himself or acting like a bigwig. He simply believed in himself. And Lily supposed that at least a measure of it had to be true; she didn't figure they'd let just anybody take pictures for *Life* magazine.

"I bet you've seen lots of exotic places," she said.

"Sure have," he replied. "Paris, Tokyo, Cairo, San Francisco. If you know its name, I've probably been there."

"So if you usually go to fancy places like those, why are you here?"

Boone's smile faltered. "That there is a doozy of a story. The reason I'm in Hoover's Crossing is because—"

"Hooper's," Lily interrupted, correcting him.

"What was that?"

"It's Hooper's Crossing, not Hoover's."

Boone laughed good-naturedly. "Sorry about that. I bet I've been saying it wrong for days. I meant no offense."

"None taken, but I still don't have an answer."

He nodded. "The reason I'm here is because I'm being punished."

Lily listened as Boone laid out the whole story, from his attempt to take an early-morning picture of the New York City skyline, to his brawl with the longshoreman and subsequent time in a jail cell, to the ultimatum his editor had given, through his long drive north with Clive and Daisy as passengers.

"Who's Daisy?" Lily asked, her eyes narrowing.

"She's my dog, not my girlfriend," he explained. "Everyone gets that wrong at first. Maybe I should've picked a different name."

Boone told her that he and Clive were letting a room at Marjorie Barlow's place, his tale finally ending when he'd bumped into her the day before.

"It still bugs me that I didn't get that picture on the dock," he added. "All those buildings in the morning sun. Would have been the cover, for sure."

Though Boone's story had certainly been interesting, there was something about him, about the life he led, that nagged at Lily. He was a man used to excitement, to adventure. He wasn't meant to spend much time in a place like Hooper's Crossing, little more than a dot on a map.

Boone had admitted as much himself. He was only here to be punished.

"I bet you can't wait to leave," she said with resignation.

"Truth is, that's exactly how I felt driving up here," Boone confessed. "I figured I'd show up, snap a few pictures, let Clive jot a few things down in his notebook, then make tracks just as quick as I could. Heck, I didn't even bother unpacking what little I brought." He paused. "That was the plan but then something changed."

"What's that?" Lily asked, wondering if she didn't already know the answer.

His eyes found hers. "I met you."

If she'd been a couple of years younger or more naive, Lily knew she would have been beyond flattered by Boone's words. She would probably have blushed, looked away, and then asked him to tell her more. But she wasn't that innocent. Here he was, a man from the city who'd been around the block more times than he could count, trying to charm her into thinking she was special. As good looking as Boone was, it was probably a con he'd used many times before to some success. Right then, Lily had a flashback to the man she'd bumped into outside the bank, remembering how creepily he had come on to her. Maybe he and Boone weren't so different after all.

Boone's eyes narrowed. He leaned forward and crossed his arms on the diner table. "I bet I know what's swimming around in your head right now," he told her. "I reckon you think I'm a wolf on the prowl, that I saw myself a pretty girl and decided to make a play for her."

Lily shook her head in denial, even though he was absolutely correct. "I wasn't thinking that," she lied.

"Sure you were. It's written all over your face."

This time, Lily didn't argue. Maybe it *was* plain to see.

"Let me tell you something," Boone continued. "I may have been all over the world, and yes, I've met dozens, heck, hundreds of good-looking gals, but I've never been as captivated by any of them as I am by you."

She couldn't help but laugh, unable to fully believe him.

"It's true," he insisted, his tone a bit forceful.

"Why me?" she asked, staring hard into his eyes, needing him to answer truthfully. "What about me could be that interesting?"

Boone again leaned back. "Honestly, I don't know," he answered. "Maybe it's the sound of your voice or the curve of your smile. Or maybe it's just the way things were meant to be. In the end, what does it matter? All I know is that I want to spend as much time with you as I can, to get to know you as well as you'll let me. So what do you say? Am I worth taking a chance?"

For all the reservations Lily had just felt, she found herself wanting to say yes. Boone Tatum was unlike any man she'd ever met; he was about as different as possible from those she knew in Hooper's Crossing. Even though they had only spent a short time together, she'd had a good time. He made her smile, to say nothing of the fact that he was as handsome as could be. Besides, he'd only be around for a couple more days. What could it hurt to have some fun? And after everything with Garrett, Jane, her father, and even Ethel, maybe she deserved a distraction.

"All right," she said with a smile.

But before Boone could respond, the waitress brought their food and the two of them began to eat. Small talk filled their conversation.

Still, Lily couldn't help but feel excited.

She could only wonder what the next couple of days might bring.

Garrett Doyle tipped his policeman's cap at a group of older women as they walked by on the sidewalk, then leaned back against the hood of his squad car. Working the festival could be plenty tiring, with long days and longer nights, but he liked being out among the public in uniform. Serving as a policeman entrusted him with authority, a responsibility he took seriously. It was his job to uphold the law, and he'd done plenty of that just that morning. He'd already issued two speeding tickets, helped Arlene Watts round up her stray dog, settled a dispute between Tom Gregor and Joel Hargrove about where one festival booth ended and the other began, and arrested two middle-aged men from Maine who'd spent the whole night drinking, which might explain why a simple disagreement over the best way to cook eggs had ended in a bloody brawl. All before noon.

But the whole time, Garrett had been distracted, his mind elsewhere.

He couldn't stop thinking about Lily.

So what else is new?

The last time they'd been together, when Garrett had driven Lily home from the library, she'd asked him a fateful question.

"Are…are you asking me on a date…?"

Garrett's heart had raced faster than the pistons in his squad car's engine. Right then and there, he hadn't had a clue how to answer. Was she asking in an *I've been waiting my whole life for you to notice me!* sort of way? Or was it more of a *You can't be serious!* type of thing? Having no way of knowing for certain, Garrett had chosen not to risk it. At a time when he had needed to open the door to his heart and tell the truth, he'd instead been a coward and closed it.

But maybe all hope wasn't lost, at least not yet.

In two days' time, the festival's dance would be held. A parquet floor would be installed in the middle of the park. Strings of white lights would be hung above it with tables for refreshments off to the side. Couples young and old would dance to live music, enjoying a night under the stars before the weather turned too cold. And if he could just find the nerve to ask her, he and Lily would be there. Garrett could see it now plain as day, the two of them, their arms wrapped around each other, moving under the lights and stars. Maybe, if things went as he hoped, they'd even share their first kiss. Other people would look at them and smile approvingly. After all, they *were* the perfect couple, if only Lily would open her eyes and see it.

She was the smartest, kindest woman he'd ever known.

She was the prettiest, too. On top of all that, she was also—

—coming out of the diner and headed right toward me!

For a second, Garrett's spirits soared. He stepped away from his squad car thinking that this was the perfect chance to talk to her, to make up for the awkwardness of their previous conversation, maybe even to bring up the dance. But just as soon as his heart leaped like a rocket, it then sank like a stone.

Lily wasn't alone. A man was with her, someone Garrett didn't recognize.

Unlike in the car when Garrett had opted for the safer choice, he now started walking straight toward Lily and her companion. Quickly.

Garrett was only a couple of feet from the pair and Lily still hadn't noticed him. Her head was turned toward the stranger, laughing at something he said; seeing it sent a jolt of jealousy coursing through him.

"Hey, Lily," he said, announcing himself.

She quickly looked at him, her eyes widening with surprise. "Garrett!" she exclaimed. "I...I didn't see you coming..." Noticing how his attention kept darting toward the man at her side, Lily introduced them.

"Nice to meet you," Boone said warmly enough, extending his hand.

Garrett took it, squeezing a little harder than his usual greeting. "Sure," was all he offered in return.

"Boone's a photographer for *Life* magazine," Lily explained, sounding far more impressed by that fact than

Garrett would have liked. "He's here to take pictures for an article about the festival."

"Is that right?" Garrett said, not in the least bit impressed. "Then maybe he should go and talk to your dad. I'd imagine that the mayor would have lots to say, enough to fill an article in no time flat." He offered this suggestion not to be helpful but rather in the hopes that the guy would get lost.

"Way ahead of you," the photographer replied with a smile Garrett found himself wanting to punch. "I spoke with him yesterday. Well, actually I didn't do much talking. My partner, either, for that matter," he added with a chuckle. "It's hard to get a word in edgewise once Morris works up a head of steam."

"Garrett knows *exactly* what you're talking about," Lily said.

"Yeah? The two of you go way back, I take it?"

Listening to them talk, Garrett considered jumping into their conversation to explain his relationship with Lily to the photographer; he wanted the slick out-of-towner to know that he'd always been there for her, through the good times and the bad, and that no one would ever be closer, to either of them.

But before he could open his mouth, Lily reached over and squeezed his arm, silencing the thought. "Garrett grew up across the street from me," she said as pleasantly as could be. "He still lives there, as a matter of fact. He's family."

That old uneasy feeling welled up again in Garrett's gut.

He knew that she'd meant well, but Lily's words weren't quite what he had wanted to hear. "That's right," he agreed anyway, unable to contradict her.

"And a police officer, to boot," Boone added, as if he was impressed.

Yeah, one who threw a couple no-good out-of-towners like you into a jail cell a few hours back. Hell, I bet there's room in there for one more.

"For a couple of years now," Lily said for him, "and about the best in—"

She was interrupted by someone shouting Garrett's name. They all turned to see Cliff Turner, covered with a bloody butcher's smock, hurrying toward them as fast as he could.

"What's wrong, Mr. Turner?" Garrett asked.

"There's . . . there's been an accident . . ." the butcher managed, pausing to wipe a copious amount of sweat from his brow with a handkerchief. "A truck . . . backed into a couple of cars on . . . on Lincoln Avenue . . ." he explained. "I don't think anyone's hurt . . . but tempers are gonna . . . are gonna flare if someone . . ."

"I'll take care of it," Garrett said, patting the man's shoulder, not needing to hear the rest. Turning to Lily, he added, "I've got to go."

"It's time for me to get back to the library anyway," she replied. "No need in making Ethel any angrier at me than she already is."

"Nice to meet you," Boone said.

"I'll talk to you later," Lily added, then the two of them walked away.

Garrett watched them go for a moment, even though he knew he should be hurrying to the accident.

He didn't like what he was seeing. Not one bit.

Lily and Boone left Garrett and began walking back to the library. They took the long way since Lily was in no hurry to get back, skirting the park and looking at the festival. They talked and laughed, enjoying the sunshine as well as each other's company. Lily was surprised by how comfortable she felt around Boone; it was as if she'd known the handsome photographer for years, instead of just a couple of days.

"Garrett seems like a good guy," Boone said when they'd reached the far end of the park.

"He is," Lily agreed, though she thought that her friend had seemed overprotective, what with the way he kept sizing up Boone.

"How long did you say you've known him?"

"For as long as I can remember, really. He moved in across the street when I was little and we've been close ever since."

"He's probably been planning your wedding for ten of those years," Boone said, then chuckled at his own joke.

But Lily frowned. She knew he had only been trying to be funny, but with the recent strangeness between her and Garrett, there was nothing to laugh about. Boone noticed.

"Hey, I'm sorry," he said, stopping beneath the dappled shade of a nearly leafless maple tree. "I shouldn't have said that."

"It's all right," she replied, trying to blow the whole thing off.

"No, it isn't," Boone insisted. "You know, one of the bad things about traveling all over the world is that you pick up lots of bad habits. While something might be funny in one place, it isn't somewhere else," he explained. "Occasionally, the things that fall out of my mouth would have been better off staying inside. This is one of those times."

Lily smiled. "Apology accepted," she said, and meant it.

Boone tenderly took her hand. "Let me make it up to you," he said, then pointed across the street to the Grand Theater; the movie marquee advertised *High Noon* starring Gary Cooper and Grace Kelly. "How about I take you to see a picture tonight? Come on, what do you say?"

She searched his face, unsure of how to respond. "I...I don't know..."

The smile that he flashed was completely disarming, wiping away any reluctance Lily felt and causing her heart to beat a little faster. "Don't think about it too much," he said. "We're supposed to be having some fun, remember?"

"All right, then," she answered with a smile of her own. "Although that means you'll have to come to my house to pick me up."

"No problem," he said confidently.

"You say that now, but that means you'll have to talk to my father."

Boone shrugged. "So? I've already met him."

"But that was when you were taking his picture for *Life*

magazine," Lily explained. "That's a far cry from taking his daughter out on a date."

The photographer's smile faltered, if only a bit. "Hmmm," he mused. "Well, then I guess it's like my grandfather used to say, forewarned is forearmed. As long as he doesn't meet me at the door with a shotgun."

"No guarantees," she teased.

"To spend more time with you," he said, stepping closer and looking down into her eyes, "it would be worth it."

Lily imagined what would come next: Boone's hand would touch her waist, pulling her closer until their bodies touched; he would lean down, tilting his head slightly; she would watch him come nearer and nearer, closing her eyes at the last second, right before their lips touched, a first kiss begun.

But none of those things happened.

Instead, Boone gave her hand a soft squeeze, let go, and stepped back. "I'll pick you up at six," he said with a smile, then walked off. Lily watched him go, both unwilling and unable to move. She knew that Boone had behaved like a gentleman, that he thought kissing her now would've been too bold, but a part of her was disappointed. She wouldn't have turned down his advances. She would've enjoyed a kiss. Apparently, all of that would have to wait.

For now, at least.

Chapter Thirteen

Y OU'RE GOING *WHERE* with *whom*?"

Lily looked across the table at her father and found him wearing an odd expression of both surprise and suspicion. Morris had arrived late for dinner, his mayoral duties keeping him at the festival longer than expected, and had just sat down to eat when she'd told him her plans for the evening. Instead of answering the question right away, Lily put down her fork, daubed her napkin against her mouth, and steadied herself, hoping to avoid an argument.

"I'm going to the movies tonight with Boone Tatum," she repeated.

"Tatum, Tatum…" Morris said as he wadded up his own napkin, his appetite apparently ruined. "Why does that name sound familiar?"

"He works for *Life* magazine," Lily explained. "You met with him yesterday in your office."

"The quiet one who spent the whole time scribbling in his notebook?"

"No, Boone was the photographer."

And he's really, really handsome, she left unsaid.

Lily wouldn't have thought it possible, but when her father realized who she was talking about, his expression grew cloudier than the early-evening sky outside their window. "When in heaven's name did you meet him?"

"Yesterday on the street. I accidentally bumped into him and then we started—"

"It doesn't matter," Morris said dismissively. "You're not going anywhere with that man," he declared as if the matter had been settled, then retrieved his fork and turned his attention back to his plate.

"And why not?" Lily asked, her ire rising; she may not have wanted to argue with her father, but she wasn't going to allow herself to be walked on, either.

"Because you don't know the first thing about him," Morris replied between bites. "I didn't like the look of him. He seemed like a rotten apple."

"Well, he's not," Lily countered, "and I know plenty about Boone. For one thing, he lives in New York City but his job takes him all over the world. I know that he has a dog and that the reason he's here in town is because—"

"But you don't have a clue what sort of man he is," her father interrupted.

"He was the perfect gentlemen this afternoon during lunch."

Lily's revelation stopped her father's fork short of his

mouth. "Wait...what now...?" he sputtered. "You had *lunch* with him?"

"So what if I did?" she replied, her voice rising.

"All I'm saying is that you shouldn't—"

"I understand *exactly* what you're saying," she said, cutting him off, both unable and unwilling to hold back her frustration. "You don't think I can make my own decisions, but you're wrong. I can spend time with who I want, when I want. I'm not a child anymore and its long past time you realized that."

Usually, such harsh words would have precipitated a huge argument between them. Morris would insist that he was only looking out for his daughter's best interests, while Lily would complain that he was being overprotective. Most times, Lily's anger would eventually wither under her father's relentless pressure and she would reluctantly agree to a compromise she wasn't particularly happy with. Things would be better for a week or so before the cycle started over again.

But not this time.

Morris stared at her for a long while, then sighed deeply. "I am painfully aware of that, sweetheart," he finally said. "It's just that, well, ever since your mother died, I've...I just..." Morris managed before falling silent. For Lily, it was an uncommon sight. Her father always talked a mile a minute, rarely letting others get a word in. The only thing capable of rendering him speechless was to think about the loss of his beloved wife. "I just want you to be happy."

"I'm glad. That means we want the same thing," Lily replied with an easy smile. "And that's why you have to trust me to know right from wrong. Maybe tonight Boone will give me a reason to discover I'm mistaken about him. Maybe he'll belch during the movie or pick his nose," she said with a mischievous grin. "Or maybe he will be funny and charming, maybe he'll listen to what I have to say and even laugh at my jokes. Either way, it's up to me to decide. After all, it's my life. I should be able to live it the way I want."

Lily expected her father to disagree but instead he nodded. "All right, all right," Morris said. "I know when I'm licked. Go have fun."

"Thanks, Dad," she replied, reaching over to squeeze his hand.

"But if he tries any funny stuff, I want to know about it," her father added with a scowl.

"You'll be the first person I tell," Lily said, though from what she knew of Boone, she was confident there was nothing to worry about.

"What time does the picture start?"

"Seven o'clock."

"Is he picking you up or are you meeting at the theater?" he pressed, the questions showing how protective he was when it came to his daughter.

"Boone's coming to the house."

The thin smile that slowly spread across her father's face was enough to give Lily pause. "Good, that's good," Morris said. "That means I'll be able to take his measure before your...your *date*..." he explained, that last word clearly hard to say out loud.

When Boone had asked Lily to the movies, she'd tried to warn him about what he was getting into, about how difficult her father could be.

Now she could only hope he had listened.

"You're going *where* with *whom*?"

Boone stopped the razor that he'd been using to shave whiskers from his cheek and looked at Clive's reflection in the small mirror above the sink. The writer was half-heartedly flipping through the local newspaper. Daisy was outside tied to a tree in the backyard; not only did it give Clive a welcome break from sneezing, but the dog was happy to sniff around in the cool grass.

"I'm taking Lily Denton to the movies," Boone repeated, then went back to cleaning himself up for his date.

"Denton?" Clive echoed. "She isn't related to the mayor, is she?"

"She's his daughter."

"And that doesn't worry you?"

Once again, Boone stopped shaving midstroke. "Should it?"

Clive shrugged. "All I'm saying is that her dad talks like he gets paid by the word and has his heart set on being a millionaire," he explained. "If his daughter was cut from the same cloth, I'd be worried that she'd talk my ear off."

"Lily isn't like that. Lucky for me, this particular apple fell far from the tree."

"What picture are you seeing?"

"High Noon."

"Good movie. I saw it a month or so back at the Palladium on Seventeenth," Clive said. "I know plenty of people swear that John Wayne is the best of the Hollywood cowboys, but I'll take Gary Cooper any day of the week."

Boone didn't offer his opinion, even though he'd already seen the picture, too. He liked it enough to sit through it again, sure, but this night wasn't about watching a movie. It was about spending more time with Lily. For that, he would have gladly sat through it a dozen times so long as she was there beside him.

Once he'd finished shaving, Boone wiped his face with a towel and slipped on his shirt. As he did up the buttons, he looked in the mirror and frowned. Since he hadn't expected to be in Hooper's Crossing for long, Boone didn't have much in the way of clothes. His outfit, while perfectly suitable for taking pictures, now seemed too shabby for a date with a beautiful young woman he wanted to impress.

"Does this look all right to you?" he asked Clive.

"Sure. Why wouldn't it?"

Boone took the shirt's well-worn fabric between his fingers. "I don't want to come across like a hobo fresh off the train."

"Don't take this the wrong way," the writer began, "but you don't strike me as the sort of guy who is too concerned about his wardrobe."

"What's that supposed to mean?" Boone replied a bit defensively.

"Nothing bad," Clive replied quickly. "It's just that when you're darting through a jungle or sweating bullets in some far-flung city, you aren't too concerned about how you look in the mirror, right?"

Boone shrugged. The other man was right.

"So I wouldn't worry about it."

"That's easy for you to say. You're not the one who'll look like a bum."

Clive closed the newspaper and set it aside. "That's basically what you were wearing when the two of you met, right?" he asked.

"More or less."

"Then you're as good as gold. If she liked what she saw enough to agree to go out with you, then it's hard to imagine she'd be disappointed or surprised when you knock on her door in that."

Though Boone hated to admit it, Clive was probably right. Lily had seemed plenty interested in him just the way he was, well-worn clothes and all. Besides, she knew he was in town for business; it wasn't like he'd hauled his entire wardrobe along with him. He'd just be himself and let the chips fall where they may.

"You like this girl a lot, don't you?" Clive asked, his expression curious, finally resembling a writer who'd caught the whiff of an interesting story.

Boone could have admitted to it, but chose not to. Instead he asked, "What are you going to do while I'm gone?"

"I'll probably start writing my notes into an article,"

Clive answered. "The problem is, I have so much that I'm not sure where to start."

After walking Lily back to the library, he and Clive had spent the afternoon at the festival among the crowded booths, taking pictures and interviewing people. Boone already had more shots than he needed, but he hadn't minded snapping a few more. Meeting Lily and hearing what she had to say about her town had changed his perspective on things.

"What about writing from the reader's point of view," he suggested.

Clive shook his head. "I don't follow."

"Try to imagine what it would be like to come to the festival for the first time," Boone explained. "All the sights and sounds, smells and tastes. You could introduce some of the people you talked to today as if you were strolling through the park and met them, one after the other."

"That's a great idea!" the writer gushed, then rushed over to his notebook as if he couldn't wait to get to work. "Thanks a lot!"

"I know you're excited, but don't spend the whole night cooped up in here," Boone added as he slipped on his watch and slid his wallet into his back pocket. "You should get out for a bit, too. Take a walk or check out the festival."

"Sure, sure," Clive responded without looking up from his pages. "I'll try, but I've got plenty of work to do first."

Boone shrugged. He'd tried. If Clive wanted to waste a perfectly gorgeous autumn night scribbling out an article, that was his loss.

Not Boone. He had other plans.

But then, just before he reached the door, Clive asked, "Are you meeting Lily at her place or the movie theater?"

"Her place."

"That means you're probably going to see her dad, right?"

"Yeah."

Clive chuckled. "Good luck."

Boone's brow furrowed. "Why do you say that?" But even as he asked the question, he faintly remembered his conversation with Lily.

Had something been said about a shotgun?

The writer's warning was nowhere near as threatening, though it did give Boone pause. "That guy's in love with the sound of his own voice," Clive answered. "If you're not careful, you might miss the start of the movie."

For what felt like the dozenth time, Lily looked at herself in the mirror hanging beside the front door. She had tried on outfit after outfit, almost emptying her closet as she searched for just the right one. Dresses had been discarded for being too flashy, too drab, the wrong color or length. Finally, she'd settled on a yellow dress more appropriate for summer, adding a white cardigan for warmth. Even now, she still wasn't convinced that she had made the correct choice.

Lily pulled back the curtain and looked outside. The sun had already reached the treetops, casting long shadows across the ground. Birds swooped through the quickly darkening sky. Any moment now, Boone would come walking down the sidewalk and their date would begin.

Even though there were no butterflies outside, there were plenty in Lily's stomach. It didn't matter that she'd only just met Boone. She liked him, maybe more than she would have been willing to admit. The photographer had grabbed her attention, and Lily didn't want him to let go. She wanted their night together to get off to the right start.

Which was why she was keeping a close eye on her father.

Ever since she'd told him about her plans with Boone, Morris had been lost in thought. He had grunted and grumbled both during and after dinner, clearly still uneasy that his daughter was going to the movies with a man he considered a complete stranger. Lily expected him to pounce on Boone the second the photographer knocked on the door, badgering him about his intentions and demanding that she be brought home at a ridiculously early time. Even though Lily planned on ignoring whatever her father said, she still feared being embarrassed in front of Boone.

As Lily took yet another look at herself in the mirror, the telephone rang. She heard her father answer; though she had no idea who he was speaking with, Morris was using his "mayor voice" and talking about the festival.

Just then, she saw Boone headed toward the house.

Lily's heart leaped, mostly from the excitement of seeing him again, but also because she might not have to deal with her father confronting Boone after all. She opened the door and stepped onto the porch.

When Boone saw her, he came to a sudden stop and stared. "You look beautiful . . ." he said.

The intensity of his gaze and the sincerity of his words were too much for Lily. She looked away, unable to fully accept his compliment. "I had a hard time picking out something to wear," she admitted, self-consciously crossing her arms. "I worried that I might have overdressed."

"You're perfect," he told her. "If anyone has reason to worry about their clothes, it's me. I didn't have a lot to choose from."

Boone wore the same outfit as when they'd met. He appeared casual, as if he was about to roll up his sleeves and do some hard labor, but Lily didn't mind. Thanks to his strong features, to say nothing of a smile with enough wattage to light a dark room, there likely wasn't an outfit that Boone wouldn't be handsome in.

"You look good," Lily said. When he began to chuckle, she asked, "What's so funny?"

"Seeing you dressed like that, I've realized something," he answered. "Even if I'd brought the spiffiest outfit in my closet, I still wouldn't hold a candle to you."

Even though she remained a bit embarrassed by his praise, this time Lily accepted it. "That's kind of you to say," she replied.

Boone's gaze drifted from her to the house. "This is a nice place you've got." He hesitated for a moment, then added, "Is your father around?"

At the mention of Morris, the spell that had been cast on her after seeing Boone again was broken. "He's on the phone," Lily said even as she hurried down the porch steps and slipped her arm in the photographer's, thinking that this was their chance to get away. "Something about the festival, I think. He'll probably be busy for—"

But they were only halfway down the walk when she heard the creak of the front door.

"There you are," her father said, his voice loud in the evening air. "I was hoping I'd catch you before you left. We have a few things to talk about."

"We don't want to be late to the movie," Lily responded without stopping, looking back over her shoulder. "We'll be back around—" she continued, but stopped when Boone came to an unexpected halt.

"It's okay, Lily," he told her.

She shook her head, not wanting to let the chance to get away go. "You don't know what he can be like."

Boone smiled, then gave her a wink. "Don't worry. I've got this," he said, then started back toward the porch.

Morris smiled in a way that resembled the lion at the zoo who was about to be fed. "Tatum, was it?" he asked, extending his hand.

"That's right, sir," Boone answered, taking her father's offered greeting and giving it a good shake. "It's a pleasure to see you again."

"Of course, of course. Now about you taking my daughter out for—"

"I have to admit, Mayor Denton," the photographer

interrupted, flashing his brightest smile, "I've thought an awful lot about you since we met."

Morris's brow furrowed. "You have?"

"Your town has made quite an impression on me," Boone explained. "Working for *Life*, I've been all over the world, from places that aren't a lot more than a couple of huts, to cities filled with tall skyscrapers. Heck, I've been to so many countries that somewhere along the way I lost count."

"Is that a fact?" her father asked, seeming genuinely impressed.

"Yes, sir, it is. Now, most of these places are the same other than the language they speak or the food they eat. Some are more exotic than others. Some leave an impression," Boone said. "Hooper's Crossing is one of the latter. I'll be honest with you, I wasn't looking forward to coming here. But now that I've strolled down its streets, talked with its people, seen what it has to offer," he explained, slipping a quick glance in Lily's direction, "I'm awfully glad I came. Seems to me, some of the credit for that should go to the man who runs it."

"I'm just one person among many," Morris replied humbly, though his daughter could see that he was touched. Unlike when Boone had used his significant charms to wheedle Ethel into letting him do what he wanted, Lily heard no small amount of truth in the photographer's words.

She, and Hooper's Crossing, had made an impression on him.

"Do you think the town will come off looking good in the magazine?" Morris asked, clearly quite curious about the answer.

"It will if I have anything to say about it," Boone replied.

Morris nodded, then clapped the younger man on the shoulder. "You kids have a good time at the show."

Lily didn't say a word until they were a way down the sidewalk, the house and her father well behind them. She couldn't believe what had just happened. Thinking about it brought a smile to her face. "I don't think anyone has ever tamed my father quite like that before."

"It wasn't anything special," Boone replied. "I just told him the truth, a particular truth I knew he would want to hear."

Just as with Ethel at the library, the photographer had gotten what he wanted, albeit in a different way. Boone seemed to know exactly what to say and how to say it.

"How did you know it would work?" she asked.

He shrugged. "Easy. I read him. You see, most people are like a book. Some you have to be careful with, while others can be knocked over with a feather. Your father would have known I was blowing smoke, so I took another route."

"Like a book," Lily repeated. "So then, what kind am I?"

Boone turned and gave her a wink. "To be honest, I don't know just yet, but I'm having a heck of a good time turning the pages."

Chapter Fourteen

RANDALL TOOK ONE LAST DRAG on his cigarette, then flicked the butt out the car window where it immediately disappeared from sight. Leo was behind the wheel, driving them toward Hooper's Crossing. Even though it was early evening, with only the brightest of stars shining in the bruised-purple sky, their headlights were on, illuminating the road. The oncoming night was cool and growing colder, but Randall stubbornly refused to roll up his window. The discomfort matched his mood.

"This ain't gonna be any different from yesterday," he grumbled.

"Only one way to find out," Leo answered.

Randall sighed. "It's like lookin' for a needle in a haystack."

"Just remember, you're the one who tossed the damn thing in there."

How can I forget when you keep remindin' me?

After Randall had been inadvertently photographed by the guy from *Life* magazine, Leo had come up with a plan for them to get their hands on the picture. Yesterday, they'd returned to town around dusk, using the darkness as cover, and driven the streets, scanning the festival. Randall had looked every which way, increasingly desperate to catch sight of either the photographer or the man he'd spoken with. Hours had passed with nothing to show for them. There had been a couple of close calls, men who bore a passing resemblance to the bastard who'd been talking with Lily, but each time Randall had been wrong. With every case of mistaken identity, the tension in the car had risen. Finally, they'd packed it in and returned to their hideout.

Tonight, they intended to give it one more try. If they couldn't find the photographer, the plan to rob the bank was off.

"I still don't see why it matters if that guy snapped my picture," Randall wondered aloud, voicing a thought that had nagged at him after the initial shock of being photographed had worn off. "We're gonna hit that place wearin' costumes, like about every other person in town, so what difference does it make?"

"'Cause I don't like takin' risks," Leo answered.

"Nothin' ventured, nothin' gained," the younger thief countered.

"Problem is, I'm stakin' my life on this job. You been lucky enough not to find yourself behind bars, but I've been there and I ain't goin' back. My age, it wouldn't take much of a sentence and I'd never be a free man again. They'd be tossin' my corpse in a hole back behind the jail, just another old man too stupid to keep from gettin' caught. It ain't worth it."

Randall shook his head. "That could happen whether that son of a bitch took my picture or not."

Before Leo answered, a police car appeared on the road ahead, driving toward them, the telltale light on its roof barely visible in the dusk. Neither man said a word, staring hard as the vehicle approached, the older thief's hands slowly tightening on the steering wheel. It wasn't until the cop had finally driven past that Randall realized he'd been holding his breath.

"You're right," Leo agreed, continuing their conversation. "But my way it's a calculated risk. I case a place, I draw up a plan and then follow it to the letter, tryin' to minimize all that can go wrong. That fella shows your picture—"

"One we ain't even sure he has," Randall interrupted.

"—to the wrong person either before we do the job or after, there's a hell of a lot better chance that we end up nabbed."

"Wait a minute," the younger man said, turning in his seat to look hard at his partner. "What's this 'after the job' shit? Are you insinuatin' that if I got pinched, I'd start blabbin'? That I'd turn snitch?"

"I ain't sayin' you'd do it easy or on purpose," the older man answered, his tone cautious, as if he understood that he'd waded into dangerous waters. "But cops got a way of usin' things against you to make you tell 'em what they want to hear."

Randall shook his head. "That ain't gonna happen 'cause nobody has nothin' on me," he scoffed, believing full well that it was true. After all, he had no family, least none he cared about, and the women who weaved in and out of his life were a dime a dozen, as easily replaced as a hat or a pair of shoes.

"You don't owe any money?" Leo asked.

The younger thief bit his lip and kept staring straight ahead.

"Yeah, I know all about you and gamblin'," the other man continued. "I see it in the way you bet when we're playin' cards back at the cabin. You're too reckless, makin' bigger and bigger wagers when you get behind, hopin' that one good hand will right the sinkin' ship." Leo paused, letting his on-the-mark observation hang between them. "What if you're in deep to somebody when you get pinched?" he asked. "What if the cops offer to make your problems disappear if you roll over and give them the name of your partner? Somethin' like that might make you sing a different tune."

Randall remained quiet. It was hard enough to silently admit that Leo was right; he wasn't going to give the other man the satisfaction of saying it out loud.

"We're gonna do this like we planned," Leo continued. "We go in to town, look for our guy, and if we find him, great. If not..."

"Job's done and we go our separate ways," Randall finished.

As they rounded a bend in the road, the lights of Hooper's Crossing came into view ahead. In a matter of minutes, they'd be at the festival. Throngs of people would be there enjoying themselves, celebrating long into the night.

The guy from *Life* magazine was there, somewhere.

All they had to do was find him.

As she and Boone stepped out of the theater, Lily was nearly bursting with excitement. The film had been everything she'd hoped it would be and more. Gary Cooper had been heroic and handsome as the marshal of Hadleyville, while Grace Kelly had been a vision of beauty as his new bride. Even the villains, with Ian MacDonald as their leader, had given incredible performances. Lily had been captivated, completely absorbed by what was up on the screen.

Well, maybe not completely . . .

All through the picture, Lily had been acutely aware of Boone sitting beside her. She'd stolen the occasional glance at him, his face illuminated by the movie, more attractive to her than any Hollywood star. She wasn't the only one looking at him, either; from the moment they'd entered the theater, members of the audience had been checking them out, likely wondering who Lily Denton was with. When the movie had reached its climax, the villains making their move to gun down the hero, Lily had been so wrapped up in the story that she'd been momentarily startled when Boone had reached over and taken her hand. She'd glanced at him, his face illuminated by the light of the screen, and made no move to take her hand away, instead enjoying the pleasure of his touch.

"That was great!" Lily gushed as they passed beneath the lights of the marquee and down the sidewalk.

"You won't get any argument from me," Boone said.

"I loved the outfits!"

"And that shootout was something else."

"To say nothing of Grace Kelly! She's so beautiful!"

"Yeah, she's pretty easy on the eyes. Nice to talk with, too."

Lily's eyes widened. "Nice to talk with?" she repeated. "Wait, does that mean you've *met* her?"

"Last time I was in Los Angeles, as a matter of fact," he explained. "I had a shoot on the United lot and she was there. It's no big deal."

"But she's a movie star!"

Boone shrugged. "With my job, I've met all sorts of famous people. Humphrey Bogart, Frank Sinatra, Judy Garland, Joe DiMaggio, the list goes on and on," he said. "But the thing is, the more time you spend around folks like that, the more you realize that they really aren't that different from you and me."

"I find that awfully hard to believe," Lily disagreed.

"It's true. They get nervous, have money trouble, and they want other folks to like them more than they'd admit," Boone told her. "They might be able to sing one heck of a tune, hit a baseball a country mile, write a book, or look pretty up on a movie screen, but once you get past the glitz and glamour, most of them are kind of ordinary."

Lily had never thought of it like that, but she supposed that if anyone would know, it'd be Boone. Still, in one way it was hard to believe him.

"Ordinary, huh?" she said, her voice teasing. "I bet that when you were taking Grace Kelly's picture, that word was the farthest thing from your mind."

Boone chuckled and held up his hands. "Guilty as charged."

"I bet you hoped she might have a thing for photographers."

"She's *way* out of my league. If I was a betting man, I'd lay paper she ends up married to a big-time politician or maybe a king."

"I've always loved to watch the beautiful Hollywood actresses," she said. "Olivia de Havilland, Veronica Lake, Gene Tierney. When I was little, I used to go to the movies on Saturday afternoon with my mother and we…" Lily hadn't meant to bring up Sarah Denton, but at her mention, she fell silent. Walking beside Boone, the only sounds came from their footfalls and the noises drifting toward them from the festival. When the quiet became more than Lily could bear, she said, "My mother passed away when I was six…"

"I heard," he said.

She turned to look at him, surprised. "You did?"

Boone nodded. "After we met, I was curious," he explained. "When I asked Marjorie Barlow about you, she told me that your mother had died."

It made sense. Everyone in town knew what had

happened that bright spring day, what Lily and her father had lost.

"What was she like?" he asked.

"If I'm being honest, I don't really know," she answered, the sounds of the festival growing louder as they neared the park. "All I have are little bits and pieces for memories. The sound of her voice as she sings me 'Happy Birthday.' How she looked wiping sweat from her brow while digging in her flower garden. The two of us at the movies, laughing at Laurel and Hardy." Lily paused. "But I clearly remember the afternoon she died. It happened while I was playing hide-and-seek with my dad. I can still see the look on his face after he'd found her, after he'd called the doctor. It was the first time I ever saw him cry."

Boone reached for her hand. She gladly gave it, along with a weak smile, happy she was with him.

"I bet she'd be proud of you," he offered.

Lily didn't know how to answer. She wondered if Boone was right. What would her mother have thought of her failed plan to leave town. Would she have been disappointed in her daughter for not chasing her dream? Or would she have been relieved that Lily hadn't abandoned her father? What would she think of her spending time with Boone? In the end, Lily couldn't answer any of these questions, and thought it might drive her crazy to try. "What about your family?" she asked. "I bet they tell everyone they know that their son works for *Life* magazine."

Boone chuckled. "I doubt either of them care all that

much. My folks weren't the kind who did much bragging. They were too busy spreading the Lord's good word to notice much of what I got up to," he explained. "I bought my first camera from a pawnshop on the edge of town. I used to go tramping around the country looking for something to photograph. Old rickety barns, flocks of geese on a frozen pond, the railroad depot when the trains came in, you name it, I took its picture. Somehow, I think I always knew that camera, and the ones that came after it, were my ticket out of Saybrook, Illinois."

"That's where you're from?"

"Born and raised," he answered. "But by fourteen, I was counting down the days until I could leave. The last thing I wanted was to grow old in some little town where nothing happened, a dot on the map most people found by accident."

A place that sounds an awful lot like Hooper's Crossing...

Almost immediately, Boone understood what he'd implied. "I'm sorry, Lily," he told her. "I shouldn't have said that. I don't want you to think that—"

"You'd have to be nuts to live in a town like this?" she finished.

Boone sighed but didn't answer.

"It's all right," Lily said. "I know just how you feel. My whole life, I've wondered what it would be like to go somewhere else, to know a little excitement. It would be nice not to see the same people day in and day out."

"They why are you still here?"

Lily hesitated. The only other person who knew how

she really felt about Hooper's Crossing, her job at the library, and her complicated relationship with her father, was Jane. She'd never even revealed the truth to Garrett. But now she was considering coming clean to Boone, a man who had been a complete stranger only the day before. Lily glanced over and found him looking at her. In the photographer's eyes, she saw curiosity, a desire to know the answer to his question. But she also saw compassion. It wasn't hard to imagine that he would listen without judging, that he might understand the conflicting emotions that had influenced her decision to stay. Who knew, maybe Boone would even have an answer to the questions swirling around in her head.

"I'm not supposed to be," she admitted. "Right now, I should be far away. In New York City, as a matter of fact."

And with that, her story poured out.

Soon after she began, the sidewalk they were walking on led them to the park; Lily never stopped talking as they moved around its edges. Even with the late hour, the festival was still in full swing. The air was filled with the tantalizing smells of roasting meats and sweet treats. Musicians played to appreciative crowds, enticing a few couples to twirl in the moonlight. Barkers shouted, selling their carnival games, the night punctuated with a joyful shout whenever someone managed to knock over all the milk bottles or pop a balloon with a dart. Cars slowed as they drove past, the necks of drivers and passengers craning for a closer look.

But even with all the commotion and fanfare, Boone's

attention never wavered. He listened to Lily's story attentively, only asking the occasional question. Though they were surrounded by hundreds of festivalgoers, Lily felt like they were the only two people on earth.

"I feel like such a coward," she finished.

Boone shook his head. "For whatever reason, it wasn't time for you to go. Maybe tomorrow or the day after will be different."

Lily wanted to believe that Boone was right. Just then, with Boone at her side, she allowed herself to dream a little, to imagine a future where someone would be going with her, or waiting for her to arrive, that special person with whom she could share it all.

Boone suddenly chuckled, breaking Lily's fantasy.

"What's funny?" she asked.

"I was just thinking that I'm glad you didn't leave with your friend."

"Why not?"

"Because if you had, we never would have met."

Lily thought about it for a moment. "Yes, we would've," she replied.

The photographer's eyes narrowed. "How do you figure?"

"Something about this feels like it was meant to be," she explained, giving his hand a squeeze, loving the way that their fingers entwined, how warm his skin was to the touch. "Like our meeting was fate. Even if I'd left, we would have bumped into each other on the street or sat at the same lunch counter."

Boone shook his head, chuckling again. "You really have no idea how big New York City is, do you?"

Lily laughed at her own naïveté. "Maybe not," she admitted.

Boone suddenly stopped walking. They stood beneath the bare branches of the elm tree in front of the bakery, the festival behind them, the sidewalk theirs alone. He stepped into the dark shadows away from the street; Lily followed, her hand in his. Boone looked down at her, the smile on his face making her heart beat a little faster, then slowly ran his fingers along the gentle curve of her cheek. "You know, I think you might be right," he told her.

"About what?" she answered, feeling a little breathless.

"Us," Boone answered. "Maybe we would have found each other in the end, even in a city of millions of people. And if that's true, then maybe I was supposed to get in trouble that morning on the dock. Maybe my editor was supposed to punish me by sending me here, and—"

"Maybe we were supposed to bump into each other," Lily finished.

"Exactly," he agreed.

"If so, then what's supposed to happen next?"

"I've got an idea," Boone said, then lowered his face toward hers, moving to kiss her. With every inch he came closer, Lily's heart beat that much faster, the anticipation making it race. Just before their lips touched, Lily shut her eyes and held her breath, giving herself over to a moment that felt as magical as any Hollywood movie. At first, their passion remained in check, each of them feeling a touch of nerves and not wanting to go too far, afraid to give the other a reason to stop. But it didn't take long for whatever reticence they felt to melt away. It was then, as Lily's desire grew, her mouth opened slightly, that she unexpectedly shivered. It might have been because of the cool October night, but Lily suspected that it was more likely due to the surprise and disbelief she felt at what she was doing. The emotion was simply more than her body could handle, unlike anything she had ever felt before. Regardless of the reason, Boone felt her body shake and pulled her closer, his arms enveloping her. Lily took his warmth, as well as the eagerness of his kiss, and returned them as best as she knew how.

Lily might have spent years pining to leave Hooper's Crossing, but right then, those thoughts couldn't have been farther from her mind.

There was nowhere else she would have rather been.

Chapter Fifteen

Boone walked down the sidewalk with a spring in his step, hardly noticing the chill in the night air. He couldn't stop thinking about Lily. Their night together had gone better than he could have ever expected. From his first look at her as she stepped onto the porch, to the pleasant surprise of her grabbing his hand during the movie, to their talk as they walked around the festival, and finally the kiss they'd shared in front of the bakery.

And what a kiss it had been…

But Boone hadn't been satisfied. In fact, it had made him greedy for more.

Standing on the corner close to Lily's house but far from the prying eyes of her father, Boone had kissed her again. Like before, he'd been captivated by her touch, the soft scent of her perfume, the pleasure of her body pressed against his. He hadn't wanted it to end but had eventually let her go. Even though they had made plans to meet again the next day, Boone was certain he'd spend their time apart impatiently waiting for it to be over.

And then what, hotshot? What happens next?

Though Boone had enjoyed every second of his time with Lily, a sliver of doubt nagged at him. He and Lily came from different worlds. He lived in a teeming metropolis, the city that never slept, while she was here in a town that could best be described as just another dot on a map. He was a world traveler, a photographer whose job took him to every corner of the world. She was a librarian, someone who only saw faraway places as pictures in a book. The bonds between Boone and his family had become frayed and they had drifted apart long ago. Lily still lived with her father. Since the two of them came from such opposite directions, what chance did they have to meet in the middle? Was this nothing more than a fun time soon forgotten?

Surprising himself a little, Boone truly hoped that it wasn't.

The truth was, he still wasn't sure how all of this had happened in the first place. Just days before, he'd fought tooth and nail to keep from going on assignment to this far-off dot on the map. Now here he was, head over heels.

The list of things about Lily that captivated him was long, but Boone's attraction to her was about more than any one of them, even more than all of them put together. She'd touched him deep inside. Listening to Lily talk about her mother's death had moved him, had made him want to take her in his arms and give her comfort. She was unlike any other woman he'd known, that much was for certain. And that was why he didn't want to lead her on. They needed to talk, and soon. He had to know what she wanted from—

Boone's thoughts were interrupted by the sudden, sharp sound of a dog's bark. He froze on the sidewalk, certain that he recognized the animal who had made it. Then it came again, more insistent, angrier. This time, Boone was positive that it was Daisy; after all, an owner knew *his* pet best. He looked around. Though he wasn't that familiar with Hooper's Crossing, especially at night, he thought that he was only a couple of blocks from Marjorie Barlow's place. He started to run.

He sprinted down the sidewalk, then cut a corner beneath an elm tree, moving so fast that the bare branches rustled in the wake of his passage. Only a few seconds had passed sine he'd first heard Daisy bark, but now the sound rang out again and again, growing louder as he neared, like a fireman's siren in the still of the late hour. Boone's mind raced with every step. What was happening? He pushed himself faster and faster, determined to know.

Finally, he rounded the tall row of hedges that separated Marjorie from her neighbors. Boone skidded to a stop, nearly slipping on the wet grass. The door to his and Clive's room stood open, a bright light shining from within. It took Boone a moment to realize that someone was crumpled on the floor just inside the door, moaning softly. Then, as he watched, a figure stepped into the light, a dark silhouette from which he could make out no details other than that the stranger held something in his hand. Whoever it was, they quickly noticed Boone. Almost immediately, the intruder darted off toward the rear of the property.

Like a shot, Boone followed. "Hey, wait!" he shouted.

Sprinting across the driveway, Boone was confident that he would quickly catch his unidentified quarry. He'd have answers for what was happening, even if he had to use his fists to get them.

But even before he reached the backyard, Boone heard Daisy growl, a deep, guttural sound that made the hair on the back of his neck stand up. Squinting though the inky darkness, he saw her. The Lab was snapping and snarling at another figure, someone who had their hands raised and was quickly backing away from the dog. But the person wasn't fast enough. Boone saw Daisy tense, then lunge. The night was split by a man's pained shout.

"Goddamn mutt!" he cried, then kicked out, catching the dog in the ribs, making her yip and slink away.

Boone's anger flared as hot and sure as a match dropped into a puddle of gasoline. Overcome with rage, he made a beeline for the man who'd hurt his dog, wanting to return Daisy's pain a dozen times over. But his fury made him blind. Before Boone had taken more than a couple of steps, he saw something off to his side, then a fist was driven into his stomach, forcing the air from his lungs and dropping him to his knees. Writhing in agony, he realized that it must've been the figure he had initially pursued, the one he'd seen leaving the rented room.

And now he and Daisy were both down and at the mercy of their mysterious assailants.

But just as Boone struggled to one knee, he heard the unmistakable rise and fall of sirens in the distance. He couldn't know if they were headed in his direction, but he hoped that Marjorie had heard the commotion and called the police.

"Cops," the one who'd hit him said.

"What are we gonna do?" his companion asked, sounding panicked. "We didn't have time to grab it all. There's still—"

"Shut up," the first man snapped. "Get goin'. We can't stay any longer."

With that, the two men sprinted toward the rear of the property and were promptly swallowed up by the darkness. Seconds later, he heard the rustling of leaves, then no more. The men were gone.

And there wasn't a damn thing Boone could do about it.

Leo ran through the darkness with Randall hot on his heels. Even as he jumped over fences, slipped between houses, and dodged bushes and birdbaths, he remained alert, watching every window for movement or light, listening to the sirens that continued to draw closer. Leo willed himself to stay calm and focused. He knew it wouldn't do him any good to become distracted, not now.

And to think, the evening had started lucky.

When they'd arrived in town, Leo had done the same as the night before, driving slowly as Randall watched for either of the *Life* magazine men. He had tried to stay positive, but with every passing minute, he'd become more and more convinced that they were going to have to give up, that they were never going to find the needle in the haystack, that the robbery was off.

But then Randall had nearly jumped out of his seat. "There he is!" the younger thief shouted as he pointed out the window. "One of 'em! Right there!"

The guy was aimlessly making his way down the sidewalk, looking in the festival stalls as he munched on a hot dog. He was an odd sort, awkward in both the clothes he wore and the way he moved, the kind who'd be hard-pressed to turn a pretty girl's head. An ugly one's, too, for that matter.

"He the one who took your picture?"

"Naw, it was the other one," Randall answered. "What do we do now?"

Leo thought for a moment, a plan quickly forming in his head. "If we watch him, he might take us where we want to go."

They shadowed their quarry from the festival away from downtown and into a neighborhood. Worried that the car might get them noticed, Leo pulled over and told Randall to follow on foot.

"Once you find out where he goes, come back," he explained. "Then we'll drive over and take a closer look."

Leo watched the two men disappear into the gloomy dusk. Time felt like it slid by at a crawl. He felt nervous, exposed, worried that every pair of headlights he saw belonged to a police car. After what felt like half an hour, Randall returned and they drove past the place the man had entered.

"He went in a door at the rear, back by the garage," Randall explained.

Leo nodded, slowing down to take a closer look. "They ain't local so they're probably letting a room," he said. "Any sign of the other one?"

"Nope. Lights were off when he got there."

"Maybe he's sleepin'."

"I doubt it. He struck me as the type who'd be where the fun was."

They parked the car a couple of blocks away, opposite a church, then walked back. "I say we go in, knock his skull, and see what we can find," Randall had impatiently suggested when the house was again in sight.

Leo shook his head. "Be patient. Sometimes these things have a way of workin' themselves out."

Sure enough, less than a minute after he'd said that, the door opened and the man left, leading a dog on a leash and sneezing like he had a cold.

Once the man and dog had disappeared down the sidewalk, the two thieves hurried to the house without a word shared between them. Amazingly, Leo discovered that the door hadn't been locked and a light was still on; the dumb bastard might as well have laid the welcome

mat out before he left. Immediately, Randall set about ri-
fling through desk drawers and spilling the contents from
suitcases, searching for the incriminating photograph. Leo
took a more methodical approach, looking over the room,
trying to see what stood out.

And something did.

Peeking into the small kitchen, he hit the jackpot. Pictures were clipped to a length of string, like clothes hung
on a line to dry. Bottles and trays had been laid out on
the counter. Though Leo knew next to nothing about being a photographer, he understood that this was the man's
makeshift darkroom.

Flipping on the light switch, he was momentarily surprised by the red bulb, then started making his way
through the photos. The fourth one made Leo pause. In it,
a beautiful blonde took up most of the shot, but there, just
off her shoulder, was a face he recognized.

"Got it," Leo announced.

Randall was in the room in a heartbeat. Seeing what his
partner had in his hand, he whooped for joy. "All right,
then. Let's get out of here."

"Take more pictures, all the negatives, too, and some of
the other camera stuff," Leo said. "We gotta make this look
more like a robbery."

The two of them set about stuffing pictures and negatives in their pockets, knocking over equipment, and
making a mess of things. Leo had expected them to
still have plenty of time, so he was taken completely
off-guard when the front door swung open, revealing

the *Life* magazine man and the dog, returned from their walk. For a moment, all of them froze, staring at one another.

It was the dog that moved first.

The mutt let loose a couple of loud barks, then lunged at Randall. The younger thief barely managed to avoid being bit, then made a beeline for the door. He knocked the awkward man out of the way in his haste as he rushed into the night, the dog two steps behind. The other man seemed dazed and made no effort to move or call for help, which suited Leo just fine. It was a simple matter for him to walk over and crack the man on the chin, knocking him to the floor in a heap.

But even then Leo had known that they'd made a huge mistake.

Neither he nor Randall was wearing a mask. It was possible that this joker had gotten a good look at one, if not both of them. Standing over the unconscious man, Leo contemplated using his gun. A well-placed bullet would remove any chance of their being found out. Still, a murder would create a whole host of other problems. So in the end, Leo stayed his hand. His decision came down to the photographs. They could be carefully examined and Randall's face identified. There was no way this knucklehead would be able to do the same; odds were, he'd be too frazzled or frightened to give a good description.

It was then, as he stepped to the door, determined to help his partner rid himself of the dog, that Leo saw someone in the yard, staring at him. Immediately, he'd guessed that it had to be the photographer.

And so he had run.

Fortunately, the other man had been distracted enough by Randall to allow Leo to put a fist in his breadbasket, letting them escape.

Now, breathing hard and with a sheen of sweat on his brow, Leo split between a pair of houses, dodged a mailbox, and was at the car. He already had the keys in the ignition, the engine roaring to life, before Randall had shut his door.

"We did it!" the younger thief crowed triumphantly.

"Yeah, we did, but don't forget that the reason we had to go through all this shit is because you screwed up," Leo reminded him.

Randall groaned. "Can't you just be happy we got the damn thing?"

As he pulled the car away from the curb, moving quick but not too fast as to draw attention, Leo suppressed a smile. He *was* happy that the problem had been solved, but he didn't want his partner to know it. Let him stew for a while. Regardless, now they could finally get back to focusing on what they'd come here to do.

It was time to rob a bank.

Kneeling in Marjorie's backyard, Boone took a couple of deep breaths, the pain in his stomach starting to subside, and nuzzled Daisy. The rise and fall of sirens continued to grow stronger as they drew closer. Slowly, Boone rose to unsteady feet, then started back to the room.

"Come on, girl," he said, and the dog obediently followed.

The figure Boone had first seen slumped on the floor was now stirring. As he'd both feared and expected, it was Clive. The young writer appeared dazed, as if he had just woken from sleep. His hands gingerly touched his jaw where an ugly bruise was blossoming, a red that would soon turn dark.

"What...what happened...?" Clive asked.

"I was hoping you could tell me," Boone replied as he knelt beside him.

He shook his head. "I opened the door...and these two guys..."

"Don't hurry it, and go back further if you can."

"Okay," the writer replied, then took some time to regain his bearings; when he continued, his voice was stronger, which made him sound more sure of himself. "When I finished writing, I took your advice and went to the festival," Clive explained. "I walked around, got something to eat, and had some fun. When I came back, I decided to take Daisy for a walk. I felt bad that she'd been cooped up for so long and figured that my allergies would be better outside, but we hadn't gone more than a couple of blocks before I was sneezing as bad as ever." As if to prove the point, he sneezed, then winced from the pain it caused.

"Go on, girl," Boone said, shooing Daisy into the yard. "Then what?"

"When I opened the door, two men were in the room.

They looked as surprised as I was. The next thing I knew, Daisy went crazy and chased one of them outside. The other decked me, I guess."

Boone looked over the room. It was in shambles. Clothes and newspapers were strewn about. Furniture had been tipped over and broken. Then he noticed that the door to his darkroom was open, so he went over, worried about what he would find. It wasn't good. Most of the photographs he'd taken at the festival were gone; only a few remained on the drying line, and a handful more littered the floor. Boone knelt and opened a drawer, expecting to find it empty, but was pleasantly surprised to find his camera and lenses where he'd put them that afternoon.

Which didn't make a lot of sense.

Up until then, everything about what had happened pointed to it being a robbery. If so, then why had the most expensive thing in the room been left behind? For that matter, why were some of his pictures missing? Boone wondered if he wasn't making the wrong assumption. Had this been an act of vandalism, just a couple of guys who'd had too much to drink and decided to wreck something? Boone quickly dismissed that possibility; neither man had moved or fought like they were under the influence of alcohol. But in the end, he couldn't come up with a better explanation. Odds were the only reason his camera hadn't been stolen was because of Clive; the writer had returned before the two thieves could finish ransacking the place. Boone knew that he'd gotten lucky. Clive, too.

Just then, Daisy made a sudden, sharp bark. Boone

hurried outside, wondering if the two men were back for more. Instead, he found Marjorie cautiously peeking her head around the edge of the porch. In the scant light spilling from the door to his room, the landlady looked frail and frightened, much older than her already advanced years.

"Is . . . Is everything all right . . . ?" she asked hesitantly.

Boone nodded. "It is now. A couple of guys broke in and jumped Clive," he explained, "but Daisy and I ran them off."

Marjorie's expression showed relief. "I heard the dog bark and then some shoutin'. I didn't know what else to do so I called the police."

"You did the right thing."

As they talked, the sound of sirens grew louder by the second. Boone looked up the street just as a police car raced around the corner, the red light on its roof flashing bright in the night. It pulled into Marjorie's drive fast, then skidded to a sudden stop. Boone was surprised that he recognized the officer who got out from behind the wheel; it was Garrett, Lily's old friend whom she'd introduced to him that very afternoon.

"I got here as quick as I could," he said, addressing Marjorie. "What seems to be the trouble?"

"Someone broke into our room and attacked my colleague," Boone answered.

He led Garrett through what had happened. He showed him the destruction in their room, the bruise on Clive's chin, as well as where the two intruders had disappeared into the night. The whole time, Garrett didn't say much, asking only a couple of questions as he shone his flashlight into the bushes and not bothering to jot anything down in his notebook. Boone wondered if it was just the police officer's demeanor, if when he was on the job he was all business, but a sneaking suspicion was beginning to nag at him.

He was starting to think that Lily's friend didn't like him all that much.

"Do you know what was taken?" Garrett asked once they were back in the room. Clive was finally up off the floor and in a chair, some ice pressed against his wound. Marjorie stood near the door, absently scratching Daisy's head; the dog's tongue lolled out of her mouth.

"I couldn't say for sure just yet," Boone answered. "Some pictures, a camera bag, a few other things."

The police officer nodded. Turning to Clive, he asked, "You said that you saw the men. Did you get a good-enough look at either of them to make a description?"

Clive shrugged his bony shoulders. "I...I don't know. It all happened so fast. One was older than the other, but besides that..."

"Out-of-towners, I'd bet," Garrett said. "Here for the festival."

There was something about the dismissive tone in the lawman's voice that rubbed Boone the wrong way. This whole time, Garrett had been acting like their getting robbed was an inconvenience to him, something that wasn't worth getting worked up about. Even though

Boone knew it wouldn't do them any good, likely it would do the opposite, he couldn't help but voice his frustration.

"Good detective work, there," he said sarcastically. "Now what do you plan to do about finding the guys who did this, maybe get us back our stuff?"

Garrett looked at him with a flat stare; if he was angry about what Boone had said, or how he'd said it, it didn't show. "We'll do what we can, but this isn't like in the big city," he explained. "We don't have the manpower or the time, especially not with the festival in full swing. Usually, things are pretty peaceful around here. Outside of the occasional drunken brawl, the worst we have to deal with is a pickpocket working the crowd. Odds are, the guys who did this," he said, nodding at the disheveled room, "aren't local."

"Do you think you'll ever catch them?" Clive asked.

"We'll do our best," Garrett answered.

"That's not much of an answer," Boone said, still a bit hot under the collar.

"If I'm being completely honest, I wouldn't bet on it," Garrett answered. "What with their almost getting caught, I'd be willing to bet my paycheck that those two are high-tailing it away from here just as fast as they can. They'll know they got lucky."

"I hope Daisy bit them so bad they need stitches," Marjorie added, giving the dog's head another pat.

Clive chuckled and even Garrett broke a smile, but Boone kept frowning. Sure, the things that had been stolen from him could be replaced, all the pictures retaken, but he still felt angry, violated. He knew that he should be glad that Clive hadn't been hurt worse, but he couldn't.

So he swore silently to himself.

Those bastards better have headed for the hills, because if I ever get my hands on them, there's going to be hell to pay!

Chapter Sixteen

THE SUN WAS already a couple of hours above the eastern horizon when Garrett left the police station and headed for home. Steering his squad car through the waking streets, he yawned, feeling tired all the way down to his bones. He was looking forward to getting home, having a quick bite to eat, and then sleeping the afternoon away before getting up and doing it all over again.

In most ways, his shift had been ordinary. Garrett had written up a fistful of parking tickets, many of them to cars with out-of-state license plates. He'd broken up a fight outside the pool hall. He had even sped along behind the Hooper's Crossing fire truck on its way to a blaze that turned out to be nothing more than a bonfire that had gotten out of hand.

But even with all of that to keep him busy, Garrett had spent the night distracted, unable to get one event in particular out of his head.

The break-in at Marjorie Barlow's place.

Even though such a crime was unusual in these parts, it should've been a routine call for him, just another of the many things he had to confront as an officer of the law. Most times Garrett dealt with a tragedy or crime, he prided himself on being friendly, understanding, and as helpful as he could be. But when he pulled up to the house and saw Boone Tatum standing in the driveway, lit by the squad car's headlights, all that went right out the window.

Listening to the *Life* magazine photographer explain what had happened, Garrett couldn't stop seeing the man with Lily, the two of them smiling and laughing together on the sidewalk. It made him feel so uncomfortable, so *angry*, that he couldn't see straight. He hadn't wanted to ask any questions or jot anything down in his notebook. He had just wanted to leave.

Boone had known it, too. It had been written on his face, in the harsh words he'd spoken. Garrett wondered if his jealousy was that obvious. But it couldn't be changed. It was how he felt, for better or worse.

Garrett parked at the curb in front of his home and got out, stretching his sore muscles. He looked across the street at Lily's place, a habit as far back as he could remember, one he couldn't have changed if he'd wanted to. Incredibly, at that moment Lily stepped onto the porch to grab the newspaper. His heart beat even faster when she noticed him and waved. Tired as Garrett was, he knew that he should just wave back, then go inside and get some much-needed sleep, but he'd never been able to resist Lily; he was drawn to her, like metal to a magnet.

Walking over, he smiled as he looked at her, drinking her in. Lily stood in the early-morning sunlight, its shine making her blond hair glow as if it was gold. She was dressed as if she was about to head to the library. Garrett swore that she got more beautiful every time he saw her.

"Long night?" she asked.

"Every one of them is at festival time," he answered. "I'm glad that I only have to make it through tonight and then I get a day off."

The night of the big dance, remember? he almost added, but didn't.

"You look pretty tired."

"I am," he admitted, then stifled another yawn.

Lily laughed, a sound that was music to Garrett's ears. "You'll be asleep before your head hits the pillow."

"Have you talked to Boone this morning?" he asked.

"No, why?" Lily asked, her smile faltering, her expression curious.

Garrett sensed he was making a mistake. He knew that there was still time to fix things, but he felt powerless to stop himself and instead stepped over the edge of the cliff. "Someone broke into the room he's renting from Marjorie Barlow last night," he said. "They stole a few things and made one heck of a mess."

Lily looked dazed, her eyes widening.

"It's no big deal," Garrett continued, digging the hole deeper, clueless as to how to go about filling it back up.

"Nobody was hurt, well, not really. That other guy, Clive, got walloped on the chin, but it shouldn't be—"

Before Garrett could say more, Lily was down the stairs and past him, heading for the sidewalk. "I've got to go," she said, looking both determined and worried.

"Lily, wait! There's nothing you can..." he shouted but then trailed off since she was already a house away and not listening.

There was no doubt in Garrett's mind as to where she was going: to be with Boone. No one, certainly not him, was going to stop her; this realization was powerful enough to make his heart ache.

Garrett sighed, then shook his head. How in the heck had this happened? Only a few minutes had passed since he'd parked his squad car and all he had managed to do was make a royal mess of things. Seeing how Lily had reacted, he understood that he'd been right to worry about her and Boone. Somehow, the photographer from New York City had cast a spell on his favorite small-town gal. Whatever it was between the two of them—he couldn't bring himself to call it a romance—was growing fast and picking up speed as it went.

A sudden, sickening truth revealed itself to Garrett.

If he didn't tell Lily how he felt about her soon, he ran the risk of losing her forever.

By the time Lily arrived at Marjorie Barlow's house, she was out of breath and beside herself with worry. The whole way over, her legs churning just as fast as she could make them go, her imagination had run wild, conjuring up one terrifying outcome after another. She worried that Boone's dog had been injured or all his things stolen. Worst of all, she feared that he'd been hurt, beaten and bloodied by criminals operating under the cover of darkness.

"Someone broke into the room..."

Everything after that had been lost, her mind a swirling mess. Lily kept telling herself that Garrett hadn't seemed concerned, but then again, he was a police officer who was probably used to all sorts of horrible scenes. The moment he had mentioned what had happened to Boone, she had reacted without thinking, compelled by a feeling deep inside of her to act.

And so she had run and run and run.

Lily raced up Mrs. Barlow's drive, then pounded on the door where she knew Boone was staying. Standing there, her heart beating hard as she wiped sweaty strands of hair from her face, it felt as if the seconds were crawling by. When the door finally opened and Boone appeared without any cuts or bruises, looking exactly like she'd last seen him, Lily let out a deep breath.

"Oh, thank heavens!" she exclaimed. There was more that Lily wanted to say, a flood of joy and relief, but the words no longer seemed necessary. Instead, she put her hand on Boone's whiskered cheek, as if she couldn't quite believe her eyes and needed further proof that he was unhurt. She was reminded of the kiss they'd shared only the night before, a moment that had kept her awake for hours. Yet in some unexplainable way, this touch meant just as much.

"I'm all right," he told her. "More angry than anything else. Come on in and I'll show you what happened."

Boone held the door open and Lily stepped inside. She'd expected to find the room a disaster, a chaotic mess of their belongings and broken furniture, but everything was neat and tidy, as if nothing had happened.

"You should've seen it last night," he said as if he'd understood her confusion. "It took half the night to clean up."

"I'm just glad you weren't hurt."

"Me, too," he said, then absently rubbed his stomach.

"Do you have any idea who—" Lily began but was interrupted when the door opened behind her; she was so startled that she jumped.

A thin, awkward-looking man stepped into the room, a newspaper in one hand, a paper bag in the other. "I hope you don't mind but I got doughnuts. They didn't have any—" he said before noticing Lily. He glanced at Boone, then back at her. "I'm sorry, I didn't know you had company. I'll go and—"

"Just shut up and give me the bag," Boone said. "I'm starving."

Boone introduced Lily to Clive, a writer at *Life* and his partner on this assignment. Listening to Clive describe the events of the previous night, Lily couldn't stop herself from staring at the ugly welt on his mouth and chin; seeing it made her feel a little guilty for being so happy Boone hadn't been hurt.

"I'm just thankful Daisy was here," Clive said.

Lily looked around for the dog. "Where is she, anyway?"

"With Mrs. Barlow," Boone explained, taking another doughnut out of the bag. "She might be a tough old bird, but having two guys break in like that would've frightened anyone. Daisy makes her feel safer."

"You don't have any idea who those men were?" Lily asked Clive, unknowingly echoing Garrett from the night before.

The writer shook his head. "Not a clue."

"At least you interrupted them before anything valuable was taken."

"Depends on what you mean by 'valuable,'" Boone answered, then popped the last bite of his sugar doughnut in his mouth.

"You said they only took a bag and some pictures."

"None of which could be pawned for more than a handful of coins," he explained. "But to me, they're worth a hell of a lot more than that."

Boone led the way into the small kitchen he'd converted into a darkroom. His camera and all its lenses were laid out on the counter beside several bottles and trays, as well as a small stack of photographs.

"That pile used to be five times as high," he said, pointing at the pictures.

Lily shook her head. "Why would someone want to steal them?"

"Beats me," Boone answered with a shrug. "Maybe it was like your police officer friend said, and they'd tossed back a few drinks and just grabbed whatever they could get their hands on. Odds are, when they sobered up and realized what they'd taken, they tossed them in the trash figuring they were worthless."

Lily suddenly thought of one photograph in particular, one that had angered her when it was taken, but that she now saw in a very different light. "What about the picture you took of me?" she asked. "Is it...is it gone, too?"

"Yes and no," Boone answered.

"I don't understand."

"Well, the copy that I showed you was taken with the others," he explained, "but I still have the negative so I can develop another. It's the only sheet of negatives left. I didn't keep it with the rest. I set it aside because it was special to me."

Lily understood what he was telling her. That particular sheet of negatives was special because of *her*. He'd set it aside because *her* picture was in it, therefore making it more valuable than the others. That fact made her happy.

"Unfortunately," Boone continued, "I still have a big problem."

"What's that?" she asked.

"All of the other pictures that were stolen were for the feature in the magazine. Without them, I'm back to square one."

"So just take them again."

Boone chuckled. "It's not that easy."

"Why not?"

"Look, I'm not trying to sound like a snob or a know-it-all, but taking pictures is a lot more complicated than pointing a camera at something and clicking a button," he explained. "You have to consider the lighting and the angle, and I almost never want my subjects to even know I'm there. I take pride in what I do. I'm a perfectionist. I can't just replicate the shots I've already taken. It's impossible."

Lily thought of the story Boone told her about the photograph he had tried to take on the New York City dock, about the pains he'd taken to get it right, about how his failure had resulted in his being sent to Hooper's Crossing as punishment. He was right. He'd have to start all over.

But then she had an idea.

"What if I could guarantee that the new pictures you took would be even better than the ones that were stolen?" she said.

"How could you possibly do that?" he asked skeptically.

"Easy. We go back to the festival and I show you things that only a local could. You'll have more good shots than you'll know what to do with."

"Aren't you supposed to work today?"

Lily coughed, then put the back of her hand against her forehead, frowning theatrically. "I think I might be coming down with something."

"You'd play hooky to spend the day with me?" Boone asked.

"I'd be doing my civic duty," she answered.

He gave a thin smile but still hadn't agreed to it. "I don't know. Seems like you could end up in a heap of trouble."

"I don't think you have a lot of choice in the matter,"

Clive piped up from the other room. "No pictures, no story, that's what Walter would say."

"I couldn't have said it better," Lily added.

"Shut up in there," Boone barked at his partner. His face creased in concentration, then he shrugged. "All right, but if you end up getting grief from your dad or that sourpuss at the library, remember that this was your idea."

"It's a deal," she agreed.

"But before we go, there's something we need to talk about."

"Okay," Lily said, waiting for it.

"Not here," he said, thumbing toward the door; whatever it was he had to tell her, he didn't want Clive to overhear.

"What's it about?" she couldn't keep from asking.

Boone paused, then leaned closer, his voice low. "I want to talk about us."

Lily followed Boone outside into the late-morning sunlight. She should've been happy, excited about the prospect of spending the day with him taking pictures, but something about his tone and mannerisms worried her. So it was with no shortage of unease that she asked, "What do you have to say to me?"

Boone didn't answer right away, running a hand through his hair. Whatever it was, it clearly weighed on him. "I want to be honest with you."

"All right," she replied uneasily, bracing herself for what was to come.

"I need you to know that I like you. A lot. I'd be surprised if you had a clue how much," he told her. Lily disagreed—the passionate kiss they'd shared had told her plenty about Boone's feelings—but she didn't contradict him. "But I worry you might think I don't have the right intentions or that I'm leading you on."

"I've never thought that," she reassured him.

"I'm glad," he said, then took her hand. "But I still worry."

"Don't."

He shook his head. "I can't help it. Part of it's because whenever we're together, something reminds me of how different our lives are. I come from the city, you live here. I'm a photographer for *Life* and you're—"

"A librarian," Lily finished for him. "All of that's true, but I don't care," she explained, meaning every word as she squeezed his hand. "What matters is that I like spending time with you, listening to your stories about all of the places you've been. I wouldn't have run across town to be here if I didn't. I know what I'm doing."

"I'm glad one of us does," Boone said with a weak smile.

Lily bit her lip; it was odd to see his normal self-assurance slip, if only for a second. "I thought you were having a good time…"

"I am," he answered emphatically. "I'm having more fun than I've ever had before, which is no small order." He came a step closer, their bodies almost touching. "You have to believe me when I say that I've never felt this way about someone before. Not in the city. Not anywhere in the world. Not this fast. *Never.*"

Lily held his gaze, measuring the truth of his declaration; it took only seconds for her to believe him. "I feel the same way about you."

"I don't want this to be a fling," he told her, his voice soft yet firm.

"Me, either," she answered, as honest as she had ever been.

"The problem is, I don't know if what the both of us want is enough."

"Why wouldn't it be?"

"Because I'm supposed to go back to New York City in a couple of days," Boone answered. "And when that happens..."

He didn't finish the thought, but Lily knew what he meant: when he left Hooper's Crossing, he was gone from the town, and her, forever. It was then that she decided to give voice to something that had started to take root in her head ever since he'd placed his lips against hers in front of the bakery.

"Maybe that doesn't have to be the end of anything."

"I can't stay here. My job is—"

"That isn't what I meant," Lily cut in, taking a leap of sorts.

Boone stared at her for a moment before speaking. "Wait, are you...are you saying that you'd come with—"

"I don't know, not for certain," she interrupted again, not yet ready to hear the full thought spoken out loud.

"But I don't have to choose just yet. You said it yourself. We still have a couple of days together before then. The time will come soon enough to make decisions, but until then, why can't we keep enjoying each other's company and see where it takes us?"

She wondered if he might disagree, but instead Boone smiled. "You're right," he said. "Besides, by the end of the week, you might be champing at the bit to get rid of me."

"Maybe," Lily said, playing along, "but I wouldn't bet on it."

The two of them laughed, making her think that they had made the right choice: take nothing for granted, enjoy the moment, and let things shake out as they were supposed to. Wherever they ended up, the joy would be in the journey.

"Now go get your camera," she told him. "We have work to do."

Chapter Seventeen

LILY STRETCHED HER LEGS on the cool grass, crossed her feet at the ankles, and arranged her skirt. Birds held a musical conversation in the elm tree above where she and Boone had chosen to eat their lunch, adding their voices to the festival's many other sounds. Sunlight shone through the bare branches, making a mottled pattern on her skin and clothes. A soft breeze whispered through the air, making strands of her long blond hair dance before she tamed them, pulling them behind her ear.

What an absolutely perfect way to spend a day...

After she and Boone had gathered his camera and said their good-byes to Clive, they'd walked to the festival and gotten to work. Lily had done her best, trying to think of out-of-the-way places she knew of only because she'd grown up in Hooper's Crossing. So she had taken him to second-floor windows of the department store, with their incredible view on the park below. She'd shown

Boone the soda counter at Mott's Drug Store, sunlight glinting off the chrome fixtures and stools. Lily had introduced him to dozens of people around town: Sally Lange, who ran the bakery along with her husband, and who claimed to sell the sweetest cinnamon rolls in the whole state; Will Burton, who handed out lollipops to everyone who entered his barbershop, man or woman, seven years young or ninety years old; and Sylvester Cushing, whose bushy, snow-white beard had earned him the job of playing Santa Claus during Christmas festivities for two decades running.

"Use my picture in the magazine and I promise you'll have something nice in your stocking this year," Sylvester had said with a cackle.

Roll after roll of film had been used, so many pictures that Lily had lost count of all the times Boone had raised his camera to his eye and clicked the shutter open. But what interested her wasn't just the shots he took, but those he didn't. Boone didn't go along with all of her suggestions, taking photographs to make her happy. Instead, he looked at each shot with a critical eye, changing an angle to improve the light, waiting for someone to leave the shot, or occasionally rejecting it; when Lily proposed a picture of the festival snapped from the far end of a long alley, Boone had turned it down, explaining that the trash cans would distract the viewer. It made Lily see what he did in a new light. Taking pictures was hard work.

Eventually, they had decided to break for lunch. Boone bought a couple of sandwiches and two bottles of Coke from a vendor and they'd stretched out in the park, watching all the people and enjoying each other's company.

"Can I ask you a question?" Lily asked.

"Shoot," Boone answered, taking a long pull of his soda pop.

"Why do you take pictures?"

"Because *Life* magazine pays me," he said, then chuckled.

Lily frowned playfully. "I'm serious."

"You really want to know?"

"I do."

Boone thought about his answer for a bit before replying. "I take pictures because they're magic."

"Magic? Like a man pulling a rabbit from a hat?" she teased.

"In a way, yeah," he said. "Whenever I use my camera, I can make time stand still. For that one moment, everything quits moving. Look around," Boone told her, waving a hand toward the crowded festival. "Everyone is in motion. People throwing back their heads to laugh, slipping their hands in their pocket for some change, or waving to a neighbor. Watching it with your eyes, you miss details, but when you look at a picture, there they are. That's when you really see the design on a woman's blouse, the chipped paint on the side of a delivery truck, or how the sun shines off the clock above the post office." He paused, finishing off the last of his drink. "Like I said, magic."

Lily believed him. Listening to Boone's answer, his words about magic, she felt he was casting a spell on her.

He spoke about his work as if he was a sculptor or painter. She thought of all the famous paintings she'd seen in books, how she had marveled at their colors and shapes, at the small flourishes meant to capture the eye. A photograph was much the same. She felt as if he was opening a door deep inside of him, allowing her to see him for who he *really* was.

"You make it look so easy," she said. "I could never do that."

"Sure you could," he disagreed. "You already did."

"What are you talking about?"

"There were plenty of times today where you saw something I didn't," Boone explained. "I loved the shot you suggested in the department store. All of the shadows, looking down on the crowd. You found that, not me."

"What about the lemon in the alley?" Lily asked with a frown.

"So what? Do you think I'm perfect?" He picked up his camera. "There will be plenty of mistakes in the pictures I took today. Maybe I misjudged the light or how far I was from the subject. Maybe I took it too soon or too late. For whatever reason, the shot won't come out the way I wanted."

"Doesn't that bother you?"

"From time to time," Boone replied. "I just hope that when I develop pictures there's more good than bad. With my talent and camera, that's usually a foregone conclusion," he added with a wink.

Lily smiled. In the short time they'd spent together, one

of the things about him that stood out was his confidence. Some people might have called Boone cocky, but not her. In fact, Lily found his belief in himself attractive.

"Speaking of seeing how these pictures turn out," he continued. "How would you like to help me develop the shots we took today?"

"Is it hard?" she asked.

"Nope. It's a piece of cake. I just thought you might have fun seeing how it all works. It's magic, remember?"

"I'd love to," Lily readily agreed. If it meant that she could be by his side for a little while longer, then she was all for it.

They were enjoying the last of their lunch when Boone asked, "What's all that for?" and pointed to the far end of the park.

Lily looked over to find workers hanging bunting along the edges of the bandstand, positioning sections of flooring, checking and rechecking strings of lights.

"There's going to be a dance tomorrow night," she explained. "It's the biggest event of the festival other than Halloween night."

"A dance?"

"With music and everything."

"Is it just for locals?"

She shook her head. "It's for everybody attending the festival. Out-of-towners included."

Boone had been reclining on his elbows, but now he sat up and turned to face her. "Let me take you. I promise I won't step on your toes."

Even though Lily's first instinct was to accept, she hesitated. While she had spent the day walking the festival with Boone, talking with dozens of people, she knew that going to the dance with him would bring a different kind of scrutiny. There they would be, beneath the strings of lights and the stars and moon above, moving in their own sort of orbit, holding each other tight for everyone to see. More than likely, her father would be there, too. What would people think? Would it be obvious how she felt about Boone? Would they know she was falling in love?

It didn't take long for Lily to shoo her worries and questions away. Though she'd been too frightened to leave town with Jane, she now found Boone's confidence infectious. It emboldened her to make her own choices.

"That sounds like fun," she said with a nod.

"Great," Boone replied, then stood and began to gather their things. He held out his hand to her. "Ready?"

"For what?" Lily asked, even as her fingers found his.

"To get back to work. These pictures aren't going to take themselves, especially if I don't have my guide to lead me. In a big city like this, a fella could get lost in a hurry and never be heard from again," he teased.

Lily smiled. She most certainly wouldn't want *that* to happen.

Lily stood beside Boone in his makeshift darkroom and watched as he developed the pictures he'd taken. It was a more complicated process than she had expected it to be, full of terms like *stop bath*, *fixer*, and *wetting agent*; Lily didn't understand half of the words Boone used but she nodded along as he talked. The chemicals he used had a sharp, unusual smell to them, but Lily didn't mind. She was just happy to be with him, to watch him work at his craft.

While they waited for the film to soak, they reminisced about the rest of their day. They'd moved through the crowded festival, taking more pictures. Boone was excited about one shot in particular. He had photographed a young boy blowing a humongous bubble of chewing gum, his eyes wide as saucers as he watched a performer juggle bowling pins; he wondered whether the image might even be good enough to make the cover of *Life*. Lily offered a favorite moment of her own, but it was just one among many. What she would truly treasure about the day was that she'd spent it with Boone, watching the autumn sunlight shine in his hair, hearing his warm laugh, and occasionally feeling his touch as he steered her through the throngs of festivalgoers. Even now, looking at him in the strange red glow of the darkroom, she was struck by how handsome he was, by how close their bodies were in the cramped space.

"I had a nice time today," Lily said after Boone had finished rinsing the film in the sink and then hung the long strips up to dry.

"I'm glad. I had a good time, too."

"Until today, I had no idea that work could be so much fun. Maybe I should've become a photographer. It sure beats being a librarian when it comes to excitement."

"It usually isn't," Boone replied. "Fun is usually the farthest thing from your mind when it's cold enough to no longer feel your fingers, when there are so many mosquitoes that you can't see a few inches in front of your face, or when you're standing around for hours on end waiting for those five seconds when a Hollywood starlet races out of her dressing room." He chuckled. "Days like today are worth their weight in gold. This one was particularly memorable."

"Why is that?" Lily asked, hoping that she was the reason for his answer.

"Because of who I spent it with," he answered, making her heart skip a beat. "With you by my side, I don't think I'd mind the cold, a few thousand bugs, or even a little waiting." Boone stepped closer, smiling as he stared into her eyes. "You're more fun to have around than Clive, that's for sure."

"I wonder what he's up to tonight."

"Beats me," he said with a shrug. "Probably stuffing his face with hot dogs and popcorn, then washing it down with some cotton candy. With as much as I've seen him eat, he should be a blimp instead of a string bean."

By the time Lily and Boone had finished taking pictures, the sky was quickly turning dark. When they got back to the room, all of the lights were off and the door was locked. Inside, Clive had left them a short note explaining that he was returning to the festival for some fun and a bite to eat. With Daisy still staying with Marjorie, that meant they were alone.

"I don't know why you're so hard on Clive," Lily remarked. "I like him."

"Actually, he's not half bad," Boone admitted. "When we first left the city, I didn't think I'd survive ten minutes in the car with him, what with all the talking and sneezing, but I'm man enough to admit that I was wrong. Clive takes the job seriously and wants to do well, even if it wouldn't hurt him to ask a well-thought-out question from time to time. But enough about him," Boone said as he came closer, placing his hand on her arm. "I'd much rather talk about us."

Even though she agreed, Lily's heart began to beat a little faster. "In that case, I'm all ears," she replied as confidently as she could.

"Sorry about that," he facetiously apologized. "I misspoke. What I really want is a kiss."

Lily smiled. "But you already had one this afternoon."

And he had, just not from her.

Moving through the crowded festival, Lily had introduced Boone to Cissy Hermann, a flamboyant figure around Hooper's Crossing. Cissy dressed in the most garish of colors, almost always with matching accessories, including purse and hat. Overweight, she had a boisterous laugh that set her ample midsection to jiggling. So when Lily mentioned that Boone was a *Life* magazine photographer from New York City, Cissy had promptly walked over and planted a big, wet kiss on his cheek, leaving behind a distinctive lipstick smear.

"That's a memento so you won't forget your visit," Cissy

had said before cackling, making her fire-engine-red outfit shake every which way.

"You're right," Boone told Lily with playful grin. "That *was* pretty exciting. Makes me wonder what the heck I'm doing here with you?" he teased. "You don't happen to have that lady's address, do you? I think I'll go over and surprise her right—"

"Hush," Lily interrupted, quieting him.

With her hand on his elbow, she gently pulled him closer, rising on her tiptoes to place her lips against his. This time, their kiss felt stronger, more intense, as if now that they'd acknowledged their feelings for each other, the trickle of passion had become a steady stream, well on its way to a flood. When they had finished, Lily leaned back, her eyes remaining shut for a few seconds as she savored the kiss, then asked, "Is it just me or are we getting better at this?"

"And here I thought I was already pretty good when we started."

Lily smiled. "Let me be the judge of that."

"While I'd love to give you another example to compare, we still have some work to do," Boone said before going to check the strips of film.

He took down the negatives and got busy turning them into actual pictures. Once again, Lily felt out of her element as Boone talked about the "enlarger" and the "emulsion side of the negative paper." She watched as he positioned a shot here and turned a knob there, moving as confidently as would be expected of a man who'd likely done this thousands of times before. When he put the print in one tray after another, moving it from developer to water to another chemical and more, Lily couldn't help but smile when the first image appeared, materializing as if out of thin air. It *was* magic, just like Boone had said.

Shot after shot was developed and then hung on a line of string to dry. The photographs were like a puzzle that revealed their afternoon together: the view from the upper floor of Dunaway's Department Store; Cissy Hermann just before she kissed Boone; a row of people lined up to buy caramel apples; and many more. Boone's picture of the boy and the juggler turned out to be every bit as spectacular as he'd hoped, the bubble of gum frozen forever, never to burst.

"One more to go," Boone said. "And this is one I can't do without."

Lily recognized the image the moment it began to appear; it was the photograph Boone had taken of her the day they'd met. Everything was just as she remembered, her mouth open slightly, wisps of hair hanging in air, her expression a bit surprised as she looked at the camera. But strangely, there was something she *didn't* recall. There was someone just to the side of her shoulder, a face that had yet to come into clear-enough focus for her to make out any features.

"Who is that?" Lily asked.

"Beats me," Boone answered with a shrug.

"Why is this picture different from the one I saw before?"

"That's because I trimmed the first one," he explained. "The only face I have any interest in looking at is yours."

As Lily watched, the image grew clearer. First, she recognized that it was a man standing beside her. He was staring at the camera, his expression as baffled as hers. But then came an unexpected surprise.

"I...I know that face..." she said.

Boone looked over her shoulder. "Yeah? Who is it?"

It was the man from out in front of the bank. Lily remembered their meeting. It had only lasted for a couple of minutes, but he had made her uncomfortable with the slick, practiced way he'd talked, as if he had been propositioning her. Though he was handsome in his own way, seeing him again made Lily's skin crawl. She felt as if the man's name was right there on the tip of her tongue, but try as she might, she couldn't retrieve it.

"I bumped into him the other day," Lily explained.

"Have a habit of that, do you?" Boone asked with a laugh.

She shook her head, sweeping away all memory of the other man, choosing to focus on the person she'd been happy to run into. "How do you think we small-town girls entertain ourselves?" she teased. "That's how we land you big-city boys."

"Like a fish on a line? Just snag one on the hook and reel him in?"

"With one practiced flick of my wrist."

He stepped closer, pulling Lily into his arms. "Well, then I promise I won't struggle to get away," he said.

"Fry me up in a pan or mount me on the wall, but whatever you do, don't throw me back in the water. I'm all yours."

Boone's words were like magic to Lily's ears. That a man as handsome, as worldly as him would have fallen for a woman like her, well, it was like something out of a fairy tale. It was just what she wanted.

When Boone bent toward her, Lily rose to meet him. This time, their kiss felt different, even more passionate. It was there in the deep, almost-guttural sound rumbling from his throat, the way his hand slid to her hip, his fingers digging into her soft flesh as he pulled their bodies closer together. Lily surrendered to her desires, matching his fervor, a part of her already wondering where the night might end. After all, they were alone. Unlike before, kissing in front of the bakery and down the street from her house, they didn't have to worry about being seen. This time, there was no one to interrupt.

Boone must have understood the same things.

"Come with me," he said once he'd broken their kiss. Now that the photographs had been developed, it was safe to open the door. He took Lily's hand and led her into the larger room. Outside, the sun had long since set, blanketing everything in darkness; though it was hard to see, Boone navigated the room safely, stopping at the foot of his bed.

But then his boldness ebbed. "I don't want to do anything you don't, Lily," he said cautiously. "If you'd rather wait, we can always—"

"Shhh," she quieted him. "I'm not making any promises, but why don't we see where things take us."

The fact was that Lily didn't have a whole lot of experience when it came to men. There had been plenty of kisses and a handful of times when a hand had roamed somewhere that would have made her father furious, but that was as far as she'd gone. But right then, Lily knew that it didn't matter if she was a virgin or not. She wanted more of what Boone could give her, and she wanted it now.

Seconds later, she was lying on her back in the bed, her lips pressed to his, their mouths open, and a hand running through his thick hair. When she felt Boone's fingers on the bare skin of her calf, slowly rising first to her knee and then to the back of her thigh, Lily gasped, shuddering with the pleasure of his touch. Quickly, she started to consider that this night would have no restrictions, that this man had captivated her enough for her to want to give herself to him. Lily marveled at how strange and unexpected life could be. Only days before, she'd intended to go with Jane to New York City. But now here she was, a man from the city come to her. It was like a dream.

Unfortunately for Lily, all dreams, both good and bad, come to an end.

And that's what happened when someone tried to open the door.

Chapter Eighteen

Boone was in heaven.

Kissing Lily, touching her bare skin, feeling her hand run through his hair, was unlike anything he'd ever experienced. The whole day had been that way, really. Walking with her through the festival, sharing lunch in the grass, and watching her smile as she introduced him to people: it all made it hard for him to concentrate on his work. And now look where they were.

As excited as Boone was, he knew that he had to be careful. He didn't want to pressure Lily into doing something she wasn't ready for. Sure, she'd told him that she was willing to go farther, to lie down with him in the bed, but it was obvious to him that she was innocent. The last thing Boone wanted was to push too far, too fast, and give Lily a reason to regret what they were doing. But that was easier said than done. Each kiss made him yearn for more, and it was a struggle to hold himself back.

And that was when he heard someone at the door.

Boone froze. Where moments before his heart had been racing from kissing Lily, it now came to an abrupt stop. For a second, he wondered if he'd imagined the noise, but then it came again, not loud but clear enough.

"Did you hear—" Lily began beneath him but he put a finger to her lips.

"Shhh," he further silenced her, straining to listen.

There came another sound from the other side of the door.

His first thought was that it was the two bastards who had robbed and beaten them only yesterday. Maybe they hadn't gotten what they'd been after or felt that no one would expect them to hit the same place two nights in a row. Either way, if they'd been casing the place and saw it quiet and dark for hours, they would've assumed that no one was there.

If so, they were in for a shock.

"Whatever happens, run away as fast as you can, then call the police," Boone whispered as he started to get off the bed, but Lily held him tight.

"Don't!" she implored him. "What if it's the same men from last—"

"I'll be all right," he interrupted, knowing that there wasn't time to discuss the matter. "Do you trust me?" he asked.

Lily nodded in the darkness.

"Then be ready to move," he told her.

Boone slipped off the bed and moved toward the door,

his eyes never leaving it, expecting it to open at any moment. He braced himself against the frame, the knob at his hip; when it swung open, he'd be right on top of whoever stood outside. More sounds came from the other side, as if something had been stuck in the lock in an attempt to jimmy it. Boone considered using the darkness inside the room to his advantage but quickly changed his mind. The greater element of surprise lay in meeting the intruders head-on. Taking a deep breath, he put his hand on the knob and then whipped open the door.

The figure standing just outside emitted a gasp of surprise. Boone grabbed a fistful of shirt and yanked the person toward him, knocking them off their feet. Together, they tumbled to the ground in a heap, Boone in control, straddling the unwanted visitor's chest, his fist cocked and ready to strike.

"Wait!" a man's voice screeched. "It's me! It's me!"

In the faint moonlight shining over his shoulder, Boone got enough of a look at the man to suspect he knew who was wriggling beneath him, the prominent Adam's apple being the most obvious clue. When Lily turned on a lamp, the sudden light glaringly bright, his hunch was confirmed. It was Clive.

"What in the hell are you doing?" Boone demanded. "I just about knocked your head off your shoulders!"

"I...I was just coming home from the fair..." the writer explained, his voice panicked. "Everything was dark and I couldn't see the lock and then my key stuck and then—"

"All right, that's enough," Boone said, trying to stem the rush of words, but Clive wasn't going to be deterred.

"I didn't think anyone was here! How was I supposed to know that you were inside with the lights off and..." Clive's words trailed off as he looked around the room and found Lily sitting on the edge of Boone's bed. No matter how naive he might have been, the writer was still smart enough to put two and two together and come up with four. "Oh no. I...I didn't realize that..." he blabbered. "I'm so sorry. I didn't know that...that you were..."

"It's all right, Clive," Lily told him with an easy smile. "You couldn't have known."

"If I had, I never would've opened that door, I promise!"

"We know that," she told him.

Boone got up off Clive, then helped the writer to his feet. By now, the younger man's cheeks had turned beet red with embarrassment.

"Why...why don't I go out for a while longer?" he asked as he stepped toward the door, trying to make up for his inadvertent mistake, but Boone put a hand to his chest, stopping him in his tracks.

"Stay," he said. It was already too late, the romantic mood between him and Lily ruined, at least as far as the rest of the night was concerned. Glancing at her and seeing her nod, Boone knew that he was right.

Clive walked around the room, unsure of what to do with himself, then drifted into the darkroom as if he was trying to hide.

"I'm sorry," Boone apologized to Lily once he thought Clive was out of earshot. "This isn't how I wanted our night to go."

"It's all right. Really," she said, further reassuring him by planting a soft kiss on his cheek. "There will be other chances for us to be alone."

He could only hope that she was right.

In a couple of days' time, Boone was supposed to leave for New York City, then off to all the other far-flung places his job would take him. While Lily had given an indication that she was considering coming along, the details had been few and far between. Was she being serious? Would she leave her hometown, the only place she'd ever known, in order to be with him? Boone really wanted to ask, but understood that now was not the time.

Just then, Clive wandered out of the darkroom as if in a trance, unsteady on his feet, his mouth hanging open like a door with a broken hinge. He held a photograph in his hand.

"Did you . . . did you take this today . . . ?" he asked.

Because of the way Clive was holding the picture, Boone couldn't get a good look at it. "Yeah. Lily took me around town so I could replace those that were stolen, remember?" he answered. "Why? Is something wrong?"

Clive turned the photograph so Boone could see it. His assumption had been wrong. It wasn't a shot he'd taken today. It was the picture of Lily from the day they'd met.

"What about it?" Boone asked.

"I know him," Clive replied, pointing at the man sharing the picture. "He was one of the men who broke in last night. He's one of the robbers."

"You're joking," Boone said, finding none of this funny.

"It's him."

"He's the guy who hit you?"

The writer shook his head. "I don't know if it was him or if he was the one Daisy chased out of the room."

"I thought you said you were sure?"

"I am!" Clive insisted. "It's just that everything happened so fast that I maybe have them mixed up in my head. But this one," he said, jabbing a finger at the photograph, "was here! Neither of them was wearing a mask."

"Mike," Lily suddenly blurted, causing both men to look at her. "His name is Mike Detmer, or at least that's the one he gave. I couldn't remember it before, but it just came back to me."

"You've met him, too?" Clive asked.

"I . . . bumped into him a couple of days ago . . ." she answered with a frown.

"We have to go to the police."

"Tell them what we know," Lily agreed.

Boone frowned. They were right, but he couldn't help but remember how unhelpful Garrett had been the night before. Still, even the possibility of getting his hands on the bastard who'd robbed and beaten them was more than enough incentive.

"All right," he said, plucking the picture from Clive's hand. "Let's go."

"...and once we're through the door—"

"We make sure all the blinds are drawn," Randall finished, his words heavy with boredom.

Ever since they'd returned to the cabin after hitting the *Life* magazine reporters' room, Leo had droned on and on about the coming bank robbery. He'd mocked up a rough model of the bank using ridiculous props like twigs, stones, bottle caps, and even a pepper shaker to mark the safe. Over and over, he talked through every step, periodically asking questions to see if his partner had been paying attention, until Randall was so sick of it he wanted to puke.

"And then what do you do?" Leo asked.

"Me and my tools head for the safe," Randall answered, then yawned.

What the hell else would I do, asshole?

But as much as he'd hoped that Leo would take the hint and shut up, he was to be disappointed. "What about me?"

Randall shrugged. "What do you mean, 'what about me'?"

"While you're crackin' the safe, where will I be? What will I be doin'?"

"Enough already, man. We've been over this crap a hundred times," he answered with very little in the way of exaggeration. "I feel like I could do this in my sleep."

"That's the point," Leo answered. "If we cover every detail, every eventuality, then we'll be prepared to do the job. This way, nothin' can go wrong."

Randall wanted to call bullshit on that. Life was full of unexpected occurrences. His tools could break while he was trying to open the safe. One of the bank's higher-ups might have forgotten something and come back to retrieve it, surprising them just the way that scrawny peckerwood had the night before. Hell, they could get in a car accident on the way to town, run over by some hick farmer who'd done too much Halloween celebrating. And none of these things could be prepared for no matter how many times you looked at some crappy model. But Randall couldn't tell Leo that. The stubborn son of a bitch wouldn't listen.

"I gotta stretch my legs," he said, wincing as he got up from his chair. He still hurt from where that damn dog had bit him. Since he couldn't go to a doctor, he'd done the best he could with alcohol and bandages.

"You try your costume on yet?" Leo asked before Randall reached the door.

"Nope," he mumbled, pulling a pack of smokes from his pocket.

"Better get on it. We gotta make sure it's not too long or you'll be trippin' on the sheet."

Leo's big plan to get them to the bank unnoticed was to wear Halloween costumes in order to blend in with the crowd. The older thief would be disguised as a cowboy, while Randall would go as a ghost so that he could better hide his bag of tools. According to Leo, no one would pay them any mind as they moseyed out of the bank, bags stuffed with cash.

But right then and there, Randall didn't give a damn about costumes or pepper shakers that were supposed to be safes.

He wanted to be alone.

Outside, the night was colder than he'd expected, though there was no way in hell he was going back inside for a jacket. The wind gusted, requiring three matches to light his cigarette; when he finally managed to get it lit, Randall inhaled deeply, then blew a plume of smoke toward the sky. All the while, he kept telling himself that his share of the stolen money would be worth putting up with Leo and his crap. Somewhere, there were dice and cards waiting for him.

When he was on his second cigarette, Randall pulled a picture from his pocket, the image of Lily he'd stolen from the photographer. Though the night was dark as coal, he stared at the shot in the faint glow of his cigarette. Randall had folded over the edge of the photo, removing himself from view; he didn't want to look at anyone but her, and that included his own mug. He drank in her long hair, pretty smile, and expressive eyes. He wanted to be alone with her, preferably in a hotel room where he could tear off her clothes, ravish her, to hear her voice screaming his name in pleasure. Randall knew he was fantasizing, that he would likely never see Lily again, but he didn't see any harm in it. Besides, who knew? Maybe she'd be at the Halloween festivities.

After another couple of drags, Randall got tired of freezing his ass off and stomped out the cigarette; with as dry as things were this time of year, if he flicked a smoldering butt into the bushes, he could start a fire. When he went back inside, Leo was still poring over his model, studying it like there was going to be a test.

"You better?" the older thief asked.

Randall grunted in answer.

"Good enough. Now get over here. We still got work to do."

Feeling a sudden urge to needle his partner, Randall answered, "Give me a second." He walked over and propped up Lily's photo on his bedside table, then stepped back to admire her. "Quite a looker, ain't she?"

"What the hell is that?" Leo asked with a scowl.

"What're you talkin' about?" Randall answered, a little confused. "That there's the reason we broke into those fellas' room last night."

"I know that, moron," he snapped. "What I'm askin' is why is it still here?"

When the two thieves had returned to the cabin with the spoils of their robbery, they'd burned everything, the pictures, the negatives, and even the camera bag; they were now nothing more than a pile of ashes at the bottom of their wood-burning stove. No evidence meant no crime.

"I couldn't bear to part with that one," Randall explained.

"'Cause you're stupid sweet on that girl."

"Her name's Lily," he said, his tone more defensive than he'd intended.

"Stop that shit. It ain't like the two of you are on a first-name basis."

Randall wanted to point out that they were, but with as bent out of shape as his partner seemed, it'd be pouring gas on a raging fire.

"Take it down," Leo ordered.

"I think I wanna keep it where it is," he disagreed.

"If you won't do it, then I will," the older man said, and got out of his chair. But before he could reach the photograph, Randall stepped in front of him. Somewhere deep down, he knew that he was being stupid and petty, that this was one of those ridiculous arguments that ended up with someone getting hurt, but Randall couldn't bring himself to back down. So far, he'd gone along with Leo's plans without much complaint, but this time he wasn't willing to give in.

To him, this was worth fighting for.

"Move aside," Leo told him with steel in his voice.

Randall shook his head. "There ain't no harm in my keepin' that picture," he said. "It don't change things one way or another."

"Someone could find it."

"No one will."

Leo pointed at the picture. "You leave that behind, whether here or the next place down the road, the cops might be able to draw a connection between us robbin' that bank and you."

"Trust me," Randall said, feeling confident, even a little cocky. "Nobody is gonna link us to that girl, to our breakin' into that room or hittin' the bank." He grinned. "I promise you that."

Chapter Nineteen

THERE ISN'T MUCH I can do with this."

Lily frowned as Garrett tossed the photograph of her and the man who had broken into Boone and Clive's room onto his desk. The three of them had walked to the police station and had found Garrett just as he was about to go out on patrol. He'd listened to their story, each of them talking over the others as they added their own piece to the puzzle, and had asked a few questions. Now he seemed to be saying that there was little chance of the thief being brought to justice.

"Why not?" Boone asked, sounding annoyed.

"Like I told you before, this isn't the big city," Garrett answered. "I can't check our files of criminals or ask among the detectives to see if anyone knows this guy. It doesn't work that way. Not here."

As she looked around the Hooper's Crossing police station, Lily thought he might be right. There were few other officers around, a couple at the coffee machine, laughing at a joke. Two out-of-towners were loudly snoring in the tiny jail cell at the back, sleeping off too much drink and the trouble it had caused. Occasional bits of static came over the radio, but no one was calling for backup or declaring an emergency. The fall festival might be the busiest time of year around these parts, but that wasn't saying much.

"Then how does it work?" Boone demanded. "Those bozos rob us, knock the stuffing out of Clive, kick my dog, and get off scot-free?"

"We're doing what we can."

"I just bet."

"I know how to do my job," Garret said, his own temper rising, staring daggers at the photographer perched on the corner of his desk.

"Doesn't look like it from where I'm sitting."

"Stop it. The both of you," Lily told them, wanting things to be civil and wondering why she seemed to be the only one concerned with keeping it that way.

Ever since they'd arrived, Garrett had been acting strangely. Though he had smiled when he first saw her, that good cheer had disappeared as soon as he'd realized she hadn't come alone. Garrett was indifferent to Clive, but with Boone his dislike was obvious, bordering on confrontational. He cut the other man off midsentence, dismissed his concerns, and often turned in his seat, acting as if Boone wasn't even there. Lily watched with dismay, unsure of what, if anything, she could do about it.

Garrett picked the picture and stared at it, his eyes

flicking back and forth between Lily and the man. "If this guy is really responsible for—"

"He is," Lily interrupted before Boone could.

"So you say."

"So *I* say," Clive clarified. Up until now, the young writer hadn't said much as he nervously chewed a nail, content to let Boone do most of the talking.

"You're sure this is the guy who attacked you?" Garrett asked for the second time since they'd arrived.

"Like I said," Clive answered, a hint of exasperation in his voice, "I don't know if he was the one who punched me or if Daisy chased him from the house. What I do know is that *that* man," he said forcefully, pointing at the photograph, "broke into our room. I'm absolutely certain of it."

Garrett looked at the picture awhile longer, then sighed. "I can always send the information out over the wire," he explained. "Maybe we'll get lucky and someone will know who he is. Stranger things have happened."

"Don't forget to mention that his name is Mike Detmer," Lily added helpfully.

"I'll write it down but I'd bet my house that he was lying," Garrett explained. "A guy would have to be pretty stupid to give out his real name if he knew he was about to commit a crime."

"That's it?" Boone asked. "That's all you're going to do?"

"The wire's a good place to start."

"It'll probably be the end of it, too."

Garrett stared hard at Boone. "What more do you want? Should I go door-to-door at the hotels or start frisking people attending the festival? And all so I can find a few canisters of film."

The photographer was off the desk in a shot, his fuse short and burning fast. "Aren't you the comedian?" he asked through gritted teeth. "Next time I'm in Hollywood, I'll make sure to warn Abbott and Costello that they have some competition. But I wonder if you'll find it funny when I kick your—"

"Boone!" Lily shouted as she moved toward him, forcing him to back up. She couldn't understand what had gotten into the two men she cared so much about, why they were at each other's throats. Out of the corner of her eye, she noticed the other policemen watching them, coffee cups in hand. "Don't ruin our day together. Not now," she said softly enough that only Boone could hear. "Not after all the fun we've had. Please."

That last word broke the spell Boone's anger held over him. He looked down at her, his eyes searching her face as all the tension drained from his expression. He almost seemed embarrassed. "I'm sorry," he told her.

Amazingly, at that moment Lily realized just how hard she was falling in love with Boone. In the short time she'd known him, he had proven to be everything she wanted in a man. She had loved spending the day with him, watching him work, sharing laughs, then later feeling his lips against hers. Even now, seeing him calm his anger, listen to her, and understand her point of view all provided Lily with hope for tomorrow. A future together seemed more possible than ever.

But that didn't mean he was off the hook, and not just with her. "I'm not the only person you need to apologize to," she replied.

Boone took a deep breath then nodded. He walked over to Garrett and stuck out his hand. "I shouldn't have talked to you like that," he said. "I was out of line. I'm just mad as hell at having my things stolen, my friend and dog attacked, not to mention letting someone get the jump on me. What do you say?"

Garrett hesitated. For a moment, Lily wondered if he was going to refuse Boone's apology. But when her oldest friend looked at her, his expression softened. "I probably wouldn't have acted all that different if I were in your shoes," he said, shaking the photographer's hand.

For now at least, a truce settled between them.

Lily, Boone, and Clive waited as Garrett made a couple of phone calls, disseminating their information about Mike Detmer to various law enforcement agencies in the hopes that someone knew of him. "Well, we've thrown out our fishing lines," Garrett said after hanging up the receiver. "Now we just have to hope for a bite."

By now it was getting late; the clock on the wall read 11:15. Lily yawned. After such a busy day, Lily was quickly growing tired.

"Let me walk you home," Boone said, noticing.

"I'll take her," Garrett interjected. "I...forgot something that I need at home. I can drop her before I start my patrol."

Lily had noticed her friend's hesitation and wondered if

he was being completely honest but saw no point in calling him on it. She was so exhausted that it really didn't matter who took her home. "That's fine with me," she said.

There was a flicker of disappointment in Boone's face but he nodded. Though she would have liked to give him one more kiss, or even share an embrace, Lily didn't think it appropriate to do so in the police station. Instead, she gave Boone a wave and promised to see him the next day.

"Don't forget the big dance tomorrow night," he told her.

Before Lily could answer, she was startled by Garrett's keys falling to the floor. He made no move to pick them up at first, looking at her, then Boone, then back again, his expression a bit confused. Finally, he retrieved them. "We better get going," he said, and started for the door.

Lily followed, stifling another yawn with the back of her hand, thankful that her day was almost at an end.

She had no way of knowing how wrong she was.

"Will it be another long night?"

Garrett didn't immediately answer Lily's question as he turned his squad car off Main Street and into a quieter neighborhood, heading for their homes. When he did reply, it wasn't with words, but more of a grunt and shrug of his broad shoulders. It wasn't that he was trying to be rude, not intentionally, but rather that his mind was reeling with things far more important than fender-benders and rowdy out-of-towners.

He couldn't stop thinking about Lily and Boone.

When they'd shown up at the police station with the

awkward writer in tow, Garrett had been stunned. Even as
the photographer explained the reason for their late visit,
Garrett had struggled to keep his eyes and attention off
Lily. This was the second time he'd seen them together,
and as bothered as he had been on the first occasion, this
one made him feel worse. It was obvious that something
was growing between Lily and Boone, more than a simple
acquaintance or fleeting friendship. But because Garrett
took pride in his work as a policeman, he'd fought down
his worries and turned his attention back to Boone's tale.

Which lasted right up until he saw Lily's picture.

As reluctant as he was to give the other man credit,
Garrett had to admit that Boone's photograph was incredible. In the image, Lily was more beautiful than ever; her
expression, the wind in her hair, even the light and angle
were all perfect. She was so captivating that Garrett had
trouble focusing on the other person in the shot, the one
Lily said was named Mike Detmer, now accused of breaking into Marjorie Barlow's house.

Besides, Lily was more important to him than some
petty robbery. That was why Garrett had offered to drive
her home even though he had no reason to do so. Well,
that and a little jealousy. He wanted to get her as far
away from that slick photographer as possible. When she'd
agreed to go with him, he had been elated. But then his
victory had turned into the harshest of defeats.

"Don't forget the big dance tomorrow night..."

Boone's words had left Garrett dumbstruck. Many
different emotions had raced through him: disbelief,

confusion, even fear and sadness. But the one that overwhelmed all the others was a surprise in and of itself. Anger. It grabbed hold like a rabid dog, sinking its teeth in deep, ripping his flesh while it shook him, refusing to let go. Garrett thought of the times he'd asked Lily about the dance, how he had suggested that they might go together. He hadn't imagined it, had he? Why was she rejecting him, her oldest friend, who loved her with all his heart? Why was he being pushed aside for a man she barely knew, someone who would be long gone in a matter of days?

"What's wrong?"

Garrett's trance was broken by Lily's question. Out of the corner of his eye, he saw her staring at him. "What are you talking about?" he asked with a chuckle, trying to blow off her question and doing a terrible job of it.

"You know what I mean. Something's bothering you."

"I'm fine."

"No, you're not," she insisted. "Tell me."

Garrett shouldn't have been surprised. Lily knew him better than anyone. Over all the years they'd known each other, she had seen him happy, sad, and every other emotion up and down the line. He could no more hide his feelings from her than stuff a Saint Bernard into a birdhouse. Knowing that she wouldn't let the matter drop until he came clean, Garrett chose to give her a sliver of the truth.

"The dance," he said.

"What about it?" Lily asked innocently.

"Boone mentioned it back at the station," Garrett

continued, fighting down his growing dread. "Are...are you going to go with him...?"

"I am," she answered with a smile that would have lit up the darkest room. "He asked me this afternoon and I said yes."

Garrett felt as if he had been punched right in his heart. He squeezed the steering wheel tighter and tighter, as if he was strangling it. He struggled to come to grips with not only *what* Lily had said, but *how* she had said it, giddily, like someone who'd had her greatest wish fulfilled. It was almost more than he could bear.

"I asked, too," he muttered through clenched teeth.

"What did you say?" Lily asked; she must not have heard.

"I said that I asked you, too," Garrett snapped, loud enough to startle them both. Now that those first words were out, more followed, as if he was on a slippery slope and picking up speed. "When I picked you up at the library after work, I told you that I have tomorrow night off," he explained, a tremor in his voice. "I said that I thought we could go together and you agreed, remember?"

"But—but that's not right," she argued.

"Yes, it is," Garrett insisted.

"No, you said that if neither of us had someone else to go with, we'd go together," Lily told him. "But just then, no one had asked me. I never would have accepted Boone's offer if I'd already committed to going with you."

Garrett's head spun. For as often as he rehearsed conversations with Lily in his head, trying out a new word here, a hearty laugh there, he had trouble remembering what was imaginary and what was real. Had he told her that? Or was she mistaken? He had no way of knowing for sure.

But even as he struggled to make sense of things, Garrett realized that they were rapidly nearing their destination; he'd just crossed Eisenhower Avenue, which was only two blocks from home. He couldn't turn a corner now, hoping to prolong their talk, without it being blatantly obvious. He was running out of time.

"I'm sorry if I said or did something to confuse you," Lily apologized, filling the void of his silence, then punctuating it with a yawn.

And then the ride was over. Garrett pulled the squad car to the curb. Before he could even pull the parking brake, Lily gave his arm a squeeze, thanked him for the taking her home, and opened her door. He watched helplessly as she stepped in front of the headlights and was momentarily bathed in light, like an angel. He had the undeniable feeling that she was walking away from him for good.

The next thing Garrett knew, he was pushing open his own door and stepping into the street on unsteady legs. "Lily, wait!" he shouted.

She had just about reached her front walk when she stopped and turned back toward him. "What is it?"

"There's...there's something I've been meaning to tell you..." he managed, his heart pounding.

Lily stared, waiting for him to go on.

For a moment, Garrett feared that this would be like

all the other times he'd built up his confidence only to
chicken out and spend the rest of the day kicking himself
for being such a coward. But somehow, almost miracu-
lously, this time was different. The strength to finally confess his feelings welled up from deep inside him. Maybe it
was because he understood what was at stake, that it was
now or never, that he had to speak now or forever hold his
peace. So even though his mouth was as dry as cotton, the
words he spoke came out loud and clear, a burden lifted
from his shoulders.

"I love you..."

Lily stared at him in disbelief, unable to move or speak.
Her heart banged hard against her rib cage. She'd heard
Garrett's words clearly, but now it felt as if they had washed
over her like a wave and were now racing off into the distance, fading away, losing their shape. "What...what did
you say...?" she asked, hoping that she'd heard wrong or
that there was a misunderstanding.

But there wasn't.

"I love you, Lily," Garrett repeated. High above, the
clouds parted, bathing them both with bright moonlight,
shining off his silver policeman's badge. "I've been in love
with you for as long as I can remember, ever since we were
kids," he explained, taking a small, tentative step toward
her. Where during the whole drive across town he'd appeared distracted, Lily thought Garrett now seemed to be
focused, sure of himself. "If I had a dollar for every time
I've wanted to tell you, for all the times I tried, I'd be the

richest man in Hooper's Crossing." He laughed, though there wasn't much humor in it. "But I could never bring myself to go through with it. Until now."

"Ever since we were kids..."

The weight of Garrett's words rattled around inside her head like marbles in a tin cup. Lily thought of all their years together. They'd been inseparable, one memory on top of another as far back as she could recall. Her life was entwined with his, two peas in a pod, two sides of the same coin, growing up a stone's throw from each other. All that time, Lily had believed she'd known Garrett inside and out, but just like that he had proven her assumption wrong.

"The last time I tried to tell you was when we talked about the dance," he explained, "but I clearly didn't do too good a job of it."

Lily still couldn't speak. Her mind raced along the course of their friendship, trying to find something, a clue, a sign of how Garrett claimed to feel about her, but there was nothing. Had he really been pining away for her all this time? How had she never noticed? Most important, what happened now? There were so many questions, but no matter how hard she tried, Lily couldn't come up with a single answer.

"I know this has to be a surprise to hear," Garrett continued, uttering one of the biggest understatements Lily had ever heard. "But I couldn't hold it back any longer, not now, not with..." he began but never finished.

Lily suspected that she knew what Garrett had meant.

This was because of Boone. After all, the timing of his declaration coincided with his learning that the photographer had asked her to the festival dance. The more she thought about it, the stranger Garrett's behavior had been, ever since running into her and Boone outside the diner.

"I . . . I just . . . this is so . . ." she stumbled, finally finding her voice, but Garrett didn't let her get far.

"Lily, please," he interrupted. "I've been trying to tell you these things for so long that I can't stop. Not now. If I do, I may never start again. When I'm finished, you can say whatever you want."

She nodded.

"From that first time you waved at me from across the street, you've always been the best person I've known," he continued, taking a step, then another. "Every time I see you, whether you're here on the porch or sitting in the sun outside the library, I can't help but stare. You're so beautiful it takes my breath away," Garrett told her, though Lily was still too stunned to be embarrassed. "But you're more than your looks, much more. You've always been as funny as you are smart, kind as well as caring. Whenever I needed to talk about the death of my parents, you listened, just like I did when you spoke of your mom." By now, Garrett was close enough to tenderly take her by the hand. "You're everything I've ever wanted, Lily. Then, now, always. I'm in love with you." He paused, his eyes searching her face, his expression pleading, his words insistent. "I just need to know if you can love me back."

Listening to Garrett bare his heart moved Lily. Tears

filled her eyes and her lower lip trembled. In that moment, she understood a truth so well, so completely, that it hurt all the way down to the center of her.

She did love Garrett.

Just not in the same way. Not how he wanted, how he needed her to.

"I...I can't..." Lily said, stepping back and taking her hand from his, as strangely uncomfortable with his touch as she'd been with his words. "I care about you, Garrett, I really do, more than you know, but not like that."

"Don't say that. The two of us—"

"You've always been there beside me," she interrupted; now it was her moment to speak, to tell him how she felt. "I don't want to imagine what my life would be like without you in it. You're family, the younger brother I never had, which is why there isn't that kind of love in my heart for—"

"Stop!" Garrett shouted, his policeman's voice loud in the still of the night; the intensity of his response momentarily startled Lily. From where she stood, his eyes looked wet in the moonlight as his hands bunched into fists at his side. "You...you can't say that..." he muttered while he shook his head. "I...I don't want to hear that. Not now. I have to..."

Abruptly and without another word, he turned and walked away.

"Garrett, don't go!" Lily yelled, but he ignored her. He didn't so much as look back before he got into his squad car and sped away, leaving her staring after his headlights until they were lost to sight.

In a way, Lily understood.

He had taken a risk and bared his soul to her, revealing his deepest secret, all in the hopes that his love would be returned. But when it wasn't, when it became clear that things weren't going to go his way, Garrett had been unable to face that painful truth and so he ran from it. Though her own thoughts were riddled with confusion and sadness, Lily knew that Garrett was in even greater turmoil, angry and in pain. She realized that there was nothing she could do for him, not now. Maybe later, when he'd had time to come to grips with what she'd told him, they could sit down and talk, to try to heal what had just been broken. She certainly hoped so.

Until then, all Lily could do was wait.

Chapter Twenty

OUTSIDE THE LIBRARY'S WINDOWS was a gorgeous October morning. Sunlight streamed down from a cloudless sky, warm enough for people walking by on the sidewalk to stop, slip off a jacket, push back a hat, and raise their face with a smile. Birds and squirrels still went about their preparations for winter, storing food and padding nests, although maybe without as much intensity. Only a few leaves fluttered to the ground to mix with their orange, red, yellow, and brown kin. It was a perfect day.

But inside Lily a storm raged.

"I love you... I've loved you ever since we were kids..."

Ever since Garrett drove away, Lily had thought of little beside his declaration. Fortunately, her father had been in his office dealing with festival business, allowing her to climb the stairs without a conversation. Unfortunately, her room had provided little sanctuary. For hours, she had lain in darkness, staring at the ceiling above her bed, thinking.

She replayed their conversation, back to how Garrett had spoken to Boone at the police station, how he'd acted in front of the diner, and so on, one moment after another, all the way to when they'd been kids.

What Lily had come to realize as the dawn sky began to lighten made her feel like a fool. All of those times when she'd thought Garrett was just staring at her, smiling and laughing out of friendship, had been something more. He had always been protective of her, not in the smothering way of her father, but more like a brother. Now she saw that differently, too. Dozens of other examples all led to the same conclusion.

Garrett had always been in love with her, just as he'd said.

But she'd been too blind to see it.

Now she had no idea what to do next. Garrett's police car hadn't been out front when she got up; even if he'd been home, Lily doubted he would have wanted to see her. Normally, this was when she would've talked to Jane, but she didn't have her friend's phone number in the city. Confiding in Boone was out of the question since there was already enough friction between him and Garrett. No, she was on her own, which made sense since—

"Who were the authors of the Federalist Papers?"

Lily startled, blinked a couple of times and turned to find Sherman Banks standing beside the checkout desk, crossword puzzle in hand; she'd been so lost in thought that she hadn't noticed him shuffle across the library.

"The what now?" she asked.

"The Federalist Papers," the older man repeated. "I know that two of the writers were Alexander Hamilton and James Madison, but neither one of them fits and I can't remember the name of the third."

"I'm sure it will be right there in the encyclopedia," Lily said, her tone short and sharp. She was so consumed by what had happened with Garrett that she didn't want to be bothered, especially for some silly puzzle answer.

From the strange look on Sherman's face, equal parts surprise and embarrassment, Lily understood that her words had unsettled him. "I . . . I'll go see if I can find it . . ." he muttered, then started to trudge away.

Lily was ashamed of herself. Just because her life had become so complicated didn't give her an excuse to take her frustrations out on others. "Mr. Banks, wait," she said as she stepped out from behind the desk. "I'm sorry. I didn't sleep well last night and I'm afraid it's making me a little crabby," she apologized. "Now, how about we go find your answer."

After Lily had gotten Sherman the right volume, the phone rang. Halfway back to the front desk, she heard the old man exclaim, "John Jay! I should have known!" Smiling to herself, she answered the telephone.

"Hooper's Crossing Library. Lily speaking."

"I want you in my office as fast as you can get here," her father grumbled on the other end of the line.

Stunned, Lily managed, "But . . . but I'm working . . ."

"Right this minute, young lady!" Morris snapped, then hung up.

Lily stood with the receiver in her hand for a long time, as if hoping that it still had more to say to her, that it might explain what had just happened. Her father could be a demanding man, but this was unusual, even for him. His tone, rough and allowing no room for disagreement, bothered her every bit as much as what he'd said. She wondered what he wanted, grasping at any possibility.

Was he upset about how much time she had been spending with Boone?

Had word gotten around town about the robbery?

Or had he spoken with Garrett? Did he know how the policeman felt about her? Was he disappointed that she'd turned him down?

Whatever the reason, Lily knew that it was in her best interests to do as her father had asked. Morris Denton didn't like to be kept waiting.

Just as she was about to go find Ethel to tell her she was leaving, the older librarian stepped from between two stacks of books. Her expression was as unfriendly as ever. When Lily arrived that morning and offered a kind-enough greeting given her rough night, Ethel had mumbled a response and then stalked off. Lily doubted this conversation would go any better.

"I'm sorry to do this, Ethel, but I need to leave," Lily said. "My father called and needs me to come to his office."

Ethel glared at her fellow librarian with an expression frostier than a January afternoon. "Do you really expect me to believe that was your father on the phone?" she asked with a derisive snort. "I bet it was that fancy magazine

photographer you've been running around with. He calls
and you snap to heel quicker than a dog. You'll be jumping through hoops by the end of the week!"

Lily felt her temper rising, but after so many years
of putting up with Ethel's snide comments, she was well
versed in turning the other cheek. She grabbed her purse
and started for the door. "I'll be back as quickly as I can."

"Your mother would be ashamed of you."

Ethel's words made Lily stop in her tracks. It felt as
if her heart stopped, then began beating double-time.
"What... what did you say...?"

"I'm merely pointing out that you are the perfect example of what happens when a girl grows up without a
mother's firm hand to guide her," the librarian explained.
"Sarah would have tamed this recklessness out of you,
made you more respectful of your elders and not so prone
to flights of fancy."

Like too much air in a balloon or too much water in
a cup, Lily's anger was too big to be contained. In mentioning her mother, Ethel had finally gone too far. Moving
quickly toward the other woman, Lily knew that this time
it would be impossible to hold her tongue, but the truth
was, she didn't want to.

"How dare you talk to me that way," Lily said without
raising her voice, though it seethed with anger and men-
ace. "But why should I be surprised? You've been nothing
but horrible to me since the day I started here. You turn
your nose up at everything I say, as if I'm a child or an
idiot. You belittle everything I do, making me repeat jobs

again and again, claiming that it isn't good enough. You're the nastiest, most bitter woman I've ever met in my life."

As she spoke, Lily continued to come forward, forcing Ethel to retreat, but when the older woman bumped into the card catalog, she was trapped. Lily leaned close, her finger just beneath the librarian's nose. Years of resentment and frustration poured out of her like water rushing over Niagara Falls.

"But I'm not the only person you're rotten to. Far from it," Lily continued. "You treat everyone who walks in here as if they're stupid. You act like you're a queen and we should all feel lucky you let us in your castle. For too long now, all of us, including me, have let you get away with it. But no more," she declared, her voice finally rising, her vow emphatic. "If you can't treat me with respect, if you can't stop being such a . . . a *witch* to people, maybe you're the one who needs to find another job!"

Lily fell silent, letting her words sink in. Ethel stared at her with a look of horror and fear, her face white as a sheet.

Though she wouldn't have been proud to admit to it, Lily was pleased with herself.

She started to do as she'd intended and go to her father's office, but when she was halfway to the door, Lily turned back to Ethel. "One more thing," she said. "Don't you *ever* mention my mother to me again. Understand?"

Ethel nodded, then scurried off to the stacks, her kingdom of books.

It was then that Lily noticed Sherman Banks staring at

her, his crossword puzzle clutched in his hands. He must have heard the whole thing.

And he was smiling.

Morris Denton's office was on the second floor of City Hall, facing the park. The view from his picture window was spectacular, showing the heart of downtown. Most times Lily visited, her father would be holding forth before that window, ruminating about where Hooper's Crossing had once been, where it was currently, and especially about where he was leading it. Even in those few quiet moments of his day, when he wasn't on the telephone or didn't have any guests, Lily suspected that her father stared out the window and daydreamed. That's what she would have done. The view was especially magnificent this time of year, what with the festival, its vendors and visitors, its sights and sounds.

And so Lily was surprised to find her father sitting at his desk, his back to the window, his face creased with an angry frown.

But even more shocking was who he was with.

Dave Dunaway sat in the chair opposite Morris. The owner of Dunaway's Department Store was a wiry man. His always-rolled-up shirtsleeves revealed the lean muscle of a man always in motion, always at work. Like her father, Dave knew every person in town by name, and odds were he knew most of their family trees and birthdays, too.

He was also Jane's dad.

"Mr. Dunaway..." Lily managed. "Hello..."

"Take a seat," Morris told her. "We have lots to talk about."

Even as Lily lowered herself into the chair beside Mr. Dunaway, her mind raced to come up with an explanation as to why he was there. Had something happened to Jane? Living in New York City could be exciting but it had its share of dangers, too. Had her friend been in an accident or gotten robbed? Every possibility made her more and more worried.

"If you don't mind, Dave," her father began, "why don't we back up a bit so Lily knows what brought you to my office."

"All right," Mr. Dunaway answered. "A couple of mornings back, I was gettin' ready to go open the store. I was drinkin' a cup of coffee, lookin' out the kitchen window like I usually do, when I noticed that Jane's Oldsmobile wasn't in the drive. When I went upstairs to her room, it was empty. Her bed was made up, like no one had slept in it. That's when I found the note she'd left on her pillow," he added, then pointed at a piece of paper lying on her father's desk.

Lily felt the bottom fall out of her stomach. That fateful night she had written a message of her own, explaining where she'd gone and why, hoping that her father would understand when he found it. Fortunately, when she had gotten cold feet, she'd managed to reach it before Morris. But since Jane had actually gone through with their plan to leave Hooper's Crossing, her message had been discovered. The problem was, Lily had no idea what Jane had written.

She didn't have to wait long to find out.

Her father picked up the letter and leaned forward, extending it to her. Lily took it, looked at both men, and then began to read:

Dear Mom and Dad (Susan and Emily, too!),

If you're reading this note, then that means I'm off chasing my dreams. By tomorrow morning, I'll be in New York City. I think you all know how badly I've wanted to leave Hooper's Crossing. Well, it's gotten to the point that if I stay here much longer, I'm going to go out of my mind! I need to be somewhere else, somewhere bigger, a place that's exciting! And Dad, maybe you're right. Maybe I'll fail and come crawling back. But I have to try to make it. If I don't, I'm going to regret it for the rest of my life. As soon as I'm settled, I'll let you know. Who knows, maybe you'll even come for a visit!

Love, Jane

P.S. Don't worry! Lily is going with me and with the two of us watching each other's backs, nothing will go wrong. She's the responsible one, remember?

"She's right, you know," Mr. Dunaway said after Lily raised her eyes from the note. "I always understood that someday, no matter how hard I tried change her mind, Jane was going to leave. If I'm bein' honest, I'm surprised it took this long. Well, a couple of hours after I found the note, the phone rang down at the store," he continued. "It was Jane callin' from a pay phone right there in Manhattan. She'd done just like she said. I couldn't understand half of what she was sayin' 'cause of all the people and a bad connection, but it as clear as day to me that she sounded happier than she had in a long, long time."

Lily nodded. She'd received a similar call at the library, Jane's voice cutting in and out, giddy about life in the big city. Faintly, Lily remembered her friend saying something just before she was gone for good. Had it been a warning? Had Jane been trying to caution Lily about what was in the note?

"While all of us were plenty worried about Jane, my wife and I were comforted by the fact that she hadn't gone off alone," he said, looking right at Lily. "That's why I was so confused when I saw you in the store yesterday."

With that, things clicked into place in Lily's head.

Yesterday, she and Boone had gone around town, taking pictures to replace those that had been stolen. One of the places Lily had been happy to show him was the view from the upper windows of Dunaway's Department Store. She hadn't seen Jane's father when they'd entered, but on the way out Lily had noticed him coming out of the storeroom and waved; Dave had stared at her, his expression strangely blank. Now she knew why.

"I struggled to make heads or tails out of you still bein' in town for the rest of the day and most of the night," Mr. Dunaway said. "In the end, I reckoned that the only thing I could do was bring the note to Morris. I'd been meanin' to do it regardless, to see how he was copin' with you gone, but the darn festival's had me runnin' 'round in circles. Now I wish I'd picked up the phone soon as I found Jane's note to see if he knew anything."

He didn't, not then, but now he knows it all.

Lily realized that she was caught as surely as a mouse in a trap. All of the precautions she'd taken, slowly taking her money out of the bank, hiding her suitcase first in the back of her closet and then in the bushes in front of the house, and then racing upstairs to destroy her own note, had all been for nothing.

"I think you owe us both an explanation," her father prodded.

Lily took a deep breath, trying to settle her rattled nerves, and then said, "It's true. I was supposed to go with Jane to New York City. We planned it for weeks. I...I got in the car with her that night, but just as we were leaving town, I couldn't go through with it. I don't know why, not exactly, but I couldn't," she told them, the shame of her weakness as fresh as when it had happened. "But Jane wouldn't wait. She said that she couldn't stay any longer and that she was going whether I came with her or not. So she dropped me back at home and drove away. I got a call the next day, just like you. She *did* sound happy," she said with a small grin.

"At least now I know the whole story," Dave told her. "And while I wish you were there watchin' out for her, I've gotta let Jane try to make her own way. Heck, even if I managed to find her in the city and haul her back, she'd just hate me for it, then take off again the first chance she got." He shook his head, then rose from his seat. "I better get back to work. The store isn't gonna run itself, 'specially not at festival time. Thank you, Lily. You, too, Morris," he said, then left.

But when Lily rose, hoping to follow and get back to the library, her father spoke. "Sit down, young lady," he said, his tone making it obvious that he wasn't in the mood for any disagreement. "You and I aren't done, not by a long shot."

That's what Lily was afraid of.

Chapter Twenty-One

"Did you write me a note that night?" Morris began.

Lily nodded.

"What did it say?"

"The same things as Jane's," she answered. "I told you where I was going, who I was with, and that I didn't want you to worry."

Her father was silent for a while, his brow furrowed. "This was the night I found you outside talking with Garrett, wasn't it?"

"He startled me when I came home," Lily explained.

"Did Garrett know what you were planning to do?"

"No. The only person who did was Jane."

Morris got up out of his chair to stare out the window. Lily was thankful for the respite, no matter how brief it might be. But while the questions had stopped, her father was hardly done talking.

"Your mother has been gone now for more than fifteen

years," he began, "and not a one of them has been easy for me. There were a lot of times, especially in the beginning, when the responsibility of raising you nearly overwhelmed me. I didn't know what to do and made my share of mistakes. But I fought on. For you. For Sarah. Through it all, I longed for someone to talk to about raising a child, someone who could give me advice when you were unruly, when you disobeyed, those difficult moments that every parent faces. I even entertained the idea of remarrying," he said, a revelation that momentarily stunned his daughter, "but I knew that it wouldn't be fair. I could never love someone else like I did your mother. So, in the end, I chose to share my life with just one other person." He turned to look at Lily. "With you."

Her father surely didn't realize it, but he had perfectly described the guilt that gnawed at her. Every choice Lily faced, no matter how badly she may have wanted to make it, had to be balanced against her fears of hurting him, worrying that she would be abandoning him.

That burden had never felt heavier than now.

"I hate to imagine what your mother would say if she were here," he continued. "Seriously, Lily? Running away in the middle of the night? Going off to live in a dangerous place like New York City? Sarah would've expected you to have more sense than that. She would have thought it the most foolish, irresponsible thing she'd ever heard of in her life. Why, I dare think she—"

"You're wrong," Lily blurted, cutting off her father midsentence.

In the silence that followed, she wondered which of

them was more surprised that she'd spoken. Something inside Lily had changed. Before, she had always worried about her father's feelings, afraid that she might hurt him, that by following her dreams she would leave him alone. But now she could no longer ignore the desire to live for herself, to find her own happiness.

She couldn't stay silent. Not anymore.

"What . . . what did you say to me . . . ?" Morris asked.

"That you're wrong," Lily answered. "She would've wanted me to be careful, like any mother would, but in my heart I believe that the most important thing to her was that I make my own decisions. That I live my own life."

"You don't know what you're talking about," her father answered dismissively. "Your mother wasn't the sort of woman who—"

"All my life I've been told that I didn't know her, that I couldn't because I was so young when she died," Lily interjected, again daring to interrupt, realizing that she'd come too far to stop now. "But I *do* remember her," she insisted. "I may not have more than a moment here and there, like the time she backed the car down the drive and knocked over the mailbox, or that she always smelled like lilacs," Lily explained, each recollection raising a wellspring of both happiness and loss inside her, just like always. Her father also seemed moved, though Lily didn't know if it was because he remembered those moments, too, or if he was surprised his daughter remembered them at all. "Mom was kind and understanding," she finished. "In in the end, she would've wanted me to be happy."

"Are…are you saying you aren't happy here?" Morris asked.

Lily took a deep breath. "You know, Dad, I'm a lot more like Jane than you think," she began. "I may not be as impulsive, and I'll never be the prettiest girl in any room she's in, but just like Jane, I have dreams of my own. I wanted to leave town just as badly as she did. And while I may not have gone through with it this time, that doesn't mean I never will."

Maybe even sooner than you think…

All day, even as she struggled with Garrett's revelation, through her confrontation with Ethel, to her confession to Jane's father and her own, Boone had never been far from Lily's thoughts. Things between them were moving fast, but she didn't mind, not one bit. She cherished every moment they were together. Every one they weren't, she found herself counting down the minutes until their separation would end. Boone had told her that he was concerned about what would happen to them when his time in Hooper's Crossing came to an end. Ever since, the possibility of going with him to the city had become more and more attractive. What would her father think if he knew what she was considering?

"As much as I want to continue this conversation," her father said as he glanced at the clock and then reached for his coat, "I'm needed elsewhere. I'm supposed to judge the Biggest Pumpkin Contest and have plenty of hands to shake. But we're going to talk about this later. When I get home—"

"I have plans tonight," Lily interrupted, feeling a touch

of anger him for trying to dismiss her, for wanting to retreat to his work rather than confront the problems that
now stood between them.

Morris paused, an arm halfway in a coat sleeve. "What
plans?"

"I'm going to the festival dance," she told him.

"With whom?"

"Boone Tatum," Lily said.

Her father's eyes narrowed suspiciously. "That photographer again? No. Absolutely not. You've been spending
too much time with him. I won't allow it."

Lily couldn't believe what she was hearing. Jane had
often complained about her own father, about how he
was always meddling in her business, but Dave Dunaway
wasn't going to interfere as his daughter tried to make her
way in the world. In comparison, Lily's dad wanted to control who took her to a dance.

"It's not up to you to decide," she said defiantly. In a
heartbeat, she was out of her seat and headed for the door.

"Lily, wait!"

"I'm going to the dance with Boone and that's final!"

Even as her father continued to call her name, Lily
quickly made her way down the hallway. She never once
looked back.

"Is that what you're planning to wear to the dance?"

Boone was just winding up, ready to throw a rubber
ball, Daisy excited and expectant at his feet, when he
stopped and looked at Marjorie. The two of them stood in

her yard, enjoying the beautiful afternoon while Clive did a little writing. The older woman had taken such a shine to the Labrador retriever that she'd gone down to the department store and bought a ball for the dog to chase. Though Marjorie had claimed she was too old to have a dog, Boone would've bet his life savings that she would have reconsidered within weeks of their leaving town.

"I was thinking about my other shirt," he said, looking down at his outfit, "but basically, yeah."

Marjorie nodded but not in a way that said she agreed with him.

"Why?" he asked. "Do you think it's a bad idea?"

Boone then launched the ball, sending it bouncing across the yard, speeding toward the bushes on the opposite end of the property. Daisy was off like a shot, a panting, whirling dervish of legs, tail, and hair. She was so fast that she easily caught the ball well before the boundary, securing it between her snapping teeth, then cutting a sharp turn to run back to where she started.

"All I'm sayin' is that this dance is probably a bit fancier than you're expectin'," Marjorie explained. "Don't get me wrong, it won't be one of those fancy gown-and-tuxedo deals you see in the movies or the rich people hold on Park Avenue. But it won't be a bunch of yokels in overalls slappin' their knees while they mosey around hay bales, either. You need to be prepared."

Daisy dropped the ball at the older woman's feet; Boone smiled, thinking that the dog wanted to make sure they were all taking part in the fun. Marjorie picked up the slippery, drool-covered thing without the least bit of disgust and tossed it. While it didn't have the same speed or distance as Boone's throw, Daisy pursued it with the same wild abandon.

"You don't want to disappoint Lily, do you?" she asked.

That was the *last* thing Boone wanted. That morning, he'd gone to see Lily at the library, but she hadn't been behind the counter or among the stacks of books. Walking back, feeling a bit discouraged, Boone realized that she had snared his heart, but he would do nothing to pull it free. He was right where he wanted to be.

"No, I don't," he answered.

"Then let me give you a bit of advice," Marjorie began. "A lot of years have passed since the last time a suitor came to court me, but there's something to be said for a man who presents himself well, who shaves his whiskers and dresses nice. Seeing that he'd made the effort always spoke louder to me than any words he might say." The older woman nudged him with her elbow, then winked. "Women notice these sorts of things."

Boone chuckled but he took Marjorie's words to heart. He wanted to make a good impression on Lily, to show her how seriously he took what was growing between them. A plan began to form in his mind. If he was going to pull it off, he had to hurry.

There was no time to waste.

Lily stepped back from the mirror, turned one way and then the other, her eyes never leaving her reflection.

She wore a red dress that started just below her knee, rose to a cinched waist, then climbed until it ended in straps across her shoulders, revealing a just-appropriate amount of skin. She liked the dress because it was stylish not old-fashioned, fancy yet not showy. Almost a dozen outfits lay in a heap across her bed, rejected for any number of reasons: wrong color, wrong cut, wrong season, wrong whatever. She'd chosen not to wear stockings, thinking that between her excitement and all the dancing she would manage to stay warm, but had added a white cardigan just in case.

She hoped that Boone would like it as much as she did.

That afternoon, he'd called her at the library to tell her he was running late and would have to meet her by the park, giving her the time and place. She had spent the rest of the day on pins and needles, obsessing about the festival dance. Fortunately, Ethel appeared to have gotten the message from their confrontation and had largely stayed out of sight, allowing Lily plenty of time to think.

And her mother had been on her mind.

If Sarah Denton were still alive, this moment would've been very different. The two of them would have gotten Lily ready together, talking about clothes, hairstyles, and all the other things that bound mothers to their daughters. Lily couldn't help but wonder if Sarah had been as nervous and excited when she and Morris had started dating. Sadly, she had no way of knowing. Instead, she would just have to listen to her heart for guidance.

Still, in one small way, Lily did feel as if her mother

was there with her. For the dance, she had chosen to wear pearl earrings that had once belonged to Sarah. Though Lily had been given them shortly after her mother's death, she'd never put them on, always telling herself that she was waiting for just the right time, that one special occasion to take them out of their box.

This was that moment.

Boone was worth it and more.

Lily took one last look at herself in the mirror, tugged at the hem of her dress to make it fall just so, and nodded. She was ready.

As ready as I'll ever be…

She grabbed her purse and left the bedroom, but no sooner had she set foot on the landing than she heard the door open downstairs.

"Lily?" her father called out. "Are you here?"

All afternoon, Lily had considered getting ready for the dance early enough to be sure she was out of the house before her father returned home. By doing so, she was sure to avoid further confrontation. But it would also make her a coward, a little girl running away from her problems. Their talk in Morris's office had been the beginning of a conversation many years in the making.

Now she had to bring it toward its end.

"I'm here, Dad," she answered.

Morris came down the hallway from the kitchen, his ample girth making the wooden floor protest beneath his heavy foot. He ran his hand over the well-worn newel ball at the bottom of the banister, then stopped to watch her descend. But Lily halted halfway down, wanting a bit of distance between them.

"You...you look beautiful, sweetie," he said with genuine sincerity.

"Are you still going to try to stop me from going to the dance?" she asked.

Her father sighed deeply, then shook his head. "No, I'm not," he answered. "Ever since you left my office, all through an afternoon spent working out the thousand details for tomorrow's Halloween parade, judging that silly pumpkin contest, I kept coming back to how I behaved toward you, the things I said, how I acted..." He paused as if, amazingly, he wasn't sure what to say next. "I wasn't fair to you..."

"You're just being overprotective," Lily replied, defending him even when she agreed with what he'd said.

"Then that's a problem. Maybe it's always been the problem," he said. "I don't know if it's because of all the years I spent raising you or it's how young you were when your mother died, but I have a hard time seeing you as the woman you've become. I can't help but see you as six, playing hide-and-seek in the laundry, laughing and laughing."

"I do the same thing, in my own way," Lily admitted, coming down the rest of the stairs. "I'm so worried about upsetting you that I forget I should be making my own way. Every baby bird leaves the nest, after all."

"I've always considered myself more papa bear than bird."

"Male bears don't raise their cubs," Lily said. "That's the mother's job."

"Really?" her father asked. "Are you sure?"

Lily shrugged. "I'm a librarian, remember?"

Morris laughed hard enough to shake his considerable bulk. But then he fell silent. He looked at Lily intently, then tenderly touched her ear, his thumb running over the pearl ornament in its lobe. "These... these were your mother's, weren't they?"

Lily nodded. No words were needed.

"I gave them to her for our one-year wedding anniversary," her father explained. "I saved and saved for them. I even skipped a meal or two," Morris said with a chuckle. "I can still see the look on her face when she opened the box. Happy, of course, but she knew they were expensive and was mad at me for spending so much money, but I didn't care. She was worth every penny."

A lone tear slid down Lily's cheek, but she made no move to wipe it away; when it neared her chin, her father did it for her.

"You like this guy, don't you?" Morris asked.

"I do," she told him truthfully.

"Must be quite a lot if you're going out wearing those earrings."

I think I'm falling in love with him.

"Think he'd ever buy you a pair?" her father asked.

Lily thought about it for a moment. "I don't know," she answered truthfully. "But from the moment I met Boone, when I bumped into him and he took my picture, he's made me feel special, as beautiful as any of the Hollywood actresses he's photographed, important as any king or president. Not even getting a handful of diamonds could be better than that."

At that, the sternness that often filled Morris's eyes fell away, revealing someone who knew firsthand how powerful love could be.

When Lily slipped into her father's open arms, squeezing him tight, it felt as if, after years of trying, they'd finally managed to turn a page.

Now they just needed to read the rest of the book.

"A hundred miles for an outfit. This girl must really be something special."

Boone glanced at Clive as the two of them leaned against the back of a bench, taking in the festival. After leaving Daisy with Marjorie, he'd spent the early afternoon on the telephone searching for a store that sold decent clothes. Once he'd finally found somewhere promising, he had dragged Clive away from his writing and set off, the Chrysler flying down the rural highways. He'd burst into the small boutique in Creston, a larger town more than an hour to the northeast, like a man possessed, hoping that it hadn't been a wasted trip. But Boone had been pleasantly surprised by what he found. He'd purchased a stylish blue shirt, a slightly darker shade of tie, black dress pants, and the fanciest pair of shoes he had ever owned. No overalls for him. His wardrobe problems solved, they'd raced back toward Hooper's Crossing, only making a quick stop at a gas station so that he could call Lily at the library and tell her he was running late.

"She's worth all this and more," Boone answered. "Trust me."

"Correct me if I'm wrong, but didn't you complain the whole drive up here from the city?" Clive asked. "Didn't you tell me not to unpack because we were going to go right back? That you had to get to Havana?" He laughed good-naturedly. "Seems to me that if we had, you would've missed out in the worst way."

"Yeah, yeah. Keep reminding me, why don't you?"

"Oh, I plan on it. Believe me."

As unexpected as meeting Lily had been, it wasn't the only crazy thing to happen on this assignment. Slowly but surely, Boone had realized that he actually sort of liked Clive. Stunned as the people back at the *Life* office would have been to hear it, Clive could even be funny; Boone had laughed at a couple of jokes during the day's drive.

Somehow, some way, they were becoming friends.

"This dance seems like a pretty big deal," Clive commented.

"That's what Marjorie told me."

The crowd had swelled in the short time they'd been there. Couples walked arm in arm, dressed nicely, smiling and laughing, excited about what was to come. A band warmed up beside the open-air dance floor, the snare of a drum here, the rising and falling scales of a trumpet there. Though the sun still colored the sky with a last smear of purple, the strings of lights had been turned on, glowing among the trees and stretching over the park.

"You owe me five bucks, you know," the writer said. "Or at least I think you do. You kissed her, didn't you?"

"I sure did." Boone glanced across the crowded park at the bakery; only a few nights before, after the movie, he'd taken Lily in his arms and touched his lips to hers. Strangely, it felt as if it had happened a month ago and yesterday, both at the same time.

He pulled out his wallet but Clive waved him off.

"No, no, no," he said. "I was just kidding. It was a joke."

"Come on. A bet's a bet."

"I don't want your money, Boone. Honest. I'm just really happy, for the both of you, even if I'm a little disappointed for myself."

"How so?"

"The whole way up here, I kind of hoped I might find someone to spend some time with," he explained. "Nothing serious. It's not like I expected I'd meet the girl of my dreams, but, well, you know what I'm talking about. The problem is, with a face like mine..." Clive began but didn't finish. Boone thought he knew the rest; even without the bruises, he wasn't much of a looker.

"What about what's-her-name? The one in Maryland? I thought she was the girl of your dreams?"

"The one who's married to another guy? The girl whom I never had the courage to tell how I felt?" The writer shook his head. "If I spend all my todays pining for what happened yesterday, I'll miss out on tomorrow."

"That's pretty deep, Professor."

Clive shrugged in answer.

"Take it," Boone said, holding out the money. "Buy yourself something to eat, or better yet ask some pretty girl if you can buy her a drink."

His partner shook his head. "Keep it."

But Boone made no move to put the bill back in his wallet.

"Can I ask you a question?" the writer said.

"Shoot."

"Would you have made me pay up if I'd lost?"

"Absolutely," Boone answered with a chuckle, then stuffed the cash into Clive's shirt pocket, where it remained.

With that, the two of them silently watched the crowd for a while longer, until Boone decided to broach a sensitive subject.

"Speaking of kisses," he began. "Back at the room—"

"I still feel terrible about what happened the other night," Clive interrupted. "How was I supposed to know that the two of you were in there? I was so embarrassed I could have died!"

"I'm not talking about then," Boone explained. "I mean tonight."

"Wait...you mean that...oh..." the writer stumbled along, finally putting it all together. "You're thinking that tonight you and Lily might..."

"I'm not assuming anything," he said emphatically. "For all I know, I'll only be lucky enough to hold her hand, which would be fine. I'm just saying that if the evening does head in that direction, our room is the only place we can go."

Clive nodded. "I understand what you're saying."

"I'm sorry to put you out."

"Don't be. Look at all this," he said, sweeping an arm across the crowded festival. "There's more than enough here to keep me busy."

"Thanks," Boone told him, and meant it. "You know, I'm not the kind of guy who easily admits he was wrong, but I didn't have you pegged right. I may not have been thrilled to get this assignment, but I'm glad I got the chance to know you a bit. You're a good guy."

Clive chuckled.

"Something I said funny?"

"I was just thinking that you're not quite what I was led to believe, either."

"Oh, yeah?"

"Walter told me that you were a conceited horse's ass who probably wouldn't give me the time of day." Clive flashed a thin, teasing smile. "But he was wrong about you. You're not all that conceited."

"Still a comedian," Boone said, then playfully slugged the writer in the arm.

The way that friends sometimes do.

Just then, as the two of them laughed, Boone noticed Lily. She stood fifteen feet away, there one moment, gone the next, then visible again among the moving people. He couldn't get a good look at her, not really, but from what he *could* see, she was more beautiful than ever. A smile spread across his face, every bit as bright as the one she was flashing at him.

"That's my cue," Clive said, seeing her and pushing off the bench. "Have fun," he added, then clapped the photographer's shoulder and melted into the crowd.

Not for the first time, Boone was glad he'd listened to Marjorie, that he hadn't assumed anything about the dance, that he had bought new clothes.

Tonight was going to be special.

Chapter Twenty-Two

LILY MOVED AS IF the music was controlling her, like she was a puppet on a string. She raised her arms, shook her hands, and tossed back her head, seeing the artificial lights blend in with the thousands of stars filling the nighttime sky. She twirled around and around, the hem of her skirt spinning. Her feet pounded out the rhythm, dancing in time to the beat until sweat glistened on her forehead and chest, quickly growing cold in the October air, though she hardly noticed. She was far too busy having fun to pay it any mind.

And so was Boone.

He was a much more experienced dancer than Lily; it was there in the confidence of his movements, how he snapped his fingers in perfect time, the way he knew just when to take her hand, pull her close, and then let her go again. Boone seemed tireless, letting one song lead straight into another, making no move to leave the dance floor. The bright smile on his face was intoxicating.

But time and again, ever since she'd spotted him leaning against the bench with Clive, there was something about Boone that kept drawing her attention.

The clothes he was wearing.

Lily knew that Boone had come to Hooper's Crossing without much more than a few things tossed into a suitcase for a trip he hadn't wanted to make in the first place. Nowhere had that been more evident than on the night of their movie date. Boone had looked nice enough but he'd been wearing the same shirt as on the day they had met. Tonight was a different story altogether. He looked stylish, like a model in a magazine. She had already noticed quite a few of the other ladies in the crowd glancing Boone's way. Clearly, he'd gone to some effort to get what he was wearing. Lily was touched, not just because it made him look that much more attractive, but because it said that he cared about her, that he'd wanted to make a good impression.

The song ended and everyone clapped.

"I need a breather," Lily said, finally feeling a bit tired.

Boone led the way to the long table of refreshments that had been set up beside the dance floor. He poured her a glass of punch that she quickly drank.

"Are you having a good time?" he asked.

"I am," she answered. "It's been a long time since I've gone dancing and it doesn't hurt that I have a partner who knows what he's doing."

He smiled and shrugged. "I've picked up a thing or two

over the years. I'm just glad I haven't stepped on your toes once," he joked.

"And I appreciate it," Lily told him. "But what was that dance step you were doing? The one where you tapped your foot, then went backward."

"It's a swing step but I have no idea what it's called," Boone explained. "The last time I was in Hollywood, I saw a fella doing it and it looked like fun. I tell you, things go in and out of fashion so fast that I can't keep track of it all. By the next time I'm out there, everyone will be on to something else."

Lily smiled on the outside, but inside she felt uneasy. Boone hadn't meant anything by it, but by mentioning Hollywood she was reminded of all the exotic places he went for *Life*. Doubt nagged at her. What could a girl from Hooper's Crossing have to offer him? But Lily fought her worries down. He was here. Now. With her. That that was all that mattered.

"Well, will wonders never cease," Boone suddenly declared, his attention drawn to something in the crowd.

"What is it?" Lily asked.

"Clive found himself a girl to dance with."

"Really? Where?"

"There," Boone said, and pointed. While the two of them had been taking a much-needed break, the band had resumed playing and the dance floor was again packed with couples. Lily looked and looked but there were too many people.

"I don't see him," she said.

"He's right there," Boone insisted, then pulled Lily closer, pressing their bodies together as he pointed straight ahead. She was no closer to noticing Clive, her view still obscured by the crowd, though she was enjoying the nearness of the photographer.

But then, just like that, she saw the writer. Clive was dancing, or at least Lily supposed he thought he was, his moves as awkward as he was, all odd angles and jutting elbows and knees. It took a little longer for Lily to see who he was with, but when she did it was a recognizable face.

"He's with Missy Lanham," she said. "She's a nice girl."

Boone paused, then asked, "Do you think she'll give him a kiss before the night is out?"

Lily considered it, then said, "Probably. The festival can be a romantic time of year, and it's not like Clive is ugly."

"Looks like he was right to give up on what's-her-name after all."

Before Lily could ask what he was talking about, the song ended and the next one began. This time, instead of a faster tune, the band began to play a slow melody.

"May I have this dance?" Boone asked and held out his hand.

"Of course," Lily said as she took it.

Boone led the way and Lily followed. With the change in the music's tempo, many couples had taken the opportunity to rest or get some refreshments, leaving plenty of room on the dance floor. When Lily placed her hands on Boone's shoulders, then took a deep breath as he put his on her waist, it felt like a spotlight was shining on them, as if everyone was watching.

But she didn't mind. Not one bit.

They moved in unison, one step at a time, their eyes locked on each other, smiling as the band played on. To Lily, it felt like a dream, one of those fantasies that she never wanted to wake up from. But she knew she didn't have to worry. This was real. Boone Tatum was here, with her, dancing. She hoped that she'd always remember the soft feel of the hair at the back of his neck, the almost-mournful wail of the clarinet, the sensation of his hands on her waist, the way the light danced in his eyes, all of it, every last detail. Even as Lily reveled in the moment, she wondered what tomorrow might bring, or the day after that, a week from now, a month, a year, a lifetime. Right then, anything seemed possible. It didn't matter if they were in Hooper's Crossing, New York City, or Rio de Janeiro; as long as they were together, everything would be all right.

"Tomorrow's Halloween, isn't it?" Boone asked, leaning down so that his lips brushed against her ear.

"Did all the pumpkins give it away?" she teased.

"You and Clive should start a comedy act," Boone said with a chuckle. "Just like Hope and Crosby."

"Why did you ask?"

"Because I'm convinced you're a witch."

Lily was a bit taken aback. "What's that supposed to mean?"

Boone's expression grew serious. "Don't take it the

wrong way," he told her. "But you've cast a heck of a spell on me."

He put his thumb beneath Lily's chin and gently lifted her face to his. Their kiss was soft, not as passionate as the one in front of the bakery and an even farther cry from those they'd shared in the darkness of his room, but it shot through Lily like fireworks all the same. She didn't care that there were other dancers swaying to the music beside them or that people in the crowd could be watching. To Lily, it felt as if she and Boone were alone beneath the twinkling stars, kissing.

No one else mattered.

Garrett walked toward the park with his hands stuffed deep in his pockets and his spirits much lower. All around him, people were celebrating, enjoying the fall festival, but he was miserable. Ever since the previous night, when he'd driven off and left Lily standing in the street, his head and heart had been in turmoil. He'd learned the hard way that his fears about revealing his romantic feelings for her had been well founded.

Lily didn't love him.

All day, Garrett had thrown himself into his job, desperate to keep the memory of his rejection at bay. Not having much of an appetite, he'd worked right through lunch, fielding every call he could, and then staying on a couple extra hours until the chief had shooed him out the door.

But it had all been for nothing. He'd heard Lily's words

over and over again in his head, like a needle skipping on a scratched record.

"I care about you...but not like that..."

It had left a bitter, angry taste in Garrett's mouth. So then why was he walking toward the park? Why, when he knew that Lily was there with Boone, the man who'd succeeded where Garrett had failed? Hadn't he suffered enough already?

As usual, he had no answers, and so he kept on walking.

Garrett could hear the band from blocks away, the notes echoing off the buildings, sounding across town. Now that he was beside the park, it was loud enough to drown out conversations, which was fine because the last thing he wanted was to have to talk to someone. The song seemed familiar, although the name escaped him, the sort of tune he'd dreamed about, twirling under the lights with Lily in his arms. The closer Garrett came to the dance floor, the more he looked, unable to resist.

And then, just like that, there she was.

They were both well dressed, like a couple out on a big date, wanting everything to be just right. Lily had her arms around the photographer's neck, while Boone had his hands on her waist. Garrett could see that they were talking, though he didn't want to guess at what was being said. Pangs of jealousy tore through him, making him gnash his teeth in anger.

But as dark as this nightmare already was, it suddenly grew darker.

Garrett watched as Boone tilted Lily's face to his, then kissed her. He stared, dumbstruck and numb, as the stark realization that he'd lost Lily forever slid inside him like a knife stuck between his ribs. He was frozen in place, unable to move, to blink, to breathe. Then he noticed an older woman standing just off the dance floor, smiling at the young couple as if she approved of the bold expression of their love. This, in some ways more than the kiss itself, made Garrett want to scream or be sick to his stomach. Maybe both.

Instead, Garrett tore his eyes away and pushed his way through the crowd, leaving more than a few people grumbling in his wake. Baring his heart to Lily had been a mistake. Coming to the park had been an even bigger one. Nothing had worked out the way he'd wanted. All his hopes and dreams were a shambles, broken into tens of thousands of pieces.

And he had no idea how to put any of it back together again.

The moon and stars looked down on Lily and Boone as they walked home, hand in hand, after the dance. Somewhere in the near distance, an owl hooted, which was followed by a dog's bark, the symphony of the night. A gentle breeze had risen, stirring the tree branches above their heads, carrying with it a chill that made Lily glad she'd brought a sweater.

What a wonderful time, better than I dreamed it could be . . .

After Boone had kissed her, they'd continued to dance,

four or five fast songs for every slow romantic one, only taking an occasional break. It had been a time of talking, laughing, and a few kisses, each of them basking in the other's company. Hours had sped past like minutes until the clock was just shy of midnight.

"I'll walk you home," Boone had told her after the bandleader announced that they were playing their final song.

But Lily had shaken her head. "I'm not ready for the night to be over yet."

He had looked at her for a while, the two of them having an unspoken conversation, then nodded. And so when they left the park, the large crowd slowly dispersing, they headed straight for his place.

Lily had no illusions about where the rest of their evening might be headed. Just because she was inexperienced didn't mean she was naive. The last time they'd been alone together at Boone's, they had ended up in his bed, sharing passionate kisses, their hands roaming across each other's bodies; who knew what would've happened if Clive hadn't interrupted them. Lily tried to convince herself that she had no reason to be nervous, that Boone was the man she'd been waiting her whole life for, but she was only partially successful. Still, if things went as she expected they would, if she ended up giving herself to him, she'd do so willingly, a young woman who made her own decisions.

When they reached Marjorie Barlow's home, the window to Boone's room was dark and the door locked. "Clive must not be back yet," Lily said.

"Maybe he's still with that Missy gal."

"What if he stumbles in on us like last time?"

"He won't," the photographer said, so confidently that Lily was certain the two men had talked about it before-hand.

That meant Boone was thinking the same way she was.

Inside, Boone turned on a light while Lily slipped out of her cardigan and wandered the room, unable to stay still. Her mind whirled, thinking about where the two of them had begun, as well as where they were going, both tonight and all of the tomorrows she hoped they would have. Walking past the table, she noticed a lone photograph; when she picked it up, Lily was a little surprised to discover that it was that first fateful shot of her on the street, the one that had started it all.

"I thought you gave this to Garrett," she said.

"I made another copy," Boone answered, coming to stand beside her. "I look at it all the time. Even when you're not around, I can't keep my eyes off you for long," he explained. "The funny thing is, I used to think that this picture was unique, that it captured something I'd be hard-pressed to see again. But the more I think about it, the more I believe that I could take a dozen shots of you and all of them would captivate me." He paused. "This shot isn't one-of-a-kind. You are."

Lily shook her head, her blond hair swinging. "I find that hard to believe."

"What makes you say that?"

"Because I'm ordinary. I've never seen myself as pretty."

Boone chuckled. "That's not up to you to decide. My opinion's the only one that matters and I say that you're the most beautiful gal I have ever laid eyes on."

She had been looking at him, but now turned away, embarrassed.

"You have a hard time taking a compliment, don't you?" he asked.

"A little," she admitted.

The truth of it was, Lily had never been on the receiving end of much romantic attention. With her glamorous looks and outgoing personality, Jane had always monopolized the boys' interest, pulling them into her orbit as if she was the sun, leaving little left over for Lily. The only compliments she'd ever really heard had come from Garrett and up until a day ago, she had always thought them to be innocent, the kind of things said between friends. So much of this, the rituals of courtship, was new to her. Lily wasn't entirely sure how she was supposed to act.

"What about you?" she asked.

Boone's eyes narrowed. "What *about* me?"

"Aren't you ever uncomfortable when someone praises you?"

"Heck no!" he declared, though she suspected he was teasing, if only a bit. "If there was a line of young ladies a city block long who wanted to tell me I was good looking, I'd stand there and listen to every last one of them."

"They'd be right," she said. "You're the handsomest man *I've* ever met."

Surprisingly, Boone looked away.

"I thought you said you could take a compliment?" she asked.

"I can," he said, "except when it comes from you."

"Why?"

"Because you're the only woman whose opinion matters," Boone told her, taking the picture from her hand and placing it back on the table. "When you're the one doing the complimenting," he continued as he slid his arms around her, pulling her close, "then it must be true."

Their first kiss was tender and soft but soon escalated into something more. Lily's lips parted, allowing their tongues to touch, which sent a shiver of excitement barreling down her spine and across her skin. Whatever reservations she might have felt about being here with him, about what could soon happen, evaporated like a puddle of water on a hot summer afternoon. She pressed her body into his, wanting to be closer, then closer still. His hand slid up her arm, across her shoulder to the skin at her collarbone, and then began to push the fabric of her dress to the side, as if he meant to begin removing it, which made Lily hold her breath.

But then he abruptly stopped.

"What's wrong?" she asked, searching his eyes for the answer.

"I want you to be sure about this," Boone told her. "Completely sure. I don't want to pressure you into doing something you aren't ready for. I don't want you to have any regrets."

A smile slowly spread across Lily's face. "I know what

I'm doing," she said, trying to reassure him. "There's nowhere else I want to be than right here, right now, with you. I know what comes next. My eyes are wide open." Staring up at him, the soft light from the lone lamp bulb throwing their shadows across the room, more words burst out of her, ones she'd always wanted to say but had never expected would be directed at a photographer from New York City. "I love you," she told him, her admission filling her with joy.

She hadn't given much thought to what Boone's reaction might be, how he might respond, but what she got was perfect. "I've never heard those words before," he told her. "I've never had the urge to say them, either. But you, Lily Denton, you make me want to shout them from the top of the Empire State Building." He rubbed his thumb across her cheek, brushed it against her lips, and then slid it down to her chin. "I love you," he said. "I love you with all I am and have."

Lily let the silence that followed linger for a moment, basking in its glow, then told him, "Shut off the light and hurry back."

Boone did as he was told, plunging the room into darkness. For Lily, the next few minutes were a blur of kisses and discarded clothing. When it was over, her dress and undergarments lay in a heap, mingled with the fancy outfit Boone had just bought. They stood before each other, naked. In the faint light, now that her eyes had had time to adjust, Lily drank him in, the muscles of his shoulders, chest, and stomach, as well as much, much more.

Once they were on the bed, lying side by side, they resumed kissing, but now it was different, hungrier, more insistent. Their hands roamed across each other's bodies, lingering briefly at one spot before moving on. Nowhere was off-limits. Lily gasped when Boone's fingers danced across her ribs and found her breast, his thumb tracing a circle around her nipple that made her skin rise in gooseflesh. She moaned into his open mouth when that same hand slid down her spine, then arced across the curve of her backside. After that, it moved between her legs, touching her in a way that no other man had, slippery in her wetness, a clear sign of how much she yearned for him. She moved her knees apart, wanting more.

"Oh, Boone..." she said, then bit her lower lip to keep from crying out.

Wanting him to feel every ounce of pleasure she did, Lily explored Boone's body. She squeezed the thick muscles of his arms. She ran her hand through his hair, her fingernails grazing his scalp. She was so intent on touching him everywhere that she eventually moved between his legs. The hardness of him surprised her, but when Lily grabbed hold and squeezed, he reacted so unexpectedly that she half expected him to leap out of the bed.

"Careful," he told her.

Covering her hand with his own, Boone guided her along the length of him, up and down, over and over, a slow rhythm that grew steadily faster. Eventually, he let go, leaving Lily in charge. She was amazed at how much pleasure she could give him. But when she picked up the pace, going faster than ever before, he abruptly stopped her midstroke.

"Not...not just yet..." Boone breathlessly told her.

He rose up, positioning himself above her, supporting his weight on his powerful arms. Lily spread her legs to allow him entry, her hands on his waist.

"Are you ready?" he asked.

Lily nodded. She was ready to become a woman.

Boone lowered himself and slowly slid inside her. At first, Lily felt an intense pain but she bore it, refusing to show discomfort or ask him to stop; she knew enough to understand this was to be expected. Inch by inch, he continued forward until they were completely joined. For a while he stayed still, allowing her time to adjust, kissing her tenderly. When he felt like she was ready, Boone began to move. There was still a bit of pain but it didn't take her long to discover the joy of lovemaking. As he slid in and out of her body, Lily felt as if she was being hauled up a mountain, higher and higher still, the air growing thinner, making her light-headed. She worked to match her movements to his, both of them headed to the same destination.

"I love you..." he gasped into her ear.

Lily wanted to reply, to tell him that she loved him in return, but when she opened her mouth no sound came out. Unexpectedly struck mute, she tried to show him how she felt through her actions, squeezing his arm as droplets of his sweat rained from his body to mix with her own. Boone moved faster and faster and the next thing Lily knew she had reached the top of the mountain; she sailed over the summit and it was like she was flying through the air, buffeted by one blast of pleasure after another, a fall leaf fluttering this way and then that on its way to the ground.

"Lily...I...I can't last any..." was all Boone managed before his body shuddered and he spilled an intense warmth inside her.

He hung above her, his arms trembling, then carefully lowered himself until he was fully on top of her. She put her arms around him and held tight.

Lying there with Boone, Lily found herself wanting the night to go on forever. The dance, their laughter, the kisses, making love to him: it was all straight out of a fairy tale. She was like Cinderella, Snow White, and Rapunzel. She'd found her handsome prince and now she wanted what all the other princesses got.

To live happily ever after.

Chapter Twenty-Three

Go GET IT, girl! Fetch the ball!"

Boone smiled as Lily tossed Daisy's ball into the yard, the retriever getting her morning exercise. Halloween had dawned brilliant and bright, though the weatherman on the radio had said that clouds and a light rain would roll in sometime that afternoon. But Boone didn't mind. Not at all.

Nothing was going to ruin his good mood.

Making love to Lily had been better than a dream come true. While Boone had been disappointed that she'd needed to leave—he would have preferred she spend the night with him in his bed—he understood that she hadn't wanted to upset her father. Besides, on the walk back from Lily's home, he had found Clive shivering on the sidewalk; the poor guy would've rather caught pneumonia than interrupt them again. Amazingly, before Boone had drunk the morning's first cup of coffee, Lily was there at the door, a bag of doughnuts in hand, ready to start another day together.

"Give me that disgusting thing," Lily said with a laugh, picking up Daisy's soggy ball and throwing it away.

The dog barked once, then was off, living up to her breed's name.

With all that had happened the last couple of days, Boone was surprised to realize that this was the first time Lily and Daisy had met. But the two had quickly made up for lost time. The dog had taken an instant liking to Lily, running to her, barking playfully, then rolling over onto her back for a belly rub. Lily returned the retriever's affection, doing lots of petting and tirelessly tossing the ball.

As if Boone needed another sign that she was special.

The dog loves her just as much as I do.

His thoughts were interrupted by the phone in his room ringing. At first, Boone didn't move, assuming that Clive would get it, but the noise persisted. Thinking that the writer must be in the shower, he excused himself and went inside to answer it. "Hello," he said into the receiver.

"I gotta admit, I figured you'd be long gone from there by now." Boone immediately recognized the voice on the other end of the line: it was Walter Bing, his editor back at *Life* magazine. From the sounds in the background, shouting voices and typewriters, he was calling from his office.

"This place is more interesting than I expected," he replied.

"I don't know how that's possible, but I suppose I should be glad. Did you get me some good shots?"

"Rolls of 'em. One in particular might be good enough for the cover."

Walter chuckled. "Figures that I send you to the middle of nowhere and you still manage to snap something great," the editor said.

"And I didn't even get arrested to take it."

"You ain't outta there yet," the magazine man kiddingly cautioned. "Anything else happen worth mentioning?"

Boone considered telling him about the robbery but decided against it. In the end, they hadn't lost anything of consequence, and besides, the new pictures he and Lily had taken might even be better than the originals. If needed, he could always tell Walter later. "Not really," he answered.

"How's Clive working out?"

"He's good. A hell of a lot better than I expected," Boone admitted truthfully. "He still asks too many questions, but his writing looks sharp." A memory from the previous day came to mind, something that Clive had told him. "He said that you'd warned him about me. That I could be a conceited horse's ass."

Walter paused, but only briefly. "He did, huh?"

Boone found the editor's response slick, neither an admittance nor a denial. Like the robbery, he decided it wasn't worth talking about.

"Look, today's Halloween so I'm gonna expect the two of you to be back here by the day after tomorrow at the latest," Walter continued, barely skipping a beat. "We'll take a look at your shots, Clive can put the finishing touches on his article, and that'll be that. I've already got both of your next assignments lined up."

"Havana?" Boone asked, remembering how badly he'd wanted to go only a week earlier, how it was the only thing that had mattered to him.

"You've earned it, kid," Walter told him. "I gotta admit, I had my doubts. I figured you'd crack and give the higher-ups a reason to send you packing, but you've really come through. And what a reward! Just think about all those sandy beaches, those drinks with the little umbrellas in 'em, and all the girls! Heck, maybe I oughta be the one goin' instead," he added with a hearty laugh. "We can iron out all the details when you're back. Day after tomorrow, got it?"

"Sure," Boone managed before Walter hung up.

He stood there for a long time, the receiver buzzing in his hand, thinking about how much his life had changed in such a short time, how coming to Hooper's Crossing had been like a fork in the road, forever altering his life's trajectory. Boone no longer cared about the Caribbean sand or other women.

And it was all because of Lily.

In a matter of days, Boone would return to the city. He'd fill the Chrysler's trunk with their belongings and put Daisy in the backseat while Clive rolled down his window, probably stifling a sneeze. But Boone hoped that there would be another passenger joining them, someone he couldn't bear to be without.

He wanted Lily to come with them.

Halloween had always been Lily's favorite time of year. It wasn't just because of all the fun she'd had as a kid trick-ortreating with Jane and Garrett, running down the sidewalks, dragging a wagon to haul their candy. And it also wasn't on account of the decorations that hung in store windows and on porches, paper ghosts, pumpkins, and ugly witches. It wasn't even because of the scary films she used to watch at the movie theater, nervously peeking through her fingers at Dracula, the Wolf Man, and other cinematic terrors.

To Lily, the best thing about Halloween had always been the festival parade.

She and Boone were part of a huge crowd massed along Main Street. It felt like all of Hooper's Crossing was there, as well as plenty of out-of-towners. Much of the parade was the expected fare: veterans who'd served during the Second World War and in Korea wore their uniforms as they marched in formation; a band played, the autumn sun shining on trumpets, tubas, and trombones; town dignitaries rode in the back of convertibles, Lily's father in one of the first cars, waving wildly to their constituents and the outsiders who brought plenty of money to town.

But what set this parade apart, what made it *unex-pected*, were the touches that reflected the day's holiday: a "headless" horseman galloped up and down the street, far from Sleepy Hollow but still plenty scary; one float depicted a graveyard, with tombstones blanketed in a creepy fog created by buckets of dry ice; Vince Rollins, the local postmaster, did his best Victor Frankenstein on another float, shouting "It's alive!" as Cliff Turner, the town's butcher, rose from a table and stumbled around, the mad scientist's creation come to life.

"This is amazing!" Boone said as he looked through the camera's viewfinder, snapping pictures.

And he was right. It *was* amazing.

But try as she might, Lily was having a hard time concentrating on the parade. Her mind raced, her thoughts returning again and again to her time in Boone's bed, the warmth of his body against hers, the passion of their lovemaking. When added to all of the emotions he inspired in her, the laughter they'd shared, Lily realized that Boone had become a treasured part of her life. She was determined to keep it from ending.

So how did they stay together?

The answer to that question was amazingly simple. It just required a difficult decision.

Lily leaned toward Boone, the noise from the parade echoing between the buildings and making it hard to hear. "Can I ask you a question?"

"Sure," he answered, still taking pictures.

She paused. "It's important."

Boone lowered his camera and looked at her, giving Lily his undivided attention. "What is it?"

Before she could answer, the band began to play another song. Knowing that she'd never be heard over the din, Lily took Boone's hand and the two of them made their way through the crowd. Incredibly, they found themselves back in front of the bakery; Sally Lange leaned against her doorway, enjoying the parade. It was still loud, but it would have to do.

"Do . . . do you remember when I suggested that I might want to go with you to New York City?" she asked.

"Of course I do. How could I possibly forget?"

"I've given it a lot of thought," Lily began, worried about how he might react, knowing full well what she was asking of him, "and I want to do it."

She braced herself, fearful of rejection.

"Yes!" he emphatically shouted, smashing her doubts to pieces.

"Are you sure?" she asked, still not completely convinced. "I wouldn't want to be a burden."

Boone shook his head. "You wouldn't be, not in a million years," he told her. "I was thinking about it ever since you first mentioned it. I *want* you to come with me. I want to show you the city. Central Park. This dress shop I took pictures of on the Upper East Side. There's this Italian place on Mulberry Street that has the best spaghetti sauce I've ever had, even in Rome. I want to show you all of it."

Even as a smile began to spread across her face, Lily tried to hold it back, worried that this was all too good to be true. "I'm serious."

"I am, too," he insisted. "I told you before that I'd never lead you on and I meant it. I don't want this to end. Come with me. Let's take a . . . a leap of faith . . . and start a life together." He paused. "I love you, Lily."

Relief flooded her heart. She was about to accept when Boone's smile unexpectedly began to fade. "What's wrong?" she asked.

"I just remembered something."

"What?" Lily pressed.

Boone ran a hand through his hair and asked, "The

last time you wanted to leave town, you got cold feet, right?"

Whenever Lily thought about the night she'd planned to go with Jane to the city, she was filled with shame. Even though staying in Hooper's Crossing had resulted in her meeting Boone, changing her life forever, she still felt like a coward, a terrible friend for abandoning Jane. But this wasn't like before. Far from it. Lily had found new strength and conviction. She wasn't the same person.

"I don't want to end up disappointed," Boone continued. "I'd rather you back out now than get my hopes up."

"This *is* what I want," Lily told him, taking his hand and squeezing it, trying to prove her sincerity. "I've never wanted something more."

Boone paused, thinking, but a smile began to slowly spread across his face. "All right. Then this is your last day in Hooper's Crossing for a while," he explained. "Tomorrow, we leave for the city."

Nervous excitement coursed through Lily. Even though she'd spent her whole life here, a lot of that time spent dreaming of being somewhere else, Lily was finally ready to go. She felt it deep inside. She would miss her father, friends, and familiar places, but with Boone at her side, she was determined to see what the rest of the world had to offer.

"I'll be ready," she said. "But that's tomorrow. What about tonight?"

"What about it?" he asked, his eyes narrowing.

"Tonight is the Halloween party, the end of the festival," Lily answered. "You have a costume, don't you?"

"Costume? No one said anything about a costume. Besides, I'll be busy working."

"You can do both at the same time."

"I don't know ..." he said, looking a little uneasy.

"Don't be a stick in the mud," Lily told him. "Come over to my house this afternoon and we'll see if we can't come up with something."

"Clive's going to need one, too," Boone said, as if he didn't want to suffer alone.

"I'll come up with a costume for Daisy if I have to."

The photographer laughed, then lowered his head and gave her a gentle kiss; out of the corner of her eye, Lily noticed that Sally Lange was watching them, a pleasant smile on her face. But Lily didn't mind the attention. She no longer worried about who might notice them. Not now. Not ever again.

But when Lily stepped back, ending their kiss, she saw something over Boone's shoulder that made her realize she'd been mistaken.

There, at the edge of the crowd, wearing his policeman's uniform, was Garrett. He was looking right at her.

He'd seen everything.

Lily stared at Garrett, horrified to think of what he'd just witnessed. He looked hurt, angry, even disappointed, all at the same time. Briefly, she wondered if he would come over and make a scene, but he did the opposite, turning on his heel to walk away. Lily knew that she had to talk to him. Right now.

"I have to go," she told Boone.

"Why?" he asked, then looked over his shoulder, trying to understand what had grabbed her attention. All he caught was Garrett's back as he disappeared into the crowd, but it was enough. Lily thought he might not want her to leave, that he might be a little possessive, jealous even, but Boone surprised her. "I wish he hadn't seen that," he said with a grimace.

"Me, either," Lily agreed, suddenly realizing that she'd never told the photographer about Garrett's declaration of love for her. In the end, she decided that it didn't matter; the trouble between she and her lifelong friend didn't interfere with her love for Boone. It was her problem to fix.

"Are you going to tell him that you're leaving town?" he asked.

Lily nodded. She had to. By this time tomorrow, it might already be too late. She couldn't imagine leaving Hooper's Crossing without settling things with Garrett. He was too important to her.

They quickly made plans to meet later that afternoon to work on costumes, but when she turned to leave, Boone put a hand on her arm. "Good luck," he told her. "I hope things work out, for the both of you."

"Thank you" Lily said, then set off in search of Garrett.

She entered the crowd, pushing her way in the direction Garrett had gone. Her head turned this way then that, hoping for a glimpse of his uniform. She craned her neck but saw nothing. It was as if the parade had swallowed him up. But just when Lily was about to give up hope, the throng of people briefly parted in front of the drugstore and she saw him. Garrett was talking with someone; from the way he pointed down the street, it looked as if he was giving directions. Seizing the opportunity, Lily hurried to him.

"Garrett, wait," she said as he turned from the out-of-towners.

He seemed genuinely surprised to see her, then looked around as if he expected Boone to be there as well. "I'm working, Lily."

"I don't care," she replied defiantly. "We need to talk."

"No, we don't," he disagreed with a shake of his head. "Not anymore," he added and made to walk away, but Lily grabbed his arm, holding him fast.

"That's the way you're going to deal with this?" she demanded. "By ignoring me?"

"What do you expect me to do?" Garrett snapped, finally showing some of the emotion she was sure was churning around inside him. "Should I take it all back, tell you that I don't really love you, that it was all a joke? Would that make you feel better when you're kissing *him*?"

Lily recoiled from his hurtful words. But she wasn't going to back down. "Of course not," she said. "I'm glad you told me."

"Glad?" he repeated incredulously. "What, did you enjoy breaking my heart?" His pain overflowing, Garrett tried to pull his arm from Lily's grasp, but as strong as the young policeman was, her determination to mend what was broken between them was stronger.

"I didn't know you felt that way!" she insisted. "Maybe

I was too blind to see it, maybe I was stupid, but all these years, I had no idea! To me, you were—"

"Like a brother to you," Garrett finished for her, then sighed deeply. He looked tired, worn down, as if revealing what he'd kept hidden in his heart had aged him. "Can't we talk about this later?" he asked. "Once the festival is done, I'll come over and we can sit on your porch and—"

"It can't wait," Lily interrupted. The first blow she'd struck against Garrett had been when she hadn't returned his feelings, but what she needed to tell him now would be just as much of a shock, maybe more. She took a deep breath, then said, "I'm leaving town..."

"What?" he blurted, as stunned as Lily had expected him to be. "When?"

She looked him in the eyes. "Tomorrow."

Garrett's initial surprise quickly turned into anger. "This is all because of Boone, isn't it?" he demanded. But rather than give her a chance to answer, he kept on. "No. No, you can't. It's too much, too fast. You don't know him well enough to make a decision like that. If he's pressuring you to go—"

"It isn't like that," Lily told him, her voice steady as she tried to calm him. "I've wanted to leave for a long time. For years. As a matter of fact, I should already be gone."

"What are you talking about?"

"Do you remember that night you scared me with your flashlight out in front of my house?"

He thought about it for a moment, then nodded. "What about it?"

"Twenty minutes before, I'd been in Jane's car, both of our suitcases in the backseat, headed out of town to try to make it in New York City."

"You're joking," he said with a skeptical chuckle.

"No, I'm not."

Garrett's brow furrowed. "So why are you still here?"

"Because I was afraid," Lily admitted. "I couldn't bring myself to leave my father, you, the only life I've ever known. I got cold feet and Jane went by herself."

"And now you're no longer scared?" he asked.

Lily shook her head. "I'm still afraid, at least a little," she answered. "But I'm not going to let it define me or keep me from doing what I want."

"I suppose you have Boone to thank for that…"

"He's the reason for some of it," Lily agreed. "But this is about more than Boone. If I don't take a chance now, then I'm going to spend the rest of my life wondering about what might have been. I don't want those kinds of regrets." She paused, then gave him a thin smile. "And maybe I'll fail," Lily said, echoing what she'd told her father. "Maybe the city and all the cars and people will be too much for me and I'll come back home, but at least I would've tried. Can't you understand that?"

But then, just as Garrett was about to answer, a man rushed over to the policeman and pointed back in the direction he'd come. "Officer, there's a woman over there who feels faint," he said. "I don't know if it's too much sun or too many people, but I think she needs a doctor."

Garrett turned back to Lily. "I have to go, but we'll talk

again soon," he said, already rushing away. "Whatever happens, don't leave until we do."

Lily watched him go as the band continued to play, the crowd still cheered, and the monsters on the Halloween floats kept doing their best to scare, little changed from last year, and the year before that, and so on.

But for Lily, nothing was the same, and she doubted it ever would be again.

Randall took one last look at Lily's picture before putting it in his duffel bag. He and Leo had spent the morning and early afternoon packing up all their stuff, checking and rechecking the cabin to make sure they hadn't left anything behind. No trace of them being there could remain, not even their trash. After tonight, after they'd robbed the Hooper's Crossing Bank and Trust of piles of cash, the police would be looking for them, so the fewer leads they had to go on, the better.

"Let's go over the plan again," Leo said, taking a seat at the small table.

His partner sighed. "We been over it plenty."

"One more time won't hurt."

"Look, I know you think I'm impulsive, that I don't pay as much attention as you'd like, but I could do this job in my sleep," Randall told him. "We can talk 'bout whatever you want on the ride to town, but you gotta trust me on this. I ain't gonna let you down."

The older thief looked at him for a long moment, his expression hard to read. Randall expected him to start in on the plan anyway, but Leo surprised him. "Fair enough," he said, then added, "You got your costume?"

"It's in the car," Randall answered, though he wished it was in the bag with the rest of the trash. He felt like a god-damn idiot with it on, even if he had to admit that Leo had a point, that by dressing up in Halloween getups they'd be able to move among the crowd without attracting attention.

"How about your gun?"

Randall pulled the pistol from the rear of his waistband and held it up to catch the light of the slowly setting sun. He'd diligently cleaned it, swabbing out its chambers, and putting every last bullet back where it belonged; he might run wild with his own body from time to time, but he'd always taken immaculate care of his weapons. "It's ready to be used if needed."

"Let's hope it don't come to that," Leo said. "The last thing we want is to shoot someone. It'd bring all the sorts of attention we're lookin' to avoid."

Randall nodded even if he didn't share his partner's concern. If someone was stupid enough to get in his way, they'd catch a bullet, attention be damned.

Leo got up out of his chair. "Let's go."

They had a bank to rob.

Chapter Twenty-Four

I'M GOING TO look like an idiot."

Lily looked up from where she sat on the floor of her living room, surrounded by a pincushion, scissors, pieces of cardboard, masking tape, pens, and a dozen other items she was using to create a pair of Halloween costumes. Boone's face was full of displeasure as he stared at the white sheet in his hand; a couple of holes had been cut into the old, worn fabric so that its wearer could see.

He wouldn't be a particularly scary ghost, but a ghost he would be.

"There's only one way to find out," she replied.

Boone's frown deepened. "I think I'd prefer the mystery of never knowing."

"Do you want to trade?" Clive asked from the couch.

The writer had been braver than his colleague and actually tried on the costume Lily had come up with. With a liberal use of aluminum foil and cardboard, she'd made him look like a robot from outer space, something straight out of a Saturday matinee. His helmet, with two huge antennae made from an untwisted coat hanger, sat beside him, as of yet unworn. He hadn't been *that* brave.

"No thanks," Boone answered with a laugh, making no effort to hide how ridiculous he thought his friend looked. "I'll keep the sheet."

"Come on," Clive pleaded, shaking his silver arms. "Be a pal."

"Forget it." Turning his attention to Lily, Boone asked, "Are you sure we have to wear these silly getups?"

"You want to fit in, don't you?" she replied.

"Technically, we're supposed to be working tonight," Clive chimed in.

"What he said," Boone agreed.

"You can do both."

"I wonder what Walter would say about this?" Clive asked.

"He'd probably fire us on the spot," Boone answered.

Lily smiled. As much as the two of them complained now, she was sure that they'd be singing a different tune later. After all, they'd never been to the festival's Halloween night celebration before and didn't know what was in store for them. "If you're coming with me tonight," she said, "then you're going to have to dress for the occasion."

"You still haven't told us what you'll be wearing," Boone pressed.

"That's because it's a secret."

"I suppose that means we're supposed to guess," the

photographer said with a shrug. "How about the Bride of Frankenstein?"

"Dorothy from *The Wizard of Oz*?" Clive suggested.

"How about Rita Hayworth in a slinky dress?" Boone asked. "Now, that's an outfit I'd be all in favor of and then some."

"Guess all you want," Lily told them, "but my lips are sealed."

But as fun as the afternoon had been, Lily felt distracted, her attention periodically torn from the good times and taken back to her conversation with Garrett. She had wanted to fix what was wrong between them and didn't like that she'd failed, at least for now. Would she see her old friend tonight? Or would she leave town without making one last attempt to heal Garrett's wounded heart?

Shaking off her nagging thoughts, Lily got to her feet and took the sheet from Boone's hands. "Enough complaining," she said. "Try this thing on and make sure it fits." Lily draped the sheet over the photographer's head, adjusted it so that the eyeholes were where they were supposed to be, and stepped back to examine her work.

"I can't see a thing in this," Boone grumbled.

"Then I'll make the holes bigger."

"How am I supposed to take pictures?" he kept on, raising his arms as if he wanted to bring a camera to his eye, finally managing to look a little spooky.

"You'll figure something out," Lily said.

More than likely, Boone would just take off the sheet and that would be that. Still, that he'd go along with it even for a while, that he was willing to have some fun, said a lot. It was one of the things she liked most about—

Lily was interrupted by the opening of the back door near the kitchen.

"Honey? Are you here?" her father called out.

Even as she'd extended the invitation to Boone and Clive to come to her home, Lily had known that her father could appear at any moment. After their talk the day before at the bottom of the stairs, she felt as if they'd taken a step forward, but if Morris was in the same room as the photographer who had captured his daughter's heart, there was no telling what might happen. But that didn't necessarily mean it shouldn't.

"I'm in here," she answered.

Morris came through the door focused on the folded newspaper in his hand, then stopped short when he realized that Lily wasn't alone. "Oh, I didn't know you had company," he said.

Clive managed to stand up in his robot costume, then tottered, finally losing his balance and falling back onto the couch. "It's good to see you again, Mr. Denton," he offered.

"That's some outfit you have on, son," Lily's father said with a chuckle.

"Thank you," the writer replied, clearly feeling plenty foolish.

"Don't be embarrassed. Tonight, you'll fit right in."

Boone pulled off his sheet, crossed the room, and extended his hand to Morris. "I hope we aren't intruding, sir."

Lily's father hesitated a moment before taking the offered greeting. "Not at all," he said pleasantly enough, although Lily noticed that some of the humor had left his voice. "As a matter of fact," Morris continued, "I'm glad you're here. I was hoping the two of us might have a talk."

"Dad..." Lily said, not liking the idea one bit.

"It's all right," Boone told her, then turned his attention back to the older man. "I'd be happy to."

"Why don't we step outside?" Morris suggested, then headed for the front door without waiting for an answer. Boone followed, showing no hint of concern, as if having a chat with Lily's father was the most natural thing in the world. Before he closed the door behind him, he gave Lily a smile and a wink.

"Is that something to be worried about?" Clive asked after they were gone.

Lily didn't reply.

For the life of her, she had no idea how to answer.

Boone followed Lily's father outside, then shut the door behind them. Morris walked to the far end of the porch, his hand running along the railing.

"You know, I always wondered what you would look like," he said, his back still turned to Boone. "I didn't know if you'd be blond or dark-haired, tall or short, heavy like me or thin. I hoped that you'd be a lawyer, a doctor, or a policeman," Morris explained, staring across the street. He paused, then looked directly at Boone. "I never considered that you would be a magazine photographer from New York City. The thought never crossed my mind."

Though Boone's first instinct was to speak up, it was obvious to him that Lily's father had more to say.

"I'm talking about the man who would come along one day and steal my little girl's heart," Morris continued. "The man who'd finally convince her to leave the only home she's ever known."

"Lily's not a girl anymore," Boone said. "She's more than capable of making her own decisions."

Morris leaned his considerable bulk against the railing and sighed deeply. "Lily has made that abundantly clear to me," he explained. "Even though to me she'll always be six years old, she's all grown up now, a young woman, plain and simple. With all that's happened lately, I'd have to be blind not to see it." He paused, as if weighing his words. "Did you know that she almost ran away to the city with her friend?"

Boone nodded. "I'm glad she didn't. If she had, we never would have met."

"But she plans to go eventually, doesn't she?"

His question put Boone in a tough spot. On the one hand, he didn't want to betray Lily; it was both her right and responsibility to tell her father. On the other, he didn't want to lie. "That's her intention," he admitted, choosing to give some but not all of the story.

"Because of you." Morris hadn't asked a question; to Boone's ears it sounded more like an accusation, as if he was being blamed.

"You may not know me well, Mr. Denton," Boone began, "but you strike me as a good judge of character. As mayor, I'm sure you've met hundreds, heck, thousands of people. From the moment they shake your hand or look you in the eyes, I bet you get a pretty good read on them. Some are honest, friendly, and hardworking. Others might be liars, complainers, or lazy. Most are somewhere in between. Knowing all that, when we first met in your office, I'd be plenty surprised if you came away with a bad impression of me."

Morris didn't answer; to Boone, it was the same as saying he was right.

So he decided to get right to the point.

"I'm in love with Lily," he said.

Her father's reaction wasn't severe, but it was noticeable. Morris's eyes widened and his lips parted as his jaw dropped open.

"Because of my job with *Life*, I've been all over the world, from Paris to Shanghai, and I've *never* met a woman like her," Boone continued, smiling as he thought of all the ways Lily had unexpectedly changed his life. "She's smart, funny, everything I've ever wanted and a whole lot more. Lily has made me think about where I've been, where I am, and, most important, where I'm going. Amazingly, she's even made me realize that I'm not always as right about things as I think I am," he added with a smirk. "That day I bumped into her on the street? Most people would think it was an accident, but I'm starting to believe it was meant to be. And as to where we go from here, I can honestly tell you, wherever it is, I want Lily to be by my side."

"In New York City," Morris said, again not asking a question.

"If that's what she wants, then that's where we'll be," Boone answered. "Wherever it is, I promise you that I will take care of her, that I'll be true to Lily and love her more and more every day. You won't have a reason to worry."

The older man barked out a humorless laugh. "But I *will* worry," he contradicted Boone. "That's what a parent does. A father knows what's best for his child, which is why I'm still not convinced that this is the right decision for Lily."

Boone paused, contemplating whether he wanted to ask the question that had sprung to mind as he listed to Morris; in the end, he decided to go through with it, believing Lily to be worth the risk. "What would your wife have said?"

"Excuse me?" her father asked, his tone unhappy with a hint of anger.

"I asked about Lily's mother. I wondered what she would—"

"Don't even begin to think you'd know what Sarah would say about this," Morris interrupted, pushing off the railing.

"You're right. I wouldn't have the slightest idea what she would say or think," Boone admitted, his voice calm, standing his ground, his eyes never leaving those of the other man. "But Lily claims she knows."

Morris's unhappiness stalled when he heard this. "She does?" he sputtered. "What... what did she tell you...?"

"That her mother would've understood why she wanted to leave," Boone answered. "That when you got right down to it, she would have wanted her daughter to be happy." He paused, letting his words hang between them for a moment, then added, "But Lily couldn't know, not really. How old was she when her mother died? Eight?"

"Six," her father corrected.

"I'm sure she has some memories, a snippet here and there, but Lily couldn't possibly know the kind of person your wife was, how she would feel about an important decision like this. The only person who *would* know is you."

Morris looked away. Silence settled on the porch, but Boone wasn't about to be the one to break it. When Lily's father finally spoke, his voice lacked its characteristic timbre. "She told me something like this yesterday," he began. "When she said it, I didn't give it much thought. I was too busy being telling her I was disappointed and that she couldn't go with you to the dance. But maybe I should've listened closer. Maybe she did know her mother.

"You see, Sarah was the most amazing woman I'd ever known," he continued. "When we met it was like a thunderbolt shot across my heart. She was always beside me, guiding me, willing to tell me I was wrong even if I was convinced I was right. She taught me what was really important in life, and that's family." He paused, gathering himself. "After . . . after she died, I did the best I could, raising Lily in a way that I hoped Sarah would have approved. I wanted our girl to grow up the same

as if her mother hadn't been taken from her, from us."
Morris shook his head. "I know that's impossible, but I
tried all the same."

"The way I see things, you couldn't have done any better," Boone told him.

"Maybe you're right," Morris agreed. "You and Lily
both."

"About her mother?"

The older man nodded, then took a deep breath. "Sarah
would have wanted Lily to be happy," he said. "To chart
her own course in life, even if she made a mistake here and
there. If Lily wanted to go, if she was committed to leaving
Hooper's Crossing, Sarah would've encouraged her to do
just that."

"If Lily leaves, it will be her choice to make," Boone
said. "But if that's what she decides to do, I'll do everything
I can to keep her happy and safe."

Morris smiled, then clapped a heavy hand on Boone's
shoulder. "You better, or this angry papa bear will be down
to the city to set you straight."

Boone had no doubt that Lily's father would do exactly
that.

By the time Lily, Boone, and Clive arrived at Main Street,
the fall festival's Halloween celebration was in full swing.
Candlelight danced from inside dozens of hollowed-out
pumpkins; some of their faces had been carved to display
smiles, while many others showed scary, toothy grins. Stations for games had been set up all around downtown,

with tubs of water so that people could bob for apples, and blindfolds to make it hard to pin the tail on the donkey. The moon kept sliding in and out of thin rows of dark clouds, a spooky sight given the date. A lone violin produced a mournful sound, like something a troupe of traveling Gypsies might play in a Hollywood horror picture, at least before the monster showed up.

But what really caught the eye was all the people.

Men, women, and children walked around in costume. Lily saw princesses and witches, Superman and Dick Tracy, goblins and vampires, President Truman and Joe DiMaggio. There were plenty of ghosts like Boone, other people who hadn't given their outfits much thought or had run out of time, and a few robots like Clive, some more sophisticated and others less, but the two magazine men fit right in, as if they were locals.

As for Lily, she was dressed as Little Red Riding Hood. She had a skirt, a crimson cloak, and a matching hood that covered her blond hair. She'd even brought along a picnic basket as a prop. Lily had been working on her costume for months but had set it aside when she thought she'd be going to New York City with Jane. All it had needed was a few stitches along the seam of the hood, which she'd completed that afternoon.

"I guess this means I'm the wolf tonight," Boone had said when he saw her.

"You better hope not," Clive told him.

"Why not?"

"Because the wolf gets killed at the end of the story," the

writer had explained. "You want to be the woodsman who rescues her."

"Fine with me," Boone had said, then joked, "You can be Red's grandma."

They walked around the festival to take in the sights, grabbed a bite to eat, and marveled at the costumed crowd. Clive wanted to interview people, but kept dropping his pencil before he could ask any questions. Worse, he needed Boone to pick it up because his clunky robot outfit made it impossible for him to bend.

"Next time it falls," Boone said, "I'm gluing it to your hand."

Nearing the park, they noticed that there was a costume contest. Entrants walked across a stage so the judges could get a good look at them.

"That *has* to be in the article!" Clive exclaimed and then hurried off, hobbling as fast as his cardboard-covered legs would let him.

But Boone held back. He took Lily's hand, the act a bit awkward since he was covered in a sheet. Even though she couldn't see his face, his eyes spoke volumes; they roamed over her full of happiness and love, the gaze of a man wanting nothing more than to be where he was. "I haven't had a chance to tell you, what with Clive around," he said, "but I think you look beautiful tonight."

"You're handsome yourself," she teased, "at least the parts I can see."

He chuckled. "Still the comedian."

Lily smiled, but then her expression grew more serious.

"I wish you'd tell me what you and my dad talked about on the porch."

When Boone and Morris had stepped back inside, both of them looked happy, as if whatever issues there were between them had been ironed out. But later, when Lily had pressed the photographer for details, he'd explained that it didn't matter, that they'd each had a chance to say what needed to be said.

"We came to an understanding," Boone told her.

"About what?"

"You," he answered. "If you decide to come with me to the city—"

"Not *if*," Lily insisted. "*When*."

"All right, all right," Boone said as he raised his hands beneath the sheet, which made him look more spectral than ever. "When we leave town, I don't think your father will get in the—"

But before he could say more, Boone was once again cut off, this time by Clive. "Come on, will you!" the writer exclaimed as he returned to tug at his partner's sheet. "You need to take some pictures! There's a shot we can't afford to miss!"

Boone slapped Clive's hand away, then turned to Lily. "Duty calls, I suppose," he said. "Want to go check it out?"

"I'm going to stay here," she answered with a shake of her head. "Since this is the last I'll see of this place for a while, I want to take it in on my own."

His head nodded beneath the sheet. "That sounds like a good idea. I'll come find you when we're done." Boone started after Clive but then stopped. "Make sure you keep an eye out for the big, bad wolf, okay, Red?"

Lily smiled. "If I see him, I promise to yell."

"Come at the bank from the north."

"I know."

"I'll make my way from the east and meet you by the door off the alley. If you see any cops or people hangin' around, move to the corner of Eighth and Roosevelt. We'll wait awhile and keep tryin' till the coast is clear."

Randall looked over the roof of the car and, for the first and likely only time, was glad he was wearing a sheet over his head. Staring at Leo, the older thief dressed like a cowboy, a real gun in his holster, he sneered then rolled his eyes, fed up with all the endless planning and worrying. It was probably for the best that Leo couldn't see his face.

As Randall made to leave, Leo couldn't resist adding one last order. "Remember, don't use your gun unless you ain't got any other choice. This whole thing will go straight to hell in a handcart if someone gets shot."

Randall took a deep breath, nodded beneath his sheet, then walked off.

The closer he got to downtown, the busier things got. Parents led children door-to-door, the costumed brats screaming "trick-or-treat" and sticking out their buckets and bags the second someone answered. With the white sheet turning him into a ghost, his bag of safecracking tools hidden beneath, Randall moved easily among the people, just another festivalgoer, enjoying Halloween.

On the north end of Main Street, he doubled back, headed for the bank. Randall had to admit that Leo's plan made sense. There was a door near the alley that was partially obscured by a bush and some trash cans. If no one was around, they could pick the lock, slip inside, and get right to work. Once finished, it'd be easy to carry off bags of cash under their costumes. They would be long gone before anyone got wise to the robbery.

And then I can find a game of cards, a good-time gal, and a drink.

Walking down the sidewalk, Randall barely managed to dodge a pint-size Indian warrior decked out in a feathered headdress and face paint as he whooped and hollered his war cry. He chuckled. After all the time spent crammed in the cabin with only Leo for company, it was nice to be outside, to be among other people. He couldn't help but enjoy himself.

But then Randall saw something that stopped him in his tracks.

"Holy shit," he said out loud.

There, standing on the corner no more than ten feet away, was Lily. She was wearing a costume, but it was definitely her; with the cape and hood, it wasn't hard for Randall to figure she was supposed to be Little Red Riding Hood. Crazy as it was, seeing her dressed like that made Lily even more attractive to him, a bit exotic, in a way. Randall carefully looked around, but there was no sign of the *Life* magazine photographer. Maybe the son of a bitch had already left town. Maybe they'd split up. Whatever the reason, this was his chance to see her again, maybe even touch...

Still, Randall hesitated.

Right now, he was supposed to be on his way to the bank. If he was late, Leo would be worried, angry, or both. It could put the robbery in jeopardy. But the more Randall looked at Lily, the more convinced he became that he had a few minutes to kill. He was only a block or so away. What could it hurt to take a closer look? When he was done, he'd go to the bank, and Leo would be none the wiser.

So Lily wanted to be the girl in the fairy tale?

That was fine by Randall. He had no problem being the wolf.

Chapter Twenty-Five

GARRETT DRUMMED HIS FINGERS on his desk at the police station. He leaned back in his chair and stared at the ceiling. He doodled in a notebook. He did anything and everything he could think of to take his mind off Lily, Boone, and the fact that the two of them were going to leave town together. Tomorrow.

But nothing worked.

For as long as Garrett could remember, he had loved this night, the fall festival in full swing, everyone in costume, celebrating Halloween. But now he just wanted it to be over. A couple of weeks ago, he'd had high hopes that he would confess his feelings to Lily and his life would change forever.

And in a way it had. Just not the way he'd wanted.

Still, he hadn't given up, not completely. Garrett tenaciously clung to the hope that he could convince Lily to stay. All he needed was time. If they were alone, he was sure that he could—

His thoughts were interrupted when the station telephone began to ring. Garrett would have preferred that
someone else answer, but the only other officer was busy
putting a drunk in a cell. Garrett sighed, then picked up
the receiver. "Hooper's Crossing Police."

"Evenin'. I'm trying to reach an Officer Doyle," the
caller said.

"Speaking."

"This is Detective Joe Edinger over in Buffalo. I'm callin'
about the photograph you sent out over the wire," he explained. "I recognize the man you're lookin' for."

"You do?" Garrett asked, unable to hide his surprise.

"I got his picture right here in front of me," the lawman
said. "That there is Randall Kane. He's caused his fair share
of trouble in these parts over the years."

Garrett's instincts had been right: the man hadn't given
Lily his real name. "What did he do?" he asked.

"Randall's a thief down to the bone. If there's somethin'
good to be got, he'll walk away with it if it ain't nailed
down. Says here he's a suspect in a robbery?"

Garrett gave the detective the details of the case: how
two men had broken in and ransacked a room, stealing a
few things, but had been surprised when one of the occu-
pants had returned, resulting in violence. The photograph
was the only clue he had to go on.

"Huh. That doesn't sound like Randall's usual play. He's
more of a bank robber. Has a knack with safes. Tumblers,
keyed locks, you name it, he can finagle a door open faster
than you can snap your fingers. If you've got a bank in

town, especially one that has a lot of cash on hand, my advice would be to keep a close eye on it. Odds are, Randall's sizin' it up."

Garrett thanked the other policeman and hung up. But instead of leaning back in his chair, thinking about Lily, he was up and moving toward the door, doing math in his head.

The fall festival.

Hundreds of people in town spending money.

The Hoover's Crossing Bank and Trust.

A noted bank robber.

It all added up to trouble.

Lily walked through downtown and revisited old memories. There was the newsstand where she'd bought her first comic book; she couldn't recall the title, but there had been a scary monster on the cover. She stepped over the curb in front of the shoe store that had once tripped Garrett, giving him a bloody gash on his forehead when he fell. She glanced in the window of Dunaway's Department Store, thinking of all the Decembers she'd pressed her nose to the cold glass, dreaming of what Santa might bring. Since she was leaving with Boone the next day, Lily didn't know when she'd see any of these things again. In a matter of hours, she would be among the sights and sounds of the city. The Empire State Building. Millions of people. Grand Central Station. Tomorrow and the days that followed, she would become Jane on the other end of the phone line, bursting with excitement.

But for now, she still had Hooper's Crossing.

Standing on the corner in front of the grocery store, she wondered how Boone and Clive were doing. Turning around, she got her answer. A ghost was walking toward her. Lily smiled brightly. She hurried to him and threw her arms around his waist, squeezing tight. "I'm so glad I met you, Boone."

There was a pause, then, "Wrong name, but I agree on the meetin' part."

Lily quickly stepped back, more than a little embarrassed at the mistake she'd made. There were a dozen sheet-wearing ghosts walking around and she had been foolish enough to assume that the one in front of her was her favorite photographer. "I'm sorry," she said. "I thought you were someone else."

"That's fine by me, Lily," the man answered, stunning her by using her name. "You can put your hands on me anytime you want."

Peering at the holes cut into his sheet, Lily searched the stranger's eyes, looking for a hint of recognition, something that would give away his identity. Even his voice sounded strangely familiar, but try as she might, Lily couldn't place it. Her face must have reflected her confusion because the man tugged away the sheet, pulling it off his head and revealing his face. Lily gasped.

It was the man who had made her so uncomfortable in front of the bank, the same man who'd later robbed Boone and Clive.

"Surprise!" he said with a grin that was more menacing

than friendly, the sheet over his shoulder, neither completely on nor off.

"It's . . . It's you . . ." she managed, backing a step away.

"Good-time Randall, in the flesh," he said, following her.

"Randall?" Lily asked, utterly confused. "You said your name was Mike."

Almost imperceptibly, the man shook his head, as if he couldn't believe the stupidity of his own mistake. "Whatever," he told her. "Happy to see me?"

"You . . . you robbed Boone's room . . . you hurt Clive . . ." she kept on, unable to stop herself from saying aloud the things he'd done. "You and another man . . ."

Randall's smiled faltered. He looked at her curiously. "How do you know about that?" he asked, not a denial but an admission.

"Because of the picture . . . the one of you and me . . ."

Now all of Randall's good cheer vanished, replaced by an ugly frown. As Lily started to move farther away, he closed the distance between them and grabbed her wrist, squeezing hard. "I stole that picture," he hissed. "How do you know about it?" When she didn't immediately reply, he shook her, demanding an answer.

"There was a negative . . ." she told him. "We gave it to the police."

Lily had hoped that might scare Randall enough to let her go, but his expression grew even darker. "That was a mistake," he said. "And here I was hopin' we could have us some fun, but things have changed." He looked around, his attention focusing on an alley twenty feet away.

"You're comin' with me," Randall growled. "Don't try anything stupid, not unless you wanna get hurt." To further make his point, he raised his shirt and showed her the gun tucked into his waistband.

Fear flooded Lily's chest. Even though there were a hundred people around, none of them had noticed what was happening to her. While everyone was celebrating, she was in danger. Lily knew that if she went along with Randall, if she allowed him to take her somewhere no one could see them, she'd be hurt, badly. That left her with only one choice, so she took it.

Lily started screaming.

Boone raised his camera to his eye, thankful he'd removed his sheet. He was just about to take the picture of the contest winners, a young girl dressed as a farmer, her little brother decked out like a pig, curly tail, snout, and all, when a woman's scream split the night. Instantly, deep down in his gut, Boone *knew* that it was Lily.

"Clive!" he shouted; the writer was jotting notes as he interviewed the kids' mother about their Halloween costumes. "Come on!"

Without waiting to see if his partner was following, Boone took off like a shot, running as fast as he could. Half a block later, he realized that he wasn't carrying his camera; he had no idea if he'd dropped it or handed it to someone, but he couldn't have cared less.

The only thing that mattered was Lily.

Boone weaved in and out of the crowd as more screams

rose, echoing off the buildings, making his heart pound. He dodged a family then squeezed between a mailbox and a fire hydrant and suddenly there she was. A man had her by the wrist, looking panicked as Lily continued to shout. Sneering, he roughly pushed her to the ground then took off running for a nearby alley, a white sheet momentarily trailing along behind him before it fell to the pavement.

The crowd seemed frozen, stunned by what they were seeing. But not Boone. He raced forward, wanting to go after the man, but he reined in his anger.

Lily first, that son of a bitch second!

Damn it, damn it, damn it!

Randall shoved Lily the second he saw the photographer, as angry at her as he was at himself, and ran for the alley. Her screams had taken him by surprise. To be honest, he hadn't thought she had it in her; she'd struck him as the type who wouldn't fight back. Hearing that the police had a picture of him had been unnerving, but Randall had thought forcing Lily away from the crowd would give him some time to figure out what to do next. Unfortunately, the bitch had had other plans.

So now he ran.

He sprinted into the alley's mouth, his footsteps loud between the buildings as he headed for the bank. Randall's mind raced faster than his legs. Even as he clung to the hope that the robbery could go on as planned, deep down he knew that it was too late. Leo was going to be furious. All that planning, planning, and more planning had gone up in flames, all because Randall couldn't resist getting close to a girl who'd caught his fancy.

"Shit!" he hissed through clenched teeth.

Running fast through the dark, Randall glanced back over his shoulder, half expecting Boone to be right behind him, but no one was there. He touched his waistband, reassured by the gun. If it came down to it, he wouldn't hesitate to use it. All he had to do was get to Leo and then they could—

A figure suddenly appeared before him, as if they'd come out of nowhere, forcing Randall to skid to a stop. His first thought was that it was just another festivalgoer, but he was quickly proven wrong.

"Freeze! This is the police!"

When Randall shoved Lily to the ground, she hadn't been angry or frightened but happy to be free of him. Screaming had been risky, but she'd convinced herself that he wouldn't harm her, not in front of so many people. Fortunately, her bet had paid off. Even as she landed on the pavement, skinning her elbow and hurting her backside, Lily was flooded with relief.

That feeling grew when Boone knelt beside her.

"Are you all right?" he asked, his expression and tone full of concern. "Who was that? Did he hurt you?"

Lily shook her head, her heart pounding. "It was Mike, I mean Randall!" she shouted. "One of the men who robbed your room! The one in the picture!"

Boone's head shot up, looking toward the alley. His eyes

narrowed. "Then I'm going after him," he declared as he started to rise to his feet.

"No!" Lily shouted, grabbing Boone's hand and holding him tight.

"Why not?"

"He has a gun," she said, remembering the fearsome look of the dark weapon and thinking of all the pain it could cause.

At that moment, Clive finally arrived, completely out of breath. He put his hands on his knees and began to suck in huge gulps of air. Parts of his costume had either fallen off or been torn away. "What...what happened...?" he wheezed.

"Watch Lily," Boone told his friend, determinedly pulling his hand from hers, then looked her in the eyes. "I'll be careful. I promise."

Before Lily could respond, the photographer was off, running toward the same alley that had swallowed Randall and was soon lost from sight.

"Who...who...is he after...?" Clive asked, late to all of the excitement and lacking in details.

But Lily wasn't listening. She was already up off the ground, not bothering to wipe off her costume, and moving away. She was vaguely aware of the writer calling to her, telling her to wait for him, but she wasn't listening.

She wouldn't be left behind. Not now.

Not if Boone's life was in danger.

When Garrett left the police station, he headed straight for the bank with the detective from Buffalo's words echoing

in his head. He'd hoped he might run into another officer on the way, someone who could back him up, but they
must have all been busy elsewhere. He was on his own.

When he arrived at the bank, nothing seemed amiss.
There were a handful of people nearby in costume, but
most of the celebration seemed to be closer to the park.
Garrett tried the front door, but it was locked. He peered
in a window but saw no one moving, no flashlight beams
illuminating the safe, nothing.

What's going on? Was the other cop wrong? Am I?

He was checking out the side of the building, peering
into the shadows, when he heard footsteps coming quickly
toward him from down an alley. The hairs on the back
of Garret's neck stood up, his instincts telling him that
this was trouble. Seconds later, a man came into view. He
didn't have on a costume. Taking a deep breath, Garrett
pulled his weapon from its holster and stepped into the
alley.

"Freeze!" he shouted. "This is the police!"

Caught off-guard, the man struggled to do as he'd been
told, skidding to a stop, his hands above his shoulders.
"Whoa there, pal!" he exclaimed. "No need for any of that!
I'm just runnin' to meet up with a friend of mine! I'm late
so I figured I'd come 'round the back to make up some
time, that's all."

At first glance, the man's reply was believable enough.
After all, Garrett was taking a stab in the dark assuming he
was up to no good. The lawman was about to lower his
gun when something caught his eye; every few seconds,

the stranger looked back over his shoulder, as if he was nervous someone else might arrive. No, something was wrong here, he was sure of it.

"Keep your hands where I can see them," Garrett ordered.

In the dark of the night, especially in the gloomy alley, it was hard to get a good look at the man. Was it Randall Kane?

"What's your name?" he asked.

There was a short pause. "Jake," he answered. "Jake Taylor."

Garrett's grip on his gun tightened. The man was lying. "Walk toward me, slowly," he said forcefully. "Don't make any sudden moves."

"No need to be like that, Officer," the stranger replied, his tone friendly enough. He came forward but he did so reluctantly. "I'm just enjoyin' the festival like everybody else. Why don't you—"

The night was suddenly broken by the roar of a gun. In the split second after, Garrett was filled with confusion. He hadn't pulled his trigger and the stranger's arms were still raised. And that was when the bullet ripped into the meat of his shoulder, spinning him sideways, corkscrewing him to the ground.

He'd been shot.

As he'd waited for Randall, Leo had grown more frustrated with every passing second. He was right where he was supposed to be, exactly as they'd planned, just as his partner had assured him he understood. So where the hell was Randall?

Leo kept to the shadows, moving around a bit, watching, always keeping the bank in sight, never getting too close to any festivalgoer who wandered past.

And that was when the cop showed up.

Goddamn it…

Leo's instincts told him to slip away, to go to the designated meeting spot and hope that Randall showed. But the policeman was too near; Leo worried that if he moved, he'd be seen. He was glad the cop didn't have a flashlight.

Then the pounding of footsteps rang out down the alley. A man appeared, stopping when the policeman told him to. From where he was hidden, Leo could tell that it was Randall, even if he'd ditched the bedsheet. The dumb bastard had waltzed right into the cop's arms. It seemed a foregone conclusion that the younger thief was going to find himself locked inside a jail cell. If he did get caught, it would be only a matter of time before he broke. Once Randall spilled his guts, Leo would spend the rest of his life on the run. He'd never know peace.

But maybe there was a way out.

Leo could be violent when he needed to be. Sometimes, life didn't leave him much of a choice. He pulled the gun from its holster, careful not to make a sound, and aimed it at the cop's head. One bullet, no witnesses. With the lawman dead, he and Randall could escape in the confusion. And maybe later, down some quiet country road in the middle of nowhere, his partner would get a bullet of his own.

Squinting through the darkness, he felt confident he could make the shot. But just before Leo pulled the trigger, he heard something off to his side and a heavy weight suddenly slammed into him, driving the air from his lungs. The gun fired and then flew out of his hand.

Pursuing Randall, it didn't take Boone long to become disoriented in the dark. He reached a fork in the road, guessed, and went right. But no matter how fast Boone ran, no one appeared in front of him. He'd stopped, trying to get his bearings, when he heard a voice shout nearby; it sounded like Garrett. He cautiously made his way toward the sound, uncertain of what he would find.

When he came out near the bank, Boone saw Garrett talking to someone in the alley. His gun was drawn. Boone was pretty sure it was pointed at Randall. He was about to walk over and offer his help in taking the bastard in when he saw something out of the corner of his eye that stopped him cold.

There was another man lurking in the shadows, watching.

With a gun of his own.

Without thinking about the danger of what he was doing, Boone ran, putting himself on a collision course with the armed man. In those first few steps, he realized that this was probably Randall's partner in the robbery. He also understood that the bastard meant to shoot Garrett; while

Boone had his share of problems with Lily's old friend, the hell if he was going to let him get shot.

If I can only get there in time…

Boone lowered his shoulder and bowled into the man's side. The gun fired, the muzzle inches from Boone's face, the sound deafening, but he ignored it. Instead, he hit the ground swinging, throwing punches with bad intentions. His right hand thudded into his opponent's surely already-damaged ribs, a left hit the hard bone of an elbow, and another blow struck its target's nose, resulting in the crunch of cartilage.

But even as Boone rained down punches, Boone hazarded a glance at Garrett. The policeman was lying on his side and didn't appear to be moving. Had the bullet found him? Had Boone's mad rush to save him been for nothing?

Boone knew that the other gunman would be closing the distance between them. He had to end this fight, fast. Rising to his knees, he threw a wicked punch with every ounce of his strength that connected with his foe's chin. His head snapped to the side and his hands fell limp to the ground. He was out, unconscious.

One down, one to go.

Knowing that he didn't have much time, Boone shot to his feet and spun around, determined. But he was too late.

"Ah, ah, ah, there, champ," the man said, his gun leveled at Boone's belly. He stepped forward, which allowed enough light from a nearby streetlight to illuminate his face. It was Randall, all right. "Don't even think about it."

Boone was stuck and he knew it. Every option he

considered ended with him catching a bullet. Maybe if he could bide his time, something, some miracle might present itself.

"I have to admit, I'm surprised," Randall said.

"About what?" Boone asked, hoping to keep the robber talking.

"I'd have thought that Lily would have been more interested in a real man," he said, meaning himself, "rather than some magazine photographer."

There was a time, not that long ago, when Boone would have told the creep that Lily had already shared his bed and liked it just fine. But he no longer felt the need to be that brash and cocky. What he and Lily had found together was much more than physical, something that a man like Randall couldn't begin to understand. Boone loved Lily. That was all that mattered.

"Better than some common crook," he said.

Randall chuckled. "I wonder if she'll cry at your funeral."

Then he raised the gun higher.

Lily hurried down the alley, hoping that Boone and Garrett were safe even as she worried what Randall might do to them. At first, she'd heard Clive huffing along as he tried to keep up with her, but he had long since disappeared somewhere behind. A sudden, sharp bang, like a firecracker, rose in the distance, making her flinch, but Lily fought down her fear and pressed forward. She eventually came out of the alley near the bank.

What she saw made her gasp.

A man lay on the ground, his back to her, not moving. Looking closely, Lily was sure that it was Garrett. Had what she'd heard been a gunshot? Was he hurt? Was he *dead*? A moment later, she noticed Boone. He was in the deeper shadows, his hands raised, his face a mask of determination. Randall stood before him, the gun he'd shown her now pointed at the man she loved.

And so once again, Lily screamed.

Both men's heads turned to the shrill sound. Randall's gun lowered, if only a little. "Lily?" he asked, as if it could be anyone else.

Boone didn't say a word. Instead, he used the distraction she'd provided to close the gap between him and the criminal, ten feet gone in an instant. At the last moment, Randall must have heard him coming because he looked back. But he wasn't fast enough and caught a vicious punch to his jaw. The blow staggered Randall, but somehow he didn't go down. As if by instinct, he whipped his gun hand around and clipped Boone with the pistol. The hard steel opened a deep gash on the photographer's cheek, sending him to one knee in the grass.

"You ain't gonna have to worry about Lily cryin' at your funeral," Randall growled as he rubbed his jaw, then pointed the gun at Boone. "I'll give her somethin' to bawl about right—"

Two quick gunshots made Lily jump out of her skin. Instantly, a pair of bloody flowers blossomed on the back of Randall's shirt. The criminal tried to look over his shoulder as if he wanted to see them, as surprised by their appearance as anyone. It was then that Lily noticed Garrett. The policeman had raised himself up on an elbow. Smoke rose from the barrel of his gun. Randall's mouth moved but nothing came out. He dropped first onto his knees, then pitched forward on his face as his own weapon dropped harmlessly from his hand.

Lily ran to Boone and knelt beside him, wanting to see if he was all right. The cut Randall's gun had caused was ugly and dripping blood, but he waved her off. "Check on Garrett," he said.

The policeman had managed to sit on the pavement, his service revolver on the ground beside him. The hand pressed against his shoulder was stained crimson with blood. When he saw her, he tried to smile but Lily could see that he was in tremendous pain.

"You've been shot!" she exclaimed.

"I'll be all right," Garrett said. "It could have been worse." He looked toward Boone. "I think your boyfriend saved my life."

Lily didn't know what surprised her more: Boone's heroism or the fact that Garrett had acknowledged their relationship. She took off her Little Red Riding Hood cloak and gently pressed it against the wound, trying to stanch the bleeding. She helped Garrett to his feet just as Boone arrived.

"That doesn't look so hot," he said, nodding at Garrett's wound.

"Neither does your cheek."

"I'm just happy to be alive." Nodding at the policeman's gun, he added, "Looks like I have you to thank for that."

"I was just returning the favor," Garrett said.

Lily looked at the crowd that was slowly forming, drawn by the sound of the gunshots. As if on cue, Clive finally showed up, his costume now in tatters, only a piece of cardboard here and there to show he'd been a robot earlier in the evening. His cheeks were bright red and his forehead was dotted with sweat. When he saw Randall's crumpled body, he asked, "Is . . . is he dead . . . ?"

Before Lily or Boone could answer, Garrett said, "I need to go find another officer." Looking at the photographer, he added, "Take good care of her."

Watching Garrett walk away, Lily's heart ached. Their friendship had hit a bump in the road when he'd revealed his feelings for her, and she didn't know if things could be mended. But she was determined to try. Only time would tell, but just then, she allowed herself to be optimistic.

"Is . . . is this one dead, too?" Clive exclaimed. He'd moved away from Randall and was now staring at the thief's partner, sprawled in the grass.

"No. I coldcocked him," Boone answered.

"What do I do if he wakes up?" the writer asked, worry in his voice.

"Knock him out again."

"Punch him?"

"Sit on him for all I care, just don't let him go."

The sudden enormity of all that had happened finally began to weigh down on Lily. She stepped toward Boone, wanting to feel his touch, his warmth. The photographer wrapped his arm around her, pulling her close.

"You saved me, too, you know," he said. "If you hadn't screamed when you did, that bastard would have shot me."

She shook her head. "We all saved each other."

Boone thought about it, nodded, but then started to chuckle.

"What's so funny?" Lily asked.

"When I was first given this assignment, I didn't want to come because I thought it'd be the most boring town on the planet, and I've been to some really dull places in my travels," he explained. "Instead, I wind up meeting you and getting mixed up in more excitement than you can shake a stick at."

"Are you complaining?"

"Not in the slightest," Boone said. "As long as I have the girl of my dreams at my side, there's nothing I wouldn't take on."

Lily smiled. Boone was right. Their time together had been quite the ride. And soon they'd be going to New York City to start a new life.

As far as she was concerned, the excitement had only just begun.

Epilogue

New York City
April 1953

OH, LOOK AT THIS! Isn't it beautiful?"

Lily joined Jane at the boutique's window and stared through the glass at an exquisite, and no doubt expensive, summer dress. Behind them the city continued about its day. Countless people poured down the sidewalk on their way to work, school, or wherever else it was they needed to be. The streets were clogged with trucks, cars, and taxis honking their horns, everyone in a hurry. Skyscrapers lived up to their names, rising high toward the cloudless spring sky.

"You'd look great in that," Lily said.

"I was thinking more about you," her friend replied.

"Wouldn't Boone's eyes fall out of his head if you walked into the room wearing that?"

"They'd fall out when he saw the price tag."

Jane laughed. "Let's at least go in so you can try it on."

"I can't," Lily answered. "If I do, I'll be late to meet Boone at the park."

"Next time, then." Jane slipped her arm in Lily's and they set off, just as they'd done when they were kids growing up in Hooper's Crossing.

But now, six months after both of them had left, neither of them was the same girl she'd once been. Not exactly.

For Jane, the change was pronounced. In the big city, she had blossomed into the woman she'd always wanted to be. Within days of arriving, Jane had landed a job as a typist in a secretarial pool, which had put enough money in her pocket that she could begin enjoying some of what New York had to offer. She went to parties and dances, movies and the theaters, out shopping and to fancy restaurants. Somewhere along the way, Jane had attracted the attention of an advertising director and she was scheduled to have her first photo shoot next week. Maybe Jane would end up on that billboard after all.

"Seven o'clock," Jane whispered to Lily, nodding toward a businessman leaving an office, decked out in a charcoal-gray suit. "Just my type, too."

One way in which Jane's life differed from Lily's was that she'd yet to find a man to share it, not that she wasn't looking. Hard. She still turned the heads of plenty of potential suitors, but she was being picky, hoping to land the big fish. The first time Jane had met Clive, the writer had been so tongue-tied by the dark-haired beauty that he'd introduced himself by the wrong name; unfortunately, Clive was the minnow who didn't stand a chance and was tossed back in the water.

"Are you sure you know the way?" Jane asked when they'd reached her subway station. "I can walk with you some more if you want."

"I'm fine," Lily said. "It's straight up Fifth. I couldn't miss it if I tried."

"All right," her friend said, her heels clicking down the steps. "Now, remember, there's a party on Saturday. Don't be late!"

Lily headed for Central Park, moving among the crowd. Even after the months she'd lived in New York City, it still felt strange, like a dream. So far, it had been everything she'd hoped it would be and more. Every day had been a new adventure. So far, she had only returned to Hooper's Crossing twice. Once for the holidays, the second time for the trial.

In the aftermath of the failed bank robbery, Leo Burke had faced a court of law to be sentenced for his crimes. He was accused of shooting Garrett, a police officer, and planning to make off with bags stuffed with money, much of it originating from the festival. Sitting in the courtroom, waiting for her turn to recount the events of that fateful night, Lily had learned that Leo was a lifelong criminal with a list of offenses longer than her arm. When he was eventually found guilty, the bank robber was sentenced to seventy years behind bars. He would never know freedom again.

As for Randall Kane, whom she had known as Mike Detmer, with no family to claim him his body had been buried in an unmarked grave. Strange as it was, Lily had felt a shred of responsibility for the man's death. If Randall hadn't been so interested in her, if she hadn't mistaken him for Boone and thrown her arms around him that Halloween night, he might still be alive. That was an awful lot of "ifs." Too many. Besides, the criminal had made his own choices in life, most of them bad, and it had all come to an end before her very eyes.

Being back home, even if it hadn't been under ideal circumstances, had been fun and familiar, like curling up in a favorite blanket. Lily had been happy to discover that her father was doing well. Though Morris still fretted about his daughter, sending a steady stream of calls and letters to see if she was doing well, checking to see if Boone was keeping her as safe as he'd promised, he had succeeded in letting Lily chart her own course for the most part. Word around town was that he crowed over each postcard she sent, proudly telling anyone who would listen about what she had seen, where she had gone, or who she had met. Though letting go had been hard, it seemed have been good for the both of them.

While she hadn't gone to the library on either visit, Lily had heard that Ethel remained as much of a sourpuss as ever. She still complained about everything under the sun, chastised patrons for the smallest of infractions, and ruled her "kingdom" with an iron fist. Whatever change Lily's tongue-lashing might have brought about in the older woman, it was short-lived.

As for Marjorie Barlow, Boone's premonition had been right. For Christmas, the landlady had gotten herself a dog to share in her days, a golden retriever she'd named Betsy. At their first meeting, Daisy and the puppy had sniffed each other warily, but then seconds later become the best of friends, barking and chasing through the snow.

But without question, the person Lily had been the most nervous about seeing on her return was Garrett. In those crazy days after he had been shot, understandably delaying her leaving town, the two of them had talked, a conversation that had continued even after Lily had moved away. By the time Christmas had rolled around, their fences seemed to have been mended. They exchanged gifts and Lily had been happy to see the police officer and Boone getting along, their tenuous bond growing stronger on account of each saving the other's life. Still, deep down in her heart, Lily knew that things between her and Garrett would never be the same. They couldn't. She couldn't help but wonder if he still loved her. It colored everything he said, each glance he gave her, every move he made. But because she didn't want to lose Garrett in her life, Lily had to hope that things would change with time.

When Lily reached Central Park, she smiled. The huge expanse of nature inside a city of concrete and steel never failed to brighten her mood. Now, in the early springtime, buds were popping on the trees, the grass was growing greener by the day, and an occasional flower was tentatively opening its petals to the sun. Blankets had been spread on the lawn as city-dwellers said good-bye to another winter. Horse-drawn carriages weaved through the park carrying tourists or couples who wanted a romantic moment together.

And speaking of two people in love…

Just as Lily came within sight of her and Boone's favorite bench, the photographer appeared from around a curve in the walk. He had Daisy on a leash, the Labrador pulling hard, wanting to go this way then that, overjoyed and overwhelmed by all of the smells the park produced. When they reached each other, Lily threw her arms around Boone and hugged him tight, nuzzling her face into the crook of his neck, acting like she hadn't seen him for a month instead of only that morning.

"You didn't have to wait, did you?" he asked.

"No, I just got here," she answered, giving Daisy a scratch hello.

"Good," Boone said, then kissed the top of Lily's head. "I got hung up at the office and had to race to get Daisy and then back here."

"Trouble at work?" she asked.

"Yeah, but there shouldn't have been. Walter had Clive and me in for a chat about our trip to Mexico City. You know, the usual stuff about hotel reservations, how we'll be getting around, what he's looking for in the article, but then Clive starts asking every question under the sun and then some."

Lily smiled. "He's excited. It'll be his first international assignment."

"He wanted to know whether they sold his brand of toothpaste in Mexico," Boone explained with a shake of his head. "He's worried he'll run out."

"What did Walter say?"

"That he should bring an extra tube." When Lily laughed, he added, "It's not funny. With the way Clive packs, we're going to need an extra plane."

In the aftermath of the failed bank robbery and shooting, Clive's star had soared. Being first on the scene, he'd written an account that had been picked up by newspapers and radio stations across the country. His and Boone's article on the Hooper's Crossing Fall Festival had gotten a prominent place in *Life* magazine; Boone's photo of the boy blowing a bubble of gum had even made the cover. Clive was still just as awkward as ever but he was getting better, like a turtle slowly coming out of its shell. His partnership with Boone had grown to the point that they were being paired together more and more often. Walter called them his "dynamic duo."

"Like Batman and Robin!" Clive had exclaimed.

"More like Superman and Jimmy Olsen," Boone had joked. "One of us is doing all the work while the other keeps tripping over his own feet."

"Jimmy Olsen's a photographer, you know," the writer had pointed out, then laughed so hard he started coughing.

"Still a comedian."

Lily had smiled. Against all odds and expectations, the two of them were becoming the best of friends.

"When do you leave for Mexico?" Lily now asked.

"The day after tomorrow."

"That means we still have a little time together. What do you want to do?"

"Anything and everything," Boone said, pulling her close to give her a tender kiss on the lips. "Do you have something in mind?"

"Not really."

Boone chuckled. "If only this place wasn't so boring," he joked. "All these people and buildings but nothing to do."

"If only it was as exciting as Hoover's Crossing, right?"

"Or whatever its name is."

In the months that they had been together in the city, Lily truly believed that she'd come to love Boone more and more with every day. She had moved into his tiny apartment, almost entirely without furniture, and set about turning it into their home. Plants decorated the windowsills. A fresh coat of paint livened up the kitchen. She framed some of his pictures and hung them on the walls against Boone's protests; he didn't want it to seem like he was conceited. They hauled groceries up the flights of stairs. They went out with Jane, Clive, and other friends. They made love in the middle of the afternoon when Boone wasn't away on assignment. Though he made a good living taking pictures for *Life*, Lily was determined to do her part and had set about getting a job; with her experience, she'd been hired at the New York Public Library within a week. When Boone was off snapping photographs, she took Daisy out for walks, counting down the days until his return. Step by step, they set about starting a life.

And through it all, they had loved and laughed and learned.

Lily was convinced that it wouldn't be long before Boone proposed; Jane guessed that it would be before he left for Mexico. She didn't know if he would pop the question when they were on the observation deck of the Empire State Building, get down on bended knee in front of their Central Park bench, or blurt it out one morning while they were brushing their teeth in the bathroom. Whenever it happened, Lily would say yes. She would want to get married in Hooper's Crossing so that she could be surrounded by her family and friends. She'd wear her mother's pearl earrings. Her father would give her away. She hoped that Garrett would attend. Jane would be her maid of honor, Clive the best man. Daisy could even be the flower girl.

Somebody else would have to take the pictures.

ABOUT THE AUTHOR

Dorothy Garlock is one of America's—and the world's—favorite novelists. Her work has consistently appeared on national bestseller lists, including the *New York Times* list, and there are over fifteen million copies of her books in print translated into eighteen languages. She has won more than twenty writing awards, including an *RT Book Reviews* Reviewers' Choice Award for Best Historical Fiction for *A Week from Sunday*, five Silver Pen Awards from *Affaire de Coeur*, and three Silver Certificate Awards. Her novel *With Hope* was chosen by Amazon as one of the best romances of the twentieth century.

After retiring as a news reporter and bookkeeper in 1978, she began her career as a novelist with the publication of *Love and Cherish*. She lives in Clear Lake, Iowa.